31
8/08

# Melissa

*Sara Hylton*

St. Martin's Press ≋ New York

Library of Congress Cataloging-in-Publication Data

Hylton, Sara.
Melissa / by Sara Hylton.
p.     cm.
ISBN 0-312-14677-9
I. Title.
PR6058.Y63M45    1996
823'.914—dc20    96-27972
CIP

First published in Great Britain by
Judy Piatkus (Publishers) Ltd.

First U.S. Edition: December 1996

10  9  8  7  6  5  4  3  2  1

# Prologue

The soft wind swept across the headland, bringing with it the scent of the mass of flowers spread before me. The sun felt warm on my face and below me the sea looked like molten gold as it swept inland towards the shore.

How Melissa would have loved this adulation! And yet, if her tortured, uneasy ghost moved among us, she would have found it strange, for there was no deafening applause, no ecstatic cheering, only a quiet sadness and a shocked disbelief that Melissa Francesca was no more. Never again would the magic of her voice echo across the hillside and make the inhabitants leave their vineyards to listen enthralled to the talent that had thrilled the world.

Overlooking the Bay of Solerno, the ancient cemetery straggled the hillside, embellished with ornamental statues, turrets and monuments, vulgar to my English eyes in their display of grief. It was normally a place of quiet, brooding sadness but today the paths were lined with darkly clad people waiting for the cortège to arrive.

I knew that many of the people grieving here had never seen Melissa on the stage. They were peasants living in the shadow of her white villa set high up on the mountainside, but they had heard her voice when she entertained her guests, and I had seen them peering through the wrought-iron gates. Now they had come to pay her their final homage.

I had chosen a place where I felt I would be unobserved, in the shadow of a massive monument and in the midst of a group of local people with their children, each one clutching a small posy of summer flowers. They had made room for me among them, staring at me curiously, knowing that I was not one of them with my pale hair and delicate colouring.

There were people I knew among those waiting nearest to the church. Opera singers like Melissa, tenors larger than life, even on a day like this conscious of their fame and their talent, and many others I had met during different stages of my involvement with her, men and women I would remember but who would be unlikely to remember me.

From the shadow of the monument my eyes searched the crowd until suddenly I saw Alistair. He stood alone, aloof from people he had never understood or wanted to understand. He looked older than I remembered him, his thin, sensitive face with its shock of fair hair reminding me poignantly of the boy I had loved and all the pain it had caused me. He seemed, as always, lost in Melissa's world. For one blinding moment I felt I should go to him, stand beside him to show the others that we were different, that we were the two people who had known Melissa longer than any of them, and perhaps known her better, but how could I be sure? Melissa had had too many faces, a personality that was too complex both for Alistair and for me.

I stayed in the shelter of the monument, hurting for him but unwilling to put my hurt into words.

There was a sudden stir near the gates and at first I thought the cortège had arrived, but it was too early. Along the path I saw three men marching towards the church, their eyes looking neither to right nor left. The crowd stood back almost fearfully. At the church door they turned and looked straight before them, ignoring the stares, the man in the middle standing almost defiant. Antonio Brindisi, Melissa's Italian husband, flanked by two policemen.

He stood with nonchalant grace, imperious to the hostility surrounding him. On Alistair's face I saw only curiosity; this was the man Melissa had turned to after their affair had run its course.

There was another ripple of interest, caused by a man walking alone along the path from the gates. He was tall, his dark hair silvered with grey, and my heart lurched painfully at the sight of his handsome, remote face. Although the famous people around the church surged forward to greet him, he merely acknowledged their presence with a stiff bow and went, like Alistair, to stand alone.

Only minutes after his arrival, the cortège came and the crowds around me surged forward to meet it. I was left alone to gaze down at the little procession wending its way along the main path. There were few mourners: Melissa's housekeeper and her maid, her butler, her chauffeur and her gardeners. She had no family.

Places in the tiny church had been reserved for the notables. Those who could not find a place inside stood near the doors so that they could hear the service. I went to stand alone on the terrace overlooking the sea. My Italian was good enough to understand the funeral service, but I wished to comfort myself with memories. Many memories were sweet, though there were others that had been bitter.

Startled, I heard Alistair's voice saying softly, 'Ginny.'

I turned to see him standing a few yards from me, his expression wary and unsure. Before I could speak, he said quickly, 'I saw you come into the churchyard; didn't you see me near the church?'

'Yes. I wanted to be up here on the hillside.'

'Didn't you want to talk to me?'

I didn't answer. I didn't know. What was there to say?

'This is a wretched business, isn't it? Why have they allowed him to come here?'

'I don't know.'

'The newspapers are full of it.'

'"Famous prima donna shot by her husband in romantic Italian villa". Unfortunately there's a great deal more to come,' I said bitterly.

'The awful thing is, I can understand why he did it, in some strange way. She could be the most maddening creature in the world, she could make me hate her one minute and adore her the next — but I don't suppose you want to listen to this.'

I didn't speak, and he went on, 'Brindisi was like her. Their life was a tinderbox from the first day they met. One or the other of them was doomed.'

'I know.'

I was remembering her pacing the room in my villa, telling me things I didn't want to hear. She was making defiant assurances that she could handle things, that she only had to confront him to get her own way. Then came that last frantic message asking me to go to her.

I shall remember it for the rest of my life, the rain-soaked streets and tossing trees, the sudden flashes of lightning illuminating the long windows. I shall remember the footsteps on the landing above and his face as he came running towards me down the stairs.

Alistair was saying, 'Well, Melissa would be gratified if she could see all these people. I wonder which of them were her lovers.'

'Alistair, if you're ever to be at peace about Melissa, you should stop torturing yourself with possibilities. Melissa is dead, and whatever secrets she had should be allowed to die with her.'

'I always thought she was in love with Mellini and he with her. She hinted at it when she wanted to hurt me. And look, he is here.'

'It would be surprising if he had not been here — the world's most famous conductor and the world's leading diva.'

'Were they ever in love, Ginny, did you never suspect it?'

Without replying, I held out my hand, saying, 'They're leaving the church now. Perhaps you should go down.'

'Aren't you coming?'

'No, I'll stay up here. There's no place for me down there.'

I watched him walk away from me down the hill to take his place with the others round the graveside. Antonio Brindisi stood between his two guards, his handsome face contemptuous. Riccardo Mellini was standing alone, distancing himself from these people who adored him as they had adored Melissa. Alistair stayed on the edge of the crowd, the sunlight gleaming on his fair head.

In the still morning air I could hear the voice of the priest from where he stood over Melissa's coffin. From inside the church, organ music swelled dramatically but failed to drown the sonorous sound of his voice.

I looked down the hillside, my eyes following the exquisite curve of the coast as it swept northward towards Sorrento and the Isle of Capri, bathed in sunlight, wrapped in peace, an incongruous backdrop for sudden death and murderous jealousies.

Yet suddenly that calm sea reminded me of a lake lying frozen under sharp winter frost, on the day when I first laid eyes on Melissa Francis.

# Part I

# Chapter One

Although it was only November, there had been snow on the Lakeland mountains for several weeks. It had snowed in the night and when I pulled back the curtains in my bedroom, I found myself looking out on a sparkling white world. Snow clung to the trees so that the branches of the conifers seemed like sweeping ostrich feathers, and I laughed at the antics of the ducks as they slithered ungainly across the frozen lake.

I was pulling my sweater over my head when the door was flung open and my sister Edith said, 'Hurry up, Ginny! Everybody's up but you.'

'I am up,' I protested.

'Only just. Surely you haven't forgotten what's happening today?'

'Of course not. I'm coming as soon as I've put my shoes on.'

'Well, just get a move on. Cloonie's in a bad mood and Mother's rushing round trying to do two jobs at once.'

It was 1939 and the war had been on for eight weeks. So far, nothing out of the ordinary had happened. There had been no enemy aircraft overhead, no invading armies, but we were prepared for them, and today a horde of children would be descending on us from the large cities at risk of attack.

Every household, if it were at all possible, was expected to take in at least one evacuee. The children would be arriving in a special train early in the afternoon, and for days we had been preparing our welcome. They would be met at the station and escorted to the village hall, where they would be fed before going to their respective new homes. Edith and I had walked down to the station only the day before to see welcome banners flapping in the wind that swept down from the fells, and Cloonie had spent every day preparing cakes and scones, which the Women's Institute ladies had collected, to swell what others had contributed.

Father had decided to take a boy. My brother Rodney had threatened to leave home if another girl came into the family, and Edith didn't much want a girl either. 'I don't like city girls,' she had protested. 'She'd probably be superior and bossy.'

Father's eyes had twinkled at me across the table before he said, 'You're a bit of a bossy-boots yourself, young lady, and you don't know any city girls, so how can you say you don't like them?'

I had no preference either way and was quite content to listen to the arguments. Edith was fourteen, Rodney was twelve and I was only ten. I doubt if anybody would have taken much notice of me anyway, so I kept quiet and the other two got their way.

Naturally we hoped the strange boy would be somebody we could all get along with, and I could understand Mother when she said, 'It's rather like adopting a child, isn't it? No doubt he'll be homesick, he'll be comparing country life to the sort of life he's been used to, and it'll be so awful if he hates it here.'

'Well, he'll have to get accustomed to it,' Father said. 'Try to think that he might love the country. The lakes are beautiful and it won't always be winter. Think about the spring — lambs gambolling, trout in the streams, boats on the lake — it's a boy's paradise.'

'But he might hanker after cinemas and concert halls. We can't provide those.'

'We can provide safety, though. Isn't that the issue at this time?'

That put an end to the argument and Father was allowed to retire into his study with the newspaper and his coffee.

Edith and Rodney sat at the breakfast table grinning at me. Rodney said, 'We're having a rota for the bathroom, Ginny, and you're the last on it.'

'That isn't fair,' I protested. 'I was here before the evacuee.'

'It goes by seniority and you're the youngest,' he explained.

Edith spelled it out: 'That means I'm first, and no new boy is going to jump the queue.'

The sound of the telephone shrilling in the hall sent Mother

4

to answer it. Cloonie came in from the kitchen to collect some of the breakfast dishes. Her face was flushed with exertion and from the way she slammed the dishes on her tray we all deemed it was wiser to keep quiet.

Mother came in from the hall with a frown on her face, saying, 'Really, today of all days! That was Mrs Rocheforte demanding to see your father as soon as morning surgery's over, earlier still if possible.'

'Didn't ye tell her the children were arrivin' today?' Cloonie said protectively. 'He'll 'ave his hands full. Everybody in the village 'as given some sort of 'elp, but not 'er, not the lady o' the manor.'

'Ginny, I want you to run down to the surgery and tell your father what's happened. I'll leave some lunch out for you and I'll see him at the village hall as soon as he can get there. I've tried to ring him but the line was engaged.'

I wasn't sorry to get out of the kitchen and into the clear, frosty air. The snow was several inches thick along the village high street and the early-morning traffic had not had time to turn it into slush.

I knew that people would be as busy as Mother and Cloonie in every kitchen along that straggling village street. Only the postman was visible, trudging up the hill from the tiny post office, away from the village.

By the time I reached the surgery, my face was rosy and, inside my warm woollen gloves, my fingers were tingling. A log fire burned in the waiting room but only two people were sitting there; Mrs Wellan and old Mr Humphreys. Mrs Wellan smiled at me warmly but Mr Humphreys didn't lift his eyes from his newspaper. Father always said he went to the surgery every morning merely to read the paper, there was never anything wrong with him.

'I'll bet you've bin enjoyin' the snow, Ginny. I did miself when I was your age, but not any more. It's no good for mi bronchitis.'

'Does my father have anybody with him, Mrs Wellan?'

'Ay, that Dolly Jamieson and 'er youngest. I can't think 'ow she'll be copin' wi' two evacuees, it takes 'er all 'er time to care for 'er own two.'

'Are you having anybody, Mrs Wellan?'

5

'I've promised to take in a brother and sister fro' Liverpool. You're 'avin' a lad, I believe.'

'Yes, Rodney said he couldn't put up with another girl in the house.'

She laughed. 'Do ye know anythin' about the lad you're 'avin'?'

'No. My father might know but he hasn't said. May I give him a message before you go in there?'

'Ay, if it won't take too long. I 'ave to get back to get the 'ouse ready.'

Just then Dolly came out with her youngest child, a sickly little girl who was always ailing with asthma. I took advantage of her conversation with Mrs Wellan to go into the surgery, where Father was busy adding coal to the fire.

'Hello, Ginny, what brings you here? I'd have thought Cloonie would have kept you all busy this morning.'

'Mrs Rocheforte telephoned. She wants you to go up to the Hall as soon as surgery's over.'

'Damn the woman!' Father exploded. 'She must have forgotten every word I said to her about this morning. Did she say why she wanted to see me?'

'No.'

'Oh, well, I suppose I'll have to go up there. Come with me if you like, I shan't be staying very long. How many more in the waiting room?'

'Mrs Wellan and Mr Humphreys.'

'Well, Mrs Wellan won't keep me long and I can soon get rid of Mr Humphreys, I expect he's more or less exhausted the morning papers by this time.'

In a quarter of an hour I was sitting in the front seat of Father's car while he drove along the country road towards the big house halfway up the fell. As we turned in at the large wrought-iron gates, I shuddered a little.

He laughed, saying, 'I know you children talk about the Hall as being haunted. I can assure you it isn't.'

'But it looks so big and gloomy.'

'It's a very fine building. You'll be able to say you've been inside, you'll like what you see.'

'Won't Mrs Rocheforte mind my going in with you?'

'You're not sitting out here in the cold, Ginny.'

We drew up in front of the Hall and I followed him up the stone steps leading from the terrace to the front door.

A very tall, darkly clad man opened the door for us. Standing in an oak-lined hall, looking up to a wide, shallow staircase, I was aware of pictures and ornaments, large bowls of hothouse flowers and the smell of furniture polish. A log fire burned brightly, its flames reflected in shining brass and copper. The tall man led us across the hall to a door, knocked softly and a woman's voice said, 'Enter.'

Mrs Rocheforte was often seen riding in the back seat of her large black car, or driving the smart pony and trap along the country lanes. She was prominent at church festivals and village fetes, and was invariably invited to present the school prizes. She always dressed in black, and usually wore a large-brimmed hat which accentuated her silver hair. She was a pretty woman — Father maintained she had been a great beauty — but there was sadness in her face, especially after Brigadier Rocheforte died a few years earlier.

She sat in a deep easy chair in front of a log fire, a small King Charles spaniel on her knee. 'Come in and sit down, doctor,' she invited. 'I'm sorry to call you out on such a morning.'

'I'm sorry you're not feeling well, Mrs Rocheforte,' Father replied, crossing the room to sit facing her. I followed shyly. Turning towards me, Father held out his hand. 'This is Virginia, my youngest daughter, we call her Ginny. She brought me your message so I brought her along with me.'

She smiled. 'I've seen you at your school, Virginia. I shall call you Virginia, it's a pity to shorten such a lovely name. Sit down beside your father, my dear. Would you like coffee?'

'No thank you, Mrs Rocheforte, we don't really have a great deal of time. I have to get down to the village hall as soon as possible. Now what is the trouble?'

'Nothing to do with my health, doctor, but I've been thinking very seriously about the children arriving today. This is the largest house for miles and yet I haven't offered to have a child here. I'm not at my best with children. My own children were tucked away upstairs in a nursery until they went away to school, but children who would expect to live here, and play here, was something I couldn't begin to think about.'

'There was no pressure on you, Mrs Rocheforte,' Father said

7

gently. 'Most of the villagers were agreeable to take the children, and in any case this house is rather grand and could easily put a child at a disadvantage.'

'It could also give the right kind of child a very great advantage, doctor.'

'Of course, but until we see the children we really don't know what to expect.'

'They are from several of the large cities expecting attacks, aren't they?'

'Yes, London, Birmingham, Manchester and Liverpool, I believe.'

'Children from all walks of life should be arriving, then.'

'Today I believe they'll be from Manchester and Merseyside, probably from the dockland area. Some of them may never have seen the countryside, never had anything to do with farmyard animals or seen the mountains. Life is going to be very strange for them all. What had you in mind?'

'A girl. A girl about Virginia's age. A girl who knows how to be quiet, and is willing to learn. A girl who has potential — surely it isn't too much to ask?'

'I rather think it is. I'm not sure if homes have been found for all of them yet, but Miss Brownson has it all in hand.'

'I preferred to take it up with you, doctor. If you can find me a girl who looks as if she would fit in here, then I'll have her. I will educate her if that isn't already taken care of, and if she has special talents I will see that they are encouraged. She will be well fed and clothed, and she may bring her friends here. The nursery is exactly as it was when my children were small, with games, toys and books.'

'I take it you're only interested in taking one child? Many of them arriving today are brothers and sisters.'

'One girl, Dr Lawrence. My own children were two boys and a girl. The boys were disruptive, they were noisy and ran wild over the place whenever their father and I were out of the house, and the poor servants had great difficulty in coping with them. My daughter and I were never close even when she was a child.'

'With such memories, I'm surprised that you're contemplating taking in a strange child.'

'Don't be too complacent, doctor. Your own children are

8

still at home, still schoolchildren, but who knows what the adult world will do to them. You and your wife will do your best, as I did. You'll hope and pray that they will grow up to be decent, honest and caring, but you can't be sure that they will. Only time will say if you were right.'

'I suppose so.'

Father turned to me and took my hand in his own. 'We squabble among ourselves, don't we, Ginny? We say things we really don't mean, but we are a family, aren't we, love? Is there anything you'd want to change?'

'Not really. If Edith wasn't bossy she wouldn't be Edith, would she?'

Even Mrs Rocheforte smiled, and after a few moments Father said, 'I'll take a good look around this afternoon, Mrs Rocheforte. Ginny will help me — won't you?'

'Somebody you can be friends with, Virginia, a nice girl like yourself, and you will be able to visit her here and have her visit you. I'm sure you have many friends — choose for me a girl your friends would like.'

I smiled at her doubtfully before we left her staring moodily into the fire.

For a few minutes Father sat back in the car gazing through the window and I sensed that he was troubled.

'She's going to be disappointed, Ginny. I've seen the evacuees that went to some of the villages across the fell, nice enough kids, but hardly Rocheforte material. Harum-scarum kids with city voices and city vices. A youngster such as that could be miserable up there at the Hall.'

'I'd hate to live there,' I said. 'I'd be afraid of dropping crumbs, sitting on the cushions and walking on the carpets.'

'Mm. I'm sure you're right.'

He started the car and we drove slowly back along the drive.


Lunch was a plate of sandwiches, a bowl of soup and fruit to follow.

Father said, 'Are you coming with me to the village hall or going to the station?'

'To the station, I want to see them arrive. Edith and Rodney will be there. I wonder what he'll be like?'

'I've left it all to Miss Brownson. All she's said is that he'll suit us fine — background, age, a boy.'

'Is he older than Rodney?'

'I don't know anything else, love. You know Miss Brownson. I'm very reluctant to tread on her toes about a girl for the Hall. I'll have to be very diplomatic.'

'If I see anybody at the station who looks as though she'd fit in, I'll tell you.'

'That's my girl.'

I ran along towards the station with my scarf flying behind me and the pompom on my woollen beret bobbing on top of my head.

There was a lot of activity around the village hall. The vicar was helping his wife to carry in trays of food from the vicarage and I saw Miss Brownson setting out towards the station, armed with a large register and accompanied by two of her helpers. She was a large, bustling, formidable woman, head-mistress of the village school and lay reader for the local church. I wasn't sorry to have left the village school behind me two months before.

Now I was at Copelands, a private school with a good reputation, where my sister had been a pupil for four years. The school was in the next village, Elmsworth, and Edith and I caught the bus every morning which deposited us at the school gates. Rodney was at the grammar school in Kendal and I wondered if our evacuee would be able to go there with him.

A group of girls greeted me outside the station. Then I saw Edith standing with two of her cronies. She called out to us, 'We can go on the platform to watch the train come in, and we're all to give them a welcoming cheer.'

'Your sister knows everything and everybody,' Mary Allen said snidely.

I didn't answer. Edith had that knack of finding out where things were happening, but she was good-natured and seldom truly malicious.

It was cold in the fresh wind that swept down from the fells, but it was beautiful with the watery sun shining on the mountaintops and the dark conifers heavy with snow. What would they make of it, these city children? Would they enjoy our long country twilights, silent lanes and the lake frozen under the first sharp frost of winter? Surely they would come to love it as I did, and surely there would be more sadness on leaving it when the years of war were over.

# Chapter Two

Groups of children stood along the length of the platform, their cheeks rosy in the sharp wind, their ears strained for the arrival of the country train.

We did not have long to wait. Before it came to a stop, the air was filled with our cheering, and then the doors were opening and other children were climbing down to the platform.

Some of them were warmly clad against the cold and carried neat valises. Others wore inadequate clothing and clutched paper bags or makeshift parcels. Many pinched faces looked wistful and tearful, but some stared with awe at the glistening snow and the mountains towering above them. All of them carried over their shoulders the square box containing the gas masks they had been issued with.

We surged forward to meet them, while the teachers formed them into an orderly column, a difficult procedure, since a great many of them clutched the hands of brothers and sisters and seemed loath to part from them.

While we handed out sweets and smiled our greetings, I looked towards the back of the train, where a solitary girl was climbing out of her compartment. Miss Brownson gave me a little shove, saying, 'Tell her to hurry up, Virginia, and see if there's anybody left in the train.'

The girl made no attempt to hurry. She sauntered complacently along the platform and when I reached her side she eyed me carelessly. About my age and height, she had long dark hair and was very pale. She was wearing a navy-blue macintosh and carried a paper parcel along with her gas mask. She continued to walk slowly ahead and did not return my smile.

'Please hurry,' I admonished her. 'We're going to the village hall to eat. I expect you're very hungry.'

Again she gave me a swift, uninterested glance.

Somewhat put out, I said, 'My name is Virginia Lawrence, most people call me Ginny. Who are you?'

Without answering my question, she asked, 'Do they all have somewhere to go?'

'I'm not sure, but I think so.'

'Are you having somebody?'

'Yes, a boy.'

She spoke quietly and with deliberation, and from her accent I could not tell if she was North Country or not. A little annoyed that she had not vouchsafed her name, I urged her again to walk quickly. When we caught up with the end of the procession, she walked alone, disdaining the other children, and I rejoined my friends.

'She's awfully difficult to talk to,' I complained to Edith.

In the village hall, the children stared wide-eyed at the long trestle tables laid with sandwiches, scones, cakes and bowls of jelly, all donated from family rations. My spirits lifted as they ran round the tables jostling for seats; then small hands were extended to take what they wanted from the plates and those helping at the tables encouraged them with warm smiles.

The girl sat at the end of one of the tables, and there was nobody next to her. I saw her extend a slim hand to take a scone from one of the large plates and eat it delicately, unhurried, while the rest of them crammed food into their mouths as though starving.

'Who is that girl sitting alone?' Miss Brownson asked me.

'I don't know. She didn't tell me her name.'

At that moment my father was passing and Miss Brownson called out, 'Did you find your boy, doctor?'

'Yes, Alistair Grantham. He's sitting over there near the window.'

I followed his gaze and saw my brother talking to a boy sitting with his back towards me, so that all I could see were thin shoulders and a shock of fair hair, brighter than my own.

'That girl over there, doctor, can we find out who she is? I'll have her name down somewhere and she'll need to be taken to the family who are expecting her.'

The girl had taken a small iced cake and as before was breaking it into small pieces before putting them into her mouth. Father looked down at me with a grin. 'Mrs Rocheforte material, do you think, Ginny?' he asked.

'Could be. She's a bit stuck up.'

'Well, you and I will go and have a few words, she's got to talk to somebody.' To Miss Brownson he said, 'Leave it to me, I'll get round to you later.'

I followed my father to where the girl was sitting. As we took our places opposite, she looked up and I noticed her beautiful eyes, the colour of my mother's jade necklace. Framed by dark, shining hair, her face had the quality of a cameo, luminous and exquisite.

'Hello,' Father said gently. 'I'm Dr Lawrence and this is my daughter Ginny. Didn't you want to sit with the others?'

'I don't know any of them,' she replied in her soft voice as if searching for words.

'Don't they come from the same place, the same school?' he encouraged.

She merely shrugged her shoulders.

Father said gently, 'Apparently you're not registered with the other children. Didn't your parents know they had to agree to your going away?'

The silence was defiant rather than sulky, and Father continued, 'Well, we'll make a start by knowing your name, where you come from and where your parents can be contacted.'

He stared at her appealingly. After a few seconds she said, in a voice hardly above a whisper, 'I'm Melissa Francis.'

'And your parents, Melissa?'

'There's only my grandmother.'

'You mean you live with your grandmother?'

She nodded.

'I'm afraid we shall need to know a little more about you, Melissa. All these children have accommodation to go to, families who agreed to take them weeks ago. In some cases their parents have been here to meet the host families. Will your grandmother be able to visit you?'

She shook her head.

'Why is that?'

'She's old, she hates travelling.'

14

'Are your parents dead?'

'My father's dead, my mother lives away.'

'I see.'

At that moment Miss Brownson came to us, holding her sheaf of papers and wearing a flustered expression. 'Have you made any headway here, doctor?' she demanded. 'All the children are accounted for except this one; it really is most irregular. How anybody can send a child without knowing she has a home to go to is quite beyond me. Obviously I'll have to find somebody willing to take her.'

'I don't think that will be necessary, Miss Brownson. I spoke to Mrs Rocheforte this morning and she's agreed to take a girl about Ginny's age. This is Melissa Francis and it seems she fits the bill.'

'Gracious me! Mrs Rocheforte was adamant the last time I spoke to her that she wouldn't take anybody. What's made her change her mind, I wonder? We can't send her just anybody, Dr Lawrence. Are you quite sure that you're doing the right thing?'

'Quite sure. I have evening surgery but there's time to run Melissa up to the Hall. Ginny can come with us.'

'Well, I would appreciate it, doctor, but do let me know if there are problems. We all know what Mrs Rocheforte's like — if she's agreed to take somebody, we have to make sure it's the right somebody.'

Importantly she moved away. Grinning at us, Father said, 'Well, girls, let's get going. The Hall is a few miles away and I don't want my patients standing waiting for me in the cold. Where is your luggage, Melissa?'

She pointed to the paper carrier bag.

Picking it up, Father said, 'There's not much in here, my dear. We'll have to see about some warm clothing for you. The winds that sweep down from the fells come right from Siberia.'

Without answering, she rose from her seat and walked beside us out of the hall.

'I'll sit in the back,' I said. 'You'll be able to see the country-side better. It's beautiful this morning.'

Without answering, she climbed into the front seat. As we drove off along the village street, Father said, 'This is all a far cry from the city, I suppose?'

She nodded. Father gave his full attention to the roads,

15

which were still treacherous, and Melissa sat gazing out of the windows at the mountains, the frozen lake and the road that wound upwards to the Hall with its turrets and terraces.

If Melissa was awed by the sight of the great stone house, she did not show it. She left the car and walked up the steps towards the house, and when I stole a look at her face I found her expression bland and unconcerned.

Somewhat nonplussed, Father said, 'Don't let the house intimidate you, Melissa. You'll find Mrs Rocheforte very nice. Answer her questions as well as you can and she'll soon come to see that you're exactly the sort of young lady she's hoping for.'

There was no answer from Melissa, and in silence we followed the butler across the hall and waited until Mrs Rocheforte's voice asked us to enter the room.

As before, she was sitting in her favourite chair, the spaniel at her feet. Only a quiet waft of his tail acknowledged our presence.

Mrs Rocheforte smiled. 'Do sit down, doctor, over there on the sofa, and perhaps you will sit here, my dear.' She smiled at Melissa. 'Would you all like tea?'

'I doubt if we have room for either tea or food,' Father was quick to say. 'The food at the village hall was more than adequate and we all did justice to it. This is Melissa Francis, Mrs Rocheforte. She wasn't on Miss Brownson's list but Ginny and I think she'll fit in very well here.'

Melissa sat calmly in her chair, her hands clasped together in her lap, enveloped in a strange maturity, seemingly unconcerned by the waiting.

'Where are you from?' Mrs Rocheforte asked her.

'Near Liverpool, ma'am.'

'And I expect you're sad to have been asked to leave your home. Your parents must feel that you will be safer here.'

There was no answer from Melissa.

After a few moments Mrs Rocheforte said, 'Have you brothers and sisters in Liverpool or are they also evacuated for the duration of the war?'

'I haven't any brothers or sisters,' Melissa replied.

'An only child will be very much missed. Perhaps it will be possible for your parents to visit you here, to reassure them that

16

you are being well cared for and are happy in your new environment. Would they like that, do you think, Melissa?'

'I have a grandmother. She doesn't like travelling.'

'What about your parents?'

'Mi mother's away and mi father's dead,' Melissa replied tersely, and for the first time I was aware of an accent that was not entirely genteel. In the next sentence she covered it up by saying, 'I don't know when my mother's coming home, she's working away.'

'I see. Do you have friends who came with you today?'

'No. I didn't know many of them.'

'Didn't you go to school with them?'

'We didn't live in Liverpool very long. I would have been going to a new school soon, but now I don't know where I shall go.'

'Of course, my dear, you will go to school here. Virginia's school, perhaps. I'll have a word with the headmistress to see what arrangements can be made.'

For the first time consternation showed on Melissa's face. 'Mi grandmother hasn't any money, she wouldn't be able to pay for my schooling.'

'We'll talk about that during the next few days, Melissa. For now I'll get one of the servants to show you up to your room. Virginia can go with you if you like.'

'I've got to get back, Mrs Rocheforte,' Father said quickly. 'I have evening surgery. Ready, Ginny?'

I turned to smile at Melissa. 'We live at the big house in the middle of the high street,' I told her. 'I do hope you'll come to visit us.'

Mrs Rocheforte pressed the bell beside her chair and a young housemaid appeared to show Melissa up to her room. She left with only a brief smile in our direction, and after she had gone Mrs Rocheforte said, 'What a self-contained child she is, Dr Lawrence.'

'We have to think that this has been quite an ordeal for her,' Father said quickly. 'Some of the children were in tears, others were frightened; at least she seems to be holding up very well.'

'More than well,' Mrs Rocheforte answered dryly. 'Ah, well, I'll do all I can for her, I can't do more.'

'No, indeed. You can telephone me at home about nine

o'clock if you have any problems, or Miss Brownson, who has had the evacuation problem in hand.'

'I will telephone you, Dr Lawrence, and I hope Virginia will make a friend of Melissa. A friend of her own age will do wonders for that young lady, I think.'

My father was unusually silent on the way home and I too had a lot to think about. Mrs Rocheforte had put the responsibility for Melissa in my hands and I was unsure if Melissa wanted my friendship.

Something of my thoughts must have conveyed themselves to my father. Before we left the car, he said gently, 'It's early days yet, Ginny. Reserve your judgement until you know her better. Now let's find out a little more about the boy we've taken under our wing.'

When we got home, our evacuee was out on the fell with Rodney, and Edith had elected to go with them which was a sure sign of her approval.

Mother said, with a smile, 'He's a very nice boy, darling, he'll fit in very well. His father's a heart surgeon and he's already made sure that Alistair has got a transfer to the grammar school here. The two boys will be able to go together. How did you get on with your girl?'

'Well, she's installed up at the Hall. Not a very forthcoming girl, I'm afraid, but it's been a difficult day for her. She'll settle in, I'm sure.'

'Did you like her, Ginny?'

'I probably will like her when I get to know her better.'

At that moment there was the sound of chatter and laughter from the garden and then Edith and Rodney were in the kitchen accompanied by a tall, fair-haired boy who smiled at me and held out his hand. My first thought was that he was nice. He had already captivated Edith, who sat next to him at the evening meal and monopolised him to such an extent that Father said jovially, 'Give us all a chance, love, we all want to know Alistair. My wife tells me you'll be going to school with Rodney?'

'Yes, my father arranged it when he knew I was coming here.'

'And are you doing well at school?'

'I think so. My father was pleased.'

'Any ambitions?'

'Yes, I want to be a doctor like my father, and like you too, sir.'

'I don't want to be a doctor,' Rodney asserted. 'My father works silly hours and he's at everybody's beck and call.'

'We have yet to hear what you do want to be,' Father said.

'I'll know when it's time to make up my mind.'

'You're not clever enough to be a doctor,' Edith snapped spitefully.

Rodney retaliated by saying, 'My reports are better than yours, and Ginny's are better than yours.'

'Do you have brothers and sisters, Alistair?' Mother asked, smiling.

'No, I'm an only child.'

'Lucky you!' Rodney said feelingly.

Meeting my eyes across the table, Alistair smiled.

The evening passed uneventfully. Father went off to his evening surgery before visiting his patients. Mother worked on her embroidery and we children sat round the dining table playing Monopoly. Mother had made sure we had done our homework before the arrival of the evacuees. Promptly at nine o'clock Cloonie came in with steaming cups of cocoa.

Edith said, 'Don't forget I'm first for the bathroom! But as it's Alistair's first night here, I don't mind him going first tonight.'

'No, please, Edith, I'd much rather you went first,' he said gallantly. 'It's best we keep to the rota.'

'Oh, well, if you insist.'

But Mother was quick to say, 'I think Ginny ought to go first in the evening as she's the youngest, and she can go last in the morning. I don't want Ginny up after the rest of you have gone to bed.'

The other three saw the logic in this. Not to be outdone, Edith said firmly, 'Don't take all day, Ginny, remember we're waiting.'

In some annoyance, I retorted, 'Then don't you take all day in the morning, I have to go to school as well as you.'

'Aren't you glad you didn't have brothers and sisters?' Mother asked gently.

Alistair merely smiled.

19

Later, in the bedroom I shared with Edith, we made peace. Sitting up in bed and hugging her knees, she said, 'I think he's nice, don't you? Much nicer than the boy Mary Allen's family are having.'

'How is he nicer?'

'He's much better-looking. I saw Mary Allen looking at him in the village hall, and when I saw their boy I could understand why.'

'What's wrong with him?'

'He was small and pimply, I was hoping he wasn't the one we were having.'

I wasn't very interested in the boy staying with the Allens. I was sleepy, it had been a long day, but before I drifted off, I thought about Melissa in that great house surrounded by tall trees with the forest of Bowland sweeping down to the fells.

# Chapter Three

Weeks passed and the children settled down in their new homes. Some of them were terribly homesick and others adapted easily, loving the cold, crisp mornings and starlit nights. We joined them at the weekends as they played in the snow on the lower fells and our laughter could be heard echoing on the still, icy air.

It soon became apparent that Edith had developed a crush on Alistair since she didn't like any attention he bestowed on me. Alistair took it all in his stride, he was kind and charming to both of us, and he and Rodney became inseparable. Father had good reports of him from the school; indeed, they were far better than Rodney's, which had the effect of making Rodney try harder. Father said that was a very good thing.

Of Melissa we saw nothing, neither in the village nor on the lanes leading up to the Hall. It was Miss Brownson, who came to see us one evening in some distress, that made us all think about Melissa.

We had just finished the evening meal and Father was about to set out for his surgery when Cloonie brought Miss Brownson into the dining room.

'She's wantin' to see you urgently, doctor. I told 'er you were due to go out but she's right upset, she is.' Miss Brownson hovered behind Cloonie in the doorway.

'Come along in, Miss Brownson,' Father said. 'Sit here near the fire and Margaret will give you a glass of sherry.'

While Mother poured the sherry, Miss Brownson sat with her hands clenched in her lap and a look of the utmost frustration on her face.

'I'm sorry to bother you with this, Dr Lawrence, but I am responsible for the children who were sent here. I told Mrs Rocheforte this but all I got in reply was that since she sat on the Education Committee, she knew what she was doing.'

'And what is she doing?' Father asked.

'It's the girl she's taken to live at the Hall. She isn't going to school and Mrs Rocheforte has got in a private tutor. I saw the girl, who seems particularly aloof. It's difficult to say if she's happy or unhappy, but she does need to be with other children. It's unnatural that she isn't mixing with the children she knew in Liverpool.'

'I doubt if she mixed with them in Liverpool,' Father said. 'From the little bit she told us, she hardly knew any of them. There was some sort of mystery attached to the girl, or she wants to put the past behind her quite deliberately.'

'But a tutor, Dr Lawrence! A tutor in this day and age! I suppose a private education is all right for the royal family, or even for Mrs Rocheforte's own children, but this girl is only an evacuee from a provincial city.'

'I'm due to pay Mrs Rocheforte a visit. I'll have a chat with her about Melissa and I'll be sure to keep you informed. Try not to worry too much, I'm sure there's a very good reason for everything Mrs Rocheforte is doing. I'll take Ginny up to the Hall with me, maybe she can get closer to Melissa than either you or I.'

After Miss Brownson had gone, the rest of the family had their say.

'We don't want her here if she's that stuck up,' Rodney asserted.

Edith said, 'I didn't like her at all, she was too superior and she's not that pretty.'

'I thought she was lovely,' I said defensively. 'She was different — different from anybody we know.'

'She's probably very shy,' Mother said. 'It must have been a wrench having to leave her home, and then to find herself in that huge place with a woman who isn't the easiest person to know.'

'She's really quite a charming woman, Margaret,' Father demurred. 'She's possibly a very lonely woman who wants to do the best for a young girl who has suddenly been thrust upon her.'

The next evening Father and I drove up to the Hall. He made out it was a routine visit, enquired about Mrs Rocheforte's health and checked her pulse and her blood pressure.

'Quite normal,' he said with a smile. 'Have you been taking care during this cold spell?'

'Yes, of course, Dr Lawrence. You know I seldom go out in the winter, but I did go into Lancaster with Melissa to choose some clothes for her. The poor child had very little in that paper bag she brought.'

'How is Melissa?'

'I rather suspect she is the reason you and Virginia are here. Miss Brownson came to see me and left in some impatience. She does not approve of the tutor I have been employing for Melissa and after she'd gone I felt pretty sure she'd be informing you before the day was out.'

'But why a tutor? What's wrong with the schools around here?'

'Nothing at all. But I didn't know how bright she was. Somehow or other I couldn't think she'd fit in at the village school and there was no point in sending her to your daughters' school if she wasn't up to it. A tutor for the first few weeks seemed the ideal solution. He is a retired headmaster from a boys' public school. I have great respect for his judgement and he is only here until Christmas. After that I will follow his advice on which school Melissa attends.'

'And which do you think that will be?' Father asked.

'He tells me she is intelligent and learns well, so I rather think it will be Copelands. I have already spoken to the headmistress on the subject.'

'Then it seems Miss Brownson has nothing to worry about.'

'That is what I told her, Dr Lawrence.'

'And where is Melissa now?'

'She is in the old nursery. She spends most of her time up there, doing her schoolwork or reading. Occasionally she walks in the garden but it is very cold out there.'

'The other children play on the fell, Mrs Rocheforte. They love the snow and the lake.'

23

'I am aware of it, doctor. Virginia, perhaps you would like to go up to the nursery to see Melissa? You will make a pleasant change from her school books. It's on the second floor, the door directly opposite the top of the stairs. And you and I will drink a glass of sherry, I think, Dr Lawrence.'

I climbed the stairs, awed by the size of the house, my feet making no sound on the deep pile of the carpet, and on the way there were pictures that claimed my attention. A young girl sitting on a garden swing, a small kitten in her arms, her pretty face smiling, her blonde hair tied back in a blue ribbon; two boys in school uniform, their faces similar; and at the head of the first flight of stairs, the portrait of a tall man in military uniform. There was also one of a very much younger Mrs Rocheforte in a white satin gown with three feathers in her hair. She had been very beautiful, and some of that beauty still lingered in the face of the woman below.

I faced the nursery door, doubtful of my welcome. However, there was no help for it, and after a brief knock I opened the door and went in.

Melissa was sitting on the window seat with a book on her knee. She looked across the room as I entered and I smiled a little tremulously at the sight of a face that showed no sign of welcome, only an adult acceptance.

'Hello, Melissa,' I said. 'Mrs Rocheforte told me to come up here, she thought you might like some company.'

'I'm doing my homework. Mr Arden is coming tomorrow and he will expect me to have memorised everything he taught me.'

'I'm sorry if I'm interrupting you. I can go if you like, I can tell her you're too busy to see me.'

She put the book down quickly on the window seat and, jumping to her feet, came towards me and suddenly smiled. Melissa's smile was unlike any other smile I could remember. It illuminated her face, chased the coldness from it, made me feel that she had been waiting for me all day.

'Come and sit near the fire,' she said, 'and get warm. I sit on the window seat because it's lighter there.'

'Can't you sit near the fire and put the light on?'

'The maid comes up to put the lights on. Usually I go down

24

for afternoon tea and when I come up in the evening the lights are lit and the fire's been stoked up.'

'I see.'

I stared at her curiously. She spoke differently now, the inflection in her voice reminiscent of Mrs Rocheforte, as was the air with which she indicated the chair opposite hers. 'How long can you stay?'

'I'm not sure, my father will tell me when he wants to leave.'

'Did you get an evacuee?'

'Yes, a boy, Alistair. He's very nice.'

'Is he going to school?'

'Yes, with my brother Rodney.'

'I'm to go to school after Christmas, your school, I think. I shan't know anybody but you.'

'Well, you'll soon get to know the others.'

'Mrs Rocheforte is paying the school fees. Are they very expensive?'

'My father says so.'

She grinned. 'She's really very nice and generous. I like living here. I like the house and the servants, I like being waited on, and she's bought me some clothes. Come to my bedroom and I'll show you.'

Obediently I followed her out of the nursery and along the corridor to her bedroom. The room was huge with a large bed, dressing table and chest of drawers. Off it was a pretty, pink bathroom. On the floor was a thick, pale-green carpet and there were long velvet drapes at the windows.

'But it's beautiful!' I exclaimed.

Melissa smiled.

'It makes our little bedroom look like a rabbit hutch,' I said.

Melissa was opening the large wardrobe doors to show me a rail filled with skirts and blouses, dresses and warm winter coats, while a rack at the bottom of the wardrobe displayed several pairs of shoes in different colours.

'Mrs Rocheforte bought you all these?' I asked in surprise.

'Yes, and if I'm to go to your school she'll buy me the uniform.'

'You've been very lucky, Melissa. The other children are going to the village school and the families they're billeted with haven't this sort of money.'

25

'I know. I must be the sort of girl she was hoping for.'

If there was vanity in her voice, she hid it very well, making it seem merely a commonplace expression of her suitability for her new life.

I wondered how she would fit in at Copelands. Most of the girls had been friends from years back, even the girls from the other villages, but Melissa was different, with her confident air.

'Are you looking forward to coming to Copelands?' I asked curiously.

She shrugged her shoulders delicately. 'I really don't care,' she said. 'Shall I like it? Do you like it?'

'Yes, very much. I have a lot of friends there.'

'Then you won't have time for me?'

'Of course I will. I'll introduce you to the others and you'll soon make friends.'

At that moment a young housemaid put her head inside the door, saying, 'Your father's ready for leavin' now if you'd like to go downstairs.'

On the way back I told him about Melissa's room and her wardrobe.

He grinned cheerfully. 'It would seem she's fallen on her feet. Is she any more forthcoming?'

'Oh, yes, and she speaks exactly like Mrs Rocheforte.'

'Then it would seem we don't have to worry about Melissa,' he observed dryly.

As the days and weeks passed, it seemed that the evacuees had always been with us. They mingled with the village children in the school playground and attended each other's birthday parties. They revelled in the snow, skating precariously along the icy pavements, and excitement shone in their faces as they viewed the decorated church hall and the Christmas tree brought down from the fells and placed in the centre of the green.

The tree was a stately Norwegian spruce, and as usual everybody in the village took a hand at decorating it. Lights were now forbidden, but there was no dearth of tinsel and shining baubles. Parcels were arriving daily from the evacuees' families in the cities, and I wondered if there had been anything for Melissa from her grandmother.

When I mentioned it to Father, he said Mrs Rocheforte had told him Melissa received no letters but there had been a small parcel. When Mrs Rocheforte had asked if it was from her grandmother, she merely said 'Yes' and took it up to her room. Nothing more was said about the parcel.

'She's a mystery,' Mother said. 'I wonder how she's going to get along if she goes to Copelands in the new year?'

'If she's going to be aloof and stuck up, nobody'll like her,' Edith said firmly, 'and if you're going to get stuck with her, Ginny, you'll lose all your friends.'

'She's probably very shy,' Mother said. 'After all, it must be a little intimidating to find yourself living at the Hall.'

Alistair surprised us by saying, 'I'm glad to have come here. I'd have hated to go somewhere like the Hall where there are no other children.'

Father smiled, well pleased with his comments. 'So you don't really mind this wretched brood then?' he said jokingly.

'Well, no! We always had a quiet time at Christmas. This will be the first time in my life I've ever been part of a family.'

'What did you do at Christmas, then?' Edith asked curiously.

Alistair didn't answer her immediately. His face was thoughtful, his fork chasing the food around his plate. Then, with a shy smile, he said, 'We always had my grandmother for Christmas, and Uncle Martin. Grandmother was very deaf and didn't hear anything that was said to her, and Uncle Martin grumbled all day about the expense of Christmas. My parents hardly spoke to each other and then three years ago my mother went away.'

'Where did she go to?' Rodney asked, though cautioned by a warning look from Mother.

Alistair answered him quietly, 'She said she'd had enough. Father was immersed in his work, and I knew she was unhappy. I think she must have been unhappy for a very long time.'

My eyes filled with tears for Alistair and his mother, for a boy who had no brothers and sisters to love and quarrel with.

Seeing the tears rolling slowly down my cheeks, he smiled. 'There's no need to cry for me, Ginny, I'd never known anything else. Now I'm really looking forward to Christmas here with you.'

'It won't be like the old Christmases,' Rodney said dolefully.

27

'There's rationing, and Cloonie's grumbling all the time about her Christmas cake and there not being enough of anything to make Christmas dinner.'

'I think you'll discover that Cloonie will cope very well,' Father said dryly. 'She grumbled when there was plenty. We'll just let her get on with it and not forget to tell her what a wonder she's turned out to be.'

As predicted, the kitchen table disappeared under a mountain of mince pies and a cake every bit as large as any cake I could remember. Cloonie warned us that it wouldn't taste the same, powdered eggs and powdered milk couldn't possibly produce the same result, but Father cheerfully upended it and poured in a large glass of his best brandy.

It was the season of coughs and colds and he was kept busy in his surgery and on his rounds, but we were all together in the village church for the carol service on Christmas Eve, and were on our way home when he dropped his bombshell.

I was invited to eat Christmas lunch with Mrs Rocheforte and Melissa at the Hall. In spite of my tearful protests, he was adamant that I should attend. It was almost like a royal summons. Father would drive me there in the morning and collect me in the early evening, and I was admonished not to sulk, since there would still be festivities around our own fireside waiting for my return.

Rodney and Edith thought it was a huge joke, Alistair was sympathetic, but Mother said gently, 'Think about Melissa, love, a young girl all at sea in that great house. At least you can cheer her up a bit.'

Personally I didn't think Melissa needed any cheering up. She sat at the table, calmly eating her lunch while I felt completely overawed in that vast dining room. Mrs Rocheforte sat at one end of the long table while Melissa and I sat opposite each other. The table glowed with crystal and silver, but its only decoration was a bowl filled with dark-red roses and not a trace of holly.

We had been bringing holly into the house for days, bright with so many scarlet berries that Cloonie said it was evident there was a hard winter ahead of us.

We talked about school, about my ambitions for the future, and I learned that when Christmas was over Melissa would be joining us at Copelands. In genteel tones Melissa asked about my friends there, about the teachers and what she might expect to find in the way of social activities. All the time Mrs Rocheforte listened, occasionally smiling.

After lunch the servants came to clear away and Mrs Rocheforte went to her room for her afternoon's rest, saying she would return to the drawing room in time to hear the King's speech. The three of us listened to it in front of a huge log fire and I thought of my family at home listening to it in our living room, surrounded by Christmas presents and hearty camaraderie.

After the speech was over, Melissa asked permission for us to walk in the grounds. We were advised to wrap up warmly and not stay out too long. The wind hit us like a knife as we emerged into the winter afternoon and we walked quickly along the frozen paths surrounding the house. Melissa talked about Mrs Rocheforte's jewellery and furs, things I wasn't really interested in at that time.

Later, in her room, I asked Melissa to show me her Christmas presents. She said hastily, 'I've had chocolates and a new dressing gown. What have you had?'

So I told her about my modest presents from my brother and sister, my pleasure in a book that Alistair had given me that morning, and the bedroom slippers from Cloonie and articles of clothing from my parents.

'Did your grandmother send you anything?' I asked curiously.

'No, I expect she forgot.' She added, 'She hasn't anything to send, she left all her money and her jewels behind when she had to leave Russia in a hurry.'

I stared at her wide-eyed. 'Tell me about it! When did she leave Russia?'

'All the aristocrats fled. My grandmother was married to a Russian grand duke who was shot and killed and grandmother had to get out, leaving everything behind. She was lucky to escape with her life. Now she's old and forgetful. She wouldn't even think about Christmas.'

'But she writes to you, surely?'

'She hates writing letters. I never expected her to write to me.'

'Was your mother in Russia, too?'

'Oh, no. My mother was born in England. My grandmother married an Englishman for her second husband.'

'Hasn't your mother sent you anything for Christmas?'

I was suddenly aware of the hostility in her eyes and realised that my questions were unwelcome. Without answering, she said sharply, 'I expect your father'll be here for you soon.'

He came for me in the late afternoon. It was already dark and had started to snow, thin powdery snow that was caught up with the wind in flurries of white. Under the full moon the parkland seemed an enchanted place, like a huge, beautiful Christmas card, creating a scene I thought I would remember always.

We drove in silence. Father devoted all his attention to steering the car on the frozen road. There were no lights along the winding lanes and straggling village street, so that the moonlight seemed doubly beautiful.

As soon as we were home, I was bombarded with questions about how I had enjoyed my day at the Hall. I rushed to tell them about Melissa's grandmother's exciting life in Russia and her escape. I embroidered on it a little, on the sleigh ride across the snow, her furs and her jewellery, her husband who had been a relative of the tsar.

Edith was impressed, the boys interested, but I did not miss the swift glance of amusement that passed between my parents and I realised that they were sceptical about Melissa's story.

It was only much later, when we were in bed, that I remembered the small parcel Melissa had received, which she had never mentioned.

Edith brought up the story again over breakfast and this time Father said, 'I think we should take Melissa's story with a pinch of salt.'

'You mean you don't believe it?' I cried.

'I mean that I think our Melissa is a young lady with a good imagination and an inventive frame of mind. Perhaps there is some truth in her story but I wouldn't say too much about it at Copelands. The other girls might give her a hard time.'

'Why would they give her a hard time if her story's true?' I demanded.

'Girls can be very unkind to each other,' Mother said gently.

'They might think she's a bit of a show-off. I've already heard some of their mothers going on about her private tutor, and the fact that she's living up at the Hall doesn't exactly endear her to some of them.'

'Mary Allen says she's sure to give herself airs and graces,' Edith said.

'And Mary Allen rules a gaggle of girls who will agree with her,' Mother said quickly.

'Well, I don't care what Mary Allen's going to think,' I replied staunchly. 'I think Melissa's all she says she is, and I think Mary Allen's going to have to watch out.'

'At any rate life isn't going to be dull,' Father added.

Later in the morning, when Miss Brownson arrived, it seemed to have started already.

'I suppose you're aware Melissa is going to Copelands?' was her opening gambit.

'It would seem so,' Father said diplomatically.

'Matters were taken completely out of my hands,' Miss Brownson went on, 'but I think the tutor was a grave mistake and I'm not so sure about the girl herself. She's more aloof than ever, and now she speaks with an upper-crust accent she certainly didn't have when she arrived here. Living at the Hall has given her ideas of grandeur the other children could resent.'

I opened my mouth to speak but Father cut in quickly, saying, 'Two months of living with Mrs Rocheforte must have had some effect. We shouldn't judge Melissa too harshly. None of us knows what her life was like before she came here, and I admire the girl for trying to improve herself.'

'Well, she's seen nothing of the children who arrived with her. How do you suppose they'll view the new Melissa?' Miss Brownson wondered.

'I doubt they'll be interested. Anyway, Melissa's a bit of a mystery and she appears to like it that way.'

I longed to tell Miss Brownson about her aristocratic grandmother but by this time I knew Father wanted me to keep that story to myself. I knew I was right when he later instructed Edith and me to say nothing to any of the girls at school.

'If Melissa wishes to tell them, then that's her affair, but it shouldn't come from either of you two,' he said firmly.

'I'd love to tell Mary Allen,' Edith said. 'She thinks she

knows everything and she's the one who's been going on all over the school about the private tutor.'

'Let Melissa handle Mary Allen,' Mother advised. 'From what I hear of that young lady, I feel she's quite capable of doing so.'

# Chapter Four

The Christmas holidays were over and I waited with others for the small bus that would take us to Copelands, while Rodney and Alistair crossed the road to go to the station for the local train.

There was no sign of Melissa, and Edith whispered, 'How's she going to get there? It's a long way from the Hall.'

My eyes scanned the road leading away from the village, but only the baker's van trundled down the centre. The snow was piled high on both sides.

We left the bus at the gates to Copelands, and there we greeted our friends, chattering about the holidays and how we had spent them. While we were laughing together, Mrs Rocheforte's large Daimler drew up at the school gates and the chauffeur got out to open the door for Melissa.

Everybody stopped to stare at the slender girl walking alone along the path. She wore her new uniform with an air of elegance in advance of her years. Under the wide-brimmed hat she looked us over with calm detachment.

Giving me a little push, Edith hissed, 'Go and meet her! She's your friend, isn't she?'

I went forward, strangely unsure of my welcome, and said hurriedly, 'I looked for you at the bus stop. I wondered how you'd get here.'

'Mrs Rocheforte said I had to come in the car. The bus doesn't stop near the Hall.'

'Come along, I'll introduce you to the others.'

I was amazed at her composure, remembering my own first morning at Copelands, when I had known hardly anybody

33

except my sister. On Melissa's face there was no sign of anxiety. This was the Melissa I had seen alighting from the train on the day of her arrival, with all the wariness of a queen about to face her enemies.

Right from that first day, Melissa was unpopular with Mary Allen's set, but it appeared not to worry her. Snide remarks drifted over her head without any ruffling of that enigmatic composure, and my sister said that for once she agreed with Mary Allen, Melissa had too big an opinion of herself.

In spite of the private tutor, she was not particularly clever but she managed to hold her own in the central stream. The Daimler continued to bring her and pick her up in the evening. My father had a quiet word with Mrs Rocheforte, suggesting that Melissa came on the bus like the rest of us or she could find herself unpopular. But Mrs Rocheforte merely said, 'While my chauffeur is driving Melissa to the bus stop, he might just as well take her all the way.'

She was chastised by the music mistress for not opening her mouth to sing at assembly or in the school choir. 'I'd be interested to know what exactly are your interests, Melissa?' Miss Carter said sharply.

Melissa merely looked at her and didn't bother to reply.

Apart from the evacuees, war seemed not to touch the Lakeland villages, although at night from the fells we could see the sky was red over Barrow and further south, and we knew that cities were suffering under Hitler's bombardment. Many of the children had sleepless nights, because their families lived in those cities. There was much talk in the village that spring about the terrible fears that somehow brought death close to all of us.

When I asked Melissa if she was worried about her grandmother, she said calmly, 'She's gone through worse things than this, she'll cope.'

I was there when Miss Brownson told my parents she had brought sad news to a brother and sister that their parents had been killed in an air raid on Liverpool, and to a little girl whose mother had been killed when a hospital was bombed where she was working.

'What will they do when the war's over?' Edith asked

curiously. 'They'll have nobody to go home to.'

'That's for the future,' Miss Brownson replied. 'None of us knows how long the war will last, and with luck the children have relatives who'll take care of them.'

'But they can't go home for the holidays,' Edith persisted.

'They'll be safer here,' said Miss Brownson. 'That reminds me, what do you suppose Melissa will do while Mrs Rocheforte's away with her sister in August?'

'Are you sure she's spending August with her sister?' Father asked.

'Well, it'll be the first time if she doesn't. I can't think that Lady Barton will want a strange girl about the place, and to leave Melissa in that great house with just the servants doesn't seem right.'

'What's the alternative?' asked Father.

'I was wondering if perhaps you would have a quiet word with Mrs Rocheforte. Melissa and Ginny are friends, perhaps between you, you could come up with something. Don't your family go to the coast for the school holidays?'

'We've always rented a house in north Devonshire, ever since Edith was a baby, but this year is different. We don't know if it's safe to travel all that way by train, and the petrol ration even for a doctor won't stretch to the West Country.'

'I see.'

'Holidays and Melissa, Miss Brownson, you've lumped them together — I wonder why.'

Miss Brownson had the grace to blush and appear flustered.

'Oh, it's nothing, really, doctor. I was simply thinking it might be rather nice if you had room for Melissa. The two boys are happy together, and Edith is so much older than Ginny.'

'And Edith has older friends, and Ginny might like to have Melissa, and it would mean you don't have to worry about her,' Father said with a wry smile.

'I'm sorry, Dr Lawrence, it was only a thought. Of course I can't expect you to take Melissa with you. I'll have to think of something else.'

'Leave it with me,' he replied. 'I'll have a word with Mrs Rocheforte and between us we'll take care of Melissa.'

\*　　\*　　\*

35

The music mistress decided to stage *The Mikado* at the end of term. Auditions for the parts would take place on Friday evening after school, she announced.

A keen admirer of Gilbert and Sullivan, Father entertained us to a gramophone selection from *The Mikado* and told us about the story. I had a small, sweet voice which was always acceptable in the chorus, but Edith had a stronger and wider range and usually got one of the small parts.

The lead soprano was sure to go to Joyce Miller, the vicar's daughter. She had had singing lessons from her aunt for many years and she was pretty and popular, so usually it was a foregone conclusion that Joyce would take the leading role in anything the school produced.

Edith informed us that she intended to audition for the part of one of Yum Yum's sisters and father remarked dryly that Mary Allen might make a very creditable Katisha. The male parts were always sung by the teaching staff. Mr Weller, the art master, fancied himself as a useful tenor and Mr Longrod and Mr Gerrard were baritones. If we didn't have enough male singers in the school, Mr Weller always seemed to have friends who would step in.

On Friday evening I waited outside the school doors to walk down to the gates with Melissa. There was no sign of the Daimler, and after a little while the bus driver came to the gates and waved at me to hurry to the bus. It was not until Edith arrived home, bursting with excitement, that I knew what had happened.

Melissa had gone to the audition and got the principal role.

I couldn't believe it. 'Did you hear her sing?' I asked. 'She never sang in the classroom or at assembly. Miss Carter was always on to her about it, I only ever heard her mumble.'

'Well, she's got the part. Joyce Miller's got the part of one sister and I've got the other; Mary Allen's Katisha. The first rehearsal's next Monday so we'll all be able to hear Melissa sing then.'

It was the talk of the village over the weekend, and of the school all Monday. Melissa seemed completely unconcerned by the attention she was receiving.

'Why didn't you tell me you were going to the audition?' I said somewhat reproachfully.

'I didn't want the others to know. None of them really likes me, and I wanted to surprise Miss Carter. She's always getting at me. I couldn't wait to see her face when I stayed for the auditions.'

'Did you have to sing for them on your own?'

'Yes, of course.'

'What did you sing?'

'"The Last Rose of Summer". Joyce Miller went in first and I could hear her singing it. She was so sure she'd got the part, I could tell by her face when she came out, but they hadn't heard me then.'

'You sang it better than Joyce?'

'I got the part, didn't I?'

'You're awfully secretive, Melissa.'

'I had to be. Some of them have been hostile.'

'I thought I was your friend.'

'You are, but I'll probably have others now. The ones who make a goddess of Joyce Miller, they know what they can do.'

There was a smile of derision on her face. There was little satisfaction in being Melissa's friend, for she did not need me. Even as I was thinking this, she surprised me by saying, 'Why don't we do something together next weekend?'

Like a grateful puppy I agreed to whatever she had in mind, which turned out to be listening to recordings of *The Mikado*.

On Monday evening at the rehearsal I heard Melissa sing for the first time. I couldn't believe it, nor could any of the others. All those whispered and mumbled noises that we had been subjected to were suddenly replaced by a powerful, pure soprano that made Joyce Miller's voice seem feeble and childish. Miss Carter appeared as stunned as the rest of us, but there was no disguising the appreciation in her attitude. Here was a girl worthy of her efforts.

It was almost dark when we emerged from the school doors. Father was waiting for us in the company of several others. Further down the road I could see the Daimler parked and the chauffeur waiting at the open rear door.

'Well?' Father demanded as soon as we were in the car. 'How did it go?'

'She was fantastic,' Edith said. 'None of us could believe it.'

'So, what did you sing?'

'Well, the three-little-maids thing, and then she sang a duet with Mr Weller. In the past he always had to sing softly so that he didn't drown Joyce, but he had to keep his end up with Melissa.'

'And what about you, Ginny? Did you do your bit?'

'I didn't have anything to do except sing with the others. Edith and Joyce were very good,' I added loyally.

'All the village will be looking forward to the finished product,' Father assured us.

I enjoyed being in the chorus, listening to voices better than mine. But more important to me was the talk of the summer holidays.

At one stage Edith would have objected to Melissa's being included. Now, however, having Melissa on holiday was regarded as something of a feather in her cap, and we later learned that several other of the girls had issued invitations to her to spend the summer holidays with them.

At the weekends Melissa and I sat on the fells surrounded by sheep while below us the lake sparkled and glowed in the sunlight. She asked endless questions about Devonshire: why we went there, what we did there, and what sort of clothes she would need.

'Oh, summer frocks and cotton shorts — the usual holiday clothes,' I answered, but her expression was doubtful. She started to make excuses about the holiday, saying she should go to see her grandmother, or that she should stay at the Hall and wait for Mrs Rocheforte to come back.

Mother was the first to say, 'Why do you think she's losing interest in the holiday, Ginny?'

'I don't think she has the right sort of clothes.'

'There are a great many things Edith has grown out of, but we have to be very careful not to offend Melissa. I think she's probably very proud and sensitive. Perhaps your father will have a quiet word with Mrs Rocheforte.'

A few weeks later, Melissa took me up to her room to show me an array of summer clothes which far outshone anything Edith or I had in our wardrobes.

The weeks leading up to the end of term passed quickly. The

rehearsals for the end-of-term concert occupied most of our evenings and preparing for exams took care of the rest.

At the weekends we helped to paint stage scenery. Costumes were produced by willing helpers out of old curtain material, and attics were raided to reveal treasures largely forgotten. Mr Weller pored over Japanese prints and programmes of professional companies who had performed *The Mikado*. Numerous sewing machines in the village were whirring away in an effort to produce creditable kimonos and other costumes. Mrs Rocheforte contributed the material for Melissa's costumes, causing Mrs Allen to grumble that she shouldn't be allowed to overshadow Mary's part in the show.

By the first night of the concert, the classrooms were hives of activity where anxious mothers gathered to see that their daughters were as good as everybody else's. My kimono was in rose pink and round my head was a bandeau decorated with two floppy artificial flowers Cloonie had taken from one of her hats. Edith was wearing a kimono in bright peacock blue with slightly larger flowers in her hair, from another of Cloonie's hats.

None of us saw what Melissa wore until it was time for her to enter the stage. Sure enough, her costume was made of pale-blue, heavy satin, and the flowers in her hair were real chrysanthemums, their soft pink setting off her dark hair.

'We're supposed to be sisters,' Edith complained, 'but she makes Joyce and me look like poor relations.'

'Well, she is the lead,' I said gently.

'Don't we all know it,' Edith retorted.

Miss Brownson made an appearance backstage to inform us that the hall was filled to capacity and Mrs Rocheforte was sitting with the headmistress in the middle of the front row.

'I hope that won't make you nervous,' she said to Melissa, who responded with a half-smile and a small shrug of her shoulders.

We listened in the wings to the men performing their parts. What they lacked in tunefulness they made up for in enthusiasm. We were greeted with delighted applause when it was our turn to enter the arena, and even more applause when the three little girls from school shuffled out on the stage, fluttering their fans, rolling their eyes and enchanting the audience with their voices.

'We have a huge success on our hands,' Miss Carter informed us at the first interval. But it was Melissa's solo that clinched it. I listened entranced as she sang, staring provocatively into her hand mirror, her expression chillingly vain, her pure soprano unashamedly proclaiming:

'Pray make no mistake,
We are not shy.
We're very wide awake, the moon and I.'

The applause was rapturous. Even Mary Allen's accute bitchiness in the role of Katisha had no power to detract from the sheer poetry of Melissa's performance.

Afterwards, when we were driving home in Father's car, he started to sing:

'I mean to rule the earth as he the sky,
We really know our worth, the sun and I.'

Looking at his face, I saw that he was smiling. Catching me looking at him, he grinned, saying dryly, 'And that young lady meant every word of it. Oh, pray make no mistake, she is not shy, she really knows her worth, does Melissa.'

'We can expect to hear more of this, David,' Mother said firmly. 'Either you'll receive a royal summons to go up to the Hall or Miss Brownson will call to see us. Either way, it promises to be very interesting.'

By this time we had reached the house and the dogs were barking a welcome. Rodney and Alistair were sitting at the kitchen table, their school books open before them. Grinning, Rodney said, 'How'd it go, then?'

'You said you didn't want to see it, so there's no need for you to know,' Edith was quick to retort.

'So it was a flop?' Rodney went on.

'It was extremely well done,' Mother said. 'Melissa was wonderful; they all were.'

'Really? Perhaps we will go.' He exchanged a look with Alistair. 'I thought she'd be a disaster.'

'You'll be lucky if you can get seats,' Edith said. 'Tomorrow everybody will want to go when they hear what a success it is.'

'Well, you've got a part and we're family. Surely you can get a couple of seats?'

'I'm not promising,' she said, with a smirk on her face.

'Then Ginny'll get tickets for us,' Rodney said.

'She won't if I won't,' Edith asserted.

Father said, 'Stop your squabbling! You were annoyed when they decided not to come; now they want to come, you're being difficult. Get the tickets and satisfy their curiosity.'

# Chapter Five

Father's summons to the Hall came two days later. Mrs Rocheforte complained that her blood pressure was too high, but Father thought he knew what had brought it on.

It was Friday, and the last night of the concert. When it was time for us to leave for the school, he still hadn't returned and we had to beg a lift from Mr Miller. Edith had managed to get tickets for the two boys, but they had decided they would set out early and walk up to the school.

After the concert we sat and listened to the speeches extolling our performance. Flowers were handed up to the lead singers, Melissa in the centre of them, gracious and smiling. That night I had no idea how often I would see her thus.

In the way of brothers, Rodney was noncommittal about the concert, but Alistair was enthusiastic. He thought the entire thing had been very well done and Melissa spectacular.

'What about me?' Edith demanded.

'You were great,' he assured her. 'You too, Ginny. You looked so pretty singing your heart out in the chorus.'

I smiled at him warmly. I thought a lot of Alistair. He was kind and warm, never made me feel inadequate, the way Edith often did, and I was glad that he had come to be part of our family.

'What did Mrs Rocheforte want?' Edith demanded to know as soon as we entered the living room, where Father sat with his newspaper and his whisky nightcap.

'Just a chat about her blood pressure,' he answered.

'What did she say about Melissa?'

'She was pleased with her performance, of course.'

He was saying nothing more and we had to be content.

At the end of July a taxi arrived to take us to the station. Cloonie did not come with us. 'I shall hate goin' by train,' she had said firmly. 'Ye can't possibly take the animals and who'd be lookin' after them poor things?'

'They could go into kennels, or we could get somebody to take them until I get back in two weeks,' Father said.

'They're not used to kennels, they'd fret,' Cloonie said. 'Besides, other folks'll be on holiday like you. No, I'm not goin'. It'll not be like it was afore the war. Shoppin'll be difficult and there'll be no lights along the promenade because o' the blackout. I prefers to stay 'ere where things are more or less normal. You don't know what you'll be rushin' into down there.'

Men and women in uniforms filled the compartments and the corridors, and we had to split up. I sat next to an army sergeant, who grinned at me cheerfully and said, 'Off on holiday, then?'

'Yes. Where are you going?'

He laughed and pointed to a notice stretched across the luggage rack. 'See that, love? I'm not supposed to tell you.'

'Careless talk costs lives' I read, although I couldn't really see how my knowing where he was going could harm anybody.

'How long are you going for?' he enquired.

'A month.'

'Is that a fact? Yer father's a lucky man if 'e can leave 'is job for a whole month.'

'He's not,' I defended him. 'He's only going for two weeks. He's a doctor, he has to get back.'

'Sorry, love. No offence meant.'

After that he settled down in his seat and closed his eyes. A young soldier sitting opposite gave me a broad wink and next to me Edith hissed, 'What did he say to you?'

'Nothing much. Did you see where the boys and Melissa went?'

'They're next door, and Mother and Father are further up the train. You'll have to stick close to me when we get there or we'll be separated in all this crush.'

43

It was almost dark when we reached our destination. It had been a long, wearisome day with stops and starts, a change of train, and long delays for reasons none of us could know. The strain was evident in Mother's face, but Father said cheerfully, 'Well, we're here in one piece. Now all we need is a taxi to take us up to the house. Have we got all the luggage?'

The two boys were sharing a large suitcase, as were Mother and Father. Edith and I had a small one each, but Melissa had two expensive leather suitcases. The boys coped cheerfully with the weight.

By the time we reached the headland it was dark, a darkness like none I could remember. We slid and struggled along the path towards the large, white house, dragging our luggage behind us.

Edith grumbled, 'We'll never be able to find our way about the house if the curtains have been left open and we can't put the lights on.'

'I can remember the layout,' Father said. 'I want you all to stay in the hall until I see if the curtains are drawn.' At the front door, I heard him searching anxiously for the keyhole.

We stood at last in a small group in the darkness of the hall and suddenly the hall sprang into light.

The blackout curtains in all the rooms were shut tight, so after we had eaten it was possible to explore the house and decide where we were going to sleep. Edith was given the single bedroom on the first landing, but the two boys and Melissa and I were expected to share. Rodney wanted the room overlooking the sea, but Father said we should toss for it. Melissa and I won the toss, much to Rodney's annoyance.

It took Melissa a long time to unpack her two suitcases. I sat on the bed watching her take out her dresses, placing them carefully on hangers in the wardrobe.

'Mrs Rocheforte's awfully generous,' I couldn't help saying. 'You are lucky, Melissa!'

'Well, she wouldn't want me to come on holiday with the things I brought from Liverpool, would she? It would be a reflection on her,' she replied.

'Not all the evacuees have been so lucky, though,' I persisted.

'I'm not like the other evacuees, am I?' she said. Although her words jarred on me, I knew that she spoke the truth.

Her unpacking finally finished, she turned and smiled, and her smile made me forget the vanity in her words. It was a smile in keeping with the elusive beauty of her face, a beauty that made me feel suddenly uneasy because it promised so much and gave very little.

'What do you do all day here?' she asked, sitting beside me on the bed.

'We go down to the shore, we walk along the promenade, we explore. The boys will probably go off on their own, they go fishing and sailing, and Edith has some friends here. We can do whatever you like.'

'And at night when it's dark and we're here in the house?'

'We play games. There's a piano and we gather around that and sing. I've never been bored here, there's a lot to do, I promise.'

In the days that followed, I was never sure if Melissa was enjoying herself or not. We walked along the beach and scrambled over the rocks in search of shell pools. We strolled along the promenade and in the gardens listening to the band, and it was like every other holiday I had ever known until it went dark. Then everything was different. Now there were no fairy lights strung out along the margin of the bay, no strains of music coming from the bandstand in the illuminated gardens. But in the house we made our own amusement and became closer than before. Mother was an accomplished pianist and Melissa entranced us all with her singing. We played charades and Melissa excelled in every part she enacted.

On the last evening, there was a full moon. I let myself out of the house and walked through the gardens to stand on the cliff. Below me the sea rolled in gently in silvered crescents.

I sat on the short, dry grass drinking in the sight. After a little while, Alistair joined me. I turned to smile at him.

'Isn't it beautiful?' I said. 'I never realised how beautiful when the lights were shining.'

'I've had a great time here. I'll never forget it.'

'We'll come again next year. The war won't be over for ages, so you'll be with us a long time.'

'Perhaps.'

'Well, of course you will. For the duration, Miss Brownson said.'

'The longer I stay, the harder it'll be to leave.'

'Have you heard from your parents while you've been here?'

'I got a postal order from my father, and Mother sent me some money from Cheltenham. She's got some sort of shop there, selling pictures and gimmicky things. She says she's not doing badly and after the war it will be a gold mine. Mother was always wanting to put money into something like that.'

'Does she ever see your father?' I asked curiously.

'When Father writes, he doesn't mention her at all. When she writes, she sounds very bitter, it's embarrassing.'

'Why is she bitter when she's the one who went away?'

'She thinks he has somebody else, his secretary, I think.'

'Do you know her?'

'Yes. Alison. She's worked for him for several years.'

I wanted to know about Alison but I felt dreadful asking so many questions. As if he sensed my embarrassment, he said gently, 'We were never a family like your family. Father was always immersed in his work and Mother did all sorts of things with local charities. They were always quarrelling, it was pretty horrible.'

There was something painfully mature in Alistair's expression. I could never imagine my brother Rodney speaking like this to a girl, but then Rodney had never experienced an unhappy home life. To change the subject, I said, 'Melissa has a lovely voice. You can even hear it in the garden with the doors and the window closed.'

'Yes. She should have real training.'

'I wonder if she's really enjoyed this holiday.'

'I'm sure she has. She'd be a funny girl if she said she hadn't.'

'I never quite know with Melissa. Perhaps one day she'll be famous and we'll be able to see her on the stage.'

'I don't think it's really up to Mrs Rocheforte to have her voice trained. Her family might not even agree to it.'

'That would be terrible.'

'I know, but she's not had a single letter since we came here, and when anybody mentions her mother she simply changes the subject. Wouldn't you think her grandmother might have written to her?'

'Perhaps her English isn't good enough.'

To my dismay he threw back his head and laughed. 'Oh, come on, Ginny! You surely don't believe all that nonsense she told you about her grandmother escaping out of Russia?'

'How do you know it's nonsense? I'm not surprised she doesn't talk about her mother or her grandmother when she knows none of us believes a word of it.'

'Except you.'

I didn't answer. I was aware of the laughter in his eyes and the amusement in his voice.

'Now you're annoyed with me,' he said softly.

'I just think we shouldn't laugh at Melissa. Maybe she tells us these things because she believes them herself; maybe she has nothing else.'

He was saved from answering by the appearance of Rodney, who sank down on the grass with us.

'I'm fed up with listening to Melissa every night,' he complained. 'OK, so she's good, but it's got to be a bit too much.'

'Just because you don't like music doesn't mean we shouldn't enjoy it,' I snapped.

'I do like music. I just think we should do other things for a change. I don't suppose we'll go on coming here. Things'll change before next year.'

'Why will they change?' I didn't like the idea.

'Well, the war will change things. The war's changed this place. Just look over there — that isn't the sunset.'

Our eyes followed his pointing finger to where the sky glowed dully with shades of flame and tragic crimson. Harshly I said, 'But what is it? Something is on fire?'

'Didn't you hear the planes droning in the distance? We heard them from inside the house, that's why I came out here.'

'But what is there out there?' I cried. Then we were silent and in the distance we heard the throbbing sound of aircraft. Sudden light flashes illuminated the sky.

'It's probably Plymouth,' Alistair said. 'The naval dockyards.'

We stood in silence staring at a night sky illuminated by flashes of flame followed by dull, rose-glowing embers. To all of us for the first time the war seemed very close.

In the morning we would be returning to our homes, to the

47

peace of the countryside and a life virtually unchanged, and Rodney's words took on a real and frightening significance. Everything could have changed drastically before another year came round.

Rodney drifted back to the house, leaving Alistair and me staring across the silvered sea towards the crimson sky. Alistair said, 'People are being injured out there. Many of them will be dying.'

I didn't speak. My throat felt tight with unshed tears. This beautiful place had somehow gone for ever and strangely I pictured myself standing in this same spot in another life, another age, in a thousand years perhaps. Would I recognise the exquisite curve of the bay? And would I look up to where the white house had once stood to find it no longer there, and a wilderness that had once been a garden? And would my heart be plagued by a strange puzzlement?

I could not have told Alistair what I was thinking about at that moment. He was staring down at me with amusement in his eyes, and took hold of my hand, saying gently, 'Time to go in, Ginny. I still have packing to do, I don't know about you.'

'Of course.' Tomorrow we were going home.

# Chapter Six

Instead of Father, old Mr Grimshaw waited for us at the station with his dilapidated old taxi. As we drove to the house along the village street, it was as if we hadn't been away. The dogs barked excitedly at our arrival and Cloonie was clucking like an old hen.

Mother decided that Melissa should go straight on up to the Hall. When the rest of us got inside the house, Cloonie said, 'There's a scarlet-fever epidemic. The doctor's run off his feet, 'e is, and that Miss Brownson poppin' in all the time wantin' to see 'im. I told 'er this mornin' that 'e had enough to worry 'im.'

'Oh, well, let's get unpacked and have something to eat. The journey was a very tiring one and there was a long wait for the connection to bring us home. What are we having for the evening meal, Cloonie?'

'Chops. The butcher sent chops, and well 'e knows I'd 'ave preferred a roast.'

'Perhaps he hasn't got a roast. We're very lucky to get anything. Life is more or less normal for us and we don't have the bombers over.'

'I'll get on with the evenin' meal then,' Cloonie said. 'The dogs sensed you were comin' home today, and look at the cat there, sittin' on the front doorstep e's been all morning.'

The cat Eustace was weaving around our legs. I picked him up and felt comforted by his loud purring.

We were halfway through supper when Miss Brownson appeared, flushed and apologetic. Mother settled her comfortably in the living room with coffee after explaining that Father wasn't home yet.

'I'm a nuisance, I know,' Miss Brownson said anxiously, 'but I really don't know which way to turn and the doctor did say if I needed any help he'd be at hand.'

'I hear there's a scarlet-fever epidemic,' Mother said. 'He's probably run off his feet.'

'I know, and I'm sorry, but there's nobody else I can talk to, nobody that can talk to Mrs Rocheforte.'

Cloonie rattled the crockery with a frown of disapproval on her face. Mother said sharply, 'The poor woman is worried, Cloonie. Try not to look at her with that fierce expression.'

We finished our meal and I helped Cloonie to clear away, then went into the living room, where Mother was telling Miss Brownson about our holidays. She purposely asked no questions about Mrs Rocheforte, and we all heaved a sigh of relief when we heard Father enter the house by the kitchen door, where no doubt Cloonie warned him that he had a visitor.

He looked unusually tired as he sank gratefully into his easy chair. Cloonie was there with his whisky and soda and Mother sat on the arm of his chair with her arm around his shoulder.

'I feel quite dreadful burdening you with my worries,' Miss Brownson began. 'I know how busy you are, but I'm at my wits' end about Melissa Francis.'

'It would seem Melissa's a problem whether she's here or away. What has she done now?' Father replied dryly.

'It isn't anything Melissa's done, it's what Mrs Rocheforte intends to do for her. She doesn't listen to a word I say, but really, Dr Lawrence, we have to make her see that when the war is over, Melissa is going back where she came from. Mrs Rocheforte will only make Melissa dissatisfied with her lot.'

'I can't think that Mrs Rocheforte intends to do anything bad for Melissa, Miss Brownson.'

'Of course I didn't mean that. The thing is, she plans to shape her future by having her voice trained professionally, but Melissa's future is not her concern.'

'Not even when it's evident the girl has a great deal of talent?'

'Not even then, doctor. You won't be taking any part in shaping Alistair's future, you will leave that to his parents. All you're doing is giving the boy a safe home. His father is paying for his education, and when the war is over Alistair will go home and do whatever his parents have planned for him. He'll

50

never forget you or the village, but his future doesn't lie here. The same thing should apply to Melissa.'

'And will it happen for Melissa, Miss Brownson?'

She bit her lip doubtfully. 'No, perhaps not. I've made some enquiries about Melissa — I had to, it's my job. Her mother is a single woman living away, nobody seems to know where. She had Melissa when she was eighteen years old and left the baby with her mother. Melissa's grandmother has brought her up, but there is precious little money there. She works in a local laundry and takes in boarders. There's nothing wrong in that, I'm not saying she's bad for Melissa, but the people who know her say she's something of a recluse. Melissa never mixed with other children; she seemed to spend her time running errands or sitting in the window staring out into the street.'

'Not a particularly happy sort of life, it would seem,' Father put in.

'No, perhaps not, but you do see that it's a life she has to go back to. She's twelve years old. We're all hoping the war will be over quickly, but even if it lasts some years, Melissa could still be little more than a child. And it is her grandmother who is her legal guardian, not Mrs Rocheforte.'

'And in the meantime what are we talking about? What exactly is Mrs Rocheforte planning to do for Melissa?'

'Singing lessons. She's written to Madame Courtney, who I understand used to live in the area and was quite a celebrity.'

Across the room Father looked at Mother and they both dissolved into laughter.

Seeing Miss Brownson's consternation, Father said quickly, 'I'm sorry, but Daphne Courtney was indeed a celebrity in the village before your time. Her father was the local grocer and Daphne sang in the choir. I was only a youngster then but our Daphne was quite the *grande dame*. The old vicar paid for her training. She went away to musical college and made a name for herself singing in concerts all over the country. She performed in front of royalty and, when she visited the village, rode about in a large Rolls-Royce wearing floating draperies and large feathered hats. Are you telling me Mrs Rocheforte is hoping she'll take Melissa on?'

51

'Yes. She's retired now and living somewhere in the Yorkshire Dales. Mrs Rocheforte said she was a friend of hers at one time and she has heard she is now living in obscure gentility.'

'She could be right. Her father left her money, but she married some chap who was good at spending it. Even so, Melissa is at school here — how can a woman living in Yorkshire possibly give her lessons?'

'She's invited Madame Courtney to visit with a view to making some arrangements about Melissa. Mrs Rocheforte said she too had heard the old lady was suffering financially and you know what she's like. She's set her heart on Melissa receiving voice training and nothing and nobody is going to stop her, even if it means giving Madame Courtney a home here to achieve it.'

'I take it all your efforts to make her change her mind fell upon deaf ears, then?'

'She says she'll write to Melissa's grandmother and invite her to visit. If that isn't possible, she will keep her fully informed on how Melissa is progressing.'

'Then why are you so worried?'

'There are more than twenty evacuees in the village, and it doesn't seem right to single one out for special treatment.'

'But what if Melissa is special?'

'What do you think I should do, doctor?'

'I suggest you stop worrying about Melissa. We're all living in a sort of vacuum and none of us knows what the next few years will bring. In the meantime I think we should allow Mrs Rocheforte to have a hand in shaping Melissa's future. Her talent shouldn't go to waste. In the end, it will be Melissa herself who decides whether to use it wisely or fritter it away.'

Miss Brownson left us unconvinced; I was glad to see her go. Almost as soon as the door closed behind her, I said stoutly, 'Maybe it's because her grandmother's foreign that she doesn't allow Melissa to mix with the other children. Melissa said she was afraid they'd come after her from Russia.'

'Oh, Ginny,' Father sighed. 'Your loyalty does you great credit, but don't put too much credence in Melissa's stories. Now tell me all about the holiday and what I was missing.'

\*　　　\*　　　\*

In the days that followed, life took up its familiar pattern. We returned to school. Melissa arrived each morning in the Daimler and went home in it in the late afternoon, and she never said a single word about Madame Courtney, even when everybody knew she had arrived at the Hall.

Madame Courtney was larger than life. She wore georgette scarves edged with fox, and she seemed to float along the road like a ship in full sail. She invariably wore very large hats with brims decorated with feathers or chiffon flowers, a great deal of rouge and lip colour and her hair was a remarkable colour of red.

When she swept into the little post office, her deep, sonorous voice shut everybody else up. She informed the village post-mistress that she was visiting indefinitely and had had her mail readdressed to the Hall. One old gentleman, who had known her father, asked if she was thinking of returning to the village. She gave him a bright smile and said, 'My plans are uncertain, but the possibility is always there.'

When Edith recounted this conversation over the evening meal, Father said with a smile, 'She'll stay if Mrs Rocheforte makes it worth her while.'

'But she surely can't expect to live at the Hall?' Mother said.

'Arrangements will be made, never fear. We've known Mrs Rocheforte long enough to know that if her heart is set on something, she manages to satisfy it.'

There were many times when I saw Miss Brownson in deep conversation with Miss Carter, the music mistress, but I learned nothing from Melissa. All I knew was that she declined to take part in the next Christmas concert because Madame Courtney had said she was not yet ready for it and must confine herself to singing scales and taking deep-breathing exercises.

I was therefore more than surprised to receive an invitation to take tea at the Hall on Christmas Day as I had done the year before. I didn't want to go, but Edith hissed, 'Of course you'll go, then you can tell us about Madame Courtney, what she says and what she's wearing.'

Madame Courtney did most of the talking. She sat at one end of the dining table, wearing a long, plum-coloured dress and a jewelled band around her hair. Her long, glittering earrings danced as she gesticulated.

53

She talked about people she had known, rich, titled people and royalty. She talked about the theatre and concert halls, foreign cities and foreign men who had showered her with compliments and jewels. All the time Mrs Rocheforte sat silent with a gentle smile on her face, and I must have looked wide-eyed and overwhelmed. Melissa was outwardly composed as always.

'And are you destined to be a singer also, Virginia?' Madame Courtney asked, addressing me for the first time.

'Oh, no. I'm not a singer at all.'

'Have you no ambition to go on the stage?'

I giggled. 'No, I can't sing and my sister Edith says I can't act.'

'So what do you intend to do with your life, young lady?'

'I'd like to work for my father as his receptionist, do his books and look after his prescriptions. That would give him more time for his sick people and the visits he has to make, and it could help him to get home earlier and have more time for us.'

'Well, that is highly commendable, I'm sure. But *your* life is going to be very different, Melissa — that is, if you do exactly as I tell you and work very hard. You will be an opera singer and one day Mrs Rocheforte and I will see your debut at Covent Garden. Isn't that what you want, Melissa?'

Melissa smiled at her but didn't answer. After a few seconds, Mrs Rocheforte said, 'Don't worry, Melissa, this is all in the future. There's a very long way to go.'

'Of course,' Madame Courtney agreed. 'All the same, she must set her sights on these horizons. The Met in New York, the Garden in London, La Scala in Milan. They were my ambitions once but I had to settle for the concert hall and then I did a very foolish thing, I fell in love with a weak man who squandered my money and blighted my career. You, Melissa, will fall in love only with a man who can enhance your career, and you will remind yourself of that fact every day of your life.'

'A little mercenary, perhaps,' Mrs Rocheforte murmured.

'For ordinary people, perhaps, for a girl like Virginia; but Melissa must have the best of everything.'

The visit gave me plenty to tell them at home, and later that day they sat round the table while I imitated Madame

Courtney. I draped a bright silk scarf round my head and gesticulated with my hands, using a long pencil instead of Madame Courtney's cigarette holder. My girlish voice had none of her contralto depth, but at the end of my performance they were helpless with laughter, and father said, 'I thought you always said Ginny couldn't act, Edith, but she's just done a very fair Madame Courtney. Did you mean it about becoming my receptionist, Ginny?'

'Yes, of course, it's what I've always wanted to be.'

'To stay in the village and stagnate,' he said gently.

'I love the village, I never want to live anywhere else. All my friends are here and it's beautiful. You think so, don't you, Alistair?'

'Yes, it's the most beautiful place I've ever seen,' he replied with a laugh.

'Well, don't be getting too fond of it, Alistair. Your father's paying us a visit tomorrow. I don't think he'll be too keen on your wanting to stay on here. It's my guess he has other plans for you.'

Alistair's expression changed. Now there was no laughter in his eyes and I knew that he was not looking forward to his father's visit.

'How long is he coming for?' I asked.

'Just one afternoon. At least, I hope that's all there is.'

'That doesn't sound very welcoming, Alistair. We must make him feel at home, let him see that you're happy, that you're working hard and that he's got nothing to worry about. Have you heard from your mother?' Father asked.

'A card and some money. She's staying with Aunt Mildred, I don't suppose she'll come to see me.'

'But you write to her, Alistair?' Mother said anxiously.

'Well, yes, whenever I can.' He looked down and I thought he was hiding his feelings.

I had always loved Christmas Day. We looked at each other's presents, partook of Cloonie's mince tarts and Christmas cake, and stuffed ourselves with chocolates and sweets from our rations. I spared a thought for Melissa, surrounded by the grandeur of the Hall and the company of Mrs Rocheforte and Madame Courtney. By this time the vocal coach would surely

55

be drunk with all the wine she had consumed. Long before I left, her words had slurred and there had been a glassy look in her eyes.

I dreamed about her that night. In floating black draperies she entered my dream waving her ivory cigarette holder, telling me that my ambitions were futile. Then Melissa and I stood together in a large choir and Madame Courtney waved her baton in front of us, saying over and over, 'No, Virginia, not like that at all. Listen to Melissa, sing like Melissa.'

I woke, shouting hysterically, 'No, I won't sing like Melissa, I don't want to sing like Melissa!'

Cloonie was shaking me, saying, 'What ails ye, child? Ye've bin dreamin'. It did ye no good goin' to the 'all yesterday. I'm gettin' breakfast early, Alistair's father's comin' today.'

Alistair was unusually quiet over breakfast. Looking at him thoughtfully, Mother said, 'I suggest you and Rodney go out for a walk after breakfast. It's very cold but it's dry. Your father said he'd be here just before lunch, so please be back by then.'

He nodded, and Rodney said with a little laugh, 'You'll get a grilling about your school report. It wasn't as good as you expected.'

'No. I'll have to try harder next term.'

'Are you expecting a rollicking?'

Alistair shrugged his shoulders.

Alistair's father was a tall, fair-haired man with a remote, good-looking face which smiled seldom. Alistair was quiet after shaking his father's hand and addressing him as sir. Lunch was an unusually subdued meal. Mr Grantham complimented Cloonie on her cooking but refused second helpings. Most of the time he chatted to our parents, only occasionally asking Alistair about his schoolwork and frowning when he referred to his last report.

'He'll do better next time,' Father said reassuringly. 'The first few months were bound to be difficult — new school, new friends and a new home. He tells me he's hoping to join us in the field of medicine.'

'He'll need to work hard. I hope you'll continue to make that clear to him, Lawrence,' Mr Grantham said shortly.

'I have three children of my own,' Father said, and we

glanced at him uncomfortably. He had replied in the same cold manner in which Alistair's father had spoken to him.

Mr Grantham seemed not to have noticed anything, however, because he said quickly, 'Well, of course, but you do happen to be on the spot, which unfortunately I am not.'

'What are you exactly wanting from Alistair, then?' Father asked curiously.

'I want him to specialise. I specialised but in many ways I have been held back from doing everything I wanted. My wife refused to move away from the area when I had an opportunity to work overseas. Now it's too late for me but I want it for Alistair.'

'I see.'

'You must think I am asking too much since you've settled for being a GP. Don't think for one moment I'm belittling your accomplishments, but you must have ambitions for your own children.'

'I'm not pushing any of them. I've seen too many children pushed by parents into nervous breakdowns.'

Mr Grantham stared at him, then, turning his attention to Rodney, he said, 'And what are your ambitions, young man?'

'I'd like to go to agricultural college and be a farmer,' Rodney answered firmly. We all stared at him in amazement, since it was the first we'd heard of it.

'I should have thought the area had a preponderance of farmers,' Mr Grantham answered, 'and not too many GPs.'

Rodney blushed and pushed his food around his plate.

Edith said, 'You never said before that you wanted to be a farmer.'

'Well, I don't tell you everything,' he snapped.

To everybody's relief, Cloonie appeared with the pudding, which Mr Grantham declined. Looking at his watch, he said, 'I hope you won't mind if I leave you immediately after lunch, Mrs Lawrence? I have an appointment in Lancaster later this afternoon. It was a good opportunity to kill two birds with one stone, drive on to see Alistair and keep my appointment on the way back.'

'Of course not,' Mother murmured. 'Will you have coffee before you leave?'

'Thank you. Have you heard from your mother, Alistair?'

'She writes often.'

'And you write back, I hope?'

'Of course.'

They looked at each other. It was a long, hard look and Alistair was the first to look away.

Cloonie arrived with the coffee, and immediately Mr Grantham had drunk it, he asked to be excused. Alistair and my parents went with him to his car.

When they were safely out of the room, Rodney said, 'Gosh, I'm glad he's not my father!'

'Do you really want to be a farmer?' Edith asked.

'I don't want to specialise, I'd have had a lecture a mile long. If Alistair doesn't make it, his father'll never forgive him.'

Silently I agreed with him, but by the time the others returned to the table we were talking of other things.

For the rest of the meal Alistair was quiet and I knew he was thinking about his father's visit. It had put a blight on what was left of the day.

# Chapter Seven

We had all tried to make Melissa part of our lives but she kept aloof, emphasising her difference. For the rest of the war, I saw her only in the classroom.

Madame Courtney was now living in a cottage at the edge of the village. A gardener tidied up the garden, modern plumbing had been installed and new window frames for every window. We had watched a large removal van unloading a huge grand piano, until Madame Courtney waved us away. Her draperies flapping in the wind, her plumed hat sitting squarely on top of her red hair, she proclaimed that she had every right to expect privacy and if we didn't move off the police would be called in.

We got most of our information from Cloonie, who was friendly with the head gardener's wife.

'She demands fresh flowers twice a week,' Cloonie said over Sunday lunch, 'and everythin' she wants she gets. Nothin' and nobody 'as to interfere with that girl's music, and if she's not bein' taught up at the 'all she's down at the cottage. There's another woman goes every Tuesday to give 'er elocution lessons. They're fashionin' the sort o' girl she was never meant to be.'

'She's a very fortunate girl to have so much attention lavished on her,' Mother said.

'Well, I don't 'appen to think she's fortunate at all,' Cloonie said defiantly. 'What's goin' to 'appen to her after the war's over? She'll go back to Liverpool and be swallowed up with 'er own sort. They'll give 'er a bad time, too, if I'm not mistaken.'

'Perhaps she's never going back to Liverpool,' Edith said. 'Perhaps her grandmother will let Mrs Rocheforte adopt her.'

'I don't think that's on the cards,' Father said, 'but she has obviously given Mrs Rocheforte a purpose in life.'

'Do you suppose she's approached Melissa's grandmother?' Mother asked.

'I have no idea. I don't talk about Melissa when I visit the Hall. I realised a long time ago that Miss Brownson's arguments have put Mrs Rocheforte on the defensive, so now we talk about her blood pressure, her arthritis and the state of the war. It's part of my profession to be cautious when dealing with a lady of Mrs Rocheforte's calibre.'

Cloonie cleared away the dishes, determined to have the last word. 'Well, I don't 'old with it. She's makin' the girl dissatisfied with her lot, she'll 'ave no time for her folks when she goes back 'ome and she'd 'ave done more for the girl if she'd had somebody in to teach her somethin' that could 'ave made sure she could earn 'er own livin'.'

On Edith's seventeenth birthday she stated that she wanted to become a nurse. She had done well in her last year at school and with father's help had little difficulty in being accepted as a probationer at Lancaster Infirmary. Now we only saw her on her weekends off, which were few and far between, but she was enjoying her work as well as any leisure that came her way.

With the end of the war in Europe, the evacuees began drifting back. They went in twos and threes, leaving gaps in classrooms and church pews. They were missed at dances in the village hall, at family parties, walks across the fells and wherever young people congregated. They promised to come back and visit, but we watched them go with uncertainty in our hearts.

It was a cool spring day when Alistair's father came for him. Breakfast had been a silent meal. I felt tearful, and Alistair's glum face did nothing to cheer me up. His father arrived mid-morning and, after shaking hands with my parents, he quickly gathered Alistair's luggage together and proceeded to load the car. Rodney and Alistair shook hands very correctly, and I threw my arms around his neck in a passion of weeping. Then we watched as he took his place beside his father in the front seat of the car, his face very pale, unsmiling, and we stood at the garden gate until the car disappeared round the bend in the road.

I was too upset to eat my lunch and Rodney's appetite too seemed to have gone.

Father said, 'You both knew this was going to happen one day. Alistair will keep in touch and he'll come to see us. Didn't he promise he would?'

Promises! We'd had a surfeit of promises over the last few days.

Seeing the disbelief on our faces, Father offered a distraction. 'I suggest we have a ride up to the Hall to see what is happening to Melissa. Are you coming with us, Rodney?'

'No, I don't care what Melissa's doing. I'll take the dogs out.'

Getting into the car, Father and I saw him setting out with the two dogs across the fell.

'Perhaps Melissa's already gone,' I said uncertainly.

'I don't think so. She was having a singing lesson with Madame yesterday.'

'How do you know?'

'I passed the cottage and I could hear her. There was no mistaking Melissa's voice, nobody else around here sings like her.'

The gardens surrounding the Hall were blooming with daffodils and crocuses. There were clumps of snowdrops everywhere and their beauty made my heart ache.

The butler opened the door, saying, 'Mrs Rocheforte's in the drawing room, doctor. I'll inform her you are here.'

I was surprised when she came out into the hall to meet us, wearing a warm woollen coat. 'I was just thinking I'd like to walk down to the cottage, doctor. Have you time to come with me or are you as busy as usual?'

'We'll gladly come with you, Mrs Rocheforte. It will do Ginny good. She's feeling a bit desolate because our evacuee has gone home this morning.'

'Oh, dear! He seemed a nice boy. But he'll come back to visit, I'm sure,' she said with a smile.

'Of course he will,' Father said stoutly. 'He's promised and we always knew that one day he would have to go home.'

He looked at her meaningfully. Unconcerned, she indicated that we should follow her. We walked through the huge conservatory and took a lane through a small wood until we reached the fork leading to the cottage.

'Melissa is having a singing lesson this morning,' she told us. 'I'm expecting Miss Brownson any day now, asking a lot of questions.'

'It's her job, Mrs Rocheforte.'

'I'm aware of it, but I've made my own arrangements about Melissa. When we get to the cottage, we can discuss them,' she replied.

We heard the sound of a piano as we reached the gates of the cottage, and Melissa's soprano soaring lightly up the scales.

'Doesn't she sing anything else these days?' Father asked. 'She's taken no part in anything the school's produced since her role in *The Mikado*.'

'No. Madame Courtney forbade it and she knew better than anybody how Melissa should nurture her voice.'

'And now?' Father prompted.

'Now, Dr Lawrence, you are soon to learn about the plans I have for Melissa's future. I will leave it to you to inform Miss Brownson.'

Father said nothing, but he gave me a broad wink.

After a brief knock on the door, Mrs Rocheforte opened it and we entered the cottage. The grand piano took up nearly all the space in the living room. Madame Courtney sat on the piano stool, her fingers resting on the keys, looking round enquiringly at our entrance. Melissa stood behind her, looking older now she was not in school uniform.

'I asked Dr Lawrence to accompany me here, Daphne, since it was he who brought Melissa to live with me over six years ago. I think it would only be polite to inform him about the arrangements I have made for Melissa's future.'

Madame Courtney left the piano stool and ushered us into a small sitting room. Mrs Rocheforte took a rocking chair on one side of the hearth while Madame Courtney took the easy chair opposite. Father and I were invited to share a small sofa; Melissa sat on a velvet pouffe, hugging her knees.

'All this has been done through my solicitors,' Mrs Rocheforte began. 'I left it to them to contact Melissa's grand-mother and I wrote to her personally. Melissa's mother has not been in touch with her since Melissa was four years old, so her grandmother has brought her up without any help from that quarter. She has had to work very hard, taking in boarders and laundry, and in the normal course of events Melissa would have gone back to Liverpool to live with her grandmother and find work. For a girl of Melissa's obvious talents, I think this is inconceivable. All this has been explained to her grandmother and I have instructed my solicitors to pay her a sum of money in excess of anything she could hope to receive from any employment Melissa could obtain. She has accepted this.'

Beside me Father sat silent and expressionless. Madame Courtney contented herself with nodding her head in agreement. Melissa stared down at the floor, her hair like a dark silken curtain hiding her face.

'I have asked Miss Brownson to come to see me this evening,' she went on. 'She has done considerable work on behalf of the evacuees during the war and I think she will want to know. On the other hand, none of this is any of her affair. I have made my decision and my concern is for Melissa and only Melissa.'

'May I ask what you intend for Melissa?' Father asked quietly.

'Of course. She is to go to the college of music in Manchester. Madame Courtney accompanied her there last week. After hearing that Daphne has been her teacher for the last three years, and listening to Melissa sing, they accepted her.'

'And after Manchester?'

'Years of hard work. Melissa knows this. There are scholarships to be won, and if she applies the right sort of dedication, she will have the experience of singing abroad and may have a career in opera. I have done my part and Daphne has done hers, now it is up to Melissa, and she is ambitious. Walk back to the Hall with me, Dr Lawrence, and ask all those questions I know you're dying to ask me. Virginia will walk with Melissa.'

I could think of little to say to Melissa as we sauntered back along the narrow country lane. The cool spring day was tinged with sunlight, it fell on the distant lake and dark-green conifers, warmed the stone of Lakeland cottages and nourished the fat buds on rhododendron bushes. Primroses peeped shyly along the hedgerows and only the girl walking beside me seemed alien in the village that was becoming our own again.

We had almost reached the gates and the long drive leading

up to the Hall when I had to ask, 'Was none of it true about your grandmother, Melissa? Was it just your imagination?'

She was staring ahead, her expression a mixture of doubt and struggling pride. With a shrug of her shoulders, she said, 'I could tell you, Ginny, because you were the only one who would believe me.'

'But was it true?' I persisted.

'No, none of it.' Her voice was harsh, and I sensed the hurt in it. 'As Mrs Rocheforte said, my granny took in boarders and other people's laundry. She bought all our clothes from second-hand shops or took what people gave her and we never had enough money. As for my mother, I can't even remember what she looked like.'

'She never came to see you?'

'Not after she left. After a while people stopped talking about her.'

'And your father?'

She gave me a long, cool, direct look that made me wish I hadn't asked that question, then in that same cold voice she said, 'I never had a father, not the way you have. There was always just my grandmother and me, and the boarders who came to stay for short periods. I never knew any of them. I always used the back door of the house and they came and went to suit themselves. They were always men, working on ships or in the docks, and sometimes when they had a bit of money to spend they were generous with granny. I always knew when she was involved with one of them.'

'Involved?'

'Well, yes. She slept with them. That shocks you, doesn't it, Ginny? Now you know why I turned her into a Russian duchess with loads of money and jewels. I didn't want anybody here to know the truth.'

'I wouldn't have felt any less about you, Melissa. It has nothing to do with me.'

'You say that now, but I couldn't be sure, could I? Have you still got Alistair?'

'No. His father came for him yesterday.'

'Is he going to keep in touch?'

'We all hope he will.'

'And you more than most, Ginny?'

I could feel the warm colour dying my cheeks. 'I suppose so. I liked Alistair, we were real friends; now I'm sorry he's gone. There's an awful gap in our lives.'

'Don't you miss your sister just as much as Alistair?' she asked slyly.

'Well, yes, of course, but Edith and I squabbled all the time. Alistair was always nice, always kind.'

'He's going to be a doctor, isn't he?'

'I think so. A specialist, at least that's what his father is hoping for him.'

'They'll soon forget us now that they've gone home. I shan't forget because it's Mrs Rocheforte who is paying for my education and my singing. Whatever I make of my life, I shall owe to her, but it's funny to think that she's really nothing to me. She'll care about my music, about what I do with my life, but she won't really care if I'm sick, who I marry, why I'm me.'

'But of course she cares, Melissa! She's given your grandmother money, she's clothing you and paying for your voice to be trained. How can you say she doesn't care about you?'

'Well, she doesn't. She has her own children and she cares about them, about her grandchildren, her friends and her servants, but I'm just a cause, a piece of marble a sculptor works on, a canvas an artist paints on.'

'Oh, Melissa!' I cried. 'I don't think she thinks about you like that at all. She's so very proud of you. Just suppose you'd never gone to live with her, you'd be back in Liverpool with your grandmother now, and nobody would care about your voice. Why don't you try thinking that it was something that had to happen, part of some great big plan?'

She only laughed.

At the Hall we were entertained to afternoon tea with delicate cucumber sandwiches and cake. Melissa and I sat on the window seat looking out across the park. She grinned at me wickedly.

'I shall miss all this. If I'd gone home to Granny, we'd have been sitting down to hot, strong tea and treacle toast. I'd have been taking laundry back and making myself scarce. I knew she'd never come here to see me, she'd have looked at these teacups and these tiny cake knives with dismay. I hoped and prayed Mrs Rocheforte wouldn't persuade her to visit.'

Her words made me think about Alistair and how he was coping in his father's house. Would they be sitting down to silent meals and would that cold, austere man unbend long enough to talk to Alistair about the sort of things we'd talked about for the last six years?

Miss Brownson came to see us later that evening after spending a couple of hours listening to Mrs Rocheforte's plans for Melissa's future. She was indignant. She believed she should have been consulted instead of told, and she had little faith in Melissa's ability to dedicate herself to years of hard work.

'You don't know that,' Father said. 'She surely knows she'll never get another chance to make something of her voice. She's a lucky girl.'

'But is she?' Miss Brownson persisted. 'She has no real folks, all she's got is a Professor Higgins fashioning his Eliza. Don't you agree, Mrs Lawrence?'

Mother agreed, and when Father looked at her with raised eyebrows, she said, 'Well, it's true, David. Where's the love or friendship in all this? As I see it, there's only ambition, and fame at the end of it if she's lucky.'

'And she's the sort of girl who isn't asking for either love or friendship. I don't think I shall ever forget the face of that young girl singing her solo in the school hall, with her vain expression and her air of superiority. "Oh, pray make no mistake, we are not shy, we're very wide awake, the moon and I",' he quoted.

After that it seemed nobody had anything more to say about Melissa.

# Chapter Eight

We were all together to celebrate my eighteenth birthday. Edith brought the house surgeon she had been in raptures about for two years, a bespectacled, earnest young man with a shy smile, obviously besotted with my ebullient sister. Rodney brought a friend from the agricultural college who bored us all with his knowledge of organic farming, all except Rodney, that is. Later he invited me to be his partner at one of the college dances.

It was a lovely July day and the village was teeming with summer visitors who roamed the fells and sailed the lake. It seemed hard to imagine that only a few years before we had been involved in a terrible war.

I was showered with small gifts from Father's patients, and overwhelmed by the expensive white leather vanity case sent by Mrs Rocheforte. But as I scanned the pile of birthday cards, I had to admit to a feeling of disappointment.

Seeing my preoccupation, Father said softly, 'Nothing from Alistair, Ginny?'

I looked up and smiled brightly. 'Oh, he won't remember my birthday, why should he? Besides, he's probably forgotten most of the things we did here.'

He had not been to see us since that morning he left with his father, but we had received Christmas cards and postcards from the scenes of his travels, mostly from Italy and Switzerland.

'I saw him a few months back when we went on that sailing weekend on the Wye, he was there with another chap from Oxford,' Rodney said casually.

'You didn't tell us,' Mother accused.

'I forgot,' he said, helping himself to another piece of apple pie. 'He's doing well with his studies, he said. He asked about you all. I told him I was going home for Ginny's birthday.'

'So he knows it's today?' Edith said.

'I told him it was in July, I don't know if I mentioned the day,' Rodney said. 'We had a long talk after dinner. His parents split up. He was going to stay with his mother for a few days and then he was going to Italy with his father. The way he was talking, I wouldn't be surprised if he went to work abroad.'

'Has his father remarried?' Mother asked.

'He didn't say.'

'Alistair's father believed he'd missed out by not working abroad or in London, so he'll want it for Alistair,' Father said thoughtfully.

'He was taking a girl to the May Ball,' Rodney said. 'Some girl he'd met at a friend's house. Nothing serious.'

'Did he say so?' Mother asked.

'No, but he didn't sound as if she was special,' Rodney said complacently.

I felt unreasonably hurt that he had forgotten my birthday, hurt that there was a girl he was taking to the May Ball, angry that he had so soon forgotten those long years he had spent with us, and meeting my father's eyes across the table I knew that he was aware of the hurt.

After lunch the two boys decided they would go down to the lake and take out a boat, and Edith decided she would visit some of her friends in the vicinity to show off her young man. I helped clear away the dishes until Cloonie said, 'It's your birthday so you're not to help in the kitchen. Get out into the sunshine!'

Mother laughed at her encouragement, saying, 'Why not take a walk up to the Hall, dear, to thank Mrs Rocheforte for her gift?'

'I don't suppose that Melissa's remembered your birthday?' Cloonie put in.

'I never expected to hear from Melissa,' I replied. It was true, I hadn't given Melissa a single thought, but Alistair! I had thought Alistair would remember.

When I was ready to leave, Cloonie said, 'Do ye think Mrs Rocheforte'd like a chunk of yer birthday cake?'

When I hesitated, Mother said, 'Of course she would. A nice big slice, Cloonie. It will fit into this box I've been keeping for some occasion or other.'

I waited while they cut the cake and put it snugly in the box with an accompanying assortment of iced roses and silver bells, and Mother wrapped the box in rose-patterned paper.

I stood for a while looking down at the lake alive with pleasure craft. The main street in the village had been filled with fell walkers and others out for a day in the lakes with their families. They queued at the ice-cream stalls and hung around the tiny shops selling Lakeland slate and china. People were in a holiday mood and my spirits lifted as I climbed the lane leading to the Hall. Why should I worry that Alistair hadn't remembered my birthday? The only people who really mattered were my family and Cloonie. I was happy living in this beautiful place and all morning I had been reminded that family and friends cared enough to send me cards and gifts. People who forgot you weren't worth remembering, I told myself stoutly.

I was surprised to find Mrs Rocheforte sitting on the terrace. In spite of the heat of the day, she was warmly wrapped in rugs. Beside her was a low table and under it lay Benjie, her Yorkshire terrier. She greeted me with a warm smile, indicating a seat and saying, 'How nice of you to come, Virginia, and a very happy birthday, my dear!'

'Thank you, Mrs Rocheforte, and thank you for the lovely present you sent me. I was thrilled to receive it.'

'I'm pleased that you liked it. And the family are all together for your birthday?'

'Yes. I've brought you a piece of my cake. Cloonie made it, she thought you might like a piece.'

'Oh, that is kind. We shall have afternoon tea and I will eat your cake instead of those fairy cakes Cook is so fond of making. Have you heard from Melissa?'

'No, but I didn't expect her to remember.'

'I too would have been surprised. I seldom hear from her, but I get a very comprehensive report from the college regarding her progress.'

'Will she come here to see you, Mrs Rocheforte?' I asked curiously.

'No. As usual in August I'm going to stay with my sister.

Melissa is spending time with Daphne Courtney, who lives in the Yorkshire Dales. There Daphne will be able to tell how she is progressing and in due course inform me when she visits me in the autumn.'

I didn't speak. Melissa's life seemed unnatural to me.

'You're very quiet, Virginia,' Mrs Rocheforte said. 'You're thinking I'm cold about Melissa, that I'm only interested in her talent, not in Melissa herself.'

I had the grace to look confused, and she smiled. 'That is understandable. In all those six and a half years that Melissa was here, neither of us came close to understanding the other. Melissa did not ask for either love or understanding. She was not here long before I realised that she was a taker and it suited me to give. She would not voluntarily repay me for what I'm doing for her, but she will repay me by becoming famous. When I see her name leap at me from the walls of the world's greatest opera houses, then and only then will I consider my money well spent.'

Unable to imagine such a future for someone I had been to school with, I was silent.

'Miss Brownson would not be surprised at what I've told you today. She never approved of what I was doing for Melissa, she didn't think she was worthy of such attention because of her singular remoteness. Miss Brownson may have been right, but an old lady with too much money and not enough time should be allowed a few foibles, I think.'

I smiled, and she went on, 'Have you heard from the boy who was staying with you?'

'Not today. He does send postcards and Christmas cards, but I don't think he'd remember that it's my birthday.'

'I see. He was a nice boy, your father said.'

'Oh yes, Alistair was very nice.'

I was saved from saying more by the arrival of a housemaid carrying a large silver tray and another carrying a three-tiered cake stand.

'I have a visitor, Millie,' Mrs Rocheforte said, 'so we shall want another cup and saucer and a plate. What's in these sandwiches?'

'Salmon, ma'am, and these 'ere are chicken.'

'Thank you, Millie. Virginia has a good appetite and it's her birthday. Strawberries and cream, I think.'

The maids disappeared, to return shortly with a bowl of beautiful strawberries and dishes of cream.

In past years I had always been a little in awe of Mrs Rocheforte. Today I was able to relax in her company, enjoying the stories she was telling me of travels with her husband in a world cushioned by wealth. She talked about her travels abroad, India and China, Japan and Egypt, Samarkand and the Russia of the tsars. The sound of a car's engine eventually brought me back to the present and I saw my father strolling across the terrace towards us.

'Gracious, look at the time!' Mrs Rocheforte said with a smile. 'Did you wonder where Virginia had got to, Dr Lawrence? We've had a lovely afternoon. I've done most of the talking; I only hope I haven't bored her.'

'Oh, no!' I was quick to say. 'I've loved listening to you. I'd no idea it was so late.'

'And it's become much cooler,' she said. 'Perhaps I should go inside now. Will you help me out of this low chair, doctor?'

It was then I realised that the lady I had seen sitting serenely in her chair had difficulty in walking. She leaned heavily on her stick and my father's arm. Benjie ran ahead of us into the house and I followed with her handbag and rugs.

At the door we were met by a cool and efficient young woman whom Father addressed as Miss Stedman. She took charge, helping Mrs Rocheforte into the drawing room and to her favourite chair in the window.

'Saunders has put a match to the fire, Mrs Rocheforte,' she said deferentially. 'He thought it was going quite chilly in here. We can draw your chair up to the fire if you feel cold.'

'Don't fuss, any of you. I'm a nuisance, I know, but once I get going I'm not nearly so helpless. Are you having a party tonight, Virginia?' she added with a smile in my direction.

'Yes. Some friends and the family will be there. I'll have a bigger one when I'm twenty-one.'

'Then I shall expect another piece of cake and another visit. But I'd like to think I shall see you again before then.'

'Oh, yes. I'll drive up with my father, or come alone if that's all right.'

'I shall look forward to it. Now hurry home with your father and enjoy the rest of your day. I'll see you on Thursday or Friday, Dr Lawrence.'

'Of course. Have you tried those new tablets yet?'

'Yes. They make me very sleepy, I'm afraid.'

'Well, most of them have side effects. When you get used to them, I think you'll find they no longer make you sleepy. If you prefer the old tablets, just let me know.'

Miss Stedman saw us out.

'The others are upstairs changing,' Mother said to me when we returned, 'so you'd better hurry up or your friends will be here before you're ready.'

Edith grinned at me from the landing. She was wearing a long organza dress in lemon which suited her dark-red hair, and she held out her hand and flashed her fingers in front of my face.

'Like it?' she asked, laughing down at me.

On the third finger of her left hand she was wearing a diamond ring. I cried excitedly, 'You're engaged! When did this happen?'

'This afternoon. Honestly, Ginny, I didn't want it to vie with your birthday, but I thought it would be nice to announce it when we're all together at home.'

I threw my arms around her, laughing. 'I didn't know it was so serious.'

'I've been serious about him since the moment we met, but I wasn't sure if he felt the same about me. Evidently he does.'

'But where did you buy the ring?' I cried.

'This afternoon in Kendal. He loves me, he loves the family, he adores the village. It wouldn't surprise me if we end up somewhere like this — and to think I couldn't get away from it quickly enough!'

'Ginny?' Mother called from the realms below. 'You can talk about Edith's engagement ring when you're dressed and ready. Get a move on.'

My new long party dress was a confection in blue taffeta and had cost more money than any dress I had ever had in my life. As I stared at the finished result in the long mirror in my bedroom, I thought plaintively, It's good enough for any old May Ball. I wondered what Alistair's girl had worn.

Downstairs the dress was admired. I read admiration in the eyes of Rodney's friend and even Rodney said, 'You're looking good, kid.'

'This arrived for you this afternoon,' Mother said. 'Open it now and we'll put it with your other presents.'

I stared down at the brown paper parcel in my hands and asked, 'Where has this come from?'

'Open it up,' Edith commanded, 'and then we can all see.'

My fingers rushed to untie the knots in the string, and then Mother was there with scissors and the paper dropped to the floor. Inside there was another parcel, wrapped in soft tissue paper, and wrenching this off I discovered a gold and silver beaded evening purse, soft and beautiful. Inside was an envelope, and while the others were admiring the purse, all I could see was a small greeting card and the words, 'Happy birthday, Ginny! Sorry I can't be there. Love from Alistair.'

My eyes met my father's as I looked up and he smiled. It was the happiest night of my life; my family and my friends were around me, even Eustace the cat sat in his basket with a paper hat on his ginger head, and in my hands was Alistair's birthday present.

I was too excited to sleep that night. I opened the window and stood looking out on moonlight shimmering the lake and leaves stirring in the garden, and I wondered if Alistair had thought about me during the day that had gone.

I felt the sharp prick of tears on my cheek. I wanted Alistair to come back into my life, I wanted him back in the family, but I knew that it was a forlorn dream. Alistair was in a different world, one his father had fashioned for him, and one in which I had no part. As the years passed he would remember us less and less until in the end there would be nothing at all. If I could accept this, I could be strong. Suddenly my thoughts turned to Melissa. Melissa would never let the past shape the future, she could forget us as though we had never existed. I was glad that I was me, after all.

Edith and Roger were married in the village church six months later and went to live in the south of England, where Roger had obtained a partnership in his uncle's practice. Rodney left college and went off to Canada, where he said there was far more scope than in Britain.

I stayed in the village working for my father, but I was happy enough. I knew everybody and everybody knew me. I knew their ailments, familiarised myself with their prescriptions and told myself that I was indispensable.

Cloonie, who had always grumbled that there was too much to do, now grumbled because there wasn't enough. Village life was predictable, and centred largely on the activities at the church. The vicar was getting old and suffered from bronchitis in the wintertime; it was no surprise to anybody, therefore, when he took in a young curate. His name was Colin Bannerman, and it was his first job after leaving university. He was enthusiastic, and busied himself with the Scout group, the Mothers' Union and the Women's Institute, and any other group he could get his hands on.

He was a gangling young man with an infectious smile, and he very soon found his way to our house to introduce himself. My parents liked him immensely and Father teased me unmercifully when Colin singled me out at every church hop.

I didn't feel that I was destined to become a curate's wife, but one morning when I was working in my tiny office within the surgery, I couldn't help hearing the conversation from the waiting room. As deaf people invariably do, Mrs Scholes spoke in a loud voice.

'I see the curate's taken a shine to young Ginny,' she said to whoever cared to listen, and I pricked my ears up. 'Danced with 'er all night, 'e did. Our Edie said everybody was talkin'.'

'Well, she'll be twenty-one this year. I don't suppose 'er father'd offer any objections,' said another voice.

'She'll make a very good curate's wife,' Mrs Scholes said firmly. 'She's a quiet sort o' girl, allus time to 'ave a chat with ye and she's nice with everybody. I 'ear she even visits Mrs Rocheforte and she can't be the easiest person to get along with.'

'Well, if she marries the curate she'll 'ave a busy life. The vicar's gettin' too old and 'is wife 'as enough to do lookin' after 'im,' said a voice I recognised as belonging to Mrs Murray, the butcher's wife.

'It'll be nice to 'ave a nice weddin' in the village, there's not bin one since Phoebe 'Athersall married Joe Bradley.'

I was glad that the talk shifted to Phoebe Hathersall, who didn't get along with Joe's mother and generally antagonised the old villagers by her too short skirts, her dyed blonde hair and startling make-up.

As the morning wore on and I became less busy, I had time to reflect on how my life was going. Colin was paying frequent visits to the house. I invariably found him visiting along the village street when I walked home from the surgery and all the signs were there whenever our eyes met. Did I really want to stay in the village as the curate's wife? It wasn't what I had dreamed of as a schoolgirl. On the other hand, a good few of the village girls would consider themselves very well blessed if they managed to capture Colin Bannerman.

The conversation I had overheard from the waiting room bothered me, and instead of walking home I climbed the hill to the fell and sat on a stone wall looking down at the lake. I could see the smoke rising from the tall chimneys of Rocheforte Hall and my breath froze on the cold wind. I could see my father's car climbing the hill towards the Hall and thought about Mrs Rocheforte, who was looking increasingly frail. Melissa never came to visit her.

I had also come to accept that we would never see Alistair again, although we still received postcards from Italy. He was working there in the sort of clinic his father had wanted for him. I had told myself a long time ago that I must put Alistair firmly out of my mind, but I was unsure if I should replace him with Colin. He was nice, he was good-looking with an eager boyishness that was endearing. Yet always at the back of my mind was the thought that one day Alistair might keep his promise and come back.

# Chapter Nine

All the village was invited to my twenty-first birthday party in the small village hall. Seeing the tables piled high with food reminded me of that morning years before when we had welcomed our evacuees, but this time there were no tears, only wellwishers hugging me and smiling, bringing gifts of fruit and flowers from their gardens. I had said there were to be no presents and the fruit and flowers were destined for the cottage hospital. On the dais at the end of the room was a three-piece band. Children, wearing their best party dresses, ran back and forth across the floor and impeded everybody else. Nobody minded, it was an evening for all to enjoy.

After supper Father made a speech. Then he invited me to take the floor with him in a waltz, much to everybody's delight. Later I danced with a great many people, men I had known all my life, but most often with Colin Bannerman, and I was aware of the nods and smiles as he swept me round the floor.

It was late in the evening when I saw father walking quickly across the room with his hand outstretched, and Colin said, 'Some late arrival, Ginny. Somebody your parents are delighted to see.'

I started across the room and my footsteps faltered when my eyes met Alistair's smiling gaze, then he was striding towards me to take me into his embrace.

'Why didn't you tell us you were coming?' were the first words I thought to say.

'I wanted to surprise you all. You look lovely, Ginny, I always knew you'd grow up to be a beauty.'

I was suddenly aware of Colin standing beside me, and,

gathering my scattered wits, I introduced them. They shook hands and appraised one another.

'How long are you staying with us?' I asked Alistair as the three of us left the floor.

'Three weeks, if you'll have me.'

How selfish young love can be! I danced with Alistair and listened to the whisperings around us. I gave no thought to Colin standing miserably looking on, or trying hard to appear unconcerned as he danced with other girls. I was only aware that this was the happiest night of my life and that Alistair would be with us for three whole weeks.

During those weeks we discovered anew the scenes we had loved when he was a member of our family. We sailed the lake and climbed the fells. We drove along the lanes in Alistair's new two-seater, and wandered through ancient priories and ruined castles. Three weeks was all we needed to fall in love.

Alistair's father had remarried in the spring and was in California with his new wife. He told me his mother was very bitter and hardly welcoming. He had spent two days with her before coming to us, but it had hardly been a happy experience. She was unconcerned about her son's life or his career, all she could talk about was his father's marriage, regardless of the fact that they had not lived together for a good many years, and before that had been completely incompatible.

'I'm sorry for her,' Alistair said, 'but bitterness won't help. I've never got on with my father, I happen to think they're better apart, but her nerves are in a shocking state and the longer she goes on like this, the more chance she has of worrying herself into an early grave.'

He talked about his work in Italy and the clinic in the mountains above Lake Como. The clinic was run by a Dr Steiner, a very famous Swiss neurologist, and it didn't take me long to realise that he was Alistair's hero, the man he hoped in time to emulate.

As we sat on the hillside overlooking Thirlmere, he described the beauty of Lake Como, surrounded by mountains, dotted with timeless villages dreaming under the Italian sun.

After a while I said softly, 'Is it more beautiful than this?'

'Well, it's different. The mountains are higher, the lake is bigger, and the sun shines longer and is warmer. You'd love it.'

I knew I would love it. With Alistair it would be paradise. But was a three weeks' courtship long enough? My mother didn't think so.

'Ginny, you haven't seen each other for years,' she argued. 'We're all very fond of Alistair but we think you should wait a while. You'd be living in a different country with people speaking a different language. Alistair will be completely wrapped up in his career. What would you do while he's working? Be practical, darling, wait a little longer.'

But young love doesn't wait. I was impatient, and so was Alistair.

'I'll be miles away,' he argued, 'and that young curate'll be around every day trying to get you to change your mind.'

'At least wait until Christmas,' Father said firmly. 'Give yourselves time to think. By then you'll have some idea where you're going to live and how your career will be affected. See what your Dr Steiner has to say about all this.'

'I think that's fair,' Mother agreed. 'It's only five months away and if your love can't stand a five months' separation, then it isn't worth very much.'

My parents won their argument. Alistair returned to Italy and I had to be content with long, impassioned letters.

Colin called to see us and, sensing that he came with hope, I had to tell him about Alistair. I could see his disappointment, even when he smiled and took my hand.

Mother said, rather wistfully, 'That boy really did like you, Ginny. And I'm not too happy about all my children leaving the nest.'

I loved them, I loved the village I had been brought up in and I would miss it dreadfully, but all my thoughts were on marriage to Alistair. Our new life in Italy would be alien to anything I had ever known, and because of that it seemed more and more exciting.

Alistair came back three days before Christmas, bringing an armful of gifts and news of a small villa he had found for us on the banks of Lake Como, a few miles outside Tremezzo. It seemed to me that everything was falling into place.

We drove into Lancaster to buy my engagement ring, a sapphire surrounded with diamonds, which cost far more than

I thought Alistair could afford. We were to be married on New Year's Eve.

My father broached the subject of Alistair's parents by asking if either of them intended to be present at the wedding.

Alistair shook his head doubtfully. 'My father wouldn't come without his new wife, and the only way my mother will come is if she isn't there. I've told both of them that Ginny and I intend to marry before I return to Italy; the excuses will come any day now.'

Alistair's father's excuse came over the telephone just after we had finished supper. He said his wife was very tired after their trip to America and it was quite the wrong time of year to be travelling about the country. He sent us a substantial cheque. His mother's refusal came in a long, rambling letter, which he allowed me to read. She also sent a cheque and said she would be pleased to see us the next time we were in England.

My parents offered no comment on the situation, so it was left to Cloonie to say, 'There'll be nobody on 'is side of the church, just 'im and 'is best man. Don't ye think it'll look very odd?'

'The villagers will fill the church on both sides,' Mother said. 'We can't insist that Alistair's parents come if they don't want to.'

I was busy unpacking wedding presents in the living room but the door was open and I had no difficulty in hearing their conversation from the kitchen.

'All this rush,' Cloonie complained, 'and them with all their lives in front of 'em. I don't 'old with 'er goin' abroad to live. They 'aven't seen each other for years and now she's goin' to marry 'im.'

I listened for Mother's reply. 'It was always Alistair with Ginny, even when they were children. Now she's got what she wanted.'

'Oh, 'e's well enough,' Cloonie replied. 'He was allus a nice polite boy, but 'e's come from a broken 'ome with a father who was as cold as charity and a mother who was bitter and difficult. I liked that nice young curate, I 'oped she'd fall in love with 'im and she'd 'ave stayed in the village.'

'Cloonie, we have to be happy for them,' Mother said firmly.

79

'Ginny had to spread her wings some time, but we'll never really lose her.'

I heard Mother shut the kitchen door sharply behind her before running up the stairs. No doubt she left Cloonie muttering under her breath while she slammed the crockery about.

There was a keen wind blowing from the fells on the morning of my wedding day and a sharp frost had silvered the trees. The lake gleamed like a sheet of grey glass. It was on such a day that I had first seen Alistair alighting from the train that brought the evacuees to the Lake District.

By the time we left for the church, a fine drizzle of snow had started to fall, but it did not prevent the villagers lining the road and thronging the churchyard.

I was married in a pale-blue coat and hood edged with Arctic fox. Emmie, an old school friend, acted as my bridesmaid and our only adornment was the posies of flowers Mother had insisted upon. My sister and her husband did not come to the wedding because Edith was expecting her first baby at any time.

The vicar was in bed with influenza so Colin Bannerman married us, and I felt sorry for him. It must surely have been the hardest ceremony he had ever performed.

Mother wept, saying in a trembling voice, 'I always wanted to see you in white, Ginny, lots of frothy lace like Edith had and a bevy of your friends for bridesmaids.'

'It was a warm summer's day when Edith was married,' I pointed out.

'I know, darling, but did it have to be today? Couldn't you have waited until the spring?'

'Isn't it more important that I'm in love, Mother? We have a home to go to and Alistair has a job he loves. Surely these are the things that make a marriage? The others only make a wedding day.'

She smiled tremulously. 'I know, Ginny. It's just me chasing a dream.'

As Alistair and I drove back to the house after the ceremony, I knew I was looking at a scene I would remember for the rest of my life. The snow had turned the village street into a scene from a child's fairyland; Christmas-tree lights shone in cottage windows and in the narrow lanes off the main street the virgin snow shimmered under the lamplight.

Cloonie stood behind the table on which she had laid out the buffet wedding breakfast, and I threw my arms around her in delight at the spectacle. She was still wearing her new navy-blue coat and the fur mother had lent her, and her felt hat sat upon her head like Britannia's helmet.

Father came to put his arm round my shoulders, saying, 'You look pretty, Ginny. Forget about the wreath and veil, I'm very proud of you.'

'Alistair too, Father?'

'I'd better be, hadn't I? But you've always been my girl. Now I've given you to him and he'd better be worthy of you.'

'Oh, he is, he is! We'll come back in the summer and we'll have so much to tell you.'

'Don't be surprised if we visit you before then. Your mother's talking about holidaying in Switzerland and Italy, and I know she's making it an excuse to see where you're living and if you're happy.'

'But that would be wonderful! When will you come?'

'In the spring, if you're ready to have visitors.'

'We'll both be longing to see you. I'm too excited today but I know I'll be homesick one day. I'll be missing you and Mother, Cloonie and the animals — everybody.'

He smiled. 'Here's our young curate wanting to say a few words. It hasn't been an easy day for him.'

'I'll be kind to him, Father.'

Colin smiled shyly. Our conversation was brief. After all, what was there to say? As he walked away through the crowd, I felt sad for someone who had lost out when I had so very much.

I felt tearful as my parents embraced me on the station platform in Lancaster, but then Alistair was there and we were waving to them from the train that was speeding us towards our future together. It was a future viewed through rose-tinted glasses. We were young, we were in love, and there was no time to reflect on the past behind me.

We journeyed south through France, Switzerland and into Italy, and I exclaimed at every new vista along that beautiful route. Days filled with wonder, nights filled with love — was it any wonder that I believed I was embarked upon a journey that would enchant me for the rest of my life?

When Alistair had spoken of a villa in Italy, I had visualised a sugar-pink-icing affair surrounded by gardens on the banks of the lake, but reality was very different. The villa lay up a steep slope on the mountainside with the lake beneath us, but it was a tiny house with a living room, a minute kitchen and a bedroom. In place of the sumptuous garden I had pictured, there was a torrent of water that descended the mountain with a rushing clamour, bringing with it stones and dead bracken. The taxi that had brought us from the station in Como had to leave us at the bottom of the hill to stumble upwards with our luggage. There was an awful lot of it, and we left some in a small garage at the side of the road where Alistair's car was parked, keeping only what we would need for the night. Laughing, we climbed higher up the mountainside while trying to avoid the water rushing almost between our feet.

Although the villa dismayed me, it did not depress me. Alistair added a match to the logs in the fireplace and soon the glow from the fire fell on the white walls and the pine furniture.

'I know it doesn't look very inviting,' he said with an anxious look in his eyes, 'but we can shop for more furniture — I thought you'd prefer to choose your own stuff.'

'Who does it belong to?' I asked.

'We're renting it from one of the attendants at the clinic. It was his mother's place until she became too old to climb the hill. She's living with him now and he happened to say the villa was empty. I didn't offer to buy it, it's only a stopgap. We'll get something better when we've had time to look around.'

'Oh, Alistair, I love it. I'll enjoy looking for furniture, choosing curtains and soft furnishings. It'll give me something to do while you're at the clinic.'

I meant it. I had visions of the villa gleaming with polished pine and delicate chintzes. We would make a garden on the hillside, and by the time summer came neither of us would recognise it. No shadow of disappointment came to trouble my life as I lay in Alistair's arms, warm and contented after love.

Whenever I had thought about Italy I had visualised it sweltering under a golden sun, with lush green countryside and glistening lakes. The reality in the month of January was very different. Always in my ears was the rushing sound of water and the wind that echoed eerily round the house.

From the tiny windows I could look down at the lake stretching like a huge letter Y below me. Sometimes the lake and the islands were shrouded in mist, and rain lashed down on the road that circled the lake so that it came to resemble a canal. I was fearful of Alistair having to drive his little car up those mountain passes to the clinic.

Shopping for furniture was out of the question until the weather improved, so I had to make do with polishing what we had. Alistair had been able to bring up most of our wedding presents, and now the firelight sparkled on polished brass and china, cushion covers and tablecloths, and the tiny shower room boasted rose-pink towels and rugs. How much happiness there was to be found in small homely things!

In the English lakes, spring had come shyly; here in Italy it was more strident, warmer, perfumed with the promise of summer. Around the lakes, gardens bloomed with colourful azaleas and the lake was alive with boats of all descriptions. The villages were busy with visitors who crowded the tiny shops looking for pottery, silk scarves and music boxes. I had only to walk along the shore to hear the sound of sentimental love songs like tiny tinkling bells coming from every shop. The warm sun caressed my skin, bleaching my blonde hair, bringing warm smiles to the eyes of the young Italian men I met on my way.

I drove with Alistair to where Dr Steiner had his clinic, high up in the mountains with exquisite views of the lake. It was a long, white building with wide terraces ablaze with flowers.

Patients sat outside in long, low chairs, cushioned and with rugs about their knees, for even though it was summer, here in the mountains it was cool. Some of them sat in groups chatting together, others sat apart, indifferent to the scenery or the presence of others. Alistair explained that they suffered from varying nervous disorders. Many of them were well on their way to recovery, others would recover for a time and then return, but for a few of them it was already too late.

Dr Steiner was a slight man with a charming smile and his handclasp was warm and friendly. Proudly he showed me over his clinic and introduced me to several of his nurses. His eyes

83

twinkled as he asked, 'And have you settled down in that tiny villa? You must love Alistair very much to be content with that.'

I laughed. He spoke English with hardly any trace of an accent, and I couldn't help thinking that my father would have liked his humour and gentleness.

'We will now go into my office and drink coffee,' he announced.

It was indeed the most untidy room in the clinic. The large desk was littered with papers and files were stacked up on the floor around the room. Apologetically he said, 'My new secretary does not join us until next week, my old one left to get married. How your father must be missing you.'

I immediately felt very guilty thinking of my father trying to cope with his increasing load of correspondence from the Ministry of Health. I could almost hear his incessant complaints that Doctors weren't Doctors any more, but Civil Servants.

While we sat drinking our coffee, Dr Steiner said, 'I have had thoughts about that tiny villa on the mountainside and the tortuous roads leading up to the clinic. In the winter months they can be particularly hazardous, but it is a problem that could be easily overcome.'

'How?' Alistair enquired.

'You could live here in the mountains. It is beautiful, and in the summer you can make up for all the isolation of the winter. You can drive into the sunshine on those days when I say to you, enough is enough.'

We smiled. Alistair persisted, 'But there are no houses here apart from the clinic; are you thinking that we could live at the clinic?'

'No, of course not. There is my villa, which you have admired often. I can live at the clinic. What does an old man who never entertains want with a large villa with too many rooms? I could live here with Dr Thadeous, two old men with a lot in common and nothing to do with their time except talk about their work. What do you say Ginny?'

'It sounds wonderful but we can't possibly turn you out of your home Dr Steiner. Isn't there anywhere at the clinic?'

'No. It would not be comfortable, small bedrooms at the top

84

of the building and food from the kitchens. I shall be happy living here, I spend most of my time here, Alistair will tell you that I'm hardly ever in my home — but you Ginny, you will enjoy living in a proper house with proper furniture. You and Alistair shall go into Como and Milan to choose what you would like.'

'But we'd be happy with your furniture.'

'You haven't seen it yet. I'm an old man, set in his ways, hating change. The furniture belonged to my mother and has been adequate, but not for a beautiful girl fresh from England with ideas, I'm sure, of what she would really like. This afternoon Alistair will take you to the villa and you can make your plans.'

'I would like to have some sort of work Dr Steiner, I could feel very bored and lonely when Alistair is here all day. Is there anything here at the clinic for me to do?'

'My new secretary speaks Italian of course and fluent German, but she has hardly any English. Alistair has talked to me about you and the work you did for your father, and although that will not be possible here, you could help me in a great many ways. I have very many English patients and others from America and English-speaking countries. They are exasperated and often frustrated by nurses and orderlies who speak no English. They have worries about their business enterprises, their wives and their children, they would be relieved to find a young lady on my staff who could help them deal with their correspondence and who could reassure their families at home.'

'Are your patients well enough to deal with business matters then?' I asked in some surprise.

'Perhaps not when they arrive, but they are here to be made well, and it is then they start to fret about all they have left behind.'

'But you never thought of employing anybody in that capacity before?'

'I have thought about it yes, but that is all I did. I never had a doctor on my staff before who brought here an English wife with the appropriate qualifications.'

His smile was innocently disarming, and Alistair was looking at me expectantly. 'When would you want me to take up my duties Dr Steiner?' I asked him slyly, and the relief on his face was there for us to see.

# Chapter Ten

Every spare moment we had we spent hunting for furniture in the elegant shops of Milan, and the money we had received at our wedding diminished rapidly. In the end we were happy to refurnish our bedroom, the living room and one small guest room, and Dr Steiner told us we could make use of any of his furniture that didn't quarrel with what we had purchased.

I was introduced to the five English speaking patients several days later when they were sitting together on the terrace. Two of them were American, two were Canadian and there was one Englishman, and Alistair assured me that none of them were now giving problems and I would find them co-operative.

The Americans and the Canadians were affable, the Englishman more reserved and as I sat chatting to them, they all expressed their delight that at last there would be somebody on the staff who could understand them. Somebody who could find the books they wanted to read, air their grievances and deal correctly with their telephone enquiries. I had misgivings that they could keep me fully employed but largely they welcomed having a woman to talk to.

One afternoon I felt I must get out of the office into the sunshine for a little while. I walked along the terrace, exchanging smiles and greetings with the groups sitting there, intrigued in particular by a young woman who always sat alone.

A wealth of dark, shining hair fell around her shoulders, and she had a pale, patrician face and large eyes that gazed into the distance. A wave of pity washed over me, and without a second's thought I went towards her, pulling up a chair to sit beside her.

She showed no curiosity as I sat there; she did not even look at me. After a while I felt that I was intruding, so I left.

As I walked inside, I was aware of Dr Steiner watching me from one of the windows, and when I reached the office he was waiting for me.

'She bothers you, doesn't she, Ginny, that beautiful lost girl who ignored your overtures of friendship?'

'Yes, more than any of the others. Who is she?'

'Her name is Natalia Mellini.'

'I've seen her name in the files. She's been in many times before.'

'Too many times. Her husband is Riccardo Mellini, perhaps Italy's most famous conductor. When he returns from America he will take her home for a while and in the weeks that follow she will get a little better.'

'Can't he keep her with him all the time?'

'Impossible. He is a traveller on the world stage. He conducts orchestras here in Italy, in London, America, all over the world. Natalia has no part to play in the sort of life he must lead. I have known Natalia since she was a small girl. She was talented at the cello, and she met Riccardo at the musical college where they were studying.'

'When did she start to be ill?'

'It was in her as a child — tantrums, silences. Her mother thought it would pass with childhood but I suspected something more sinister than that. Her father died when she was ten years old and her mother embarked upon a life of self-seeking pleasure. She left the girl in the care of her grand-mother and the poor lady had a hard time of it.

'I was called in to help and at the age of twelve she came to me for treatment. For a time it worked, but I always suspected the malaise would return. However, she was happy playing her cello, and when she met Riccardo I began to hope that I might have been wrong.'

'So she was well when they married?'

'For a time. Then Riccardo had to spend a season in Verona for the summer opera festival. He invited her grandmother to stay with her. When he came home that night, he found her grandmother locked out of the villa while inside Natalia had set about systematically to destroy it. Curtains were torn, furniture was shattered, even the piano and many priceless ornaments. The day after she came here, silent and sulky, and remained that way for many weeks.'

'Does her grandmother come to see her?'

'Yes. Poor lady, she has done her best, but Natalia won't speak to her. When Riccardo comes home we shall see an improvement, then when he has to go away it will all start again.'

He shook his head sadly and left me to my thoughts.

I pitied the girl gazing out across the mountains and I pitied her husband, talented, famous and with a terrible burden.

I spoke of it to Alistair that night and he said evenly, 'You'll not get through to her, Ginny. None of us have, not even Dr Steiner, when she's like that.'

'What's her husband like?'

'I've had very little to do with him. He strikes me as being somewhat remote, a grave sort of chap not given to smiling, but then he's got very little to smile about. You'll see him when he comes for Natalia.'

I met Riccardo Mellini several days later. I was busy setting up my small office when there was a brief knock on the door, which immediately opened to admit a tall man wearing a dark-grey lounge suit. He was slim and elegant with dark hair silvered at the temples. For a moment he looked at me curiously before saying, 'Good morning, I am Riccardo Mellini. I would like to speak to Dr Steiner if he is available.'

'I'll find him for you, Signor Mellini,' I answered and hurried from the room in search of the doctor.

I met him halfway along the corridor and he said immediately, 'I saw the car. I'll see him straight away.'

'Would you like coffee?'

'No, we usually have a glass of wine, then we go to see Natalia.'

I went to the window and looked down at the terrace. Natalia sat in her accustomed place with a light rug over her knees. It was a sunny morning in early August and in the distance the lake gleamed. I could visualise the scene around the lakeside, busy with traffic, the water crowded with pleasure craft, the tiny shops seething with holiday makers. Yet here, only a few miles away in the mountains, there was a tragedy none of those light-hearted people could be aware of.

I watched Dr Steiner and his visitor walking out of the clinic and along the terrace. I saw Riccardo Mellini bend down to embrace his wife, who barely acknowledged him. The two men looked at each other unhappily. A nurse came out carrying Natalia's luggage. The little procession moved along the terrace and down the steps to the car, where a chauffeur waited at the open door. The luggage was packed in the boot, Natalia was helped into the car and Riccardo took his place beside her, then they were driving out through the gates. My eyes followed the car along the mountain road until I could see it no more.

Natalia would be back, the doctor said. I did not know at that moment that I would meet her much sooner than that.

At the end of August Dr Steiner informed us that we could both take four days holiday which he called a belated honeymoon and which we accepted joyfully.

We drove over the pass to Lugano in Switzerland, circling the beautiful lake before driving westward to spend three idyllic nights at Stresa on Lake Maggiore. I was utterly and completely happy. I was in love with Alistair and I was in love with Italy. Red-roofed old towns and startling blue water, sunlight across cobbled squares, and around every corner some new and enchanting vista.

I was sitting in the car on our way home, waiting for Alistair to come back after photographing yet another view of the lake with its wooded islands. His face was alive with excitement as he opened the door, saying quickly, 'Come and take a look at this, Ginny, see what you think of it.'

Curiously I followed him to a stone wall on the other side of the road, where a series of large posters were displayed advertising the opera in Verona and various concerts to be held in large villas around the lake. My heart quickened when I read that Riccardo Mellini was to conduct the orchestra at one of the villas.

' "Riccardo Mellini",' I read. 'Dr Steiner said he was coming back to fulfil engagements.'

'Not Mellini,' Alistair cried, 'the singer!'

' "Melissa Francesca",' I read.

'Well?' Alistair looked expectantly at me.

Suddenly my eyes opened wide and I said, 'Oh, Alistair, it can't be! Not Melissa!'

'Don't you think it would be just like her to Italianise her name?'

'Oh, I wonder if it's Melissa. Could we go to the concert?'

'I'll ask Dr Steiner if he can get tickets. It'll be frightfully upper crust, these concerts at the villas always are, but he's somebody around here, he can get tickets if anybody can.'

'Have you ever been to one of these concerts?'

'Gracious, no. They're attended by people like the Duke and Duchess of Windsor, foreign royalty — most of them no longer have a throne but they keep up their style and people fall over themselves to hobnob with them.'

'Can we find out if it's Melissa without going to the concert?'

'We'll ask Dr Steiner. He's a great lover of music, he may have heard of her.'

August was a quiet month at the clinic. After we had unpacked, we sauntered down the hillside and found him sitting on the terrace, a battered straw hat shielding his eyes from the sun and a pair of old canvas shoes on his feet. He smiled and indicated two chairs beside him.

'Now you shall tell me where you went and what you saw,' he said.

Alistair left it to me to describe our journey and the sensations it left with us, and then he mentioned the posters.

'Ah, yes, there is the opera in Verona. I have already made up my mind that I will go there for *Aïda*. I shall ask Signor Mellini to pull strings for me. Since he is conducting, who will refuse him?'

'Do you know anything about Melissa Francesca? She is to give a concert at the Villa Rosa at the end of August.'

'A new, shining light on the operatic stage, young, beautiful and immensely talented. Not Italian, I think. When Maria Spolleti threw one of her usual tantrums and walked off the stage of *La Bohème*, believing they would fall over themselves in order to drag her back, Melissa Francesca stepped into her shoes and captured the audience who had come to hear Maria. They stood and cheered at her portrayal of Mimi, and now she is here to stay. Why are you so interested in her?'

91

Alistair explained and the doctor was fascinated by our story.

'I will ask Riccardo Mellini to obtain tickets for us. No doubt he will be there to hear Melissa sing, and he will be pleased for me to talk to his wife to see if her condition is improved.'

One morning as I was opening the office door, Dr Steiner marched across the hall and said brightly, 'The tickets arrived yesterday. You must wear your prettiest gown, Ginny, because I can assure you the competition will be intense. Most of those gowns will have cost a fortune, but you will have your youth and beauty, as well as a sympathy for what you have gone to hear.'

That evening I looked doubtfully at my one evening gown in the wardrobe, made by Mrs Jolley, the village dressmaker. It fell away at the shoulders and, after its narrow waist, swept to the floor in long, graceful folds of rose-coloured silk. Unadorned, it relied on the sheen of the material and the simplicity of its cut, and yet I was troubled that it could hardly live up to the competition. When Dr Steiner saw me in it, however, he was quick to reassure me.

'You look lovely, Ginny. There will be nobody at the Villa Rosa you need to be afraid of.'

All the same, I was very nervous as we entered the marble salon of the Villa Rosa with its array of crystal chandeliers, its tinkling fountains, gilt and alabaster, and the chattering of a multitude of voices.

My eyes were drawn to two people sitting together on a gilded couch, surrounded by others, and I recognised them instantly, the man from photographs and pictures I had seen from my childhood, the woman from newspaper photographs that had scandalised our country.

The Duke of Windsor was a slight, grey-haired man with a sad, careworn face; the Duchess looked like a doll from a marionette show. Her dark hair, intricately styled, surrounded a face that was not pretty but worldly, and she was painfully thin. I was aware of all this before I appreciated the beauty of her cream satin gown and the sparkling jewels round her throat and arms. She was doing most of the talking while her husband sat back, occasionally smiling.

Alistair whispered in my ear, 'That is the woman he gave up his throne for, Ginny — his throne, his way of life, all he believed in! Is she worth it, do you think?'

'He must have been completely besotted by her, besotted or desperately in love.'

'Or a fool. A man is a fool who gives up everything for a woman.'

I looked up into his face, so sure, so confident in the present and the future. He looked so handsome in his formal evening dress that I was only aware of the rush of joy that filled my heart in the knowledge that he was mine.

Across the room, Dr Steiner acknowledged our presence and we went forward to join him. He was standing with Riccardo Mellini and on the gilt chair beside them Natalia sat with a set smile on her face.

Alistair murmured, 'I wonder how much of this is really registering.'

'You've met Dr Grantham, Signor Mellini,' Dr Steiner said. 'And this is his wife Virginia, who — fortunately for me — has come to help at the clinic.'

He bowed over my hand and shook hands with Alistair, then I bent to speak to Natalia. She stared at me without recognition.

Dr Steiner said easily, 'Dr and Mrs Grantham think they may have met Melissa Francesca in England — in fact, they're sure they have. Can you tell us anything about her, signor?'

'I know very little about her,' he replied. 'As you know, I've been abroad for several months and she descended upon the operatic scene here in Italy during my absence. This will be the first time I have heard her sing. But she is to sing at the opera in Verona during the season, so she will be rehearsing with me, starting tomorrow afternoon in Milan.'

'I hear she sang a peerless Mimi,' Dr Steiner persisted.

'I believe so. And here, I think, is our ascending star.'

There was a bustle of conversation around the dais and people were taking their places. Dr Steiner ushered us to seats at the side of the room, and Riccardo Mellini took his place in the chair next to his wife, leaning over solicitously to ask if she was comfortable.

A man was taking his place at the grand piano and then she

93

was there, acknowledging the applause with gracious smiles, bowing briefly to where the Duke and Duchess sat surrounded by their sycophants.

How could I be sure that this elegant woman was the girl who had stepped off that train years before? It was hard to believe that she had ever strolled with me along the promenade in Devonshire. Her scarlet silk gown shimmered around her feet while the lights emphasised the blue-black sheen of her hair. Long gold earrings were her only adornment. The voice that reverberated round that room was the voice of that young girl and yet amazingly developed. As it tenderly sang the love songs of Italy and arias from Puccini's operas, I searched her beautiful face for confirmation that this was the Melissa I had known.

The applause was rapturous, the audience emotional as only Italians can be emotional about music, and Melissa acknowledged the adulation with gracious smiles. Laughing, she handed her floral tributes to a servant and launched into her final encore, a plaintive rendering of 'They Call Me Mimi'.

Riccardo Mellini was leaning forward in his seat, intent on the singer and her music. Beside him, his wife sat with the fixed smile on her face, her hand resting in his, and my heart ached.

'What do you think, Ginny?' Alistair whispered.

'Oh, Alistair, I don't know. I suppose it must be, but she's so grown-up, so sophisticated. If she comes this way, we'll know.'

We had to wait. Surrounded by admiring people, she was taken immediately to meet the Duke and Duchess, who invited her to sit with them. When at last she got away, she went straight to Riccardo Mellini, who stooped over her hand, and she gazed up at him with something akin to hero worship.

'Come,' Dr Steiner said firmly, 'we shall confront this talented young lady to see if she recognises you.'

In some confusion we followed him across the room and she turned to smile. Catching my eye, she gave a delighted laugh. 'Ginny Lawrence!' she said. 'How absolutely wonderful!'

She threw her arms around me in a theatrical embrace the old Melissa would have been incapable of, and then she was embracing Alistair and we were answering her questions about why we were there and why together.

'Would you believe it?' she said, laughing. 'Ginny was my first friend in the Lakeland village where I was evacuated. I'd have known you anywhere, Ginny. You've grown up, but you still have that wide-eyed, little-girl innocence about you. So you're going to be a famous doctor, Alistair?'

'I am a doctor, I'm not so sure about the famous,' he replied modestly.

'But of course,' Dr Steiner said. 'Destined to take my place one day. I have great hopes for Alistair.'

'Ginny, we have so much to talk about,' she was saying. 'Tomorrow I have a rehearsal in Milan but there's all morning. I'm staying here in the villa as the guest of Contessa Forenzo, just for a few days. Couldn't you come to see me in the morning? We could have breakfast together, out there on the terrace, and we could talk. You can tell me all about the village, your family, Mrs Rocheforte and Madame Courtney.'

'I'm a working girl,' I protested. 'I work for Dr Steiner and I'm sure he'd never be prepared to give me a morning off when there's so much to do.'

'Please, Dr Steiner,' she urged. 'Just one little morning! After that we might not see each other for months.'

'Take the day off,' Dr Steiner said gallantly. 'Your gentlemen can manage without you for one day now that you have organised the work so well.'

'Then I shall see you at ten o'clock,' Melissa said.

Riccardo Mellini reminded her, 'And I shall expect you at the rehearsal promptly at three, Signorina Francesca. Please remember that when you are reminiscing over old times.'

# Chapter Eleven

There were three white vans parked outside the Villa Rosa when I arrived there the next morning. Men in white overalls were carrying out the debris from the night before. In the salon downstairs an army of cleaners were at work and a supercilious manservant spoke to me in rapid Italian as I edged inside the door.

My Italian was improving but when it was poured out to me in a quick stream I had no hope of understanding it. A darkly clad woman walking down the stairs saw my predicament and said, 'You wish for something, signora?'

'I have an appointment with Signorina Francesca.'

'Regarding what?'

'I was here last night, and she invited me to meet her again this morning.'

'You are not a journalist?'

'No, I'm an old friend from England.'

She stared at me for several moments before saying, 'Perhaps you will follow me. The signorina is busy with her dressmaker.'

I was ushered into an enormous bedroom where Melissa stood surrounded by four women, who draped her with silks and twittered like a flock of birds. I stood uncertainly within the doorway, wishing I was miles away. Nobody paid me any attention and the woman who had brought me up the stairs had disappeared.

When I entered the room and closed the door sharply behind me, they all looked in my direction.

Laughing, Melissa said, 'You're early. I'd forgotten for a moment that you were coming.'

'I'm not early, it's half past ten and you did say ten o'clock.'

'I'm hopeless with time, and I had to select something from this lot this morning. Go out on the terrace and I'll join you in a few minutes.'

The terrace outside her room overlooked the lake and was furnished with a tiny gilt table and several matching chairs. There was also a sun lounger, and a colourful bathrobe had been slung over the arms.

I sat on one of the chairs looking out across the lake. A pleasure steamer cruised slowly by, and I could see that the passengers clustered at the boat's rails, their binoculars and cameras trained on the villa. Did they hope to see Melissa, I wondered, or was the villa itself an object of interest, like the Villa D'Este and the Villa Carlotta?

Time passed, and I became aware of a hollow feeling in the pit of my stomach since I had had no breakfast. I could hear the chattering voices from inside the room until suddenly there was silence and the closing of a door. Then Melissa was there, smiling, in her hands a bottle of champagne.

'Poor Ginny! I'm sorry you've had to wait so long, but when I asked you to come today I'd completely forgotten about those women coming. There are three glasses here, the Contessa is joining us.'

She must have read the dismay in my face because she said lightly, 'You'll like her, Ginny, and we can talk about anything in front of Velma. Anything except my beginnings, that is.'

When the Contessa arrived I remembered that I had seen her the evening before, a large lady with bleached blonde hair. Now she was wearing a revealing swimsuit and carrying a large sombrero. She flopped down on the sun lounger and, taking the glass of champagne from Melissa's hand, said, 'You didn't say you had a visitor.' Despite her title, she sounded American. Fixing me with a bright smile, she went on, 'And who are you, dear? I don't think we've met.'

'This is Ginny Grantham, Velma, somebody I knew in England when we were both very young. Now she's married to Dr Steiner's assistant. He's divinely handsome and very clever.'

'A neurologist?' she said, addressing me.

'Yes.'

'Well, I've already had one brush with Dr Steiner, as Melissa knows. There was I suffering mental torture after I split from Alex, and do you know what he said to me? That I was a silly neurotic woman with too much money and too little to do, and I should sit back and take a good look at myself. Is your husband going to be like that?'

Melissa trilled with laughter. 'Don't take it out on Ginny, Velma. Alistair's a perfect darling. Besides, you very quickly pulled yourself together when you met Mario and he installed you in this beautiful place.'

'Well, of course. I deserved Mario after all I had to take from Alex. I suppose you've met Natalia Mellini?' she said, changing the subject so rapidly I was taken aback.

'Yes, but she is not at the clinic now.'

'No, I saw her with Riccardo last night. Poor man, the woman's a millstone round his neck.'

'I'm sure he doesn't think so,' I retorted. 'He loves her, one only has to look at them together to realise that.'

Melissa smiled and Velma looked at me in surprise. 'What a romantic little thing you are!' she said. 'Do you really know anything about the Mellinis?'

'Only that I've seen them at the clinic, I've seen his tenderness and that he cares about her. She can't help being a very sick girl.'

'He should never have married her. She's his cousin, you know. They were more or less brought up together because Natalia's father died young and her mother left to marry some Frenchman. Natalia was always highly strung and temperamental, and always in love with him. It was a marriage designed in hell and engineered by the old grandmother.'

'How do you know all this?' Melissa asked curiously.

'Alex told me. Alex's family were close friends of the Mellinis and the two boys grew up together. There were other girls in Riccardo's life — after all, he was very handsome and extremely eligible. None of them measured up and as Natalia grew up, more and more she and Riccardo were thrown together. Oh, I know people say he didn't have to marry her if he didn't love her, but the old lady was a matriarch to be obeyed. For one thing, she held the purse strings, and for another, she was pretty indomitable. The entire family was brought up to cosset and protect Natalia because of the tragedy in her life, but it's Riccardo who has suffered the most.'

I was beginning to feel slightly light-headed from the champagne and the hot sun, and was relieved when Velma said suddenly, 'I'll ring for lunch. Something light, I think, since you have a rehearsal. Before you go, Melissa, I do want you to take a look at the jewellery I wore last night before it goes back to the bank. It's absolutely dreadful that I can't keep it here, but Mario insists that thieves would kill for it.'

Lunch was a meal of salad and lobster washed down with a light Orvieto, and then we were taken to see the jewellery. Fashioned in diamonds and emeralds, there were earrings, a necklace and a bracelet. I watched Melissa fastening the necklace round her slender throat, posing and posturing in front of the mirror. Handing it back, she said, 'I'll be wearing paste on the stage for years, but I'll wear the real thing in private.'

Velma laughed. 'Will you be able to afford them, darling?'

'Of course,' she answered confidently. 'I shall be the diva, if I don't buy them for myself there will be men only too willing to shower me with them.'

'Nice to be so confident,' Velma said, replacing the jewels in their cases and putting them carefully in the safe.

'I've had to be confident,' Melissa said. 'If not me, who else? Let me see your clothes, you have so many of them.'

'I've told you you can borrow anything of mine.'

'They're too big for me, darling.' Melissa's smile did not take the sting out of her words.

Melissa threw open the wardrobe doors to take out a selection of gowns which she held in front of her, exclaiming on the material, the colour and the cut. I was wishing I had not come. I was bored by the banality of the spectacle of two women discussing clothes intended for a lifestyle that I could have no part in, and looking at my watch I suddenly realised that it was almost two o'clock.

'Don't you have a rehearsal in Milan at three?' I asked anxiously.

Melissa looked at her watch. 'Heavens, yes, we'll have to go. Ginny, you'll come with me, won't you?'

'No, please, I'd rather not. I promised Alistair I'd get back this afternoon and you don't know how long you'll be away.'

'But I want you to come, Ginny, that was the reason I invited you. And Velma won't come.'

'I should say not,' Velma said feelingly. 'Riccardo Mellini's a stickler for perfection. The afternoon could be extremely boring. I'd stick to your guns, Ginny and get off home.'

'Stop it at once!' Melissa said. 'Ginny's coming with me and she'll enjoy every minute of it. After all, not many people can say they've sat in at a rehearsal where Melissa Francesca sang and Riccardo Mellini conducted.'

The roads to Milan were busy as I drove with Melissa in her open tourer. Unconcerned, she kept up a stream of chatter as she manoeuvred the car at some speed through the traffic. At last we were parking in a place reserved for her in the open square near the opera house. I had heard all my life about La Scala in Milan and I would have liked to saunter through its long corridors and feel its atmosphere, but Melissa was hurrying me towards the rehearsal hall, where we could hear music being played.

A uniformed official held the door open for us and one look at his face was enough to tell me that there was trouble ahead.

The orchestra sat with their instruments on a large platform at the head of the room. They were mostly in shirtsleeves, as was Riccardo Mellini, waving his baton before them. Melissa swept down the length of the hall with a confidence I was far from feeling. Without any hesitation she stepped on to the platform; Mellini waved his baton imperiously and the music stopped.

He turned to face her with a stern look. She smiled. 'I'm so sorry I'm late, Signor Mellini, but I'm ready to start immediately.'

'Your rehearsal was timed for three o'clock, signorina,' he said. 'It is now after four thirty.'

'I know, I'm so sorry. The traffic was terrible.'

'You could have left earlier. Surely you must know the state of the traffic between Como and Milan.'

'I had dress fittings in the morning, it was impossible to leave earlier.'

'I see, and I have an urgent appointment at six o'clock. I have to take my wife back to the clinic and the traffic will be as busy for me as it was for you. The rehearsal can continue under the auspices of Signor Gallio, who is authorised to deputise for me. If you wish to rehearse with me, signorina, I suggest you keep to the times I specify. Now if you will excuse me?'

She stared at him dumbfounded. A slim young man took hold of the baton while Riccardo shrugged his arms into his jacket and stepped down from the platform. He looked at Melissa just once and she said angrily, 'My rehearsal was with you Signor. I am Melissa Francesca, I don't rehearse with deputies.'

'And I am Riccardo Mellini Signora and I only rehearse with artistes who obey my rules. Good day.'

As he swept past me, I could feel my knees trembling. The anger he had shown towards Melissa was apparent in the fleeting glance he directed at me.

I sat down miserably as Melissa flung her light wrap across a chair, glaring malevolently at Signor Gallio, who was calling his orchestra to order. After that I was subjected to a display of theatrical tantrums. Amusement flickered along the rows of musicians while their conductor struggled desperately to accommodate a prima donna who refused to be placated.

After several disasters, Melissa said, 'It's no use, Signor Gallio. I am in no mood to rehearse. Signor Mellini has offended me too much, I can't concentrate. If he wants me to rehearse with him again, perhaps you will ask him to contact me.'

'He'll be in Verona after today,' the conductor answered calmly.

'I too shall be in Verona, it won't be my fault if things go wrong there.'

With a frosty look in the direction of the orchestra, she swept from the platform. She did not look at me as she passed my chair and I stood up doubtfully, wondering if I should follow. Catching the amused expression in the conductor's eyes, I knew that this moment would pass, and it would be one of many. Two indomitable wills had clashed that morning, but Riccardo Mellini had the upper hand. There had been a great many Melissas in his life and he had called her bluff. She was a new girl on the operatic stage and she needed to be taught a lesson. There would be time for tears and tantrums when she surpassed those who had gone before her.

With a smile at Signor Gallio, I went out into the sunshine to find Melissa fuming in her car. 'He was insufferable!' she stormed. 'How dared he make me look ridiculous in front of all those musicians?'

'You were an hour and a half late for the rehearsal, and we could have left much earlier if you hadn't insisted on looking at Velma's clothes.'

'I was warned that he could be difficult. How could he do that to me? And simply because of that dotty wife of his! I'll make him sorry for what he's done this afternoon.'

I saw no point in arguing with her. Her anger showed in her driving, and I was glad to arrive in one piece at the gates of Dr Steiner's villa.

'Would you like to come in?' I asked her. 'Alistair will be home by this time, I could make us a meal.'

'I don't think so, Ginny, I'd be rotten company anyway. I'll send you and Alistair tickets for the opera, but it's likely to be another disaster if he's conducting.'

'Of course it won't be,' I said reassuringly. 'You'll be wonderful, he'll be wonderful and you'll both be good friends.'

'You have more confidence than I have,' were her parting words as she put the car into gear and drove swiftly down the hillside.

Alistair was hunting through the kitchen cupboards when I opened the door. Looking round, he said, 'You're late. I thought you were only going for breakfast.'

'And lunch, and the rehearsal,' I said feelingly. 'Haven't you had anything to eat since lunch?'

'It doesn't matter. I'll help you, then you can tell me about your day.'

We ate melon, followed by chicken and salad. Over coffee in the living room, I started to tell Alistair about the afternoon.

'Serves her right,' he said at last. 'He was late bringing his wife into the clinic. She was a bit tearful and he unusually apologetic.'

I told him about Velma's version of the Mellini marriage and Alistair said, 'I've heard something of that from Dr Steiner. It's a terribly hard burden for a professional man like Mellini, but I suppose what he misses in his private life, his public life makes up for. She was very upset when he left her.'

'I'll go in to see her in the morning. Perhaps one of these days I'll get through to her.'

'You're more optimistic than Dr Steiner and I.'

'Melissa is sending us tickets for the opera in Verona,' I told him and was surprised by his enthusiasm, because I hadn't thought he was all that keen on serious music.

When I said as much, he admitted with an embarrassed smile, 'I enjoyed seeing how the other half live. When did we ever expect to be eating supper with famous people, foreign royalty, the man we once expected to be our king and the woman who changed it all?'

'Didn't you find it all a little false? All those people wanting to be seen and photographed. Hanging round the Windsors, applauding every word they said, people who probably had had the most to say about them.'

'I know that you're right, they're dilettantes and sycophants, but they're larger than life and amusing. I think we should make the most of them.'

Why suddenly did I feel that first faint tinge of doubt, distaste?

I was working in my office the next morning when a boy arrived with a huge basket of hothouse flowers for Natalia Mellini, so I left my work to deliver them to her room. As usual she was sitting gazing out of the window. There was a thin drizzle of rain.

She did not turn her head to look who had entered her room so I took the flowers and placed them on the table beside her chair. She gave them a cursory glance. I detached the small envelope and handed it to her, not really surprised when she laid it aside unopened.

'Is there anything you want, Signora Mellini?' I asked, but she shook her head and there was nothing left for me but to leave her alone.

Later that morning I told Dr Steiner about the flowers and he smiled a little sadly. 'The flowers are a peace offering, I think, because he left her in some distress.'

I pitied her. She had a handsome and caring husband and yet there was nothing.

'How can I get through to her?' I asked him.

'Perserverance, Ginny. Talk to her, tell her about that village in England where you grew up and your family. Tell her about your husband and your hopes for the future. Spend a little time with her each day. She is in need of a friend, but don't be disillusioned if you feel your efforts are wasted.'

Alistair was less enthusiastic. 'It won't work,' he said firmly. 'It'll get you down, make you feel inadequate. Stick to those five male patients who are getting back to normal and who think you're heaven sent. Concentrate on them Ginny and leave the Natalia Mellinis in this establishment to Steiner and the rest of us.'

'Nevertheless I'm going to try,' I said, speaking more confidently than I felt.

My first opportunity came the following morning when I passed her room and saw that the door was open. She was sitting on the terrace outside her room, looking down at something in her hands. Uncertainly I joined her, surprised when she looked up at my entrance. She held out the envelope that had been attached to the flowers, saying in a cold voice, 'Read it.'

She watched as I took out the small card, and when I hesitated, she said, 'I have asked you to read it.'

Giving the card all my attention, I read clearly, '"To my dear wife with all my love, Riccardo."'

I handed back the card in its envelope and stared as her slender fingers proceeded to tear it up, dropping the fragments contemptuously on the floor.

'Why did you do that?' I asked reproachfully. 'The flowers were beautiful and I'm sure your husband meant every word he wrote.'

'My husband has gone away and left me.'

'He had to go away to work.'

'And to the women who idolise him.'

'Women will always idolise successful men, but you are the only person who matters in his life.'

'How can you know?'

'I've seen how much he cares for you.'

'You know nothing,' she said adamantly, and when I started to say something more, she turned her head and stared at me coldly. 'Please go now, and take the flowers with you. Give them to somebody else.'

# Chapter Twelve

I was disappointed that my parents had not been to see us now that we had room for them to stay. They wrote that Father was far too busy to leave his work but they would definitely make an effort before the autumn. Mother informed me that Mrs Rocheforte was very ill and that she had asked that her children be sent for.

When I told Alistair, he said, 'I suppose Melissa's been informed? She really ought to know.'

'They were never all that close. Melissa owes her everything, but there was no love there. I suppose if Mrs Rocheforte dies, Melissa will be informed.'

'I expect so. She hardly needs the old lady's money now, though.'

True to her word, Melissa sent us tickets for the opera in Verona and her performance as Madame Butterfly. The tickets were for a Friday evening, which I thought would suit Alistair far better than if they had been for midweek, but the night before he telephoned halfway through the evening to say that he had a very difficult patient on his hands and would be very late home.

The long night stretched on and at eleven o'clock he had still not returned. I hesitated about going to bed. He would be tired and in no mood to talk, and yet I felt I should be there to make him a hot drink or listen if he wanted to tell me about his patient.

For a long time I lay reading, my ears tuned for the sound of a car on the mountain road. At last I nodded off to sleep with the bedside lamp still burning.

The sun woke me as it invaded my room with shafts of gold, and from the clock beside the bed I saw that it was after eight o'clock.

From the kitchen I heard the sounds of cupboards being opened and the clinking of china. Putting on my dressing gown, I ran swiftly down the stairs, expecting to find Alistair. But it was Gina, our young girl from a small hamlet halfway down the mountain, who came to us three mornings during the week. She greeted me with a bright smile as she set out the breakfast things.

'You eata breakfast now, signora?' she enquired, eyeing my tousled hair and state of undress.

Her English was as minimal as my Italian, so I simply said, 'Wait, Gina,' then I returned upstairs to see if Alistair had slept in the spare room so as not to disturb me. There was no sign of him, and in some anxiety I telephoned the clinic, relieved to hear Dr Steiner's voice answering the telephone.

'Alistair is still here. It was a bad night, I asked him and Dr Vicelli to stay on until the patient was calmer. He will tell you about it when he gets home. You were hoping for a peaceful day and the opera to follow, Ginny?'

'Yes. It doesn't matter. There will be other times, I'm sure.'

Soon I heard Alistair's car in front of the house, and then he was in the living room, his eyes shadowed with weariness. I ran to put my arms around him. 'I'll get breakfast, then you must go to bed.'

Holding me away from him, he said, 'We're going to the opera, Ginny. I might fall asleep halfway through it but I need something to take my mind off the scenes we experienced last night.'

'Tell me about it.'

'I'll tell you over breakfast. I'm going to take a shower, I'll feel a lot better after that.'

The scenes of the night before had not affected his appetite, I was glad to see, and I waited patiently for him to tell me what had transpired at the clinic.

'This is the third time she's been brought in like that. Sullen, too quiet, and then suddenly she's a virago, screaming, running all over the place. In no time at all the other patients were outside their rooms, terrified, and we had to get them back to bed as well as control the girl. She sank her teeth into Vicelli's hand when he caught up with her.'

'But who is she? You said it was the third time.'

'That's right. She's young, half American, half French. Her parents have a villa near Lugano and the girl goes to school in the Bernese Oberland. She's an only child of doting parents, useless and afraid when something like this happens. The girl's a tyrant.'

'You mean she isn't really sick?'

'Oh, she's sick all right. No normal girl would want to behave like she does. But her sickness is coupled with a desire to injure her parents, both of them, and her tantrums always come on when her father has to go abroad on business. He's a banker, rich as Crœsus, somebody with that crowd we were with the other night. They dumped their daughter on us, but no doubt they'll both be at the opera tonight. They leave for the States on Tuesday.'

'But they'll have to know about her behaviour, surely?'

'When they get back they will be told, and they'll be greeted by a delightful, sweet young girl who will look as though butter wouldn't melt in her mouth.'

'Oh, Alistair, aren't you sometimes sorry you went in for this branch of medicine?'

'I was sorry last night, but today's another day. Most of the chaps I was at medical school with would give their souls for my opportunities.'

'Are you really sure you want to go to the opera? It's a fair drive to Verona and it starts so late.'

'Yes, let's go. It'll be an experience.'

'Do we dress up like we did the other evening?'

'Don't we have tickets for the best seats? We'll be hobnobbing with the socialites. I intend to wear a dinner jacket.'

When I looked doubtful, he said, 'Wear that dress you wore for our wedding. You look so pretty in that shade of blue and you won't need a coat. A silk stole or something will do.'

The atmosphere in the Roman arena was electric as we took our seats under a starlit sky. Every seat was filled, and as I looked round the arena I became one with the steady hum of excitement. Holidaymakers in summer clothing sat next to locals who chattered and gesticulated in joyful anticipation while the seats around us filled with richly gowned and bejewelled women. Most of the men were wearing dinner jackets, but here and there was one wearing dress uniform.

On entering the arena we had been handed a tiny wax candle each and Alistair whispered, 'We have to light them when the orchestra starts up the overture.'

The orchestra came to take their place in the space provided for them in front of the enormous stage, occupying almost half the arena. Riccardo Mellini mounted the dais and the audience were rapturous in their greeting. He bowed his head graciously, then waited while the last sound of tuning up ended. When he raised the arm holding his baton, Alistair lit our candles, and all round that vast arena glowed tiny flickering lights, vying poetically with the stars above us, as Puccini's glorious music filled the air.

I knew that however many wonderful moments there might be in my life, I would never forget this one. The balmy Italian night, the stillness that had descended upon that great multitude, and music that would live in my heart for ever.

We watched entranced as the tragic story unfolded: lanterns in a Japanese garden, sandalled feet padding across the patio outside a house open to the night with its cushions and delicate screens. It did not matter that the Italian tenor was stout and hardly conformed to my idea of an American naval officer, for his voice was rich and soaring over the deeper baritone of his companion.

Then Melissa was there with her retinue of geisha girls, looking more delicately Japanese than she had looked in her role of Yum Yum years before. Now she wore her dark hair intricately coiled about her regal head, and the cream satin kimono exotically disguised her willowy slenderness.

Her voice, effortlessly singing Butterfly's glorious melodies, held that vast audience spellbound, and as the first act ended with the glorious, thrilling love duet, the orchestra's final dramatic chords brought the audience to its feet, cheering wildly, waving their programmes and stamping their feet. I looked in vain for the Melissa I had known behind the white painted mask of Butterfly's face as she acknowledged the applause.

People were leaving their seats, moving out into the aisles

and heading for the exits. 'Let's go out into the square and get something to drink,' Alistair suggested.

We had just reached the square when I heard a voice calling, 'Ginny, over here! Come and join us.'

I looked across the square, and in a crowd of people taking their seats outside a bar, I spotted Velma Forenzo standing waving her programme. She indicated a table and several empty chairs.

'Who is she?' Alistair asked.

'Melissa's friend, they own the Villa Rosa. I met her the other day.'

'The Contessa Forenzo,' he noted.

We reached their table and she said archly, 'So this is your husband, Ginny? Melissa was right when she said he was handsome. The next time I decide to have a nervous break-down, Dr Grantham, I shall bypass Dr Steiner and come to you. Dr Steiner was abominably rude to me, did you know that, Dr Grantham?'

'I've heard him being very forthright when the occasion has warranted it.'

There was much laughter from those sitting around us. Velma said, with a theatrical pout, 'I can assure you I wasn't malingering, I was desperately sick. However, come along with me and meet the others.'

Taking Alistair's arm, she drew him towards the group at the next table. A man stood up to offer me his chair. I was learning Italian but conversational Italian was still very difficult so we merely exchanged smiles while Alistair was being made much of at the next table.

Bells sounded in the square and we returned to the arena. The opera moved on to its tragic close and then the singers were taking their bows to rapturous applause. They had all moved me, but as we drifted out into the moonlit square, it was Melissa I remembered most, standing alone in the centre of the stage, her arms filled with flowers, a smile of studied shyness on her painted face.

Again we were hailed by Velma Forenzo, who took hold of Alistair's arm in a proprietary manner.

'We're all going on to the Villa Mara,' she cried. 'It's a

tradition after the opera and I've been asked to invite you both.'

I couldn't believe that Alistair was accepting the invitation. I had no idea where the Villa Mara was situated, but there was a long drive home. As we drove out of the square, I said, 'Surely we're not going? You didn't go to bed last night and it'll be late when we get home as it is.'

'We should go, Ginny. These are potential customers, people with money and infidelities, people who live on their nerves and with not enough to do. You heard Velma Forenzo.'

'I know that Dr Steiner refused to do anything for her.'

'He's built his reputation on people like Velma Forenzo and now he can afford to be choosy, but I still have my way to make and I think we should cultivate them.'

I didn't argue with him, but I couldn't think that the Dr Steiner I had come to know and admire had ever been influenced by the position in life of any of his patients.

We were following the other cars along the road that swept towards the southern end of Lake Garda instead of the autostrada and the quickest way home. The sky was becoming lighter and looking at the car clock I saw that it was already half past four in the morning. Just outside Desanzano our procession of cars turned in at two tall iron gates.

It was a gathering similar to that at the Villa Rosa. An ageing Russian count and countess appeared to be the centre of attention. I was given a glass of wine and an introduction to several people standing idly round the room. I was tired and I was bored. I was also irritated at Alistair being surrounded by chattering women, older, richly gowned, bejewelled women. Velma stood in the midst of them holding Alistair's arm, while her husband sat near the window, eyeing the spectacle with cynical amusement.

After a while the opera stars began to arrive. The tenor went immediately to the buffet table. There was no sign of Melissa, but flutters of delight echoed round the room at the advent of Riccardo Mellini.

I watched him bow over his hostess's hand as she handed him a glass of wine. After a brief conversation, he circled the room, occasionally stopping to exchange a word here and there.

111

Seeing me, he came and stood over me with easy grace until I felt a stirring of unease.

'Did you enjoy the opera, signora?' he enquired politely.

'Oh yes, it was wonderful! Everything — the arena, the atmosphere, everything.'

'Yes, it is a splendid venue.'

'Melissa was wonderful,' I added.

'Ah, yes. She's a friend of yours from some time back, I believe?'

'Yes. I could never have imagined that one day the girl who sat next to me at school would sing Butterfly in that wonderful arena.'

'I suppose not.'

'Don't you think Melissa is wonderful, Signor Mellini?' I had to ask.

'She has a most beautiful voice, it is true, but I have known a great many divas with beautiful voices. I hope Signorina Francesca has not peaked too soon. Tell me, Signora Grantham, are Dr Steiner's patients receiving adequate attention when one of his assistants can linger on into the dawn with silly women with imaginary complaints? No doubt they are finding him entirely delightful.'

I was shocked into staring at him with a degree of anger made worse by my own feelings on the matter.

'My husband did not go to bed last night, signor. He had a very difficult patient. Alistair is very aware of his duty, I can assure you.'

'I hope so, signora.'

'By the same token, Signor Mellini, you are spending time with these people you evidently despise while your wife is being cared for by people as dedicated as my husband.'

'Touché,' he murmured, then with a little bow he moved on.

I felt furious that I had allowed him to provoke me into making that entirely childish accusation. He had his work, he was paying a quite exorbitant sum for his wife to be cared for at the clinic, and whereas he had every right to question our presence at the villa, I had absolutely no right to suggest that his time would be better spent with Natalia.

I felt miserable. Alistair showed no sign of wishing to leave and every sign that he was enjoying the attention. I went outside to stand on the terrace. There was rose in the eastern sky and the early mist was lifting from the surface of the lake. The lake was so wide at this point, it was impossible to see the opposite shore, and I thought how different it was from Lake Como. I thought nostalgically about the English lakes, each one with a charm of its own, but then these larger Italian lakes were also very different and were becoming increasingly dear to me.

I shivered a little in the chill morning air and was glad to return to the warmth of the salon. Across the room I looked directly into Riccardo Mellini's dark sardonic eyes, and then suddenly he smiled. It was the charm of his smile that set my heart racing with a strange and frightening urgency. It was a smile that placed us suddenly together, as if he had said, You and I are alike, Ginny, we are not like them.

I stared down at my hands clenched tightly on the back of a chair, and when I looked up he was walking away towards the door. Bemused, my eyes followed his tall, slender figure as he took his leave of his hostess, and then I turned to stare through the window until his car had disappeared through the gates and along the road in the direction of Verona.

I moved towards Alistair and those around him stood aside to make room for me. Velma said, 'Your husband's made a real hit with us all, Ginny. He should set up his own clinic in opposition to Dr Steiner and we would see that he got the business. Madame D'Journet has suggested that he sets up a beauty parlour and gymnasium instead of a nerve clinic, to cater for all these women with nerves and problems about their age and figures. A place like that would do away with any nerves they might have, and with a charming, handsome man in charge instead of that difficult, glowering Dr Steiner, well, you can imagine the outcome.'

At last I managed to get Alistair to leave. As we reached the car, I was very aware of the weariness etched on his face and the slow, fixed smile.

'I'll drive,' I said quickly. 'Have a sleep in the car. You'll have to go straight to the clinic.'

'I'm going to take the morning off. You can telephone when we get home and offer our excuses. Tell them the car broke down and we had to wait for a mechanic. For God's sake don't tell him we went to a party, you know that wouldn't go down well.'

'Signor Mellini was there. He could well tell Dr Steiner he had seen us there, so we should tell him the truth,' I argued.

He was asleep almost immediately. As I drove towards the autostrada, I was miserably aware of a frightening uncertainty. For the first time I had seen a side of Alistair I had never thought to see. A side that had been flattered by attention, lured by those sophisticated people he had professed to despise.

These same people were Melissa's friends now — she moved in their circle, she was their star — but Melissa knew how to use them to her own advantage, whereas Alistair was in danger of being used.

He slept heavily until we reached the villa, and then went straight to bed.

It was time for me to go to the clinic, and as I walked up the hill, I debated with myself what excuse I could give for Alistair. As it happened, I need not have worried. One look at Dr Steiner's face as he sat in my office leafing through the morning mail told me that he knew why Alistair had not come with me.

'So you went to the opera in Verona after all? I had thought Alistair would be too weary. Was it you who persuaded him to go?'

'We both wanted to go. Did Signor Mellini tell you he had met us at the Villa Mara?'

'I have not spoken to Signor Mellini. I telephoned your villa in the early evening to ask Alistair to return here. I thought by that time he would have been rested but there was no reply. It is you who have told me you went on to the Villa Mara. Where is he this morning?'

I had no answer, no excuses. I stared at him uncertainly and he said sternly, 'The opera I could have understood, but not the Villa Mara. You should have come straight home and gone to bed. Alistair knew the position here.'

'I'm sorry Dr Steiner.'

'When does Alistair intend to be here?'

'Later this morning I'm sure.'

'Well, I will leave you to your duties Ginny. Look in on Mr Marchmont. He was very distressed this morning, perhaps an aftermath of the events experienced here the other day.'

114

He got up from his chair and went towards the door, turning to say, 'If Alistair does not appear soon, perhaps you will telephone him.'

# Chapter Thirteen

The morning had started badly. I was unsettled by Dr Steiner's annoyance and I thought about telephoning Alistair to tell him. I hoped he would have the good sense to get down to the clinic quickly, but he was so tired there was no telling how long he might sleep.

I decided to see the Englishman, Mr Marchmont, who was the only one of the five English-speaking patients I had been unable to get close to. He was invariably gentle but uncommital. Where the others talked about their wives and families, other women in their lives, their money and their business interests, he kept a discreet silence, merely smiling occasionally, and I was no closer to him now than on the first day of our acquaintanceship.

As I stepped out into the corridor a voice, speaking to me in English, asked, 'Where are you going?'

I looked round in surprise, since the nurses spoke a more accented English, and saw that a young girl stood just outside the door, eyeing me curiously. Soft brown hair framed a childishly pretty face with delicate features and large brown eyes. She was wearing a dressing gown in quilted satin to match the satin mules on her feet.

I smiled at her. 'I'm calling to see Mr Marchmont,' I explained.

'Then I'll walk with you,' she said falling into step beside me.

'I haven't seen you before; have you just arrived at the clinic?' I asked her.

'Yes, a few days ago.'

'What is your name?'

'Amanda Girandot.'

For a few minutes we walked in silence then she said, 'My parents brought me before they went away.'

So this was the girl who had kept Alistair up for most of the night. She seemed normal enough to me, nothing like the virago he had described.

'I thought all the nurses here were either French or Italian,' she said. 'You speak English very well.'

I laughed. 'That's because I am English, but I'm not a nurse, merely a helper of sorts.'

'Do you live here at the clinic?'

'No. I live with my husband at the villa below. He is a doctor here.'

She stared at me curiously. 'When I came here before there was nobody speaking English. The nurses hardly understood a word I said to them and now you're here, and there is an English doctor. Is that the man you are married to?'

'Yes, Dr Grantham. Couldn't you have spoken to the nurses in French or Italian? I understood from my husband that you went to school in Switzerland.'

She smiled, a strangely sly smile that I found disquieting.

'Why should I make it easy for them? I wanted to speak English.'

At the end of the corridor I said, 'Perhaps you should go back to your room now Amanda, this is Mr Marchmont's room.'

'Why hasn't Dr Grantham come to see me this morning?' she demanded. 'Dr Vicelli came in early but I wanted the other one.'

'I'm sure he will see you later this morning,' I said gently, relieved to hear Dr Vicelli's voice saying, 'Here you are Amanda. We have been looking for you.'

He had spoken to her in English and he took her hand, smiling down at her but I knew he was well aware of the hostility in her face and there was a wariness in his expression that made me suddenly afraid.

A young nurse waited at the end of the corridor, and suddenly Amanda snatched her hand away and without a backward glance swept back to the waiting nurse.

117

He smiled at me wryly. 'Maria thought Amanda was sitting on the terrace but when she went to look for her she'd disappeared. I suppose Alistair told you that we had quite a time with her.'

'Yes. She looks so normal. It's hard to believe that she gave you so much trouble.'

'I've seen it all before Ginny.'

'You speak English so well, Amanda is cross that none of the nurses speak it.'

'It needn't be any trouble to her, she speaks French and Italian quite well.'

He grinned, rolling up the sleeve of his white coat, and showed me the marks where her teeth had sunk into his arm.

I stared at him in horror and he said briefly, 'It took three of us to hold her down. She was like a wild animal.'

'What makes her like that?'

'Insecurity. She has everything but it isn't enough. Something inside herself that she cannot control. I have asked myself many times if I was right to specialise in this particular branch of medicine. Alistair must do the same.'

'I don't know, it's want he always wanted.'

I was suddenly thinking about the people sitting waiting in my father's surgery with their coughs and sneezes, measles and arthritis. True, there were disasters and people died, but this sickness of the mind was incomprehensible, another dimension.

'So you went to the opera?' he said softly.

'Yes. Perhaps we shouldn't have gone, but for a little while it helped Alistair to forget the problems here. We shouldn't have gone on to the Villa Mara, that was foolish and this morning he was so very tired.'

'He's coming in later I hope.'

'Well of course.'

'There was a time when I was intrigued and obsessed by the fleshpots Ginny, but my years with Steiner have taught me that there are more important things in life, to see people as they really are. Alistair will learn Ginny. I can't afford the opera and the social life now. I have two children and a third on the way. There isn't time for anything in my life outside my work and my family.' With another smile, he was gone.

I liked Andrea Vicelli. He had a quiet sense of humour and

from our first meeting had been kind to me, if mildly flirtatious. He was also extremely handsome. When I had said as much to Alistair, he laughed, saying, 'It's part of his Italian charm, being able to flirt with a pretty girl, but he's married to a woman who knows how to look after her own.'

Mr Marchmont sat in his chair at the window and did not look round when I entered his room. There was an air of despondency about him. I took the chair opposite saying brightly, 'The others are out on the terrace, it's lovely out there.'

When he offered no reply I said, 'Is there anything you want Mr Marchmont? Did you read the book I brought in?'

He picked it up from the table next to his chair, indicating the bookmark in the early pages.

'If you're not enjoying it I can choose another for you,' I ventured.

'The girl they brought in, how is she?' He surprised me by asking.

'Amanda. I've just been speaking to her, she seems very much better today.'

'I wasn't like that you know. I was never like that.'

'No, I'm sure you weren't.'

'My mother died. We'd always been very close, just the two of us for a great many years; after she went there was nothing. Nobody to talk to, nobody to live for. I wanted to die but they wouldn't let me.'

'But you're not old Mr Marchmont, there are so many things left in life for you to enjoy.'

'But there is nobody in my life now. I had a good position and we travelled, Mother and I. That young girl has all her life in front of her, she doesn't know what it is like to be really alone. That woman who sits on the terrace staring into space, she doesn't know either. They're talking about sending me home soon but I don't want to go home, there's nobody to go home to.'

'Would you like to talk to me about your mother Mr Marchmont?'

'She was very lonely after my father died and I was only ten years old. She always said "There's just you and me now Terry

119

and we'll have to be here for one another now, just the two of us." That's how it was.'

I felt so sad thinking about that little boy his mother had condemned to a life of loneliness, building a wall around the two of them, shutting out friends and lovers, leaving him with nothing after she died.

As I left Mr Marchmont to his despondency, I thought Dr Steiner had asked too much of me. I had been able to deal with the others who were looking forward to returning to wives and normality. I had no words of comfort that this man would understand.

I had believed Dr Steiner had offered me work to please Alistair and to alleviate the boredom he had thought inevitable. I thought the work he had dreamed up for me with his patients was an excuse but then he had been able to find other things for me to do.

He had a great deal of correspondence with English speaking patients, their families, banks and solicitors, and because his new secretary's English was limited I was able to help him, making me feel far more useful and more worthy of the salary he was paying me.

I was enjoying my work at the clinic, but with Mr Marchmont I felt only failure. Despair was ingrained in him.

I left his room feeling helpless and troubled and meeting Doctor Vicelli in the hall he smiled sympathetically.

'I take it he's steeped in melancholy this morning,' he said.

'Yes. Surely he isn't fit to go home, he seems to think you'll be sending him home soon.'

'He won't be going home for some time I'm afraid. I doubt if Mr Marchmont will be one of our success stories, his neurosis is too deep-seated and we cannot unfortunately restore his mother to him.'

'How can a mother do that to her son? It's unnatural.'

'Of course. She filled the boy's mind with the belief that there was nothing and nobody outside the two of them, to love a friend or a woman would have filled his heart with so much guilt he was unable to face it, and even now when his mother has gone the memory of her reaches out to him from beyond the grave.'

'Does that mean that he will never be cured?'

He shrugged his shoulders philosophically. 'We do our best Ginny, but the patient too must help us, he must have the will to go on.'

'I must telephone Alistair,' I said quickly, 'I don't suppose he's come in yet?'

'I haven't seen him.'

I returned to my office where I found Dr Steiner sitting at my desk leafing through a pile of correspondence. He looked up and smiled. 'I've scribbled replies to several of these letters Ginny, perhaps you'll deal with them for me. I'm going to see Marchmont, he's feeling very sorry for himself this morning I believe?'

'Yes. I couldn't do anything for him.'

He paused at the door as if he were about to say something else, then with a brief smile he went out.

I tried ringing Alistair at the villa but there was no reply and I decided to try again before lunch and if there was still no reply I would walk down there. It proved to be unnecessary when Alistair telephoned me just as I was finishing answering Dr Steiner's correspondence.

'I'm rustling up some sandwiches Ginny and I'll be there in about half an hour, has anything untoward happened?'

'Dr Steiner wasn't pleased that we'd gone to the villa, the opera he understood,' I said sharply.

'How did he know we'd gone to the villa? I suppose Mellini told him.'

'No. He tried telephoning the villa and couldn't get a reply.'

'I see. Well, I wouldn't have been much use to anybody this morning but I'm fully recovered now. I'll make my peace with Steiner. How's the girl?'

'Better I think. I spoke to her this morning.'

'Why? Surely he's not asked you to take her under your wing, she's not one of your amiable pets.'

'I'll tell you about it when I see you. Do hurry Alistair.'

'Don't worry love, as soon as I've eaten lunch.'

I took a plate of sandwiches into the garden and sat near the shrubbery to eat them. The sky was cloudless and I watched two hawks circling lazily overhead, a familiar sight in this mountain region.

I looked up to where I could see Natalia sitting in her usual

121

place outside her room. She had a visitor, an elderly lady who sat patiently beside her while Natalia looked past her across the gardens towards the mountains beyond.

Four of my amiable pets, as Alistair called them, were eating lunch at one of the tables on the terrace. There was laughter and normality which lifted my spirits and I felt a sudden urge to join them, to be a part of their camaraderie. They greeted me with smiles, pulling up a chair for me to join them, and their high spirits seemed a very long way from the woman sitting near us with her companion and Mr Marchmont sitting sad and lonely in his room.

They didn't ask about him or comment on his absence and I thought they had not really missed him. He was just somebody who sat with them without contributing either conversation or laughter, somebody easily forgotten, relatively unimportant, and, unable to stand their laughter any longer, I made an excuse and walked away. Their laughter followed me, and as I turned to go through the open windows only Natalia sitting with her visitor watched me go.

I had not been in my office long when there was a light tap on my door and a young nurse stood there with a doubtful expression on her pretty face.

She spoke to me in Italian and all I could understand were the words 'Signora Mellini'. I went with her into the hall, relieved to see Dr Vicelli coming down the stairs and I listened while the nurse repeated her words which he translated in some surprise. 'Signora Mellini has said you took some flowers out of her room yesterday Ginny, she wants them back.'

'But she told me to take them away, I gave them to another patient.'

'Perhaps we'd better get them back.'

'I'll go up to see Signora Mellini, I'm sure she'll remember telling me to take them away.'

'I wouldn't bank on it Ginny, but if you think you should.'

Natalia was standing in the corridor outside her room and there was anger and truculence in every line of her slender figure.

'You took my flowers,' she accused me, 'where are they?'

'But you told me to take them away Signora Mellini, don't you remember?'

'Of course I didn't tell you to take them away, I would not give Riccardo's flowers away. You stole them for yourself.'

'That isn't true. Please Signora, you must remember asking me to take them away.'

She was advancing towards me in slow, measured steps; her eyes were hostile and as she drew level with me she said, 'I shall report you to Dr Steiner, he will tell you to return my flowers, now let me pass.'

I reached out and took hold of her hand, but fiercely she snatched it away, then she gave me a push that was so unexpected, I lost my footing on the top step and then I was falling helplessly down the stairs.

I lay there, aware of a sharp pain in my upper arm and my back and the sound of footsteps running across the hall, then Alistair was there holding me in his arms, and other footsteps were bounding up the stairs to where Natalia stood swaying dangerously on the landing above me.

Everything seemed so far away, like people talking in another world, and the last thing I remember before I fainted was Dr Steiner's face looking down at me anxiously.

Later that day, Alistair took me home, bandages round my ribcage, smothered with bruises but fortunately suffering nothing more serious than two cracked ribs. I was more concerned about why Natalia had suddenly turned on me and Dr Steiner asked, 'Had you spoken to her during the morning Ginny?'

'No. I saw Amanda and Mr Marchmont. I talked for a few minutes with the four men on the terrace, but Natalia was with her grandmother.'

'How can we know how her mind works? She heard you laughing, saw you with your friends, then for no reason at all she remembered Riccardo's flowers. Was she suddenly resentful that you could laugh? Did she think those men were admiring you and was she needing that same admiration? How can we really ever know what her thoughts were? I don't think she meant to hurt you physically Ginny.'

'How is she now?'

'Sedated. When she wakes up it is doubtful she will even remember.'

'And the flowers?'

'Others have been placed in her room.'

123

Later at the villa I asked Alistair, 'Did you really know what you'd be up against when you decided to work with this branch of medicine?'

'I was rather hoping they'd be elderly ladies with imaginary illnesses and vast amounts of money,' he answered with a smile. Seeing my look of disquiet, he threw back his head and laughed. 'Seriously Ginny, I did think there'd be women like that, but I knew there would be the other kind too.'

'So you're not sorry you came here?'

He smiled, drawing me closer into his arms until I gave a little cry and he released me.

'I should have been there Ginny. You were right we shouldn't have gone to the opera or that wretched villa.'

'You couldn't have done anything to prevent what has happened even if you'd been there, forget about the opera Alistair, it's over and done with.'

Suddenly he gave a little gasp. 'I completely forgot Ginny, your parents are arriving in two days. They couldn't be coming at a worse time.'

'But it'll be wonderful. I'm not ill, two cracked ribs will soon heal. Dr Steiner says I haven't to think of going back to the clinic until I'm completely better so it'll be a marvellous opportunity to spend some time with them. Oh, Alistair, it's the best present you could possibly have given me. I was wondering if they were ever coming to see us.'

'Your father's not going to be too pleased about your condition,' he said ruefully.

'He's a doctor, he'll understand.'

Dr Steiner came to see me the next morning and I was quick to say to him, 'Alistair is very unhappy about what happened. He feels responsible and I don't want him to feel that way.'

'I do not bear grudges, Ginny. I have said all I have to say on the subject of the opera and now it is finished. I simply hope that Alistair will appreciate that he has a duty to me and the clinic, and to you Ginny above anything else.'

'I'm sure Alistair knows that.'

He smiled. 'Your husband has embarked upon a career perhaps more exacting and complex than any other, and when he is most troubled there are temptations. He stumbles along a stony and lonely path and from time to time he will be aware of other paths leading away from it, paths that are smooth and colourful, riches more easily earned, people less complicated, pleasures in place of struggles. I too have been young and I am aware of the temptations that he will experience. When the time comes, I hope he will be able to distinguish between the valuable and the dross.'

'He will, Dr Steiner, I know he will.'

'And now you are looking forward to seeing your parents?'

'Oh yes. They'll love this place, I shall enjoy showing them around. I would like you to meet them. Will you have dinner with us one evening?'

'Most certainly. Your father is a doctor, isn't he?'

'Yes, just an ordinary GP with a large practice spread over many miles.'

'We shall have a great deal to talk about.'

As I walked with him to the door, he said lightly, 'Signor Mellini enquired about you this morning. I told him what had happened, he was very concerned.'

'When I return to the clinic I will try to make friends with Signora Mellini.' I said, with more confidence than I felt.

# Chapter Fourteen

My parents came armed with gifts: home-knitted sweaters and tweed skirts, Cloonie's simnels and feather-light cakes, her jams and marmalades, Mother's embroidered tea cloths and pillowcases, and English magazines and books. Where they had made room for their clothes was a mystery. Alistair laughed, saying they must have thought we were living in darkest Africa instead of civilised Italy.

As the car climbed the mountain road, Mother cried, 'Gracious me! I'd no idea you were living on top of the world. Have you any neighbours?'

'There's a small village about three miles away,' Alistair explained, 'but really we're not too far from Como or Lugano in Switzerland. During the time you're here we'll make sure you get the lie of the land.'

We pointed out the clinic at the top of the tree-lined drive, and then we climbed the hill to the villa. It stood bathed in a pink glow from the setting sun, and I thought it had never looked more beautiful. The sun still lingered on the mountain-tops and on the snow in the deep crevices on the highest slopes.

'Don't you think it's beautiful?' I asked impatiently, and they both agreed that it was.

When I picked up one of their bags, Alistair took it from me. 'Don't carry any luggage, Ginny,' he said sharply. The look that passed between my parents said quite plainly that they thought I was pregnant.

We put them in the spare bedroom, which overlooked the valley. Alistair put a match to the log fire, explaining that although the day was warm, the night would probably be cool.

126

Father's eyes twinkled at me across the room and in an amused voice he said, 'I suspect you have something to tell us, Ginny?'

I looked at Alistair helplessly, leaving him to explain while I watched their expressions change from delighted anticipation to acute anxiety.

'Don't worry,' I assured them. 'The pain has almost gone and I'm perfectly well.'

'But what on earth were they doing to allow the woman to get at you at all?' Father cried. 'And why you?'

'It could have been anybody, and she's sick, otherwise she wouldn't be at the clinic. Please don't fuss, it won't happen again.'

'Well, I should hope not,' Mother said. 'Where were you in all this, Alistair?'

'Alistair found me. Honestly, it's over now and I do want to forget about it. Besides, nothing must spoil these next two weeks. I thought you'd never come!'

During the evening I bombarded them with questions about home and family, the animals and the villagers. Edith was expecting her second child and Rodney had a girlfriend he was keen on in Manitoba.

'Is it serious?' I asked.

'It appears so,' Father said. 'He's talking about bringing her home for Christmas, he's not said that about any of the others.'

'Mary Allen has married a farmer from Patterdale, much to her mother's annoyance — she was hoping for a chartered accountant at least,' Mother contributed.

'Has she said so?' I asked with a laugh.

'In no uncertain terms. She's saying it cost a lot of money for Mary's education, now she's married to a man whose only interests are sheep and dogs.'

A look passed between them before Mother said, 'You'll be surprised to know that the vicar retired just after Christmas. He really is a very sick man and the curate has got his job. He's also got himself engaged to Joyce.'

'Oh, Mother, I'm so glad! And she'll be so good for him. After all, her father was the vicar so she knows exactly what's in store.'

'They do seem very happy. You always liked Joyce, didn't you, Ginny?'

'Yes, she was one of my very best friends since we were quite small.'

'Until Melissa came along,' Father added dryly.

Catching Alistair's amused expression, I cried, 'We've so much to tell you about Melissa. You tell them, Alistair.'

Alistair told them more briefly than I liked about our encounters with Melissa. After he had finished, Father said quietly, 'Well, we've seen Melissa too, three weeks ago at Mrs Rocheforte's funeral.'

I looked up in dismay and Mother said, 'We told you her health was failing the last time we wrote, Ginny. She died in her sleep two days later. Her funeral was a very large affair; after all, she was very well known and respected in the area.'

'Melissa was there?' I asked.

'Indeed,' Father confirmed. 'You can imagine the speculation that went on in the village when it was known the old lady had died. Would she come, would she send flowers, how would the family greet her if she came? There was no sign of her during the service in the church, which helped to confirm Miss Brownson's conviction that she wouldn't show her face. Then, at the graveside, we all noticed a sudden stir near the gates and we saw that a large car had pulled up and a woman was stepping out. It was an entrance that should have sent the applause echoing round the churchyard. Melissa was of course all in black and wearing a large black hat that would have done credit to the catwalk. She walked to the graveside looking neither to right nor left, and people standing around just stared at her.'

'Did she see you and Mother?'

'She smiled briefly,' Mother said, 'then after the service was over she took her turn to throw soil on the coffin before walking back to her waiting car. She didn't speak a single word to Mrs Rocheforte's family.'

'She never really knew any of them,' I protested. 'If they visited their mother at all, it was while Melissa was at school, and they never went to stay.'

'Well, somebody had informed her that the old lady had died

and the date and time of the funeral. Mrs Rocheforte would have been impressed by her performance.'

'I hope you are going to get the chance to see her on the stage while you're here, or at one of the solo performances she gives at the lakeside villas. She's in great demand.'

'She also has to conform to Signor Mellini's exacting strictures. She wasn't at the party after the opera,' Alistair added.

'*He* was there!'

'For a very short time.'

'This is a whole new world for you both,' Father commented dryly.

'One that we're not really part of,' Alistair said shortly.

In the days that followed I drove my parents along the lakeside and every bend in the road opened up new vistas for them to delight in.

'It makes our beautiful lakes seem small and the mountains too,' Mother commented, but Father would have none of it.

'Our country's small too, darling,' he said. 'Our mountains and our lakes are in true proportion.'

One afternoon Dr Steiner invited Father to look round the clinic while Mother and I drove into Como to shop. She was delighted with the range of beautiful silk scarves and lingerie in the shops and set about buying presents for Edith and Cloonie as well as her friends in the village.

'I'd pay the earth for these at home,' she exclaimed. 'I've already filled my Christmas-present list.'

Walking back to the car, we were hailed in a loud voice from a car leaving the piazza. Mother stared wide-eyed at the flamboyantly dressed woman leaving the large car and weaving through the traffic to greet us.

She was wearing a long, tight silk dress. Her tanned arms and shoulders were bare but on her head she wore a large sunhat and long hooped earrings in her ears. Quickly I introduced my mother, and with a toothy smile Velma Forenzo gushed, 'How nice to have your mother here! And how fortunate that they'll be able to hear Melissa sing at my villa.'

I stared at her uncertainly, and she trilled, 'Don't tell me Alistair didn't tell you? I telephoned him at the clinic yesterday morning and what do you think he said? That he'd think about

129

it! How can he *think* about it when you've got your folks here and with nothing else to do at that villa halfway up the mountain.'

'Perhaps he thinks he may be too busy to attend.'

'Rubbish! The concert's for charity. Mellini has promised to be there, I'm not sure about his dotty wife, but I've got a new Russian pianist everybody is raving about and Melchior, who is singing Carmen at La Scala. It's rumoured that she and Melissa absolutely hate each other, so the evening will be interesting enough without the music. Now, how many tickets can I save for you? Is your father here?'

'Well, yes, but he's not much for opera.'

'I'm not much for opera, Ginny, but they'll sing other things besides the great arias. Everybody who is anybody will be there.' Turning to my mother, she said, 'We're hoping the Duke and Duchess of Windsor will attend. They love this sort of thing and they love the attention they get. You might never have another chance to mingle with such celebrities.'

'I'm not sure about Alistair,' I said doubtfully, but she swept my protests away as of little account. 'Dr Steiner's been invited and Dr Vicelli, not that he'll come, with his wife so heavily pregnant. All their patients will be tucked away for the night by the time the concert gets under way, and I've got a friend who wants to have a quiet word with your husband.'

'What sort of word?' I asked sharply.

'A friend who's been receiving some sort of therapy from some quack or other and isn't sure if she should continue. I told her to speak to Alistair, she'll find him far more sympathetic than Dr Steiner. Where exactly in England do you come from?' she asked my mother abruptly.

'From a small village in the Lake District.'

'Really? I know it's supposed to be absolutely beautiful, but when I went there before the war with my second husband, it rained every single day and there was mist everywhere. You should think of exchanging it for this place, my dear.'

'Impossible, I'm afraid, my husband's work is there.'

'Oh, that's too bad. But I look forward to seeing you and your husband at my concert.'

With a gay wave of her hand she sauntered to her waiting car, which was holding up the traffic, causing frustrated drivers to honk their horns.

Bemused by the encounter, Mother said, 'Is she really a contessa, Ginny?'

'Yes, she really is, but don't let that bewilder you. This part of the world is full of faded royalty, struggling aristocracy and doubtful hangers-on. Her third husband is a man considerably older than she but with a great deal of money.'

'How did you meet her?'

'Melissa introduced us.'

'You mean she is the sort of friend Melissa has now?'

'Melissa is their idol, the new diva. They fawn on her, admiring her beauty and her voice, and relish any hint of scandal they can come up with.'

'Then they're not really friends at all! Surely Melissa can see through them?'

'Perhaps she doesn't want to. Dr Steiner can, he's both irritated and amused by them.'

'And Alistair?'

'I'm sure he can.'

'He's evidently not so sure he wants to attend this concert if he hasn't mentioned it to you.'

'Perhaps it will be mentioned this evening when Dr Steiner dines with us.'

It was Mother, however, who brought the subject into the conversation later that evening, when she amused Father by telling him about our encounter with Velma in the town.

Dr Steiner said, 'No doubt she inveigled you into saying you would attend her next concert. It is true the Contessa gives a great deal of money to charity, but that is not the sole incentive for her many concerts. She likes to surround herself with the rich and famous regardless of whether they have any substance. Simpering models escorted by lords, film stars and actors on the way up, people with too much money and no questions asked how it has been made. At least your friend Melissa has real talent and undeniable beauty, but is she wise enough to handle her fame and the men and women who worship her for it?'

Father smiled wryly, and after a few moments he said, 'That young lady has come a long way from that girl we met stepping

131

off the train that morning, Ginny. Do you still recognise the old Melissa when confronted by the new one?'

'Perhaps none of us has ever really met the real Melissa. I never thought I had in all those years she spent in the village, and now I don't suppose I ever shall.'

'You two ladies would like to attend the Contessa's concert,' Dr Steiner said gently, 'and who are we poor men to deny you that pleasure?'

Alistair looked at him sharply, and the doctor smiled across the table at him. 'Perhaps you will have room for me in your car, Alistair? I dislike driving on the mountain roads in the dark.'

It was his way of telling us that we could attend the concert with his blessing, and in the next few days Mother's entire conversation centred on what she could wear so that she would not look dowdy in a room filled with fashionable women. It was settled by another visit to Como; both Mother and I bought dresses and both Father and Alistair were wise enough not to ask the price we had paid.

As we drove down to the lakeside on the evening of the concert, I asked Dr Steiner if Natalia would be attending and was surprised when he shook his head, saying, 'She does not wish to go and has elected to spend time with her grandmother instead.'

'She never seems to have anything to say to her grand-mother,' I said in surprise. 'I would have thought she would want to be with her husband.'

'He tried all morning to persuade her to go with him, but in Natalia's mind she is punishing him for his absence. A wise woman, a well woman, would see that her attitude is only driving them further apart, but Natalia will not see — that, I think, is her tragedy.'

'He will go to the concert without her?'

'Of course. Like Melissa Francesca he has a duty to those people who idolise him because they are a part of all those years of dedication that have made him a subject for their idolatry. His wife is a thing apart.'

'Would she still have been a thing apart if she had not been a sick woman?' I asked curiously.

'Perhaps not. But with the right woman, we are talking of

132

substance, not shadows. Riccardo Mellini shrouds himself within a veneer of reserve that few people can penetrate. Behind it, however, lies a lonely, sensitive man, a man who has been bitterly hurt and sees no assuagement of that hurt in his future.'

'What would happen if he met some other woman he could fall in love with?'

'Ah, well, that is a question, is it not? In his profession he meets a great many women, women like Melissa Francesca who love music as he does, and yet that does not appear to be the answer. There are a great many women who desire him, but is it that sad, pitiful wife who keeps him from them or something else?'

The rest of the journey was taken in silence. I was remembering Riccardo's smile across that crowded room.

As we drove up the long drive from the lake, the villa was ablaze with light from one end to the other and my mother's face was alight with wonder.

I knew hardly any of those people kissing each other, squealing their greetings. Velma swept about smiling, embracing her guests, ordering her waiters, wearing a bright-yellow gown in silk chiffon.

'Isn't it marvellous?' she gushed as she came to greet us. 'The Windsors are here and Prince Olaf and his princess, sitting over there near the dais.'

My mother was staring across at them with wide eyes.

'How tiny she is!' she said at last. 'Like a doll. All those silly people clamouring round them. Don't they know how much decent people in England despise them for what they did?'

'What they did doesn't much matter here, Mother.'

'It matters to me. All those children waving their flags whenever royalty came anywhere near them, all those young men who went to war to defend their country when he wasn't even prepared to give up that woman for it.'

'We got a much better king, Mother,' I said, anxiously drawing her away.

It was a cosmopolitan gathering, most of them Italian with a sprinkling of American and German. We were possibly the only English people present until Melissa arrived, but I need not have worried. Everybody was too intent on seeing and being seen to care about my mother's disapproval.

It had not taken Velma long to spirit Alistair away and he now stood chatting to an emaciated woman wearing a beige lace gown. Her skeletal hands played with a long rope of pearls around her scrawny throat. She was talking to him intently, occasionally interrupted by Velma, and Alistair was listening with his head inclined to hear her words.

Leaving my parents together, I went to ask Dr Steiner, 'Who is she?'

'Baroness Thierry. She has run the gamut of Europe's neurologists and Alistair is new on the scene.'

'She looks terribly ill.'

'Drink, drugs, too many worries about imaginary illnesses, not enough to occupy her mind and too much money.'

'I didn't think it possible to have too much money. Most of these people wouldn't agree with you.'

'I know. When the Baroness was young, money bought her everything — men, jewels, excitement — but now she is old and there is nothing new under the sun, nothing to spend her money on except the disorders she has created within herself.'

'What does she expect Alistair to do for her?'

'Give her attention. Five years ago I had another neurologist on my staff, an Austrian, young, talented, handsome. He grew tired of caring for people like Natalia Mellini and young Amanda, people with real problems. Instead he deserted me to work with people like the Baroness, women who paid him enough money to build the most expensive clinic in Vienna. He would no doubt tell you he has done very well for himself, but I believe he has forsaken the real for the shadow.'

'Why are you telling me all this?' I asked anxiously.

'I want you on my side when they offer similar incentives to Alistair.'

'Alistair would never take them,' I declared stoutly.

He smiled gently, then, with an abrupt change of subject, he said, 'Ah, here is Signor Mellini escorting Gina Melchior.'

There was a stir as people surged forward to meet them. I watched Riccardo Mellini introducing the mezzo-soprano to Velma's guests. Her face was too proud, too hard for beauty, but she had a presence. Under a wealth of dark-red hair, her teeth flashed when she smiled, and occasionally she looked up at her escort with delighted awareness.

134

The crowd parted to permit Melissa to walk the length of the room, an entrance designed to detract from that made by Melchior.

She was wearing a white silk gown and no jewellery except long diamond earrings. It was a beauty untouched and unadorned. As she looked at Riccardo Mellini there was an air of triumph in her smile. Then she was embracing Gina Melchior and all around us there was applause.

Dr Steiner's expression was entirely cynical. 'There they are,' he whispered, 'two exotic cats displaying their charms, wary of each other's talent and the presence of a man they both wish to attract.'

'Will he respond, do you think?' I whispered.

He shrugged his shoulders. 'Who can say? The gauntlet has been thrown down, if he cares to retrieve it. I do not know how he thinks and how he will act. It is his wife who is my patient; Riccardo is an enigma and I am not in the business of understanding him.'

# Chapter Fifteen

Melissa and Gina Melchior sang their favourite arias and melodies and the applause was rapturous. Afterwards they were taken to chat to the Duke and Duchess of Windsor and the Duchess regally handed over gifts of jewellery to both artistes.

The Duke and Duchess were the first to depart and most of the guests lined up to curtsey to the royal couple. My parents and I were standing at the side of the room and Mother whispered, 'I wouldn't want to curtsey to her. I still feel a terrible resentment towards her, and he's not a happy man, trailing behind her like a pet dog.'

The two singers circulated among the guests, and Melissa greeted my parents, all smiles and charm.

Flashing dark eyes at Riccardo Mellini, she begged him to play the violin. He was reluctant, but those standing nearest added their persuasions to hers until with a little bow he walked towards the dais. The violinist promptly handed over his violin.

Riccardo Mellini played only one piece, in spite of the clamour for more, but as the tender air of the Meditation from *Thaïs* filled the room I could understand why this man and his music were fated and why anything outside that bond was doomed. How could poor Natalia with her tantrums and tirades, her punishing desire to possess him heart and soul, ever hope to prevail against it?

Melissa turned to me with shining eyes. 'He's wonderful!' she proclaimed. 'He seldom plays at these functions, we're so fortunate tonight to have heard him.'

'You get along with him now, Melissa?' I couldn't resist asking.

Her eyes opened wide. 'Why, of course! Oh, I know he was very cross with me that day, but that was nothing. He expects perfection from me and I have to remind him now and again that I was a woman before I was a diva. Some of the artistes are too easy, he only has to crook his finger and they would run to him. He has to know that I'm different.'

'And does he crook his finger at them?'

She threw back her head and laughed. 'That would annoy you, wouldn't it, Ginny? In your upright, moral little soul you would expect him to live like a monk and remain for ever faithful to that wife who is really no wife at all.'

When I didn't answer her, she said slyly, 'Those women are giving Alistair a number of incentives to lure him away from Dr Steiner and into a more lucrative world.'

'Alistair knows Dr Steiner is the best there is.'

'But he's not interested in making money, only in furthering the name of Steiner. Those people around Alistair would get little sympathy from Steiner, but your husband is young, handsome and vulnerable.'

'Why vulnerable?'

'Because money is a powerful motivation. With Steiner it will be years, perhaps never, before he becomes rich, but the darling of women like that could buy fast cars, villas like this one, and the world would be his oyster.'

'You may be happy in that world, Melissa, but I'm not at all sure about Alistair.'

'I think he seems enthralled by those women with their imaginary ailments and their promises of rich rewards.'

At that moment my father joined us and with a bright smile Melissa turned towards him, saying, 'I've just been teasing Ginny, Dr Lawrence. Don't you think Alistair enjoys having all those women hanging around him all evening?'

'Does he? I haven't been watching. Perhaps it's time we left, Ginny? Alistair has an early call in the morning,' he said evenly.

Other people were leaving. The guests of honour had gone and there was nobody left for them to fawn over. The singers were still being accosted by their admirers, but Riccardo Mellini quickly dissociated himself from them and joined us.

Having been introduced to my parents, he turned to me and said, 'I hope you're feeling much better, Mrs Grantham? It was a distressing time for you.'

'Thank you, Signor Mellini, the wounds are almost healed.'

'It is not always the wounds that cause us pain, it is the reason for them. The more insidious pain takes longer to heal, I fear,' he replied.

Again I was aware of the feeling of disquiet that his nearness caused in me.

More lightly he asked, 'Have you and your parents enjoyed the concert?'

'Oh yes, very much. I had heard that you played an instrument, but I didn't know it was the violin. It was very beautiful.'

'The violin, the piano, but the violin for preference.'

'I love music but I'm no performer.'

Father laughed. 'Ginny's always listened to others with the utmost wonder, but she sang very prettily in the school concerts.'

Riccardo smiled, and I wondered why he didn't smile more often. His smile was singularly sweet, robbing his face of its remoteness and sadness. His grey eyes matched the silver wings in his dark hair and his features had the calm perfection of a Greek statue. His smile deepened, and I realised that I had been staring at him. In some confusion I turned, to see Alistair saying good night to his new friends.

I was glad that I didn't have to make conversation on the way home. Mother was busy discussing the gowns, the jewels and the appearance of the Windsors. Father remarked, 'The new Melissa is a far cry from that young girl sitting in the village hall trying to hide her darned cotton gloves and her Liverpool accent.' It was only later that I realised Father and Alistair had hardly exchanged a word.

It was not until their last evening at the dinner table that Father said, 'Steiner was telling me that he had lost a very promising young doctor to a fashionable clinic and more fashionable patients.'

I looked straight at Alistair's bland face but he was giving nothing away.

'I never met him,' he said casually, 'but I believe he's doing very well.'

Father treated him to a long, hard stare but to my relief nothing further was said and for the rest of their stay the conversation between us was light-hearted.

We drove into Milan on the morning of my parents' departure and watched from the airport as their plane took off into a sky dark and stormy. By the time we returned to Como, the lake was glassily turbulent and it had started to rain. Alistair seemed preoccupied, and I was unsure if it was the bad driving conditions or some other problem that kept him silent.

Back at the villa he was quick to say he had to get over to the clinic because Dr Vicelli had been concerned about his wife, whose baby was expected any day.

'Tell Dr Steiner I'll be back at my desk in the morning,' I said.

Looking at me sternly, he replied, 'You're not well enough to go back. Wait until the ribs heal.'

'Oh, Alistair, I'll be glad to be back. They're no longer painful and Dr Steiner needs me. Besides, if I'm well enough to party, I'm well enough to work.'

'I can see you'll have your own way, Ginny.'

'Well, there isn't enough here to keep me occupied. I'd be bored just sitting around waiting for you to come home.'

One brief smile and he was gone.

The work had piled up in my absence and Dr Steiner was delighted to have me back. Dr Vicelli's wife gave birth to a baby boy during the afternoon, and the following day he came into the clinic exuberantly delighted, bringing champagne and a bunch of red roses for my desk.

I laughed as he pushed them into my hands. 'You should be taking these to your wife,' I protested.

'She has a roomful of roses; these are for you, Ginny. Shouldn't you be thinking of a *bambino* instead of working here?'

'We have plenty of time for that,' I retorted, but he would have none of it.

'Time waits for nobody. A *bambino* would stop Alistair from being so restless.'

'You think he is restless?'

'You mean you haven't noticed?'

'I don't know what you mean. He's happy here, it's where he wanted to be. Why should he be restless?'

'Don't we all get restless from time to time?' he said lightly. 'Don't we all want everything now instead of later?'

I was staring at him doubtfully, and with a smile he said, 'Come on, Ginny, bring out the champagne glasses. You'll find some in that cupboard. The last time we had them out was when Dienstein left.'

'Do you ever hear from him?'

'I hear of him. He's making a lot of money but he's lost out on other things.'

I knew what he meant, so I did not press him further but raised my glass in a toast to his new baby.

In the days and weeks that followed, I too sensed Alistair's restlessness. He was sweet and attentive, but there were times when I caught him sitting in his chair staring into space, his thoughts anywhere but in the present. Then he started to grumble about the snow and bad weather. Even on a morning when the skies suddenly cleared and the snow-covered mountains sparkled, he was discontented.

'So much of Italy dreams under a sunny sky all through the year,' he said. 'We could live somewhere better than this.'

'But it's beautiful!' I protested. 'Besides, the snow doesn't last for ever. Remember how lovely it was in the summer?'

He didn't answer, but it was the beginning of everything that came later. In those first moments he was convincing himself; soon he set about trying to convince me, and in his doing so, something in our marriage was irretrievably lost.

Dr Steiner put my fears into words when he asked one morning, 'Has Alistair said anything to you about leaving the clinic?'

'Leaving!' I exclaimed. 'Why, no. Where would he go? What would he do?'

'He would do what Dienstein did, set up on his own. I am sure he would have no difficulty in finding patients among the women who crowded round him at the Contessa's charity party, and their friends.'

140

'Oh, I hope you're wrong. Surely I would have known what he was thinking even if he hadn't put it into words?'

'And is he the same Alistair who came here so full of eagerness all those months ago? Now his enthusiasm is tempered with resentment. He looks beyond me to too many years when he will still be the pupil and I will still be the master, and sees himself as the master in his own clinic, making money, living well. He is young, he does not want to think about the people who really need him, only the ones who can pay exorbitant sums for his shoulder to cry on.'

'But you yourself have wealthy patients who pay a great deal of money for staying here, like Natalia Mellini and Amanda.'

'Of course. But these are genuinely sick people, and think how many sick people I have here who have very little money at all. You are *au fait* with my accounts, you know I derive very little from those people, but they would not be welcome in Alistair's clinic, they would be too sick and not rich enough.'

'I don't think you're being fair to Alistair. You don't know that he's even thinking about leaving you and I'm quite sure he would have discussed it with me.'

He smiled and patted my arm. 'There speaks a loyal wife, Ginny. If you are right and I have been wrong I shall be anxious to apologise, but if it is his intention to leave us, I hope he will tell me soon. I shall need to find a competent replacement.'

When I got home that afternoon I busied myself cooking dinner, making something special, laying the table prettily and making sure the cheerful glow of a huge fire illuminated every corner of the room. Alistair was later than usual, and I worried, hoping that nothing dire had happened at the clinic to detain him. When seven o'clock came and he had still not appeared, I telephoned the clinic, only to be told that Dr Grantham had left early and had not returned.

Anxious and annoyed, I watched the candles and the fire burn low, from time to time scanning the long, winding road along the mountainside. I turned off the cooker, and with every second my anger grew. He could have telephoned, he could have told me where he was going. When I heard the sound of a car in the driveway, I rushed to open the door.

Alistair was all smiles as he jumped out of the car, turning to fill his arms with flowers and other peace offerings.

'Ginny, before you say a word, let me say how sorry I am to be so late. I should have phoned but I wanted to tell you in person.'

He came into the villa, placing a bottle of champagne on the table and a bunch of roses and carnations in my arms.

'I hope you haven't waited dinner.'

'Actually, I have, but I'm sure it's completely spoiled. I'm not hungry anyway.'

'You mean you haven't eaten?'

'No, I was so worried. Every minute that went by took away any appetite I might have had.'

'I'll open the champagne and make sandwiches. You're going to be so thrilled when you hear my news.'

I knew right then that I would not be thrilled by anything Alistair had to tell me, but I sat silently in front of the fire and accepted a glass of champagne. Face wreathed in smiles, he came to sit next to me and I knew he was searching for the right words to dispel any fears I might have.

'I had to be sure, that's why I didn't want to say anything before. Now it's all falling into place. I'll have a clinic of my own. There are people who are keen to finance me and supply me with patients. We're going to be rich, Ginny, rich and famous!'

'Famous for what?'

'I'm a good neurologist and I'm fed up with living in some-body else's villa, having my wife attacked by dangerous patients and working for a salary paid by a man who is making considerably more.'

'You wanted to work for him, remember? And he's been a good teacher, always fair. Doesn't it strike you that you're letting him down?'

'No. I've worked hard for what he's paid me and I'm not ungrateful to him, but he's an old man, he thinks like an old man and we're young. We should be making hay now, Ginny, not in some mist-shrouded future.'

'What about your father? He was anxious for you to work with Dr Steiner. He'll be horrified that you've left him.'

'I have to stop trying to please my father some time. He doesn't love me anyway, he just wanted me to do all the things he hadn't done. Now I want to make my own life.'

142

'So where's this new clinic of yours going to be?'

'Not around here. I'm not competing with Steiner, I want to be far enough away. Most of the women who will be my patients will be leaving their villas now that winter is here, and going south to Rome or Naples. Melissa suggested somewhere beautiful in the hills above Rome.'

'Melissa!' I said sharply.

'Oh, she just happened to be at the Contessa's while I was discussing it with her. There were a group of the Contessa's friends there, women I met the other evening, all anxious to put money into the project, be my first patients, and the interest this will give them will probably be the best therapy for their boredom.'

'Is Melissa going to be in Rome while all this is going on?'

'Melissa could be anywhere. She has engagements to sing in Rome and Naples. But none of this has anything to do with Melissa, she's just interested as a friend of yours, Ginny.'

'I see.'

'Darling, say you're pleased for me. Think what it will mean! Our own villa and money to do what we want — travel, a new car each, and you'll be a lady of leisure instead of sitting at a desk all day.'

'I like my job.'

'Well, of course you do, but you'll enjoy being the famous Dr Grantham's wife and the social life that'll come with it.'

'What you mean is that you'll enjoy it. I was very proud of being Dr Grantham's wife, Dr Steiner's assistant's wife. That meant more to me than social position.'

The smile left his face to be replaced by a sulky little-boy expression.

'I did expect a little enthusiasm from you, but I can see I'm going to receive nothing but criticism. You mentioned my father. His complaint was that it was always my mother who had held him back with her whinging and grievances. I didn't expect that sort of attitude from you, Ginny.'

It was our first quarrel. Always before, whenever we had a disagreement, we could laugh about it, but not this time. The issue was too big, too important, and for days I suffered from his disappointment in me, his conviction that I had let him down.

It did not have the power to make him change his mind, however. I knew within days that Dr Steiner had been told that he was leaving the clinic. Alistair would have his way.

# Chapter Sixteen

Alistair departed for Rome a week later and was surprised that Steiner let him go so soon. When he said as much to me, I said that I didn't think he would have any problems in replacing him. Alistair accused me of being sarcastic and our relationship was strained in the days before he left. I was unhappy. I thought we were both taking a leap in the dark and when I voiced my fears he said reasonably, 'I want you to stay on here at the villa until I've sorted things out down there. I'll let you know what's happening and I'll come up whenever I can.'

'Dr Steiner may not want me to stay on at the villa,' I said cautiously. 'After all, you're no longer employed by him and he could quite easily get somebody to do what I do.'

'I've talked to him about that and he's quite happy to have you stay on. After all, it's me who's upset the apple cart, not you.'

At the first opportunity I asked Dr Steiner if he was agreeable, offering to leave the villa and move into one of the bedrooms at the clinic.

'That won't be necessary, Ginny. I'm in no mood for moving back into the villa with all my belongings. Here I'm on the spot if I'm needed and I may eventually hire another doctor with a wife and family.'

'You're taking on more staff then?'

'And giving them more opportunity to take on more work. Perhaps Alistair was right, perhaps I am getting too old and should delegate more.'

'Did Alistair say that?'

'Not in so many words, but two promising young men have left me and I begin to wonder.'

Alistair kept me fully informed about his new clinic and every day he had something new to report. After a month he had found what he was looking for, a large villa in the hills above Rome, close to Tivoli. The villa had belonged to an elderly, aristocratic lady who had let it run down, but it had wonderful possibilities and Alistair's backers would help to turn it into something quite special. The living accommodation would be wonderful, the views from every window enchanting, and I would love Rome, he said.

Alistair's replacement, Dr Gerrard, arrived, breezing into my office with a friendly grin and a firm handclasp. Sitting on the edge of my desk, he informed me that he was an American from Portland, that working with Steiner was the answer to a long-cherished dream, and that Alistair must have been off his head to leave.

I liked him, and because we both spoke the same language I became the person he consulted about what he should see and do on his days off. I invited him to dinner, and in turn he invited me to show him some of the local sights. We enjoyed each other's company.

One afternoon when we returned to the clinic after shopping in Como, I found Melissa standing in the main hall. She looked at us with a little smile on her face.

I introduced her to Alan Gerrard, who stared at her with undisguised admiration. She was wearing a rose-coloured pure silk dress with a matching scarf tying back her dark hair.

'I know this isn't very original,' Alan said, 'but haven't I met you somewhere? Your face is awfully familiar.'

Melissa laughed. 'My picture is all over the place, you've probably seen it somewhere.'

He stared at her hard for a long moment. 'Gracious, yes. I have some of your records. I heard you sing on the radio when you were in the States, and your picture was in all the glossies my sister takes. I always thought opera singers had to be hugely fat until I saw you.'

Not displeased with his chatter, Melissa permitted herself a small, regal smile.

'Are you here to see Steiner?' Alan asked.

'No, I'm here to see Ginny. We go back a long way, don't we, Ginny?'

I agreed that we did, and Alan said gallantly, 'I'll leave you two ladies to chat, then. I'm so happy to have met you, Miss Francesca.'

'He's rather nice,' she said when he had left us. 'Where can we talk? Not here, it's far too public.'

'My office is just along the corridor. I heard you were back in Milan.'

'For three performances of *Bohème*, then I'm off to Rome to sing Butterfly. How do you feel about going to live there?'

'I'm not sure.'

'I love Rome. I have an apartment there but I'd like a villa. At the moment I'm moving around so much I haven't the time to look for one. You'll love the villa that Alistair has chosen. Of course it needs the earth spent on it, but he's had no trouble in finding rich women to help him.'

'You've seen the villa?'

'Yes, Alistair asked me to drive up there one day with him. I wasn't singing that evening so there was plenty of time for us to look around and see all its possibilities. He wants it to be flourishing before you see it.'

'I can't think why. I could have helped him.'

'Not really. He's got an architect on the job, and an interior designer. You're better off here and well out of it. Is Natalia Mellini still here?'

'She's returning here tomorrow. She's been staying with her grandmother for a few weeks.'

'Well, Riccardo will be going to Rome after he leaves Milan and then on to Naples. Will he take her with him, do you think?'

'I don't know.'

'Will she ever get well enough to be the sort of wife he should have?'

'I hope so. Have you met her?'

'I've seen her with Riccardo. Usually sitting staring into space, uninterested in people and in music. What sort of commitment does she really want from him? If he ever loved her, it's long gone, and now she's simply a burden to him.'

147

'Then you would never know it. He's kind and attentive to her and she lacks for nothing.'

A half-smile hovered round her lips and she said meaningly, 'It's not enough, Ginny. Riccardo Mellini is a passionate, warm-blooded Italian with the capacity for living — believe me, I know.'

She walked on ahead, leaving me to ponder how she knew.

For the remainder of her visit we talked pleasantries, and Dr Steiner joined us.

After she had gone, he said thoughtfully, 'Did you know she was coming to see you this afternoon?'

'No, I was surprised to see her.'

His eyes narrowed and with a small shrug of his shoulders he said, 'That young lady has a reason for doing everything. What did you talk about?'

'She asked about Natalia Mellini.'

He smiled. 'How they all pursue Riccardo Mellini in their different ways! And that young woman is a predator. Over the years I have heard many stories about the women who have longed to possess him, always with one eye on his sick wife, and perhaps some have succeeded. I doubt if Melissa Francesca will be one of them, though.'

'Why do you say that?'

'She would glory in it, shout it from the housetops, and when it was over she would make him pay dearly for the privilege.'

'If it wasn't over?'

'It would be, Ginny, believe me.'

'She told me she had gone with Alistair to look at his new clinic in the hills above Rome.'

He raised his eyebrows maddeningly, then in a quiet voice he said, 'I don't want to lose you, Ginny, but the sooner you join your husband in his new venture, the better I shall like it.'

Natalia returned to the clinic and I was careful not to intrude upon her, but each day we spent a little longer in conversation. She now felt able to talk to me about her grandmother and the few weeks she had spent at her villa on the coast overlooking Capri. She looked well, her dark blue-black hair complementing her sun-kissed cheeks and ruby-red lips, but her eyes never really came alive.

148

One day when I was alone in the office there was a tap on the door. Almost immediately it opened and Riccardo stood in the doorway, a half-smile on his lips as he leaned nonchalantly against the frame.

'I have come to thank you for taking an interest in my wife, Ginny,' he said softly. I could feel my face blushing furiously at his use of my name when before he had almost always addressed me as Signora Grantham.

'Did Natalia tell you we talk together every day now?'

'No, Dr Steiner told me, and I'm grateful. She has no friends, people who have wanted to be her friends quickly grew tired of having their overtures rebuffed. You must have that special something she can relate to.'

'I do hope so. We talk about a great many things. Sometimes I do most of the talking and Natalia listens, but she is beginning to talk now — about her grandmother, her home, her garden.'

'Her home?' he asked in surprise.

'Why, yes.'

'Ginny, we have no home that Natalia cares for. I have an apartment in Rome that she hates, a hotel room in Milan that she has never seen, and she has only been once to the villa in Capri. I bought it for Natalia thinking she would love it as I did, but perversely she accused me of buying it for a mistress, somebody she had conjured up out of thin air. She stayed two nights at the villa, then her demons chased her away and she has never wanted to return.'

'Perhaps if I talk to her about it, casually, lightly, I could make her tell me why she doesn't want to go there. You have so little time, Signor Mellini.'

'You are right, I have very little time. My work takes up a great deal of my life, but it would be nice to have that beautiful place to return to and a wife who cared. Perhaps it is too much to ask for — contentment, fame and love.'

Our conversation had strayed into realms I was afraid of. Faced with this grave, worldly man, I was feeling increasingly ingenuous, and I found myself saying in a small voice, 'Natalia loves you very much, Signor Mellini.'

He smiled that strangely sweet smile. 'Is that what you call love? The need to possess without reservations, regardless of what might matter to the other person? No, Ginny, I do not

149

think that is love and you do not think so either, otherwise you would not be here while your husband pursues his dream, a dream that you are not entirely happy with.'

I could not reply to something that was obviously true. I stared at him miserably and he nodded, accepting that my silence confirmed his words.

'I am sorry that he has decided to prostitute his talent among the synthetic and bored people who will pay him handsomely for doing precisely nothing.'

Stirred to retort, I said sharply, 'Aren't you surrounded by the very people you're accusing Alistair of cultivating?'

'Our worlds are different. I get more pleasure from watching the poor people sitting up in the gods, straining their ears to hear the performers. These are the real music lovers, they do not come to be seen. I am not saying that those rich people in their beautiful clothes do not love music, but they do not have to suffer for it. I will always give as much of myself to the poor as to the rich, just as here in the clinic Dr Steiner treats the sick whether they be rich or poor.'

I had no further argument for this man with his straight gaze and his assurance. I hated him for being right and I hated him for disturbing me as no man had ever disturbed me before. I had loved Alistair with all a young girl's intensity, and I had been unable to see beyond him. Now in this foreign world I found myself attracted to this man with his sophistication, his soaring talent and the easy charm of his voice.

With a brief smile, he said, 'Thank you again, Ginny, for your kindness to my wife and for the way you forgave her. She and I will be sorry when you leave us to join your husband. When do you expect that to be?'

'He wanted me to remain here until the clinic and the villa are ready for occupation.'

'And he has friends who will help him in Rome?'

'I believe so.'

'I can assure you Melissa Francesca won't have time to help, for I shall be keeping that young lady very busy in the foreseeable future.'

He departed, leaving me staring bewildered after him.

\*     \*     \*

150

Later in the afternoon I wandered on to Natalia's terrace. There was a pile of glossy magazines on the floor next to her chair and a box of expensive chocolates on the table, from her husband, I guessed. Her expression was pensive as she gazed across the vista of mountain peaks and drifting clouds. She did not turn her head until I took the other chair. Then, with a small smile, she said, 'Riccardo came with these — do have one.'

'He was pleased to see you looking so well.'

'How do you know? Did he tell you he was pleased? Does he always talk to you?'

What crass stupidity had encouraged me to tell her I had seen him? Hurriedly I said, 'He called in to see Dr Steiner but there was only me in the office. He was talking all the time about you, Natalia, delighted at how well you're looking.'

'He is handsome, is he not? Women find him very attractive.'

'Then you're very fortunate that he is your husband and so obviously in love with you.'

'Did you find him attractive?'

'You know I have a husband I hope to be joining in Rome very soon. I find Alistair attractive.'

'You're leaving to go to Rome?'

'When our villa is ready. I could see you in Rome if you go there with your husband. Don't you have a flat there?'

I was aware of her eyes searching my face like pieces of gleaming agate. 'You know we have an apartment in Rome?' she said sharply.

'I think Dr Steiner must have told me. I've never been to Rome, I'm looking forward to it. Do you like Rome?'

She shrugged her shoulders indifferently. 'What does it matter where we are? In Rome, Naples, Milan, anywhere we go, Riccardo has his work, his audience, his musicians, and I am left alone.'

'I know how you feel. Alistair too has his work and I too was left alone for long periods.'

'But your husband does not have a throng of women who throw themselves at him. They feel sorry for Riccardo, tied to a sick wife, but I will never let him go.'

'He doesn't want to go, Natalia.'

151

Again she shrugged her shoulders and I was wishing with all my heart that I had not told her I had talked to him. I had to be careful not to let her see me as the same sort of threat as every other woman he spoke to.

# Chapter Seventeen

Alistair arrived just before Christmas, driving a long, low Maserati which looked as if it could have eaten my little car alive. Enthusiastic as a schoolboy, he introduced me to the car, pulling out new suitcases in ivory leather and innumerable gaily wrapped parcels and exotic plants.

Laughing together, we walked into the villa, where a decorated spruce tree stood in the hall and a log fire burned in the living room. Alistair looked around him appreciatively before saying, 'You're going to love the villa in Rome. This would fit into one corner of it but I've no doubt you'll add your own personal touches before you've been in it very long.'

'When did you exchange your battered old suitcases for this luxurious stuff?' I asked him.

'Well, this was a present to us both for Christmas. You have a set just like it.'

'Oh, really? Who has been so generous?'

'Melissa.'

'Melissa and I have never exchanged Christmas presents, not even when she lived with Mrs Rocheforte.'

'I don't suppose Melissa had much money then, but now that she is doing well she wants to be generous. It was a kind thought, don't you agree?'

Not to agree would have been childish and yet I didn't want Melissa to buy expensive presents for either of us. Uneasily, I said, 'Did you give her anything in return?'

'I sent her flowers. I don't have Melissa's money yet, but when I do, we shan't be in her debt for anything.'

153

'That's what I don't like — that we should be in her debt at all.'

I tried to make the holiday as similar as possible to the Christmases of my childhood, with traditional fare and Christmas music played on the gramophone. I had bought Alistair a pair of gold cuff links and he presented me with a gold bracelet; then we sat on the rug in front of the fire, opening small ridiculous presents which caused us to laugh, and I rejoiced in the warmth of his smile.

Two days later he returned to Rome and I spent New Year's Eve alone waiting for his telephone call. When it came, he informed me that he had been invited for dinner at the villa of people I had never heard of. In a faintly embarrassed voice he asked, 'You're going out, I hope, Ginny? Surely there'll be some sort of celebration at the clinic?'

Just before midnight I heard the sound of a car's engine on the drive and I went to the window to see who it was. The panes were white with frost and I could see nothing, but when I answered the door bell Alan Gerrard stood on the threshold, his arms filled with poinsettias and chocolates.

'What on earth are you doing here all on your own on New Year's Eve?' he said, thrusting his gifts into my arms. 'Why didn't you tell me you were alone? I'd have come for you and we could have gone out to celebrate.'

'Alistair had to go back and I didn't much feel like going out. Can I offer you a drink?'

'I've got a bottle of champagne in the car in the hope that you'd help me to drink it. Stoke up the fire and I'll get it.'

We sat and talked and drank our champagne. On the stroke of midnight he took me in his arms and kissed me, and when we stood apart, he said gently, 'Dr Steiner said I should come, Ginny. He was worried about you.'

I felt a little disappointed that Alan hadn't come of his own accord.

Back at the clinic, I saw the compassion in Dr Steiner's eyes and resented the fact that Alistair had put me in this position. One evening in sheer exasperation I telephoned him to demand that he tell me something definite so that I could tell Dr Steiner when I expected to leave.

'The clinic is completed and I've got several patients. I've got interior decorators in the villa, so you should be able to be here at the beginning of March,' he answered. I could tell by his voice that I had embarrassed him.

'Are you coming up here to help me pack everything up?' I asked brusquely.

'Ginny, I can't. Get the girl to help you pack up, and I'll arrange for a van to bring our stuff down here. And Ginny, we don't need everything we have up there — please bring only the essentials.'

'Am I expected to travel in the van?'

'Of course not. Be reasonable. Somebody will surely take you to the train and I'll meet it at this end.'

'What about my car?'

'Sell it or give it away. It's a bit of an old banger anyway and there'll be a brand-new one waiting for you here.'

That piece of information should have pleased me but it didn't. Everything I was going to was new and expensive, and I was unsure how much Alistair would have changed in keeping with our changed lifestyle.

The Canadians and the Americans had returned to their families and there was only Mr Marchmont left to say goodbye to. I doubt if my leaving even registered in his withdrawn remote world and Natalia was staying with her grandmother. Alan drove me to the railway station in Milan on my last morning. We drove round the lake in silence and my mind refused to stray from that morning when Alistair and I had arrived, happy and excited, scrambling up the hill with our luggage. It seemed to me that it had all happened in some other life, a life totally remote from what I was going to.

Dr Steiner had looked into my eyes while he held my hands in a warm grip.

'I want you to be happy in Rome, Ginny, you and Alistair, but you know where I am if you ever need a friend. I'm grateful for all you've done for me. I'm going to miss you.'

I could feel the tears pricking my eyes. I knew I would miss him too and his wise counsel.

My spirits revived on the train journey to Rome and excitement took the place of doubt. As I stepped down from the train, my eyes scanned the throng of people in the station hall. I saw

Alistair waving his arms, elbowing his way towards me; he looked tanned and very handsome. Tugging my suitcase, I walked as quickly as I could towards his embrace.

In the car, he said, 'The van arrived yesterday. I've put all the stuff in a spare room at the clinic for you to sort out. I think when you see the villa you'll realise most of it won't fit in.'

'Some of those things were wedding presents.'

'I know, darling, but the sort of things people could buy in that little village hardly project the right image.'

'What if they remind us of home and people we knew there?'

'You please yourself, Ginny, but wait until you've seen everything and then make up your mind.'

I said nothing more. Driving through the beautiful old city, I tried to remember my history lessons on the glories of Rome. I was enraptured by the sights. The weather, too, was as sunny as Alistair had promised when we endured the autumn rains in the mountains.

In spite of his many assurances, I was unprepared for my first sight of the Villa Marguerita. It was a long, low, white villa set in formal gardens and behind it, almost obscured by cypresses, stood Alistair's clinic.

'But it's so big!' I cried. 'Far bigger than Dr Steiner's.'

He smiled, not displeased by my initial shock. 'I'm banking on filling it with a great many patients. Steiner was more selective than I intend to be.'

A long, open tourer was parked outside the house and I recognised it instantly as the one in which Melissa and I had driven to the opera house in Milan. Seeing me looking at it, Alistair said with a broad smile, 'We haven't got visitors, Ginny — that's yours.'

'I thought it was Melissa's car.'

'It was, but I told her I was looking for a car for you and she suggested I had this one. She's bought a new Bugatti — a bit ostentatious, I think, but there, that's Melissa for you.'

'You seem to have seen quite a lot of Melissa,' I couldn't resist saying.

'Well, she came to look around the clinic and the villa. She was very ready with advice and it was Melissa who recommended the interior decorators. She had them to work on her own villa.'

'And where's that?'

'About five miles away. I've seen it, it really is something. Don't you want to look at your car?'

'I've driven in it. Right now I'm far more interested in where we're going to live.'

So for the next hour I was introduced to every extravagant room in the Villa Marguerita, to gilt shelves and tables, to onyx and marble and crystal chandeliers hanging over pale-peach upholstery and marble floors. Long, wide windows were festooned with turquoise satin drapes, and beyond them the gardens sloped towards a marble fountain and marble seats held up by dimpled cherubs. Making myself sound enthusiastic, I watched the wary anxiety leave Alistair's face.

'I told Melissa you were arriving today, but she said Mellini was keeping her so busy she wouldn't have time to come up here. He's working her too hard — if it's not a performance, it's a rehearsal. If I knew him better, I'd feel tempted to tell him.'

'I don't think Signor Mellini would take kindly to that.'

'Perhaps not, but there are limits to what he can expect from her.'

'I told Natalia that I would try to see her in Rome.'

'Still thinking you can contribute something there?'

'I like to think that we were becoming friends.'

'I'd like to think that you'll take the same interest in my patients here. Why not go up there and make yourself known to them? Talk to them, take them some flowers. They'd love you for it. Melissa went up there one day and sang for them, just gentle, ordinary songs, nothing operatic. They were thrilled.'

There was nothing for me to do. Alistair seemed to have appointed an army of nurses for the clinic and we now had a housekeeper and her staff to see to the workings of the villa. I was left with only the flowers to arrange, and when I suggested working as his secretary, Alistair informed me that he didn't see his wife in this role and had already appointed a young woman who was highly efficient, spoke good English and fluent Italian and had settled in remarkably well.

At Alistair's request I visited the clinic, taking flowers and magazines for his patients. I was impressed with the large, airy rooms and thick carpets. One old lady was having her nails manicured and another was undergoing a face massage. I thought it was more like a beauty parlour than a place for serious disorders, but when I said as much to Alistair, he said loftily, 'They're old and lonely. They need to be pampered, it does them more good than a cartload of pills. They'll go out feeling marvellous and looking ten years younger.'

More and more women were seeking Alistair's help as his reputation grew, women in the same mould; rich, bored and lonely. In the evenings we were invited to functions in villas similar to our own. We went to garden parties and exhibitions of crystal and porcelain, and we went to the opera. While Alistair joined in the adoration of Melissa, I found Riccardo Mellini's imposing figure more and more intriguing.

It was at one of those functions that I realised that I was in danger of falling in love with him. As the guest of honour, Mellini came with Natalia when the evening was well advanced. Looking at her pale, beautiful face, I felt afraid for both of them. He accepted the award of a marble bust of himself; then Melissa stepped forward and threw her arms round his neck in congratulation.

Calmly he detached himself from her embrace, but those standing nearby registered Natalia's resentment. Her dark eyes smouldered and as he sat down and took her hold of her hand, she snatched it away angrily. Making a pretence of showing her the statuette, which she barely glanced at, he placed it on a small table beside him.

'He should take her home,' Alistair murmured. Turning to Melissa, he said, 'I should make myself scarce if I were you, or there'll be trouble.'

'Nonsense!' Melissa snapped. 'Riccardo is my maestro and I am his diva. Am I not to be allowed to congratulate him because she happens to be here? He should never have brought her. It is I who should be beside him on this occasion.'

She stood glaring across the room at Natalia, magnificently angry in a scarlet silk gown with the gleam of diamonds against her dark hair.

Shortly afterwards I saw Riccardo pull his wife to her feet and place her mink stole around her shoulders. Melissa stepped forward again, saying, 'Riccardo, surely you're not leaving already? This entire evening is in your honour.'

He bowed stiffly, but before anybody could stop her Natalia had picked up the marble bust and flung it with all her strength at Melissa. It caught her arm before it crashed to the floor.

The silence among all those present was profound. Then people rushed forward to pick up the damaged bust and Natalia knelt on the floor, weeping.

Speaking to Melissa, Riccardo said softly, 'I am sorry, I hope the bruise is slight. Now, if you will all excuse me, I will take my wife home. Come, Natalia.' He pulled her gently to her feet.

As they passed us, Alistair said, 'If I can be of any help, Signor Mellini, please do not hesitate to ask.'

'It will not be necessary. Tomorrow I will return her to the clinic in the north of Italy.'

She was weeping uncontrollably, and in a burst of compassion I put my arm around her waist and walked with her to the door. She did not protest, and I could feel her trembling against me as I accompanied them to their car. I do not know if Riccardo knew me at that moment, but I was glad that I was being allowed to help. After he had settled her into the front seat of the car, he looked down at me with a wry smile, saying, 'I should never have taken her. I know that the least thing can cause distress, and yet she has been so much better recently.'

'Is the bust very badly damaged?' I asked him.

Bemused, he looked down at it in his hands. There was a slight crack across the shoulders and a dent in the forehead. He smiled. 'I wouldn't have known where to put it. Now I can put it away in a dark cupboard and people will understand why.'

'But it's a shame — '

'Thank you for your help, Ginny.' And with another brief smile he got into the car. I stood on the drive while they drove away. As I turned to go back into the villa, I saw Alistair coming towards me.

'You seem more concerned with Natalia Mellini than with your friend Melissa,' he said reproachfully.

'Oh, all those people in there will be fawning round Melissa, and I felt sorry for Natalia. Melissa should have known that Natalia would be upset by her attention to Riccardo.'

'Melissa was only doing what was expected of her. Now most of those people will think she and Riccardo are having an affair and Natalia has been made aware of it.'

'It isn't true.'

'How do you know it isn't true? Nothing would be more natural. It's a situation that lays itself wide open to speculation. Wake up, Ginny.'

Why didn't I believe it? Was it because I didn't want to believe it, because I didn't want Natalia to be hurt or because I wanted my idol to stay on the pedestal on which I had placed him?

I walked back to the villa, disturbed and resentful. Melissa was surrounded by comforters and she was making the most of it, tearful, pained and with her beauty strangely unruffled.

'You shouldn't sing tomorrow,' Alistair told her solicitously. 'Heaven knows you have enough understudies waiting to step into your shoes. Let Mellini realise what his wife has done.'

But Melissa did sing, more enchantingly than ever. I speculated on who had given the story of the evening before to the morning papers, so that the reviews of her performance accentuated her courage.

# Chapter Eighteen

The next two years were the saddest of my life. The disintegration of my marriage started with the appearance of Alistair's father, who made it quite plain that he blamed me for Alistair's severance from Dr Steiner.

His comments were so unjust and bitter that I couldn't summon up the will to defend myself. I didn't care what he thought about me, I didn't like him, and yet his views on Alistair's new lifestyle mirrored my own.

For days after his angry departure I had to listen to Alistair's rehash of his lonely childhood and his parents' hostility to each other.

With no job, I was bored. Alistair accused me of being childish, but it pleased him to find tennis partners for me and others to go riding with me. I spent my days watching fashion shows and celebrity concerts, and in the summer we went on holiday to the small villa Alistair had purchased in Positano. There Melissa once descended on us to say she had decided to have a villa built on the hillside overlooking the Bay of Solerno.

I witnessed Alistair's dismay when he said, 'But you'll be too far from Rome, Melissa, everybody will miss you.'

'It's my holiday villa so we shall be neighbours. It'll be somewhere to relax and I love Positano. Besides, one day I might marry.'

'Who? Who will you marry?' he demanded.

'Darling, there's an army of men I could marry. But not a musician, they're far too temperamental and our careers will clash. How dreadful to marry somebody like Mellini! A love affair is one thing, marriage is another.'

'You mean you're having a love affair with one or both of them?' he said sharply.

Her laughter trilled out across the garden. 'Darling Alistair, I'm not going to tell you. I adore Riccardo's brooding silences, on my knees I worship his talent, but I don't intend to end up like Natalia, reduced to a sad wrath waiting in the background.'

'And Brucio?'

'Heavens, no! When he embraces me on the stage I feel suffocated, and he reeks of garlic.'

Time after time I listened to these exchanges between Melissa and Alistair and in the end I knew that she teased him because she was aware that he had fallen in love with her.

It was hard trying to ignore it. I did not think she would return his affection but she was playing a game — with Alistair, with me, and for the benefit of a crowd of people who had nothing else to do but speculate on the ending.

It was Velma Forenzo who put my fears into words one morning when I ran into her on the way down to the marina. She was colourfully clad as always, wearing a large pink sombrero on her head and held two white poodles on leashes.

'Ginny, how nice!' she called out when she saw me. 'Take one of the dogs, will you, darling? I've asked the boy to save a couple of chairs, I was sure I'd meet someone.'

Complying with her request, I accompanied her to her chosen spot by the sea.

'Sit and keep me company for a while, Ginny,' she said. 'We've a lot to talk about and I never see you on your own.'

She reached into her beach bag, which seemed to hold enough sun lotions to stock half a chemist's shop, and several paperback novels. She grinned when she saw me looking at them.

'They're very steamy — not your kind of thing. Here, children,' she said, addressing the dogs and producing doggy chocolate bars and rubber bones.

I had the strangest feeling that I was soon to hear something I would not like to hear, something Velma's mischievous mind would revel in, and I was not left long in doubt.

'What do you think about Melissa's idea to build a villa just along the coast?' she asked innocently.

162

'I haven't thought about it. I knew she was interested but I hadn't realised she had definitely made up her mind.'

'She's been looking at villas for sale but hasn't found anything suitable, so now she's intent on having one built. Something that will put everybody else's to shame.'

When I didn't speak, Velma went on, 'She gave Alistair a lot of advice and ideas when he bought the Villa Marguerita. What sort of background does she come from? Nobody knows very much about her and she's cagey about her early life. She talks about her guardian and a beautiful house in the English Lake District, but she never talks about relatives or parents. You've known her a long time, so I was determined to ask you exactly what you know about her.'

'She came to our village during the war, and we were friends at school. Melissa was one of a crowd of children who came to us from the cities in danger of air raids.'

'But a guardian, Ginny! Does that mean she had no parents?'

'Mrs Rocheforte lived at the big house on the lakeside, a little way out of the village. She was a nice lady, something of an institution in the life of the community. I think perhaps I should swim now, will you excuse me?' I discarded my beach robe.

As our eyes met, Velma said, 'I'm asking too many questions, Ginny, and you're not disposed to tell me anything else. Let me give you a word of warning, though. Melissa may have been your friend at school but some friendships are not meant to last. Some friendships can be very dangerous.'

I stared at her for several seconds, then I turned away and ran down to the sea. I made myself swim for much longer than I usually did, but eventually I had to return to Velma, who was now sitting with two other women, their heads close together, their laughter echoing along the shore.

I didn't know either of them, but one of them trilled, 'How nice to meet you, Mrs Grantham. I've met your husband at the clinic when he was looking after my aunt. It's so much nicer down here at the Lido, one meets more people than sitting around one's own pool, don't you agree?'

I smiled. They had been introduced as Letitia and Martha, and Velma informed me that they were American and married to wealthy Frenchmen.

163

I started to pack my beach bag after towelling my hair. Velma said, 'You're surely not going so soon, Ginny? I've been telling my friends that you knew Melissa Francesca in England.'

The two women exchanged quick glances, and the smaller one said, 'Oh, well, that explains it then. I thought she had a new beau, but now I can see he was only being kind to his wife's friend.'

I stared at her without speaking.

'Alistair and Melissa were looking at chandeliers at a sale in Amalfi,' Velma explained, rather too quickly. 'Letty thought the man with her was someone special enough to help her choose what went into the villa.'

'I understood you to say you had met my husband at the clinic. Didn't you recognise him at the sale?'

'Well, no, not immediately. They were so intent on their purchase and on each other. So many odd things happen, don't they? And of course we hadn't met you. Now we understand perfectly why Dr Grantham was there.'

The two women said their farewells and left. Velma said, 'Why rush away, Ginny? They're two gossipy women not worth thinking about. You're surely not worried about Alistair and Melissa being seen together? Trust them to put two and two together and make five.'

'I'm not worried.'

'Not even the slightest bit?'

'What are you trying to say, Velma? You're as fond of gossip as they are, and now you keep hinting that I have something to fear from Melissa. Either tell me outright or leave it alone.'

'I was trying to be your friend,' she snapped. 'Everybody's talking about Alistair and Melissa. What do you think was going on all those months when you were in the north and he was in Rome?'

'He told me he was setting up the clinic and furnishing the villa, and I believed him.'

'And of course that's how it started, but everybody saw what was happening, and they were so besotted with each other they couldn't hide it. He tried after you arrived in Rome, but it didn't last. We all thought it would be Riccardo Mellini Melissa would fall in love with, but she got no encouragement from that quarter. Alistair Grantham, on the other hand, was easy.'

I stared at her furiously for a long moment, then, picking up my bag, I walked quickly away. I was angry and hurt, but unsurprised, and as I drove back to the villa I realised with something like shock that the betrayal to my pride was more cruel than the hurt to my heart.

For a long time I sat on the terrace watching the sun set in the bay. Later that evening I tried to telephone Alistair in Rome but there was no reply. Calling the clinic to see if he was there, I was informed that Dr Grantham had not been in since lunch-time and was given a number where he could be reached — the number of Melissa's villa. At that moment I thought everybody in Rome must know about my husband and Melissa.

After thinking about it for a few minutes, I put another telephone call through to the clinic and asked the receptionist to inform Dr Grantham that I was returning to Rome in the morning. The telephone rang a few minutes later and I was determined not to answer it, yet I reached for it in the hope that it was Alistair. It was Velma Forenzo.

'Ginny, we mustn't quarrel. You were upset, honey, and heaven knows I didn't want to offend you. I'm disgusted with Melissa, particularly as you're her friend.'

'I was sharp with you, Velma, I'm sorry.'

'Honey, you needn't be. You had every right to be angry, all the more since you evidently had no suspicions about Alistair and Melissa. He'll be here any day now and you can talk it over and make up. If it doesn't work out, talk to me, I know all about lawyers and settlements.'

'I'm returning to Rome in the morning,' I said shortly.

'Really! You didn't say so this afternoon.'

'It must have slipped my mind.'

'Oh, well. Don't forget my charity soiree on the seventeenth. I've got a new patient for Alistair, a widow, rolling in money, and very disturbed since her husband walked out on her. I've told her all about Alistair's clinic and the splendid work he does there. The Windsors will be there, and some members of the British aristocracy. It should be very interesting to see their reactions to their former king, don't you think?'

I had no illusions about Velma. Alistair was her pet protégé and this was not the time to fall out with his wife. How she would feel about me if we separated, I could only conjecture.

It was early morning when the telephone rang again. I lay in bed listening to it echoing through the quiet rooms. Then I got up and started to dress. It rang again as I was leaving the house, but I closed the door behind me without a backward glance.

It was a long, lonely drive from Naples to Rome, and I kept imagining what was waiting for me at the other end.

One of the maids greeted me with a smiling face, taking my suitcase. I changed out of my travelling clothes and entered the salon, where tea and tiny sandwiches and cakes had been set out for me. However long I stayed away, the villa would be cared for efficiently. Did it really need either Alistair or me? I wondered.

I was too proud to ask the maids if they knew when my husband was expected. I had had a bath and was sitting at the dressing table when I heard his car along the drive, and the opening of the front door. He knew I had arrived because I had left my car in front of the house, but he did not immediately come into the room. Instead I could hear him crossing the hall to go into his study and I waited with sickening impatience for what seemed hours until I heard the door of his study close and his footsteps ascending the stairs. I sat facing the door, watching like a frightened bird for him to appear. The moment I looked into his eyes, I knew that what Alistair and I had had was irretrievably lost. The pain of knowing was like a knife turning in my heart and I could only stare at him while the scalding tears rolled slowly down my face.

With a small, strangled cry he came over and took me in his arms, and I listened to his voice saying over and over, 'Ginny, I'm sorry. I'm so dreadfully sorry.'

How does any woman meet the ending of a love story? Disbelief, anger, heartbreak — all these feelings before the questions start. Why did it happen? When did it start to go wrong? Could any of it have been different? But the answers are never what we want to hear. I listened for what seemed hours to Alistair's pleas for understanding, to his assertion that he loved me and would continue to love me, but he was no longer in love

166

with me, and underneath all his heart-searching I knew he was in love with Melissa without really understanding or liking her.

'I don't know what I'll do, Ginny. In a month she's going to America to sing at the Met and I have to be with her. I can't let her go without me.'

'And the clinic, what are you going to do about that?'

'We've talked about it. I'll keep the clinic on, of course. I've a good staff there and you know I haven't put in much time there recently. Melissa needs me. She's scared of going to New York, and she's afraid of the furore this is going to make, but we both know we have to face it together.'

As I sat and listened to his excuses, his need for Melissa, the pain slowly subsided, leaving a feeling of emptiness more insidious than the pain. I was losing my husband and I was losing a friend, and all those years of loving him and waiting for him to love me became negligible.

It seemed a very long time before Alistair asked, 'What will you do, Ginny? You know you can stay on here as long as you want to. Melissa seemed to think you'd want to go home.'

'Perhaps that would be more convenient,' I said, and was pleased to see the ashamed colour flooding his cheeks.

'Ginny, we didn't want to hurt you. It was something we didn't want to happen but couldn't prevent. Melissa said she would like to see you.'

'I really can't think why. We've said all that needs to be said, I don't need any confirmation from Melissa.'

'She's as unhappy about it as I am.'

'Can you really be unhappy about something you both walked into with your eyes wide open? You'll continue to be the rich people's doctor and Melissa will still be the diva. I doubt if your friends will remember my name when you and Melissa are married and this bit of scandal has blown over.'

'You have every right to be bitter, Ginny.'

'I don't intend to stay bitter, I intend to get on with my life. I don't know how or where, but I shall.'

The next day Alistair moved into the clinic and nothing more was said. Three days later, Melissa came to the villa.

I watched her getting out of her car, extending long legs in beige slacks. Her eyes were hidden behind large sunglasses, her beige linen jacket was slung around her shoulders. For a

167

moment she glanced up at the house, tossing her dark hair back from her shoulders, then she strode purposefully to the front door.

I deliberately made myself sit at the desk as though I was busy writing letters, and merely raised my eyebrows as she sauntered into the room. I sensed her initial discomfort as I said, 'Good morning, Melissa. I didn't expect you quite so soon.'

'I told Alistair I would come,' she said softly.

'Yes, he told me. There was no need. Alistair explained everything very convincingly.'

'Are you very angry?'

'I was angry, angry and sad. I have lost my husband and my friend — two calamities at the same time.'

'I was never your friend, Ginny. You were mine, I was never yours.'

I stared at her with wide eyes, stunned by her words, cruel but casually uttered.

She walked across the room and came to stand over me, her dark eyes curiously honest.

'I resented you from that first morning I sat in the village hall listening to that bossy woman asking my name. Everybody in that village thought so much of you and your family. If I was friends with Virginia Lawrence, I was halfway to being accepted. If I grew up like Virginia Lawrence, I could count myself a lucky girl. Even Mrs Rocheforte talked about you and how I should cultivate your friendship. Well, I did, and it got me the recognition I needed, but it was my talent that did the rest. What I have become had nothing to do with you.'

'Is that why you went after Alistair?' I cried.

'To get at you? No, I'm in love with him and he's in love with me. I'll admit the situation does have a certain poignancy, but I wouldn't have been interested in Alistair simply to hurt you. That would have been a bore. You're not that important.'

Giving me a last contemptuous look, she strode out of the room. I sat at the desk listening to the sound of her car's engine as it receded into the distance.

At that moment I knew what I was going to do. I was going home.

# Chapter Nineteen

How could I have believed that it would be the same? The fells and the lakes retained their old magic, but I was no longer the same Ginny Lawrence who had skipped light-heartedly along the village street. Now I was that girl who had married a boy who wasn't local, and, worse than that, a boy who had taken her to live in an alien land.

The years had done something to me too. I no longer spoke with a Lakeland accent. My clothes were too fashionable, my make-up too exotic, my demeanour too ritzy for those solid North Country people I had known and loved.

I was unhappy. There was no work for me to do at the surgery because Father had an efficient full-time secretary-receptionist, and on those occasions when I asked if I could help Mother in her various activities, she already had more helpers than she knew what to do with.

Cloonie told me bluntly, 'Yer've bin away a long time, Ginny, ye can't expect to find everythin' exactly as ye left it.'

'I just want to get back into the life of the village. Surely that isn't too much to expect?' I grumbled.

'That it is,' she said adamantly. 'See 'ow ye gets on next week when Miss Birkett's on 'oliday. 'Elp out at the surgery, that will seem like old times.'

It was good to be back in the tiny office at the side of the surgery, and I welcomed the patients and chatted to them. It wasn't easy because they seemed wary of me, I wasn't the Ginny Lawrence they remembered, and one day I was upset to hear Mrs Scholes say to the patients at large, 'My, but she's

169

changed! She was allus such a nice girl. Now she's givin' 'erself airs and graces and she's that fashionable.'

Her voice carried clearly into the office. I stood listening, hoping somebody would defend me. Mrs Houghton said firmly, 'She's bin away some time, of course she's changed. What did you expect?'

'She'd 'ave done better to 'ave married the vicar. We all knows 'e was sweet on her afore she married Alistair Grantham.'

'Well, we shouldn't be discussin' that now,' another voice put in. ''E's wed to Joyce Miller and there's a baby on the way. Joyce 'as made a good vicar's wife and it's evident they're very 'appy.'

Several days later, Alistair and Melissa's photographs were splashed all over the morning papers. They were reporting the new man in her life and the fact that they were leaving Italy for New York, where Melissa was to sing at the Metropolitan Opera House. He was staring down at her with obvious admiration and she looked every inch the star, wrapped in furs and carrying an armful of flowers.

Mother tried unsuccessfully to hide the paper from me, but I had already seen it in the newsagents and suffered the covert glances of those I met along the street.

I heard them talking in whispers in the waiting room and I knew they were discussing me. The morning papers were spread across the table in the waiting room and every time I went to call one of the patients in to see Father, I had to see the smiling faces of my ex-husband and false friend. Old Mrs Ross, who had never been noted for her tact, said grimly, 'When I was a girl, anybody who'd done what they've done would 'ave bin given the cold shoulder. Now it's fashionable and they're treated like somebody. I never liked that girl — sulky, she was, and too full of 'erself. I'm surprised at 'im, after all your family did for 'im durin' the war.'

I smiled sadly and left them to their talk.

On the morning after, they had something else to talk about. Joyce had given birth to a little girl during the night. In the afternoon I visited the hospital with flowers.

I had always liked Joyce Miller, and she was pleased to see me.

170

'I was hoping you'd come,' she said, smiling. 'We knew you were back in the village, but Colin thought we should allow you to settle in before we saw you. The baby's here in the cot beside the bed, she's absolutely lovely.'

I duly admired the sleeping baby.

Joyce chatted on as if we'd met only the day before, and I realised it was so that I would not feel compelled to tell her anything about myself.

'Colin's busy this afternoon, two funerals,' she added. 'Some days I wonder if we'll ever have any time for ourselves, and then everything falls into place. Fortunately Father gave me a good grounding to be a vicar's wife.'

'You were perfect for it, Joyce. We all said so.'

'He was very fond of you, though. I thought he'd never look at me when you were around, but when you married Alistair, we got together.'

'I'd have been a terrible vicar's wife, and I'm so glad that you're happy.'

'Have you decided to stay in the village? There's not much here in the way of work and it must seem very tame after living abroad.'

'I'm financially independent, Alistair has been very generous, but I have to find something to do. Obviously I'm far too young to sit around at home doing nothing. I have to think very seriously about my life now.'

'I suppose you will divorce Alistair?'

'Yes. That is the next thing I must think about.'

I thought about nothing else in the days and weeks that followed, and the family firm of Solicitors were a tower of strength. I wrote to Dr Steiner. He would be aware of all that had happened, and he had told me that he would be a friend if ever I should need one. I needed one very badly now, and I wrote asking if he could find me a job at the clinic, or if he knew of someone else who would employ me. He had probably replaced me, and I had had no training as a nurse, but still there was a hope that somehow or other he would help me and I waited in desperate impatience for his answer to my letter.

I remember everything about the day the reply came. It was a summer's day when the morning mist hung low across the fells. Before the village came alive, I went to sit on a low stone wall close to the lake. Waterfowl squabbled in the shallows and in a small boat anchored out in the lake, a solitary fisherman waited.

I did not hear my father's footsteps across the short grass until he reached my side. He sat down and regarded me with concern in his eyes.

'Give yourself time,' he said gently. 'The pain isn't going to go immediately, it will take time.'

'I shouldn't have come back expecting to find everything unchanged. I've changed, so how could I ever have expected it to be the same?'

'It is the same, Ginny, it's just that we've all grown a little older, and you're the one who's changed the most. Think about it, love. All these years we've been doing the same things, talking about the same things, seeing the same scenery. Most of these people have never been further than the market town and all they know is sheep farming, stone-walling and listening to the old gossip. Oh, the young ones go off to work in the towns, and as time passes they'll go off more and more, but you're like a creature from another world with your sophistication and your melancholy. They're afraid of showing pity. They don't love you any less, they simply feel uncomfortable with the girl who's come back to them.'

'I've written to Dr Steiner, and asked if he has anything for me.'

'And is that what you want — to go back to Italy where you were happy with Alistair? Do you think if you went back he'd be there again if it doesn't work out with Melissa?'

I stared at him in some surprise and said nothing.

'It won't last with Melissa, you know. I'll give it a couple of years, no more.'

His words brought no satisfaction or triumph to my bruised pride, only a feeling of doubt.

'Why do you say that?' I asked.

'Think about it, love. What have they really got in common? He's a professional man who has put his career on hold so that he can follow in his wife's footsteps wherever they take him. He'll try to be one of her set but he'll never entirely succeed, and that is when jealousy and anger set in. He will marry a woman whose only loyalty is to herself and her audience. Without them she would be nothing, but if Alistair went there would be others glad to take his place.'

'She should have married a musician, somebody in her world, but I heard her say that wouldn't work, their careers and ambitions would clash, their temperaments would be constantly at war. At least Alistair will not have any of that to contend with.'

'He'll have the boredom, and in the end he'll have the pain of realising he's the one who has given up everything and the rewards for his sacrifice will not be very evident.'

We walked home together and entered the house through the kitchen, where Cloonie was busy bottling strawberry and raspberry jam. There were trays of small cakes on the kitchen table and several large sponge cakes waiting to be split and filled with jam.

'I'll put the kettle on,' Cloonie said. 'That letter yer've bin waitin' for's on the 'all table, Ginny.'

I recognised Dr Steiner's small, neat writing as soon as I picked up the envelope and I opened it eagerly to read the three pages of closely written words.

He wrote about the clinic, the people I knew there, the exhilaration of the mountain air and the beautiful views of the lake glimpsed through the pines on the mountain slopes, and I had to wait until the last page to be told I should return. There was something for me to do, something rather special, but he did not say what. I could imagine him smiling to himself as he sealed the envelope, anticipating my mounting impatience at his secrecy.

I sat staring into the fire with the letter in my hands, unaware of the opening of the door until Father came to stand on the rug in front of me, looking down at me with questioning eyes.

I passed him the letter and waited until he had read it through. Then he said, 'So, it's what you wanted to hear?'

'Yes. I just wish he'd said what I can do.'

'Obviously he'd like you to return.'

'Yes, at least there's that.'

'Well, you'll just have to contain your soul in patience, Ginny. When will you go?'

173

'Soon, next week I hope. I don't know if I'll be living at the villa or at the clinic. Whatever it is he has for me, it will be wonderful working again.'

Word very quickly got around that I was returning to Italy, and I became aware of the villagers' reproach and condemnation. If they'd taken the trouble, they would have discovered that I wanted their friendship and yearned for the peace and gentleness of the old life, but it was not to be. In the narrowness of their country lives they saw only the façade.

My sister and her children came to stay for a few days before I left for Italy and were made much of by the villagers. She was still the same Edith, proud of her husband's thriving practice and her boisterous children.

'I'd have thought you'd had quite enough of Italy. Living there wasn't exactly a happy experience for you,' she said in her usual forthright manner.

'But it was a happy experience,' I argued. 'I loved Italy, I loved my work at the clinic. It was sad the way it ended, but I can't blame Italy for that.'

'You'd still be married to Alistair if he'd settled down to a normal practice in England as my husband has.'

'But that wasn't what Alistair wanted. In any case, what's done is done, there's no point in raking over the past now.'

'Nobody in the village can understand why you want to go back.'

'If they've been talking to you about it, it's more than they've done to me. They don't talk to me at all about Alistair or Italy, they only speculate.'

'Oh, well, it's none of their business, is it? I never thought Melissa was your friend, she was never anybody's friend.'

'That's exactly what she said herself,' I admitted.

All too soon I was standing at the window of the country train, waving to them on the platform as Alistair and I had once waved to them when setting out on our honeymoon. Edith's children ran along the platform, their faces rosy, their little arms waving, and I could feel the hot salty tears rolling slowly down my cheeks.

There was nobody beside me today. I was setting out on a voyage of self-discovery, alone and uncertain.

# Part II

# Chapter Twenty

My heart sank as I walked into Dr Steiner's clinic at the sight of an efficient-looking young woman who came forward with a bright smile to enquire what I wanted.

'I'm Virginia Grantham,' I explained. 'I wrote to tell Dr Steiner that I would be arriving today.'

'Of course. Dr Steiner will be here in about an hour; he's with a new patient who came in yesterday. I'm sure you would like a cup of coffee, so please make yourself comfortable while I get it.'

I took a seat in the window, from where I could look down the mountain road towards the lake. Summer visitors still lingered among the shops and cafés that lined the lakeside and boats plied between the villages. Two gardeners toiled among the flowerbeds and above the tall, dark cypresses rose the mountain peaks which had become as familiar to me as the Lakeland mountains at home.

The secretary came back with coffee. 'How long have you been working for Dr Steiner?' I asked her.

'Almost a year. My sister is a nurse here, she said he was looking for someone who spoke English. He wasn't very efficient in the office, there was a great deal to do when I came here.'

'I can imagine. I worked for him for a time, and I too had a great deal of sorting out to do.'

She laughed. 'I'm very happy here. We have a new doctor on the staff, a Dr Bruchner from Munich, and the American doctor is still here as well as Dr Vicelli. You'll know most of the people here, they hardly ever leave.'

She suddenly looked embarrassed when I met her gaze. To put her at ease, I said, 'When I first arrived in Italy some years ago, there had been so much rain it gushed down the mountain-side and we were paddling in it. Today is beautiful, it's hard to imagine it on a rainy day.'

'Yes, it is beautiful. My name is Teresa, my home is in Como.'

'I wish I spoke Italian as well as you speak English.'

She laughed. 'We spoil you,' she said. 'You come here and expect us all to speak English, and for the most part we do, but you will learn Italian, I hope.'

'I was having lessons, but then things changed and I gave them up when I went to live in Rome. I intend to start again, particularly if I am to work here.'

'Oh yes, that is a good idea.'

'Have you any idea what sort of work Dr Steiner has for me?'

'I would rather he told you himself.'

'Of course.'

'Would you mind if I went on with my work? You know yourself how much there is to do.'

'Yes, please carry on with what you were doing. I'm quite happy to sit here with my coffee.'

To the sound of her typewriter, I worried about what Dr Steiner could possibly find me to do at the clinic. When he finally turned up, there was so much kindness and welcome in his smile that I felt instantly reassured.

'You look well,' he said, escorting me into his office. 'Your family evidently spoiled you during these last few months. Now I want you to tell me about yourself, those last few months with Alistair. I can tell you when your life and your marriage started to go wrong.'

'I thought it was here, long before he went to Rome.'

'Yes, I think so too. When he met those idle people with their villas, their money, their boredom. And then a young, beautiful woman with the world at her feet, enticing him in the guise of friendship.'

'Perhaps there is some excuse for Melissa — she did not betray a friendship. She told me she had never been my friend.'

'But she had not been ashamed to pretend. That, I think, is a betrayal twice over. Alistair is in New York; they will be in America for a year. People are ecstatic about her over there, so ecstatic that she may not have much time for the man who hopes to be her husband and follows her everywhere she goes.'

'But what about his clinic?'

'His staff can run it without him, but such a waste! To put aside all those years of study, all his hopes for a brilliant career, in order to follow her around the world, to watch her entertaining her audience and the people who crowd her dressing room after every performance and hardly notice him. I tell you, one day the emptiness will stare him in the face and he will ask himself if it has been worth all he gave up for it. Will he rebel, Ginny? Or even before that, will she?'

'She has got what she wanted, Dr Steiner.'

'But has she? A man living on her earnings, an onlooker, a man who is not of her world. This is the photograph that stared out of my morning newspaper.'

He pushed it across the desk, folded to show Melissa alighting from the front seat of a sports car, smiling up at the tall young man holding the door open for her.

'If your Italian is not good enough, I will read it for you. "Melissa Francesca and her latest admirer, Antonio Brindisi, an Italian banker." Signor Brindisi was in the audience to hear her sing Tosca and the following afternoon she was photographed with him in Santa Monica. Almost as an afterthought, the newspaper tells us that Dr Alistair Grantham remained in New York on business but was expected to join her in San Francisco very soon. When Brindisi was asked if he had enjoyed her performance, he merely smiled and drove quickly away.'

'But all that is ridiculous!' I was angry. 'Why do they always latch on to something that is probably perfectly innocent? Do you know anything about Antonio Brindisi?'

'Oh yes, I know about him. His mother was a patient of mine for several years. She is an alcoholic, escaping from the infidelities of her husband and the perpetual scandals surrounding her son. Her husband Nino Brindisi is a Sicilian, and it is widely rumoured he has connections with the Mafia. The son is handsome, and his affairs with beautiful society women are legendary. In the winter he skis in St Moritz, in the summer he sails in regattas and he is a great lover of motor racing, with some success, I should add. He has never married.

179

A wise woman would shy away from the responsibility of becoming Signora Brindisi.'

'Melissa is not a fool; besides, she will marry Alistair when our divorce is finalised. They can't be disenchanted with each other so soon.'

He made a wry face, then in a lighter voice he said, 'And now, Ginny, you want to know what I have in mind for you?'

'Yes, please.'

'Natalia Mellini was very sad to hear about your problems. She wept for you and has asked about you constantly ever since.'

'Really? Is she here now?'

'While Riccardo is away in America. It is not often Natalia expresses concern about anything or anyone outside her narrow little world of total self-absorption. When she seemed genuinely concerned about you, I began to see a little light at the end of the tunnel.'

'I'd like to see her.'

'And so you shall, but first tell me what you think about my idea for your immediate future. Riccardo is expected home in a couple of weeks, and then almost immediately he is going on a world tour, one he has shelved several times over the years. The last time I spoke to him about it, he was uncertain, concerned about his wife, and of course it would be impossible to take her with him. Her grandmother has said she could stay there for some of the time, but the old lady is far from well and Natalia is wearing. I want you to take her on. Make her a friend, let her see that you have risen above your personal tragedy, that she too could be strong if she follows your example.'

'But her tragedies are imaginary, Dr Steiner, mine were real.'

'I know, Ginny, but in the next few weeks you could be good friends. You could enjoy the summer together, drive into the country, see something of the many beautiful things Italy has to offer, and you could encourage her. You would be helping me, helping her husband and her grandmother, but most of all you would be helping Natalia.'

The doubt still lingered on my face, and gently he said, 'Talk to Riccardo, hear what he has to say about it. His doubts may echo your own, but ask yourself what else you would be doing. You want to work, to do something useful, something that would benefit others. Well, if you can play any part in rehabilitating that young woman, you will have achieved more than I could ever have hoped for.'

Later that afternoon, I spoke to Natalia. She was sitting in her favourite chair at the side of her terrace overlooking the mountains and the distant view of the lake. In those first few moments I was dismally aware of her lethargy. Still standing in the doorway to her room, I called, 'Hello, Natalia. Do you remember me?'

At first she turned to me without any sign of recognition, then her face relaxed into a smile and she indicated the chair next to hers, saying, 'Please sit with me. I am pleased to see you.'

I sensed in her a reserve. She could not speak of the sadness that had entered my life since our last meeting, but I made myself talk naturally about my return home, my family and the friends of my childhood. At last, in a small voice, she asked, 'Why did you come back?'

'Dr Steiner said he had some work I could do. Besides, it's nice to see the people I knew here, the doctors and nurses, and you, Natalia.'

'I was sad to hear what had happened to you. It is hard when your husband has someone or something more important in his life.'

'I would have liked it to be Alistair's career, that I could have understood. That would only have delighted me.'

'Even if it took him away from you?'

'Even then, because his success would have been my success, just as Riccardo's fame is also yours.'

'It is not me those fawning women monopolise. I am an encumbrance, a shadow in his background. They would like me to be dead! You would have had none of that. A doctor's life would have been different, but Riccardo had to be a musician and he is no longer mine.'

I decided not to labour the point. There would be many times over the next few weeks or months when I could try to persuade Natalia that music was not her enemy but could well be her friend.

That evening, Dr Vicelli greeted me enthusiastically, showing me a pile of photographs of his growing family, and Dr

Gerrard embraced me warmly before informing me that he had met a beautiful Italian girl and was hoping his parents would visit him from America so that they could meet her.

Dr Bruchner turned out to be much older than the other two. He was polite but not very communicative, and he seldom spent the evening with us in the common room, leaving directly his duties were over to spend the evening with his wife and daughter.

It was Alan Gerrard who said, rather dryly, 'He's a bit dour but Steiner thinks highly of him. I must say he seems to know what he's about.'

'Have you met his wife?'

'Yes, on the first day they were here. She's OK but the daughter's stone deaf — was born deaf, it seems. That's probably the reason they keep themselves to themselves.'

It seemed to me at that moment that one never really knew what peculiar sadnesses ordinary people had experienced behind the façade of normality.

I knew that Riccardo Mellini had returned to Italy when I saw his long tourer parked on the drive in front of the terrace. Either he was with Dr Steiner or with his wife, and I waited anxiously for the summons that I was sure would come.

I was writing a long letter home, filled with anecdotes of everyday happenings at the clinic, when I heard a knock on the door. The next moment I looked up into the steady grey eyes of Riccardo Mellini. I was struck again by the singular sweetness of his smile in a face whose stern beauty was at first unnerving.

I invited him to sit down and easily he said, 'Dr Steiner said I should talk to you alone. He did not wish to have any hand in persuading you to do something against your better judgement. He has told me that you and Natalia have formed a friendship which he sees as entirely beneficial to her welfare, and he believes some time together while I am away will encourage her to build something normal for our future. How do you feel about it?'

'It's true we're getting along well together. We talk every day. I'm trying to interest her in books, things she should see, a summer holiday. I think she's beginning to respond.'

'I see.'

'You're not very sure it would work, though?'

'Not entirely, but I can see the need to try. You're hoping to turn back the clock, Ginny, to change the obsessions of a lifetime into something approaching normality. But we both know that the only way my wife can be totally at peace is if I were to give up my music and devote my life exclusively to her.'

'Not if I could involve her in other things, make her see that she too could have interests.'

'Dr Steiner thinks it might just work, so we should give it a try. I wish you luck.'

We both rose from our seats and he walked across the room to take my hand. For a long moment he stood looking down at me and I was afraid of the sudden racing of my heart.

'I will drive you and Natalia to Rapallo on Sunday morning to stay for a few days with her grandmother. You can discuss how you intend to spend the next few weeks while you are there. There is a car at the villa. It is Natalia's car but she hasn't cared to drive it. Wherever you decide to go from there will be your joint decision. I will leave a supply of money with her grandmother and here is a chequebook on Natalia's account at her bank. Do not be afraid to use it.'

'I shan't use it unnecessarily.'

He smiled. 'You do not work for nothing, you will receive an adequate salary in line with my gratitude. Buy anything you wish, and encourage Natalia to do the same. Perhaps with your help she will recover her interest in clothes and take pride in her appearance.'

He reached out and put both his hands on my shoulders, then, to my surprise, held me close to him for a long moment. I was aware of the beating of his heart, the cool smoothness of his face above my hair, the scent of the soap he had used that morning. It was not a lover's embrace, and yet it was hardly impersonal. At last, he held me away from him, and in a low voice said, 'Bless you, Ginny. Until Sunday morning then.'

I nodded, and in the next moment he had left me alone. I heard his footsteps crossing the marble floor of the hall and the distant closing of Natalia's door.

I had no illusions that Riccardo Mellini would be attracted to me. There were already too many beautiful women in his life and there was Natalia. But I could be hurt by him, by his indifference and by my part in helping to restore normality to his life with his wife.

I would not be like Melissa. I had promised to be her friend and I would be her friend, even if it meant another crippling blow to my heart.

# Chapter Twenty-One

It was the strangest journey I had ever taken as we drove towards the coast near Rapallo. Riccardo concentrated on his driving and there was no conversation between him and Natalia. I sat at the back of the car with my eyes fixed on the scenery and my mind full of anxiety.

Dr Steiner had held my hands before I left him to get into the car. His smile was gentle, his words were conciliatory. 'It's worth a try, Ginny, anything to make that poor girl achieve some sort of normality. Show her a world where it is normal to trust, normal to appreciate the good things that life has given her without asking for the moon.'

I looked at him unsurely. 'You're asking somebody who at this moment does not have a lot of faith in the fairness of life to explain it to another,' I said a little bitterly.

'I know, Ginny, I know you've been hurt, but this is why you can show her that it wasn't the end of the world for you. You've risen above it, you've put it on one side to get on with your life. Natalia hasn't been hurt by anyone but herself.'

'I'll try, Dr Steiner, I can do no more,' I answered.

During the drive, I wished somebody would speak to me. I wanted to ask questions about the villa we were visiting, and the sort of life we could expect with Natalia's grandmother, but I doubted if Natalia would answer me, and I did not want to start up a conversation with Riccardo in case she would feel left out. I knew how easily her jealousy could be aroused.

Once I caught his eyes on me in the driving mirror, but that cool, swift glance gave no indication of his thoughts.

When we arrived, Riccardo introduced me to Natalia's

grandmother as his wife's friend who was going to keep her company during his absence. I felt decidedly uneasy, particularly when she said, 'Natalia and I have always felt comfortable with each other without the need for company.'

'Dr Steiner thinks she would benefit from companionship with a woman of her own age,' he replied. 'She and Ginny get along very well together and I have to admit Natalia is happier than the last time I brought her here.'

The old lady shrugged her shoulders and in a resigned voice said, 'I'm only her grandmother, you are her husband. I expect you think you know what is best for Natalia.'

I was shown into my room overlooking the formal Italian garden and a maid was sent in to help me to unpack. My spirits were at a very low ebb when I thought about the weeks ahead. The grandmother seemed antagonistic, and Natalia was totally lethargic.

I changed my travelling dress for something soft and more comfortable, then I went downstairs. The old lady was sitting in an upright chair facing the window, her eyes trained on Riccardo, who was standing outside on the terrace, staring out to the sea. There was no sign of Natalia. I made myself take the chair opposite the old lady, who acknowledged my presence by a brief nod.

The silence was oppressive and I was hesitant about speaking to her in English. I understood Italian better than I could speak it. I need not have worried on that score, however, because in perfect English she asked, 'Haven't I seen you in Dr Steiner's clinic?'

'I was his secretary when my husband was a doctor on his staff.'

'And where is your husband now, signora?'

'I am divorcing my husband!'

'I would have expected Dr Steiner to have sent a nurse to be with my granddaughter rather than his secretary.'

'He doesn't think Natalia needs a nurse. She is not ill, merely suffering from acute depression.'

'A depression that would leave her if her husband spent more time here in Italy than wandering the globe.'

I kept silent, but I thought her words monstrously unfair. How could she expect a man of Riccardo's calibre to forsake his career, everything he had worked for and accomplished, to be near a wife who had no interest in his life? She went on, 'I know Riccardo's money makes it possible for her to live in luxury, but it does not make up for the lack of his company.'

When I still remained silent, she fixed me with a shrewd glance, saying, 'I have a feeling you do not agree with me, signora.'

'No, I'm sorry.'

'Why not?'

'There is no guarantee that Natalia would be well if her husband gave up his career. Besides, musicians of his calibre have so much to give the world, why should he be expected to make the sacrifice? Why not Natalia?'

'You are a very forthright young woman,' she snapped.

'You asked my opinion, signora.'

'I am the Contessa Bourgini, you will address me as such.'

'I'm sorry, Contessa.'

I had not heard Riccardo come into the room until I heard him saying, 'I think we should be grateful to Mrs Grantham, Grandmother. We are asking her to sacrifice several weeks of her life to the care of a woman who may not respond as we hope. We should be grateful and polite, it is the least we can do.'

She bowed her head. 'Signora, I am sorry if you consider me impolite. Now, if you will both excuse me, I will go upstairs to see if Natalia has settled in.'

We watched her stiff-necked, slender figure walk across the room without a backward glance at either of us, and Riccardo favoured me with a wry smile.

'I'm sorry if she has upset you. I thought this might happen but I hoped she would have the grace to accept you and keep her opinions to herself.'

'She has made me wonder if Dr Steiner expects too much of these next few weeks.'

'She would have been happier if Natalia had been the world's idol and I the supplicant. Natalia was the only daughter of her favourite child; she idolised them both, spoiled them both, and when Natalia's mother died, she made her granddaughter her whole life. The results of that devotion are as we see.'

'Suppose I fail? Suppose Natalia doesn't respond to me? After all, I shall get no help from the Contessa.'

'You don't have to stay here the whole time. Take Natalia out in the car. There are some delightful places you can visit — Portofino, Santa Marguerita, even Genoa. This is a very beautiful corner of Italy.'

'I don't know it at all. I hope Natalia and I will be able to discover it.'

'Natalia knows it well from her childhood but I expect she has forgotten much of it.'

He stood looking down at me, his expression kind. Placing both hands on my shoulders, much as Dr Steiner had done, he said, 'It seems unfair of life to burden you with all this when you have had sorrows of your own.'

'They were made sorrows, Signor Mellini.'

'Riccardo, please. Do you ever hear from your husband?'

'Why, no. He's still in America, I think.'

'Yes, and Signorina Francesca has taken America by storm, as was expected. She is the darling of the American operatic stage, he a shadowy figure in the background.'

'Do you know Antonio Brindisi?'

His smile was entirely cynical. 'So you have heard something of that?'

'Dr Steiner showed me their photograph in a newspaper.'

'Brindisi is well known wherever there is money, glamour, celebrities. He is rich, handsome, supposedly a banker but really just a playboy.'

'I would hate to think that Alistair has to compete with a man like that.'

'Don't tell me you are still carrying a torch for Alistair Grantham?'

'No, I'm not, but I do remember that he was my friend. We were children together. Whatever has happened to us in adult life, nothing has destroyed the past.'

'Your husband was a fool to leave a nice, beautiful woman like you.'

He was looking into my eyes with such intensity I could feel the warm blood flooding my cheeks. I could not have looked away if I'd tried. When he released my gaze, I became aware that the Contessa stood on the terrace with Natalia, both of them watching us.

With a smile, Riccardo said, 'Come, let's join the others. Leave it to me to reassure my wife and her grandmother.'

In the event, Riccardo took the three of us to Portofino before leaving on his world tour. We left the old lady sitting in a small café while we walked round the exquisite bay. The hillside was dotted with sugar-icing villas in pink and white, pale turquoise and coral, and luxurious oceangoing yachts were anchored next to tiny fishing boats in the harbour below. We explored tiny shops selling ceramics and brocades, antiques and boats carved out of shells. I could have spent all day wandering along that harbour wall, but Natalia's face showed only boredom and the desire to move on.

'You look tired, Natalia,' was the only remark her grandmother made when we returned to her.

Riccardo said, 'Perhaps we should go home, perhaps it was a mistake to come. One should never go back — Ginny, didn't you say something similar the other evening?'

I didn't answer, but I knew what he meant. I had gone back to the English Lakeland village and wished I hadn't.

It was the last time Riccardo took us driving in the countryside around Rapallo. In the days that followed he was engrossed in his arrangements for his forthcoming tour and we rarely saw him until the evening.

Natalia sulked, and her grandmother lost no opportunity to tell me that it was Riccardo's absence that was making her fretful. I listened to her without comment until the morning I said, 'Natalia can barely be polite to him when he is here. If his presence is so necessary to her wellbeing, why doesn't she try to be a little more accommodating?'

'It is because she knows he is going away again.'

I could not fight them both, but more and more I began to see the difficulty of the task I had undertaken.

On the night before he left, I sat in my room listening to her sobs, her anger, her moans of self-pity. In the morning I watched him opening his mail with lines of weariness etched on his face and I could feel his despair as deeply as if it had been my own. He went upstairs to say goodbye to her, and once again I heard her cries of anguish.

'I'll telephone when it's possible,' Riccardo told the Contessa as he was leaving, 'and of course I'll write. Natalia doesn't answer my letters but I hope either you or Mrs Grantham will keep me informed of her progress.' Seeing me standing in the window, he smiled and raised his hand in farewell before he climbed into his car and drove away.

When lunchtime came and I had not seen or heard from Natalia, I went up to her room and found her pulling clothes out the wardrobes one by one and flinging them on the bed.

Turning round, she said gaily, 'I'm sorting out my clothes. Some of them are far too old. Perhaps we should go shopping.'

'Why, yes, Natalia, if that's what you'd like to do.'

'I have to do something to cheer me up. My husband has left me and I'm all alone,' she cried, her little girl's voice emotional.

'Natalia, your husband has not left you,' I said frankly. 'He is merely getting on with his profession. I'm here and your grandmother is here. Why don't we all go shopping?'

'Yes, why not? And please, Ginny, you must not scold me about Riccardo, you must understand me.'

'Oh, I do, Natalia, I do, and I want to help you to get well so that you can join him in whatever he wants to do as soon as he gets back. One day he's going to want to take you with him wherever he decides to go.'

She shrugged her shoulders and in a petulant voice said, 'I don't want to talk any more about Riccardo. When he basks in all that adoration overseas, I shall be the last thing he thinks about.'

I could not reach behind her curtain of self-pity, so we went shopping in Rapallo. She spent a fortune on dresses that were suitable for grand occasions until even her grandmother said, 'When do you expect to wear all these creations?'

'I shall. At the opera and all those other functions Riccardo and I go to together.'

The Contessa's eyes met mine in an expression of uncertainty.

Looking back, I realise now that many of the days that followed were happy. We drove through the countryside, admiring the rich vineyards and the haunting beauty of the lofty Apennines. We ate at tavernas we found in quiet places and I discovered the Natalia Riccardo must have fallen in love with, a woman of mercurial charm and enchanting beauty who seemed to be searching for a new joy in life, a joy that had deserted her for so long.

Even her grandmother seemed pleased at the new Natalia. I came to believe in Dr Steiner's therapy. We were friends, we laughed together and planned our days, and the summer sun lingered into a golden autumn.

Riccardo's letters came frequently. At first she laid them aside as of little importance, but I encouraged her to read them, saying we were all interested in where he was and what he was doing. Petulantly she read out extracts from his letters, and I told myself hopefully that this was a start.

We were sitting at a table in a small taverna overlooking the sea in Santa Marguerita when a shrill voice hailed me from the front seat of an open car moving slowly along the promenade, and with a sinking heart I recognised Velma. She quickly parked the car and hurried across the road.

Beside me, Natalia's face registered disapproval.

'Darling!' Velma gushed. 'What on earth are you doing here? I'd heard you'd gone back to England.'

'Yes, I did go home for a time.'

She was looking at Natalia with a broad smile on her face, and I said, 'I think you know Signora Mellini, Velma.'

'Well, of course. How are you, dear? Don't tell me you let that handsome husband of yours go off on that world tour on his own?'

Natalia smiled thinly, and I said quickly, 'I'm staying with Natalia and her grandmother until Riccardo returns.'

'Really? I didn't realise you were so friendly, but then of course you met at the clinic, didn't you, dear? You're looking very well, Natalia. How is your grandmother?'

'She is well, thank you.'

'Well, I'm so glad I've met you two. You must come to one of my charities, Ginny. We've rented a villa here for two months and I'm giving a soiree in aid of sick animals, you know how much I love animals. Just drinks and one or two entertainers. Nobody in the same category as Melissa Francesca or your husband, I'm afraid, but you can't say no. It's next Friday evening.'

191

By this time she had extracted two tickets from her handbag and was pressing them into my hands.

I hurried to say, 'I'm not sure, Velma. Natalia may not like to come out in the evening, she still tires very quickly.'

'Oh, but you must come. There'll be nothing tiring about this affair. You'll come, won't you, Natalia?'

'Thank you, yes, we shall be pleased to come.'

I looked at her uncertainly. I had been sure she would have no wish to attend a party full of people she professed to dislike. However, her expression was so determined it brooked no argument, and with a triumphant smile Velma said, 'I'll look forward to seeing both of you then. I've so much to tell you, Ginny. Can't stop now, but I'll get around to it on Friday.'

# Chapter Twenty-Two

I decided to wear a black dress. It was not new but it was beautifully cut and so discreet I hoped not many people would recognise it.

Natalia, on the other hand, swept down the stairs in a white chiffon gown that I knew had cost more than my entire wardrobe. Over it she wore a white satin stole edged with white fox, and the lavishness of her apparel gave me an idea of what she expected from the rest of the evening.

Her grandmother's chauffeur had been detailed to drive us to the function even though the old lady did not approve of our going.

'That woman is not really interested in charities of any description,' she said sourly. 'She merely wishes to get her name in the society columns. I'm surprised that you wish to attend.'

'I'd like to go, Grandmother,' Natalia said forcefully.

'Oh, well, I cannot stop you. My driver will take you and bring you home. Please try not to be too late.'

'I'm also surprised you want to go,' I couldn't resist saying when we were seated in the car.

She looked at me coolly, answering in a quiet voice, 'It will be interesting to see how some of those people behave towards me when I am not an appendage of Riccardo.'

I was discovering things about Natalia I had never suspected and I was uncertain which was the real woman and which the superficial. Her moods were as changeable as the Lakeland weather in England, and there was a maddening amusement in her eyes because she knew how much she puzzled me. There were days when I believed that a great deal of her life had been a lie, a special sort of torture she was able to inflict on a man who refused to make her his entire world, but there were other times when I pitied her insecurity and desperate need to be adored.

Velma introduced Natalia as her trump card of the evening — and to my amazement Natalia blossomed in the attention she was receiving. Many times I had watched her sit back like a silent shadow while her husband had been feted, but not tonight. She shone like a star while I was regarded with mild curiosity as the discarded wife of the man who had fallen in love with Melissa Francesca.

Halfway through the evening, Velma approached me, beaming with gratification.

'Thank you for bringing Natalia Mellini. She's positively blooming.'

'I'm glad she's enjoying herself.'

'We can have a few minutes to ourselves. I've so much to tell you and I know we didn't exactly part good friends, did we? I had a good think about it afterwards and, you know, Ginny, Alistair deserves to be unhappy after the way he walked out on you.'

'Do you think he is unhappy?'

'Of course he is. Oh, he wouldn't admit it, he puts a very brave face on things, but it's there for all to see.'

I looked at her curiously. She was engaged in piling her plate with delicacies from the buffet, her eyes greedily surveying the length of the table, and I waited patiently for her to move away.

'These caterers have been marvellous,' she said, 'better than the ones we had from Milan, but of course it's too far for them to travel when I give my parties elsewhere. Now what was I telling you?'

'You were saying that Alistair was unhappy.'

'I should say so. Look what he's given up for Melissa! That clinic near Rome is thriving, filled to the brim with rich women, and there's Alistair following Melissa like a little lamb everywhere she goes.'

'He is hoping to be her husband. What else can he do?'

'Well, sure, but he didn't know about Antonio Brindisi, did he?'

I gave my attention to the buffet, determined that no

expression or words of mine should be repeated elsewhere at a later date.

'Antonio Brindisi, Ginny — don't tell me you haven't heard what's going on?'

I stared at her blandly. 'I've been in England, I know nothing about Alistair or Melissa.'

'But all society is talking about them. They met in San Francisco where she was singing and for weeks and weeks they were inseparable.'

'And where was Alistair in all that?'

'At first he was in New York, on business, they said, but Alistair has no business in New York unless it was Melissa's career. Then he joined her in San Francisco and the trouble started. There was a terrible scene at one of the parties and Melissa stormed out in a huff with Brindisi driving her home. Alistair stayed on a while to make the best of it but he was furious.'

'What was the row about?'

'What do you think? Next, Brindisi invited them on a cruise on his yacht around the Caribbean and everybody was amazed when Alistair accepted. At the end of the cruise Melissa flew back to Italy and so did Brindisi, but nobody's sure about Alistair. When I asked Melissa when he was coming home, she said he was visiting his mother in England and would be back in a week or so. Do you know his mother?'

'No.'

'His father?'

'Yes, I've met his father once or twice.'

'They're saying he and Alistair aren't on speaking terms, but you know how people talk.'

'Oh yes, I know how people talk.'

The hum of conversation was all around me, drowning the background music, and I wondered idly how many other people were having their private lives milled over by this gathering.

'Don't tell me you've never heard of Antonio Brindisi,' Velma was saying. 'He's in all the gossip columns and usually there's some sort of scandal. Of course he's rich and very handsome. If you ask me, Alistair won't stand a chance if Antonio decides to get serious about Melissa.'

195

'Do you think that is likely?'

'Well, the Brindisis have always been great opera lovers. It would be a suitable conquest for both of them.'

I felt sorry for Alistair.

'Would you have him back, Ginny?' Velma surprised me by asking.

'How can you ask such a thing? What happened between me and Alistair is history. Neither of us could ever go back. I hope all that you've told me is merely empty gossip.'

'Oh yes, well, so do I, dear. Here's Signora Mellini, looking for you, I think,' and she went forward to meet her.

'Can I get you anything from the buffet?'

'No, thank you. I'm tired now, Ginny. Can we go home?'

'Yes, of course.' Velma looked surprised, and I explained, 'Signora Mellini seldom goes out in the evening and she tires easily.'

It was a balmy night with a full moon silvering the trees and the gardens. As we crossed the drive towards the car, I asked, 'Have you enjoyed yourself, Natalia? You seemed to be having a good time.'

'They talk about such strange things, don't they? They were talking about your husband and Melissa Francesca.'

When I didn't answer, she waited until we were sitting in the car to continue our conversation. 'They said she was involved with Antonio Brindisi — did you know?'

'I heard a little about it.'

'I always thought she was in love with Riccardo. She used to hang around him everywhere we went. One of the women I met tonight thought so too.'

I stared at her in astonishment. 'She surely didn't have the affrontery to say that to you?'

She gave a little laugh. 'She confirmed what I thought. I expressed neither surprise nor annoyance.'

'That was clever of you.'

'I enjoyed the party. They loved my dress, it was quite the nicest in the room and well worth spending all that money the other day.'

The rest of the journey was taken in silence.

The Contessa had waited up for us. She came into the hall as we entered the house, saying immediately, 'You look tired,

Natalia. If you would like to go up to your room, I will have something brought up to help you sleep.'

Her tone was reproachful and in some discomfort I watched her stiff, uncompromising figure climb the stairs to her room. She was still resenting my presence and I was becoming increasingly unsure of my future. What would happen to me when Riccardo returned from his world tour? I couldn't expect to go on indefinitely in my role as Natalia's companion but I told myself that during our time together she had seemed more alive than I had ever expected.

The next morning Natalia again raised the subject of Alistair and Melissa, tossing the newspaper across the table to me with a strange expression on her pretty face. There was a photograph of a smiling, elegant Melissa with Alistair looking down at her as they descended from a plane.

I handed the paper back to her but she insisted on reading the accompanying text to me.

> 'The diva Melissa Francesca returning to Milan with Dr Alistair Grantham after rumours that they are soon to marry. Melissa is returning to Milan in time for rehearsals for her role in *Aïda*, and they went immediately to their hotel in Milan.
>
> Later that evening Melissa was seen in the company of Signor Antonio Brindisi at a function in the city. Dr Grantham was conspicuous by his absence.'

She looked up at me. 'What do you make of it?'

'I don't know.'

'I used to read things like that about Riccardo — Riccardo and a great many women.'

'A great many women can be discounted, I think. Involvement with one person is more dangerous,' I replied.

'Do you really think so?'

'Yes, I do. Riccardo hasn't left you for any one of them.'

'That's true, but he must compare me with them and find me wanting.'

'Why do you say that? Why do you always assume that there is some woman he prefers to you? I'm beginning to think you're your own worst enemy, Natalia.'

For a long moment I thought I had said too much. She froze. Then she gave a little shrug of her elegant shoulders and said, 'In two weeks it will all start again with the start of the opera season in Milan. He'll be busy with rehearsals and performances, attending to the prima donnas with their tantrums and their vanities. You'll see. I shall be taken to the receptions as his wife and I shall have to sit there watching the admirers crowd around him.'

'You didn't sit in the background last night. You mingled with the others and I can't see any reason why you can't do this when you're with your husband.'

'It was different last night. I could be myself.'

'And what is yourself, Natalia? Where is the woman Riccardo Mellini fell in love with? Isn't it time for that woman to come back into his life?'

'You think I am play-acting?'

'You said it, not me. And don't play-act too long, Natalia. Now you only imagine that you're losing him, but if you continue like this, he might indeed find one woman who could take him away from you.'

For a moment I saw the fear cross her face, and I knew my words had got home to her. Then, with a toss of her head, she said, 'I would kill her, Ginny, and nobody would blame me. If any woman did that to me, a desperately sick woman, all the world's sympathy would be for me.'

With one fluid moment she got up from her chair and flounced across the terrace and into the villa.

Her words had left a distinct chill in my heart. I felt that she would be capable of such an act, I had seen the cold vindictiveness in her face, her long white hands clenched against her knees, and I asked myself again what I was doing among these passionate, alien people. Why hadn't I stayed home in my quiet, peaceful village? I was still the same Ginny Lawrence who had grown up surrounded by the Lakeland mountains — or was I? I knew in my heart that I was not.

Two days later Riccardo Mellini returned and almost immediately I knew that life for me would never be the same again.

He was deeply tanned from his time under a sun stronger than the one he was accustomed to, and cheerful and excited by the prospect of the opera season before him. Almost immediately he was involved with rehearsals, just as Natalia had predicted.

Until then Melissa had sung only Puccini's music and there were critics who predicted that the role of Aïda would be beyond her capabilities. *Aïda* was grand opera, and Melissa would never be able to handle the acting with all its fire and tragedy. They were unkind enough to say that although she might look the part, in all probability it would defeat her, and I found myself hoping that she would prove them wrong.

Natalia refused to attend the opening performance at La Scala in Milan.

'How can you possibly bear to hear her after what she did to you?' she asked me scornfully. 'If she'd done it to me, I would have killed her!'

I couldn't explain it to Natalia or even to myself, but I could listen to Melissa's voice without thinking about Alistair. Even when we were little more than children, her voice had always seemed like something apart, enabling me to forget her behaviour.

So the Contessa and I attended the premier of *Aïda* and I was absorbed by the magic of Melissa's voice, the power of her acting and the splendour of the scenery in that ancient Egyptian tragedy. When it was over, the audience went wild with enthusiasm. I rose to my feet with the rest of them as Melissa and Bruno Petronelli joined Riccardo in the centre of the stage.

Again and again the curtain rose and fell. The rest of the cast came forward to receive acclaim, flowers were handed up to the stage, and still the audience cheered.

'This will certainly silence the critics,' the Contessa remarked dryly. She added, with a little smile, 'I see that Antonio Brindisi is here.'

I followed her gaze towards a box where several people stood applauding. One man stood out through his delighted enthusiasm, his handsome face wreathed in smiles. Then I saw Melissa look up in his direction and a ripple of speculation ran along the front rows of the stalls.

'The newspapers will pick up that glance,' the Contessa said. 'Tomorrow we can expect to read a lot more in it than perhaps was intended and that poor man who was your husband will be forced to do something.'

The Contessa and I returned home in silence. It was a long drive and for most of it the Contessa slept while I thought about the opera and Melissa's part in it.

By the time we reached Rapallo, it was almost dawn and mist lay across the lawns. I assisted the Contessa out of the car and across the terrace. The long night and the journey had taken a great deal out of her and I wondered how old she really was. Her face was pale and strained. As we reached the house, she said, 'I'm tired. These operas start so late and go on so long, particularly that one.'

'But you enjoyed it,' I said with a little smile.

'Oh, yes. I always do before I start to complain. I will leave a note to have breakfast sent up to your room,' she added.

'Really, Contessa, there's no need. Natalia will be up and she'll want to know about the opera.'

Her eyes met mine, and with a wry smile she said, 'Natalia will show no interest whatsoever in the opera. Anything connected with her husband's profession is anathema to my granddaughter.'

Meeting my shocked gaze, she added, 'Yes, it is unfortunate, I am sparing you the need to tell me so. I am sorry for both of them, but Riccardo fills his days with a great many things and he is strong enough to stand it. Natalia is the one who needs our forbearance, I think.'

As I followed her up the stairs to our rooms, I couldn't help thinking that it might be Natalia that was the strong one. Any woman who could go on year after year punishing herself and her husband must be strong, and now I was beginning to doubt my ability to help her.

Bitterness had eaten into her soul. In those first few weeks I had shared the hopes of Dr Steiner, but now it was becoming increasingly clear that I had contributed nothing to Natalia's future wellbeing. Riccardo was home, and all her old antagonistic feelings had resurfaced. It was not in my power to prevent them.

I felt I was earning my money under false pretences. I had to speak to Riccardo soon about my role in his wife's life, and after that I could not think where my future lay. It was the feeling that I had failed that troubled me most.

# Chapter Twenty-Three

In the days when Riccardo was in Milan or concerned with his music, Natalia and I were happy enough, but immediately he came home she became remote, responding not at all to my overtures of comradeship. I was further shattered when the Contessa said, 'How long do you propose to stay here, Mrs Grantham? I see no real improvement in my granddaughter's condition. And does she really need a woman companion when she has me and her husband?'

She was looking at me with a haughty expression that made me feel terribly inadequate, but I had to agree with her.

Her face softened somewhat and, leaning over, she allowed her hand to rest momentarily on mine. 'I can see you are troubled but you need not be. You have done your best. Nobody knows my granddaughter better than I. Riccardo is an obsession with her, she both loves him and hates him. Once I believed love would be enough to erase all her insecurities, but it was not. She is unstable, I know, but it is self-inflicted because she asks too much from a man who cannot give it.'

'Do you think she has the right to ask it?'

She sighed. 'Perhaps not. She is destroying herself.'

'She would destroy him if he gave way to her.'

'Either that or she would accept his sacrifice as her right and change into the sort of woman he thought he had married.'

'It is too unfair. Marriage should be a partnership.'

'Of course. With two decent normal people, but not with people like Natalia with her self-centred desires and Riccardo with his genius.'

'As soon as possible I will speak to Signor Mellini about

leaving here. I cannot think that he will be surprised by my decision.'

The opportunity came two days later when I saw him standing alone on the terrace looking out towards the sea. Evening mist was cloaking the gardens, obscuring the far horizon. I reasoned that he was stealing this time for himself before driving to the city.

Now was the best time to speak to him alone, so I shrugged my arms into a light jacket and let myself out through the window. As I neared him, I could see that he was entirely wrapped up in his private thoughts, oblivious to the enchanting view before him. I had to touch his arm gently before he noticed me.

Surprised, he smiled. 'I'm sorry, Ginny, how long have you been here? I was deep in thought — something and nothing, I feel sure.'

'I was hoping to talk to you privately before you left the house.'

'What is it?'

'I have to ask you when it will be convenient for me to leave here.'

He looked unhappy. 'I hadn't realised you would be leaving. You think you no longer have a purpose in staying?'

'I've done all I can for Natalia. We became good friends, we enjoyed our times together, but they don't last. Every day now she is reverting to the Natalia I first met at the clinic. I could go on staying here, telling myself that Dr Steiner was right, that I could help her, but I would be deluding myself.'

'And do you know why you can't help her?'

'Yes. I can't turn you into the man she craves for, and if I had that power I wouldn't use it.'

For a long time he stood gazing in front of him, and I waited silently for his answer. I was aware of a chill little wind that stirred my hair, carrying with it the perfume of oleanders.

'What will you do, Ginny? Go back to Steiner's clinic?'

'No, there's nothing for me there. I'm not sure what I'll do.'

'Go home to England, perhaps?'

'I can't go on running home every time something goes wrong in my life.'

'So where do you want to go?'

'I'll settle somewhere and hope to find a job. I could afford to train for something.'

'And where would you live?'

'I have to think about that.'

'What about the villa in Positano? Does that belong to you or to Alistair?'

'Alistair said I could have it. I had thought of selling it because I didn't want to live anywhere near them — you know that Melissa has a villa not too far away?'

'Yes, but I very much doubt if Alistair will be sharing it with her.'

'Why do you say that?' I asked, though I could guess.

'I'm afraid that all the rumours about them are true. Brindisi is her constant companion and, although he is arrogant and unsavoury in my eyes, in hers he is everything she needs. Alistair was too nice for somebody like Melissa. Now it's her turn to be captivated by somebody as ruthless as herself.'

'Poor Alistair,' I said, 'and poor Melissa!'

He patted my cheek with a smile of dismissal.

Thoughtfully I turned away to return to the house. As I walked along the paths that edged the formal Italian garden, I looked up at the villa. My heart missed a beat at the sight of Natalia standing at her window staring at me. I raised my hand to wave, but she did not respond. She continued to watch me until I entered through the open window. I wondered how long she had stood at the window while Riccardo and I chatted, and I felt afraid.

Dinner was a silent meal. I tried friendly conversation but Natalia replied in short, stilted sentences and the Contessa sullenly pushed her food around her plate.

Afterwards, I retreated to a small drawing room to write letters. Natalia was sulking in her room. I was writing to my parents and to Dr Steiner and I was glad of the solitude. Dr Steiner's letter was difficult to compose. I could imagine his disappointment, for me and for Natalia, but I was certain that I was making the right decision.

I was so engrossed with the task I had set myself that I did not hear the opening of the door. Suddenly I became aware of a feeling of such menace that I spun round in my chair. The involuntary movement undoubtedly saved my life. Natalia stood over me, holding a knife in her hands. As I leaped to my feet, she brought it down with all her force and I could hear it tearing through the delicate silk of the chair in which I had been sitting.

I took to my heels and ran. Behind me I could hear her trying to wrench the knife out of the chair. I raced across the hall and up the stairs and in only seconds I heard her coming after me. There was no lock on my bedroom door so I placed a chair against it — only just in time, because almost at once I heard the blade of the knife striking the door again and again. The harsh sounds of her breathing were interspersed with wild, disjointed words.

I rushed across the room to shout for help through the open window, then cowered beside my bed. The sound of the knife striking the door continued for several minutes, and then there was silence. Fearing that she was coming to the windows, I shut them. But I had to be sure before I let myself out of the room, in case she was waiting, still and silent, outside my door. Sure enough, her malevolently distorted face appeared against the window pane and she began pounding at the glass with her knife. Terrified, I let myself out of the room and hurtled down the stairs. Frightened servants had gathered in the hall but I did not pause to explain. I had to put as much distance as possible between that madwoman and myself. I could hear voices and Natalia's screaming as she came after me.

I didn't turn to see what was happening behind me. I ran through the gardens and out along the road, not stopping until I came to the harbour wall. There I stood gasping for breath, scanning the empty road, hoping that someone had prevented her from coming after me.

My legs were trembling uncontrollably so I sat on the wall, waiting for the terror to pass and my brain to function again. Tears were rolling down my face.

I felt I could not go back to the house, even for my clothes. Wearing only a thin silk dress, I shivered in the chill wind that came off the sea.

I started to walk in the direction of the town; I had no idea how far I walked. Lights poured out across the promenade from hotels and restaurants. Dimly I became aware of the hooting of a motor horn and a man touched my arm to indicate a large car beside the kerb. I started, fearing that it came from the house I had left, but relief sent me running towards it when I recognised Velma waving to me from the rear of the car.

She stared at me in amazement. 'What on earth are you doing out at this time dressed like that? Get into the car before you freeze to death!'

I sat beside her, shivering, and the tears started afresh. She gave me a look of sharp curiosity but said nothing. I took in that she was wearing an evening gown and a headdress of osprey feathers.

'Velma, I'm sorry,' I blurted miserably. 'You're going out for the evening, I shouldn't detain you.'

'There's no rush. I'll take you back to the Mellini house and go on from there.'

'No, Velma, no! I can't go back there. Don't make me.'

'Gracious me, why not? Is it the Contessa? Has she been getting at you? Heaven knows she's a very difficult old woman. Or is it Natalia?'

'I don't want to talk about it now. Could you lend me some money to get a room in a small pension until I can get my things? I can get them in the morning and I'll pay you back then.'

'Honey, you can't go to a pension at this time without luggage and looking like a waif in a storm. I'll take you back to my place and you can stay there until I get home. I'll try to get away as soon as I can. I'm not looking forward to it — same old people, same old gossip — I'm only going because my reputation can't afford to stay away. My husband's away and I was all on my own.'

'You're sure you don't mind?'

'Not in the least. Spoil yourself, take a long a bath and borrow anything of mine you might need for the night.'

'You are kind,' I murmured.

'Think nothing of it, honey. You'll be quite safe with me. Does Riccardo know anything about this?'

'No, he's in Milan. Perhaps I could telephone him in the morning.'

She swept into the villa ahead of me, instructing her servants to run me a bath and see to my comfort. I felt guilty for never having liked Velma, because now she seemed like a guardian angel.

I knew that I was safe in Velma's villa, yet every branch tapping against the window, every creak, every rustle of the night wind made me start up in terror. I was dozing fitfully in front of the fire, waiting up for her, when the sound of a car brought me suddenly awake. I sat back with my eyes trained on the door, unreasonably fearful that it would be Natalia.

I was wrong, of course. Velma swept into the room, looking faintly ridiculous now in her emerald-green beaded gown, the feathered headdress a little awry. Taking off her high-heeled shoes, she sank into her chair.

'I've been dying to do that since the supper dance. I'll have to stop wearing five-inch heels, they're doing nothing for my feet and my chiropodist has warned me.'

I started to laugh. It was so mundane, this talk of high heels and sore feet in the midst of all my terror. I was in danger of becoming hysterical until I caught her look of reproach and sobered up.

'I'm sorry, Velma. I'm not laughing at you, I'm laughing with relief after what happened to me this afternoon.'

'I'll mix myself a gin and tonic, then I want to know about that. What can I get for you?'

'I don't know. I feel very strange.'

'A glass of Orvieto will help you sleep.'

Once we were settled with our drinks, she leaned back in her chair and said, 'Tell me about it, Ginny. I promise not to say a word to anybody.'

I smiled, giving her a sly look of disbelief.

She laughed. 'Oh, I know I'm a gossip, but when I make a promise, I keep it. You need to talk, Ginny, something has terrified the life out of you.'

It was a relief to tell someone about it, even Velma, whom I had never regarded as a confidante. She listened in silence and when the sorry tale was told, she said astutely, 'And what are your feelings for Riccardo Mellini? Was there something there that she recognised?'

I didn't answer.

'I think you should get right away from here, from Natalia and Riccardo,' she said, 'or you're going to be a very unhappy woman. I know why women feel they're in love with him — he's handsome, talented and they long to shatter his remoteness, but nobody has succeeded yet. Has he given you any reason to think he might care for you?'

'There have been times when I've thought we were close, but I'm sure it's as you say, the attraction of a man so evidently out of reach.'

'He'll need to be told what's happened, though.'

'I'll ring him in the morning.'

'Well, I suggest we get a little sleep. Try not to worry, dear.'

I couldn't sleep; memories of Natalia's attack were too recent, and an empty future loomed before me. Long before it was light I was standing at the window watching the dawn creeping slowly across the garden, turning the soft grey clouds into gentle rose.

It was too early to disturb Riccardo. Finally I could wait no longer. I picked up the telephone and dialled his number in Milan. The ringing tone went on and on and I was about to replace the receiver when I heard a click and his voice, slightly irritated and sleepy.

'Riccardo Mellini,' he said brusquely.

'This is Ginny,' I said breathlessly.

'Ginny! What's the matter?'

'I'm at Velma Forenzo's villa. Something terrible happened yesterday, I had to get away.'

'Why, what happened?'

'I'll explain everything when I see you. I'm not coming back, but all my clothes, everything I have is still there. I left without money, without even a coat. Velma found me wandering in the town and brought me here last night. As soon as I get my things, I shall leave here. I'm hoping you'll bring them to me.'

'Does Contessa Bourgini know where you are? Surely she can see to it that you get your clothes?'

'I don't want her to be involved, and I don't want Natalia to know. Please help me.'

'Very well, Ginny. I'm very tired, and I don't understand what's going on. Can you manage without your stuff until later this morning?'

'Oh yes, just as long as I know you will bring it to me. I'm so sorry to be troubling you.'

'You'd better have a good explanation. I'll see you later, Ginny.'

I heard the telephone go dead.

I had just finished breakfast in my room when the door opened and the maid said anxiously, 'You have a visitor, signora. The Contessa asks for you to go downstairs quickly.'

I had not expected him so soon, but I was glad. Now I would tell him all that had happened and then I would be able to leave Rapallo.

I ran down the stairs and went out on the terrace, but there was no sign of Velma. I surmised that she was entertaining Riccardo in the salon. But it was not Riccardo who waited for me there; instead, Velma sat facing a rigid Contessa, whose face was set in stern lines. When I entered the room, it showed no sign of relaxing.

'Contessa?' I said softly.

'I have had my maid pack all your clothes and I have brought them together with your money and other personal belongings,' she said icily. 'My granddaughter is quite distraught that you should have seen fit to flee the house and that you did not even bother to let us know where you were.'

I stared at her in amazement. 'You mean you don't know why I left the house?' I cried.

'I know that you had a disagreement and that Natalia created a scene, but in your position you should have understood that she was capable of this sort of behaviour. You should have known that it would pass, to be followed by remorse and terrible anxiety. That you left in a panic says very little for your suitability to be caring for her in the first place. Now that she knows where you are, she has calmed down, but we think it would be preferable if you do not see her again.'

'We?' I asked softly.

'We who have her wellbeing at heart. I suggest you leave Rapallo at the earliest opportunity.'

'I understood Signor Mellini would be bringing my belongings here, he paid my salary, I owe him an explanation for my actions.'

'It was early morning when Riccardo came home and he was

very tired, that is why I have come instead. I will tell him that you are leaving the area and that you are none the worse for the events of yesterday. No doubt he will be speaking to Dr Steiner later today.'

For a brief moment her face softened and something approaching kindness touched it. 'Try to understand Signora Grantham, I love my granddaughter. She and Riccardo are the two people who make up my universe, I will do anything and everything to keep them together, even when I know so many people feel I am already supporting a lost cause.'

'Their marriage has never been in any danger from me Contessa,' I said steadily. 'You should have known that.'

She fixed me with a long, searching look, then she rose stiffly to her feet.

'My granddaughter is beautiful, beautiful and flawed, but you too are beautiful Signora, beautiful and strong, and available. You may not think that you are a potential danger, but I suggest that you search your heart. Here is a man who carries a sad and terrible burden and here is a woman capable of love and understanding, a woman who came to care for a disturbed, perplexed wife but as the weeks passed your pity was for Riccardo not his wife.'

We stared into each other's eyes, then with a brief nod she turned to Velma saying, 'I bid you good morning, Contessa Forenzo. I regret if these last few hours have upset any of your plans.'

With a brief nod she swept towards the door. Velma, in some dismay, rose to escort her from the room.

# Chapter Twenty-Four

I stood in the middle of the room looking helplessly at my belongings — several suitcases and my vanity case. I had no doubt that their contents had been expertly packed by the Contessa's servants.

My feeling of desolation was intense. Riccardo had left it to his grandmother to bring them; he obviously didn't want to see me.

Velma came back into the room and glanced at the suitcases.

'Well,' she said flatly, 'that would appear to be the end of your relationship with Natalia Mellini. What are you going to do now?'

'I don't know, but I want to go quickly.'

'You can't just start a journey with nothing at the end of it.'

'Suddenly I feel so angry, Velma. I admired Riccardo Mellini, I didn't think he would desert me without a hearing. Is he so afraid of his wife and her grandmother that he can't at least hear what happened from me?'

'Leave it a few days, honey, maybe he'll come around.'

'No, I'm leaving today, this morning. I'll think about where I'm going on the train.'

'The train to where?'

She had a point. I was lost for an answer.

When we heard the sound of a car approaching along the drive, Velma said anxiously, 'I wonder who this is. We don't want visitors just now and it could be somebody who'll make the most out of this situation.'

She hurried out of the room with the intention of keeping any callers away. I put on a linen jacket which lay on top of one

211

of my cases. Velma would allow her chauffeur to drive me to the station, I felt sure, and I was ready to leave.

My heart sank when I heard footsteps returning. She re-entered the room, followed by Riccardo Mellini.

He raised an eyebrow at the suitcases. Before I could say a word, Velma said, 'The Contessa was here just now, bringing Ginny's belongings with her.'

'Did you ask her to come here?' I asked cautiously.

'No. She obviously decided to take charge of the situation. When I said I would see you here this morning, I meant it. And you still haven't told me what happened.'

Relief flooded my being. I spilled out the whole story of the attack. Riccardo was appalled, and agreed that I should not see Natalia again for some time.

'Thank you for your help, Contessa,' he said, turning to Velma. 'It was lucky that Ginny was able to stay here with you last night. Now, if you're ready to leave, I will drive you wherever you wish to go.'

Velma's eyes met mine curiously, but I was glad to leave with him. He could drop me off in Milan, and on the way I could think where I wanted to go from there. I thanked Velma for her help, promising to write to her. A servant loaded my luggage into his car, and soon we were driving swiftly along the auto-strada towards Milan.

Conversation was minimal, as he gave all his attention to the traffic and I was plagued by too many desperate thoughts concerned with my future. When we reached Milan, I was surprised that he did not deposit me in the city but continued to drive on towards Lake Como.

'Where are we going?' I asked.

'I am taking you to the clinic,' he said firmly. 'I telephoned Dr Steiner, so he will be expecting you.'

'But there's nothing for me at the clinic,' I protested.

'At least you'll have a roof over your head, and Dr Steiner will think of something.'

'I feel like a Gypsy,' I complained. 'Besides, I'm being a nuisance to you. I'm sure you have more important things to do with your time than drive me around.'

He neither agreed nor disagreed with me, but sat staring ahead at the winding road. My poor heart raced at the sight of his profile and his dark, sculptured hair with the wings of silver at his temples.

There were few holidaymakers staying in the villages of Tremezzo and Menaggio. It was the end of November, skies were grey and a thin drizzle of rain had begun to fall. Snow had already settled on the mountaintops. As we started to climb the road towards the clinic, my feeling of desolation returned. Riccardo turned his head to look at me, then smiled briefly and covered my hand with his own. At that moment tears were not so far away and I felt that he was aware of it.

As we drew up outside the doors of the clinic, they opened and Dr Steiner was there, a welcoming smile on his face as he hurried down the steps to greet us. In his private room a log fire burned and gratefully I held my hands out to the blaze.

He would not allow me to speak until we had been served coffee and sandwiches. I listened while the two men chatted amicably, neither of them referring once to what had brought us here. Then it was my turn to speak. Snow flurried against the long windows and Riccardo stood gazing through them, as if detached from the story I was telling to Dr Steiner.

The doctor did not interrupt, listening to my words with intense interest and unspoken sympathy. When the tale was told, he reached across and took my hands in his. 'I'm sorry, Ginny. When I suggested this venture, I had no idea that it might put your life in danger. Natalia never showed any signs that she could be dangerous. I thought you had become friends — when did it begin to change?'

'I never thought it had changed.'

'You were happy together when Riccardo was away?'

'Yes, always.'

'And sometimes when he was at home?'

'Riccardo drove us into Portofino and many other places, and she seemed to enjoy these outings. During these last few days we spent less time together, but there was no provocation for her to attack me like that.'

'Riccardo?' Dr Steiner looked for confirmation.

'She saw us talking together and that was enough to make her jealous.'

Meeting Riccardo's eyes, I could feel myself blushing. But Natalia could not have looked into my heart and seen

213

something I had thought I had locked away. Besides, it was an infatuation, nothing more, and one that its object knew nothing about.

'It's over now, Ginny,' Dr Steiner said gently. 'Now you have to put it all behind you and move on. Tonight after dinner we will talk about your future. Will you dine with us, Riccardo?'

'I have to get back to the opera.'

He came to say goodbye to me, but he did not take my hand, merely gave me a slight bow and a brief smile.

'I'm sorry you're leaving us like this, Ginny. I wish it could have been very different, but I want to thank you for trying. Dr Steiner will keep me informed of your plans for the future.'

He looked straight into my eyes, and I knew that in mine was an expression of anguish I couldn't hide. I wanted to reach out for him, I wanted him to take me into his arms, but he turned away and walked with Dr Steiner to the door.

I stood staring into the leaping flames of the fire until the doctor came back into the room. I hoped that he would ask no questions about my feelings for Riccardo Mellini, but I knew that he had looked into my heart and discovered the truth. However, he came back with smiling affability, speaking as if the last few moments had already been forgotten.

'Alistair came to see me just before he returned to London. He was here for three days, then he left, saying he would not be returning to Italy.'

'Not returning? But what about Melissa?'

'It is over with Melissa and she is to marry Brindisi; perhaps they're already married.'

'But his work, the clinic in Rome — what about those things?'

'The clinic in Rome has nothing to do with Alistair now, he gave that up when he went to America with Melissa. I feel sure he will find work in England; after all, he is well qualified.'

'Has he gone to his father, do you know?'

'He didn't say where he was going, but he will write to me.'

'What a waste it has all been.'

He didn't answer. After a few moments, he said, 'There will be three of us for dinner tonight. I have a friend staying with me, a man who once spent some time here in the clinic when his personal life was going through a crisis.'

214

'Not another lost cause, Dr Steiner?'

'By no means. This friend is a great survivor. He is a very successful American author — you may have heard of him, Steven Newton?'

'Yes, of course. My father loved his books. Doesn't he write thrillers, stories about espionage?'

'Tales of dark deeds, traumas hidden in our innermost souls.'

'Does he live in America?'

'No, he lives in Amalfi, but you would never meet him there, he doesn't hang around with the famous. He's a solitary sort of man. His first marriage failed and he married again, a woman who got out of his life but not out of his system. Now he is here to bemoan the fact that his faithful secretary has left him after twenty years to marry an Australian. Believe me, Ginny, I've had a surfeit lately of faithless wives and secretaries.'

I laughed. 'What are you trying to do, Dr Steiner?'

'I want you to meet him and see how you get on. I think you will like him. In spite of his fame I find him a very honest and unpretentious man. There is a refreshing innocence about him, an innocence you wouldn't expect from the way his books are written.'

'Do you have a room for me here at the clinic?'

'Yes, I've had a room prepared for you. You'll be very comfortable and it probably won't be for very long.' He chortled a little. 'We dine at eight. You know the way through the gardens. Wear a pretty gown, it will cheer you up.'

It seemed strange to be dining as a guest in the villa that had been my home for several years, but Dr Steiner made me welcome and I immediately took to his friend. Steven Newton was a large man with a shock of auburn hair and a shy, gentle smile. His eyes were the bluest I had ever seen and they looked into mine with a degree of understanding I found rather disconcerting.

Over our meal, expertly cooked and served by Dr Steiner's housekeeper, we spoke of generalities. I could tell that the two men were old friends by the easy camaraderie that existed between them, and I was relieved that for a few hours at least I could forget my own problems in listening to their banter.

It was when we were sitting in front of the roaring fire with our coffee that Dr Steiner said, 'I've told Steven why you're here, Ginny. Shall we allow him to tell us if he thinks you can help each other?'

I heard all about Milly who had been his secretary for a great many years and who had deserted him to get married.

'Plain as a pikestaff,' he complained, 'I thought no fella on earth'd ever take her off my hands, but then along came that Aussie and bingo.'

'You haven't replaced her?' I asked.

'No, I've just soldiered on, hoping for the best. Now no woman in her right senses would be willing to pick up the pieces.'

'Remember what a predicament I was in when you first came here, Ginny? And you sorted me out so beautifully,' Dr Steiner said encouragingly.

'I'm warning you, Mrs Grantham, and if you decline I'll understand. It's my bet you've had enough of lost causes.'

'You're a very successful lost cause, Mr Newton.'

'So I was, when Milly was there to sort me out. I'm a quarter way through my next novel but it should have been finished by now. I can work at it all right, but no agency would touch it in this rough state. Steiner says you have a house in Positano — do you feel like going back there?'

I looked at Dr Steiner and he said, 'Alistair won't want to be anywhere near Melissa if she decides to occupy the villa there. I can write to Alistair to explain why you're living there.'

'I suppose I could live in Positano and give Mr Newton's offer a try,' I said.

A broad smile illuminated his face. 'That's great! You won't see a lot of me. I write most of the night and sleep during the day, I get my best inspiration at night. I'll give you a key so you can just come in and work whenever you wish. I have a house-boy who will make coffee and cook you lunch. Do you have a car? It's a few miles from Positano to Amalfi.'

'I'll get a car, just a small one. When will you want me to start?'

'I'm going back to Amalfi in the morning. Why not come with me. I can show you where I live and how to get there, drive you to Positano, and after you've settled in you can start with me any time you like.'

216

'I'll need a few days.'

'Well, of course. I'm warning you, you'll be horrified at the chaos. I'll never be out of your debt if you can sort me out.'

'I'll do my best, I can't say fairer than that.'

As we drove south towards Naples, I sat silent beside Steven Newton. I was grateful that I didn't have to return to England with another failure to report. I was determined to put the old life behind me, Alistair and Melissa, Riccardo and Natalia. Now I was being given another chance and I would take it hopefully. A new beginning, where there would be no trace of anything that had gone before. Or so I thought.

The first posters we saw on the walls of Naples told us that Melissa Francesca was to sing there just before Christmas, and my heart sank dismally. Surely that would mean that she would be nearby with her new husband? Worse, Riccardo too would be in Naples to conduct the orchestra.

Suddenly I felt the weight of Steven's hand covering mine. 'Don't worry, Ginny, you needn't be involved. That part of your life is over.'

# Chapter Twenty-Five

I looked around me at the villa in Positano, wishing it felt more like home. A thin film of dust covered the furniture and the pale silk curtains hung limply at the windows across the closed shutters. As I pulled them back, I choked with the dust that came off them, and the windows behind the shutters were marked with a greasy film so that the view of the hillside and the sea below seemed distorted and obscure.

I had four days before I started work in Amalfi — four days to purchase a small car, clean the villa and shop for food. The villa felt cold and I set about looking for electric fires to warm the rooms, delighted when I found a jar of coffee in the kitchen and a tin of milk. Even a cup of coffee was better than nothing. I began removing dustsheets and gradually my spirits lifted. For the first time in years I felt that I had come home to something that could be mine.

I slept that first night on the couch in the living room because it was the warmest room in the house. After an early cup of coffee the next morning, I went into the town to look for a car. I found one at a small garage, a white Fiat they serviced and polished before bringing it to the villa, and although it was three years old the mileage was low.

I made arrangements for the telephone line to be restored and I shopped for food and other household things I needed. Then I wandered down to the sea, passing Melissa's villa on the way. The wrought-iron gates were locked and there were shutters at all the windows. The gardens were well tended, however, and I stood for a few minutes looking up the long drive, wondering if this was where she would stay when she came to sing in Naples within the next few days.

Two women strolled up the road laughing and chattering together, both of them armed with large baskets filled with household linen. When they saw me near the villa, they paused and stared at me curiously. I smiled briefly and hurried down the road, but when I turned I saw that they had opened the gates and were walking towards the house.

I did not want Melissa living so close to me. I did not want to meet her on the road or in the little town, and I did not want to hear her voice echoing plaintively among the pines.

Steven Newton had been right about the chaos I would face when I went to work for him. It was far worse than anything I had faced at the clinic, but it was immeasurably more interesting and I set to with a firm will.

I saw little of my employer, but I quickly became involved with the characters in the novel he was writing, and began to see the genius that had made him so successful.

My father was thrilled and delighted that I was working for Steven Newton, because for years he had read everything Steven had written. Over the phone, he told me that my parents were going to stay at Edith's for Christmas. She was expecting another baby in the new year and her toddler needed a lot of attention. Rodney was engaged to a girl in Ottawa and they were thinking of getting married at Easter. Mother pressed me to go with them to the wedding but I said I was unable to make any plans. She went straight to the point.

'Are you sure living in Positano is a good idea, Ginny? Isn't that where Melissa and Alistair will be living?'

So, as briefly as a telephone call would allow, I told her about the end to Alistair's relationship, Melissa's new husband and the fact that Alistair had returned to England.

I knew that my news would be hashed over in England during the days that followed. Among our friends and acquaintances there would be much shaking of heads and tutting that I should have been more sensible.

In the days leading up to Christmas, I attempted to make the villa more festive. Holly and mistletoe didn't feature in the shops in Positano but there were baubles of all colours. I bought an exquisite table decoration for myself and another for Steven. When he saw it, he chortled, 'You're ramming Christmas down my throat. Do you subscribe to all that nonsense?'

'I certainly do,' I retorted. 'I was brought up to subscribe to it. Do you mean that you don't?'

'On Christmas Day I shall retire to bed with a large bottle of whisky and not surface until it's all over and done with. What will you do?'

It had been my intention to invite him to a meal. Now I decided against it. 'I'm not sure. Speak to my family on the telephone, eat Christmas dinner, think about all those happy times I remember in England.'

'And then what?' he demanded.

'That might be enough.'

He grinned down at me, his expression kind. 'You deserve a few days' holiday. Why don't you go away somewhere? I'll see you in the new year, and there'll be another unholy mess for you to sort out when you get back.'

The next time I drove past Melissa's villa, two cars stood on the drive outside and lights streamed out into the darkness. I had almost reached the curve in the road when behind me I heard the screaming of tyres and a large car roared past me so that I had to swerve on to the pavement to avoid it. In that short, terrifying moment I saw that the driver was a man, a man with a brow as dark as thunder, apparently pursued by some deep, punishing anger that made him oblivious of danger to himself or anybody else.

I recognised the man as Antonio Brindisi. I had seen his pictures often enough over the last few months.

In the days that followed, I saw that car often, Melissa's also, and at times I could hear her voice as she rehearsed for the performances in Naples. Whenever I passed her villa there were people standing round the gates simply listening, and I drove on or walked quickly past.

I saw Antonio Brindisi just once in the little town. I was buying a poinsettia at the florists and he came in to order a spray of orchids.

'Are you wishing to take them with you, Signor Brindisi?' the assistant asked him. I stood back while another girl wrapped my plant.

'No, I wish them to be delivered to my wife before she leaves for Naples. I am not going to the theatre this evening.'

'Very well, signor.'

He stood at the counter while she selected a large spray of orchids, holding them out for his inspection. With a brief nod, he said, 'I suppose they'll do. I'm not sure what she'll be wearing.' He extracted a handful of notes from his wallet and put them on the counter. 'There should be enough there to cover the cost of the flowers and the delivery. Keep the change — it's Christmas.'

Turning to leave the shop, he caught my plant, almost sending it to the floor. Catching it adroitly, he handed it to me with a smile. The smile deepened as I took it from him, showing the interest of a bold man for a woman he hadn't seen before, a woman who was not Italian, a woman he might enjoy flirting with. I thanked him and left the shop. He walked behind me and I was disconcerted when he caught up with me at the corner.

'That's quite a showy plant for a nice English girl to be buying,' he said with a disarming smile.

When I stared at him, he threw back his head and laughed. 'Your Italian is very good, signora, but not quite good enough. It doesn't disguise your English accent. My wife is English, so I should know.'

I smiled. 'I like poinsettias, signor. We always had them at home around Christmastime.'

'And where was home?'

'The north of England.'

'Really? The north of England is where my wife comes from. Maybe you've met her, Melissa Francesca.'

'All the world knows of Melissa Francesca, Signor Brindisi.'

'You know who I am?'

'You're almost as famous as your wife, signor, but for entirely different reasons.'

He threw back his head again and laughed delightedly. 'Well, we can't escape the media, can we? I try my best but they're as tenacious as a pack of foxhounds. Do you live here, signora?'

'For the time being.'

'Holiday?'

'No, I work here, in Amalfi.'

221

'Really? Now I wonder what you work at in Amalfi?'

I smiled. 'Good afternoon, Signor Brindisi. I wish you a very happy Christmas.'

His audacity had cheered me strangely. I could understand why Alistair had stood little chance against his charm and his boldness. Still, couldn't Melissa have seen that charm wasn't enough? Had she been unable to measure it against Alistair's more enduring values?

Would Brindisi tell Melissa that he had met an English-woman in the town? I doubted it. By this time he would have forgotten my existence.

Christmas bells pealed out from every campanile for miles. Ahead of me stretched the loneliest Christmas Eve I could remember.

The poinsettia had not liked its position on the small table under the window and had drooped its leaves to show me so. I had removed it to another room and was missing its cheer-fulness. I had meant to cook a festive meal but I wasn't hungry, and when there was a ring on the door bell I leaped towards it joyfully, believing that it was Steven who had come to take pity on my solitude. I opened the door with a smile on my face, which quickly froze when I found myself staring into Riccardo Mellini's grey eyes.

He was carrying a Christmas tree and several boxes, and placed them in my arms, saying he was returning to the car for more. He came back with an assortment of parcels and when I stared at them stupidly, he smiled. 'They're filled with baubles to decorate the tree. If you'll tell me where to put it, I'll help you.'

'Really, Signor Mellini, this is so kind of you, I don't know what to say.'

'I remember you once called me Riccardo.'

'I'm sorry.' My heart beat so that I could hardly speak.

He started to set up the tree and for the next half-hour we decorated it, laughing when some bauble refused to hang in place, but not speaking of the things that concerned us. I watched while he hung on the lights, arranging them to his satisfaction. He plugged the lights in and the tree burst into gleaming beauty.

222

'I don't know how to thank you,' I stammered uncertainly. 'It's kind of you to come. I suppose you're conducting in Naples — isn't there a performance this evening?'

'No, not tonight.'

'Are you staying here in Positano for Christmas?'

'No, I'm driving back to Naples this evening. It is wrong of me, I should be with my wife for Christmas, but she wanted to go with her grandmother to some friends of the Contessa's.'

'How is Natalia?'

He was standing near the fireplace, looking down into the flames.

'Did she ever ask about me?' I asked curiously.

'No. I waited for her to do so and, when she didn't, I told her she had behaved unkindly to someone who had tried to be her friend. She said nothing at all.'

'If no one's expecting you, I could make dinner if you like. There's plenty of food in the kitchen.'

'Were you going to dine alone?'

'Well, yes.'

'I would invite you out to dinner but it will be difficult at such short notice to find somewhere.'

'Then you'll let me cook dinner for us?'

'Thank you, Ginny, I shall like that.'

I was glad that I'd bought plenty of food even when I had thought I was being foolish. I enjoyed cooking for two people again, and even more I enjoyed making the table look festive with crimson napkins and candles.

He ate with evident enjoyment, and I discovered a Riccardo Mellini I hadn't thought existed behind the austere face he showed to the world. He talked of his travels overseas and the famous orchestras that made up his life. I was content to listen to the charm of his voice and the story of a life filled with glamour, but a glamour shadowed by the unhappiness of his private life.

I did not want to love him. I told myself that Alistair's rejection had made me too vulnerable, and that I only thought I loved Riccardo because he was famous and, more than that, because he was lonely.

After our meal we sat comfortably with coffee and brandy. There was an aura of peace and tranquility in the room.

223

Relaxed, Riccardo seemed much younger and he smiled more. It was my turn to talk about my work with Steven Newton, and the more I talked, the more enthusiastic I became.

'So you're really happy in what you do?' he asked finally.

'Yes, very happy. I seldom see him, but he leaves me plenty to do and I enjoy the challenge.'

'Have you any friends in the town?'

'None that I have met since I came back. I suppose Velma will be back in the summer. Melissa's here, but as you can imagine, we give each other a wide berth.'

'I haven't seen her since her marriage, but we shall meet again in Venice. I'm conducting there in January. I've met Brindisi several times.'

'I met him in the town, and once he almost crashed into me when he was driving away from the villa. He looked so angry, I thought they must have quarrelled.'

He smiled. 'Two volatile, highly-strung people obsessed with their own importance. Many people say this is a marriage made in hell.'

'Perhaps they are right.'

Rising to his feet, he said, 'I have to go, Ginny, not because I want to but because I must. Thank you for tonight, it has been one of my very best Christmas Eves.'

'Thank you for coming, and for bringing the tree. It's made the house look so festive.'

'Gracious, I almost forgot,' he said ruefully and, putting his hand in his pocket, he produced a small parcel, festively wrapped. I opened it with surprised delight while he stood looking down at me. Inside the wrapping paper was a velvet box which contained a gold filigree brooch in the shape of a bow. It was beautiful, and I looked up at him with shining eyes because the gift had been so expensive and because I loved it.

'I'm glad you like it, Ginny. It's merely to say thank you for what you tried to do for Natalia, and to compensate in some small way for what happened on that dreadful evening. Here, let me pin it on for you.'

I stood while he pinned it on my dress, his hands light against my breast. He looked long and deeply into my eyes while I stood with a racing heart, my eyes searching his face. Then he smiled and, holding me gently, said, 'Merry Christmas, Ginny!'

He bent his head and brushed my lips with his. I clung to him, so he drew me into his embrace and our lips locked in a kiss that seemed to take every vestige of life away from me.

In that moment I knew that if no man ever kissed me again it wouldn't matter. This was the kiss I would remember all my life. But he put me away from him, and after a long, hard look he was walking away from me along the path to where he had left his car.

He did not look back, though I waited at the door until I could hear the sound of the car's engine disappearing into the night.

# Chapter Twenty-Six

In the days that followed I was stern with myself, determined that I would not read more into that kiss than he intended. Now I had to get on with my life, do a good job for Steven Newton and try to keep my feet on the ground.

I avoided the brightly illuminated villa on the hillside where Melissa held court night after night. I did not meet her husband again in the town, but the woman who came to look after my villa kept me fully informed about her visitors.

'Some of them Mafia, I'll beta,' she said laughing.

'How do you know that, Maria?' I enquired.

'He wella knowna, thees Brindisi. They fight alla the time, my sister tella me and she works ata the villa.'

'I don't suppose it means anything if they quarrel.'

'He hita her. She wear dresses to cover bruises, upa ere and over armsa.'

I felt sorry for Melissa and hoped it was not true.

Several days later, when I was struggling to open the front door with a large bundle of manuscript pages in my arms, I felt the parcel taken from me. Turning round in surprise, I saw Melissa.

She was smiling in the friendliest fashion, as if we had met only yesterday and with no hard words between us. She followed me into the villa and stood looking round with some interest.

'Would you like coffee?' I asked her.

'I'd love it. This looks very nice and festive. Bit small, though, isn't it?'

'It's big enough for me.'

'Isn't it the one Alistair bought? I thought he'd sold it.'

'Fortunately not. I'm working in Amalfi.'

'Working?'

'Yes, for Steven Newton, the American author.'

'Really? I invited him to one of my parties but he didn't come.'

'He doesn't like socialising, he's rather a solitary man.'

'How old is he?'

'In his fifties, I think.'

'Is there a love affair?'

'Not with me.'

'It's time you set your stall out, Ginny, life is fleeting.'

'I'm very happy with my life — how about you?'

'Happy enough.'

I poured the coffee and handed her cup to her across the table where she had elected to sit, and for the first time I really looked at her. She was as beautiful as I remembered her, but behind her beauty was a restlessness, instead of that disturbing calm that had been part of the old Melissa. Make-up had not disguised the shadows under her eyes.

Meeting my gaze, she turned away quickly and said, 'Do you hear from your family?'

'Yes, my parents are well, my sister is expecting another baby and my brother is getting married to a Canadian girl.'

'How nice. Will you be going to the wedding?'

'I don't think so. Do you ever hear anything about your grandmother?'

'She's in a home for the elderly. I pay the bills but I never go there.' She was unconcerned. Melissa was not one to look back.

'Are you happy in your marriage, Melissa?'

'We fight like cat and dog. He likes his own way and he's been accustomed all his life to getting it. I make a lot of money and if it's given me nothing else, it's given me independence. Naturally we quarrel, but we're two of a kind, we deserve each other.'

'It doesn't sound a very secure basis for the rest of your life.'

'Perhaps not, but I live each day as it comes.'

'But you love him, don't you?'

'Yes, but we're too much alike, with towering egos and violent tempers. I'm afraid he could kill me.'

I stared at her, amazed that she could have married a man she was afraid of.

Sensing what I was thinking, she said with a little laugh, 'I've only just learned about his temper. One has to live with someone to be aware of their eccentricities. He fell in love with my fame, my music, and now he wants me to give it up.'

'But why?'

'Because he's jealous of the attention I get, the men who flatter me, even the men who sing with me. I won't give my music up for anybody and he has no right to ask it.'

I wondered why she had come. There was a uncomfortable silence.

'Did you hate me very much, Ginny?'

'I think I hated Alistair more at first. I didn't know what to think about somebody who had pretended to be my friend without even liking me very much.'

'I did like you, Ginny, but I resented you. It wasn't true when I said I'd never been your friend. I just wanted you to feel it had been easy to betray you. I never had a friend until I met you, I didn't know how to treat a friend or what a friend could expect from me. When I said I'd never been your friend it made me feel less guilty. Now I'd like us to be friends again. After all, why not? Alistair is out of our lives, and when I'm here it would be nice to think that we could meet. I'll invite you to my parties and you could meet somebody really devastating to fall in love with. Say you'll come, Ginny!'

'Oh, Melissa, I don't really want to come to your parties. I won't know anybody and I'd be unescorted. But we can be friends again.'

'You could ask Steven Newton to bring you.'

'He wouldn't want to come and we don't have that sort of relationship.'

'Well, I'll invite you anyway,' she said gaily. 'Now I must go. I'm glad we're friends again, and I'll send you tickets to my performances. Please yourself whether you come to them or not.'

'You'll be leaving for Venice very soon, I hear. Will your husband be going with you?'

She shrugged her shoulders, then with a small smile said, 'This concert will be the highlight of the operatic year, in the palazzo of Princess Gabriella Setrovisi on the Grand Canal. Oh yes, I think for one night Antonio will forget how much he hates my music in order to mingle with the bluest blood in Europe.'

'Who else is singing in Venice?'

'Everybody who is anybody in opera, and Riccardo Mellini will be conducting the orchestra. Why don't you go?'

'I have work to do.'

'I shall send you an invitation, and one to Steven Newton. Maybe you'll both come.'

She gave me a last smile, then walked quickly down the path towards her car. With an airy wave, she was away.

The invitation came a few days later. I put it in a drawer and thought no more about it. I had no wish to go to Venice even if it had been possible.

When I arrived in Amalfi the following morning, I found Steven staring morosely at the sea, greeting me only absent-mindedly. After a while he drifted away and I saw him walking broodingly in the gardens.

His notes were in a bigger muddle than usual, and I was having difficulty in sorting them out. Words were jumbled, whole pages were crossed out, some crumpled as though he had discarded them and then thought better of it. I had not heard him return to the terrace when he said, 'I can see you're having trouble with that lot, I'm not surprised. I'm reaching the end but I can't find an end, I seem to be going around in circles. What sort of Christmas did you have?'

I was becoming accustomed to his rapid changes of subject, but before I could answer, he said, 'That book started so well, one of my best, I thought. But it's losing impact, going nowhere.'

'Perhaps you should leave it alone for a few days, then come back to it?'

'My dear girl, I left it alone all over Christmas. I ate and drank and walked in the hills, waiting for an idea that never came. I even wrote a few letters. I can't understand why people send me Christmas cards year after year. Oh, and there's this. Reply to it, will you? Make some excuse. I suppose I should be gracious, the woman might even buy my books.'

It was Melissa's invitation to Venice. I took the beautifully printed card and he said, 'I hate opera and I hate functions like that. I'd have to dress up. Tell her I'm honoured but it isn't convenient.'

'Most people would give a lot to be invited to this,' I pointed out.

'Would you?'

'I've been invited, but I intend to decline.'

'Why have you been invited? Oh yes, I forgot. Isn't Melissa Francesca the woman who waltzed off with your husband? She's got a bit of a nerve, hasn't she?'

'I suppose she has. Most people would think so.'

'What excuse are you going to give?'

'That I have work to do here, that I can't possibly visit Venice at this time. I've already said as much when she visited me.'

He stared at me, then he started to pace about the garden, a frown on his face, and I thought that was the end of the matter.

It was almost time for me to leave when he came back to the terrace and grinned at me cheerfully.

'We're going to Venice, Ginny. You can do what you like about the concert. I'm not going for that, I'm going to finish my book.'

'In Venice?' I echoed stupidly.

'In Venice. I know now where the book's going. Have you ever been to Venice?'

'No, never.'

'Forget the Grand Canal and the other tourist sights. Behind them are dark, winding passages edging deep, stinking canals, sinister tunnels and alleyways that have been dragged out of your most terrifying nightmares. In places like that I can find the ending to my book, weird, haunting places that tourists never see.'

'You want me to come with you?' I said incredulously.

'Certainly I want you to come with me. You shall dress up in your prettiest dress and go to that damned concert. I know a small hotel we can stay in where I don't have to dress up for dinner and where the staff will leave me alone to get on with my book, but near enough to civilisation for you to get to know Venice. Decline my invitation, accept yours.'

I wanted to go, I wanted to see Venice, to hear Melissa and see Riccardo, but I knew I was a fool.

Venice enchanted me from the first moment when I stood on the balcony looking out over the Grand Canal, surely the most romantic thoroughfare in the world. I discovered the glory of St Mark's and walked entranced along the row of shops that edged the square. I laughed in delight as children clapped their hand to watch the pigeons soar heavenwards above the towering campanile.

In the sunlight I ventured along the narrow alleyways that led off the square and I understood what Steven meant when he spoke of dark deeds that might be committed in those meandering passageways and on the bridges that spanned the narrow canals.

As the day of the concert grew near, I regretted that I hadn't had the courage to decline the invitation. I was not looking forward to going alone, but when I said as much to Steven he only laughed, saying, 'My second wife would have revelled in it. She never tired of celebrity functions and was furious when I wouldn't go to them. If Gloria's in Italy, she could well be at tonight's affair.'

I was wearing a gown Alistair had always admired, a confection in rose-pink chiffon, and over it a black velvet cloak that had been a birthday present from him. It was only a very short distance from our modest hotel to the Princess's opulent palazzo and, although Steven wanted to order a gondola, I decided to walk along the path that edged the Grand Canal.

It was dusk, and Venetians hurrying home from their daily toil looked at me curiously, a woman obviously dressed for some pretentious occasion. Groups of people stood looking out to where a steady stream of gondolas were arriving at the steps below the ornamented façade of the palace. I caught my breath sharply as a gondola passed conveying two women, both of them gowned in black, with dark lace covering their hair, one of them like a beautiful porcelain statue, the other proudly aristocratic. Natalia and her grandmother.

I knew at that moment that I could not go to the concert. I could not meet Natalia's accusing eyes across that crowded room, I could not look at Riccardo without the memory of that one passionate kiss and also the memory of that terrifying afternoon when I had fled from the villa in Rapallo.

The man standing at the reception desk in the hotel stared at me curiously when I re-entered, but I ran swiftly up the stairs to my room, my hands fumbling in my purse for my key, suddenly aware of the sobs in my throat.

# Chapter Twenty-Seven

I sat on my balcony until it started to rain. People were running for cover, and water was dripping from the canopy on to my arm.

I went back into the room, and then to my surprise I heard a knock on my door. Hurriedly I went to open it, and Steven stood there looking concerned.

I stepped back so that he could enter. 'What happened to you? The last time I saw you, you were leaving the hotel dressed like a princess, and now here you are like Cinderella. What happened at that wretched function, and why have you been crying? Was it Melissa?'

'I didn't go,' I murmured miserably.

'Why not? There was nothing to be afraid of.'

'I didn't want to go on my own.'

'Oh, come on, Ginny, it's more than that. Who upset you?'

'It was seeing some of the guests, I didn't want to meet them.'

'Who, for heaven's sake?'

'Natalia Mellini and her grandmother.'

'Was it them you couldn't face, or Natalia Mellini's husband?'

'All of them, I couldn't face any of them.'

There was silence except for the rain beating down on the top of the balcony and the sighing of the wind that had arisen. He put his arms around me and his voice was kind. 'You're in love with him, Ginny. Maybe that poor woman in her derangement saw it and you did not.'

'But she couldn't have, I gave her no cause. I was her friend, I never showed it, never for a moment. How did you know I was here?'

'Your room key was gone from the front desk. I was afraid you were unwell. It isn't like you to run away.'

'There was something so sinister about that black gondola with those two black-clad women sitting inside it — something about the dark canal and the thunder echoing above it.'

He smiled. 'Didn't I tell you that this beautiful city could suddenly become one of your weirdest nightmares? Isn't that why we're here?'

'How soon can we leave Venice?'

'Two days, only two days more and my book is finished.'

Two days! Two days to walk in the sunlight with the crowds, two days to absorb the culture and the beauty of Venice without having to think about the shadows behind the sunlit squares and those sinister figures in dark gondolas.

As if sensing my thoughts, Steven said lightly, 'Forget them, Ginny. Most of the people who were there tonight will be sunning themselves at the Lido and hashing over old scandals and new flirtations.'

Steven was right, of course. I had been foolish to stay away. I had done nothing wrong, nothing except fall in love with a man who had probably by this time forgotten my existence.

I would enjoy what was left of our time in Venice and show Steven Newton that I was not the silly, distressed girl he thought me to be.

So I strolled across the Rialto and gazed in the shop windows, I wandered through the Doge's Palace while light filtered through the windows, but I did not linger long in the darkness of the cathedral.

Steven had told me that this was the best time to see Venice, when the tourists were few and the city was crowded with real Venetians intent on enjoying their city. There was little warmth in the January sun when it emerged flirtatiously on my last afternoon. I drank coffee sitting at a table inside Florian's in St Mark's Square, and all around me there was laughter and the lilting sound of Italian voices. Returning to the arcades, I stood looking in a window furnished with crystal chandeliers and an assortment of Venetian glassware when a man's voice said incredulously, 'Ginny!'

I turned and looked up into Riccardo's smiling face.

'I saw you leaving Florian's, so I followed you. What are you doing in Venice?'

I explained briefly.

He placed his hand under my elbow, saying, 'It's cold out here. Let's return to Florian's and have a glass of wine.'

I was aware that people were looking at us as we took our places at one of the small tables, but then Riccardo's face was well known wherever he went. Oblivious of the attention he was attracting, he asked, 'And how do you like Venice?'

'I love it, even in January.'

'Are you staying here or over at one of the hotels on the Lido?'

'Oh, here. Steven hates the Lido, he says it'll be crowded with people who want to be seen, and there's a distinct possibility that his wife may be among them.'

Riccardo laughed. 'I'm here to conduct my orchestra. You've probably seen the posters.'

'And the concert at the Princess Setrovisi's palazzo.'

'Yes — how did you know about that?'

'We had invitations to attend.'

What had possessed me to tell him that? Coolly he said, 'I didn't see you there, Ginny; why didn't you come?'

'Steven wanted to finish his book. He doesn't like functions like that, so we decided against it.'

'You didn't feel like coming on your own?'

'No.'

'Who invited you to the concert?'

'Melissa, she came to see me.'

He raised his eyebrows in surprise. 'Is she handing out the olive branch?'

'I think so.'

I was anxious to leave the question of why I had not gone to the concert, but he was not to be put off.

'If you're friends again, why not attend her concerts? Or are you not prepared to meet her halfway?'

It was a question I couldn't answer. Instead I looked around me at the square, lashed by a sudden shower of rain.

Riccardo said gently, 'At all times Venice is enchanting, even in a rainstorm. When are you returning to Positano?'

'Tomorrow morning.'

'Then it's no use inviting you to come to the opera.'

'I'm afraid not.'

The silence that followed troubled me. I wanted to ask him about his wife but the words would not come, and he was staring out at the crowds hurrying for shelter, twirling the stem of his wineglass absent-mindedly. Nervously I picked up my handbag from the chair next to me, saying 'I should get back. I have some packing to do before dinner and I've been out all day. Steven will wonder what has become of me.'

'Where are you staying?'

'At a small hotel near the Rialto Bridge, the Della Flora.'

'I know it. Will you have dinner with me tonight? Signor Newton too, if he is free. I know a small place which boasts excellent food and wine and which even he will not find too pretentious.'

I should have been strong enough to say no, but instead I found myself saying I would ask Steven.

Riccardo said with a smile, 'I'll call for you at eight. There is no opera this evening, perhaps my only free evening before we leave Venice.'

He walked with me to the landing stage and put me on the vaporetto, saying, 'Until this evening, Ginny.'

When I informed Steven of the encounter, I was aware of the amusement in his eyes, and when I extended Riccardo's invitation to dinner he threw back his head and laughed.

'I wouldn't dream of accepting and you'd be angry if I did,' he said.

'I'd like you to come. And won't he think it discourteous if you decline?'

'I'm sure Signor Mellini will think it far more insensitive if I accept. Enjoy yourself. Tonight at least you're the woman in his life.'

'What shall I tell him about you?'

'I'll tell him myself that I'm at the end of my novel, that I've almost cracked it and can't be dragged away from it. I'll be at my most convincing, rely on me.'

When I reached the foyer at eight o'clock that evening, I found Steven already in conversation with Riccardo. They both smiled, and Steven said easily, 'I've just been apologising for being such a killjoy, but you know how I'm placed. This book really is important, the publishers are screaming at me, and now that it's getting there I should get on with it. Enjoy yourselves. You look very beautiful, my girl.'

I was wearing my favourite black gown, which flattered my colouring. Alistair had never liked black, saying it was funereal. Now all I could see was the gleam of admiration in Riccardo's eyes as he draped my stole around my shoulders.

He took my arm as we descended the steps to the waiting motor launch. When he took his place besides me in the launch, he said easily, 'You looked surprised, Ginny. Did you expect a gondola?'

'I wasn't sure.'

'Gondolas are for tourists or occasions like the Princess's function, when they are part of the scene.'

Riccardo was a charming and delightful host and the moments fled swiftly as he talked about his work and his travels but not his private life. As we left the restaurant, I could only think how impersonal it had all been. Steven Newton would never have felt *de trop* in our company.

As we stepped down into the launch, Riccardo said, 'There's a full moon tonight.'

He gave instructions to the man at the wheel and we glided down the Grand Canal towards its mouth. White and mysterious, the moon shed veils of thin cloud before sailing alone into a clear, starlit sky. From the lagoon, we could look back at a fairy-tale city with floodlit campanile and churches. Ahead of us, islands appeared, and a cruise ship lit from stem to stern towered over us while dance music came softly from its ballroom. It was enchantment I had never known, rapture I could never forget, and as I lay back in my seat I felt his arm around my shoulders and there was no yesterday, no tomorrow, only tonight.

But all too soon we were speeding back, with the city shimmering before us, and once more we were sailing up the Grand Canal. At the landing stage for St Mark's Square, the launch stopped and Riccardo held out his hand to help me ashore.

There were lovers strolling across the moonlit square and nobody stared at Riccardo. We were just a man and a woman drinking in the sight in companionable silence, savouring a last

237

moment together before the short journey to the Rialto and the end of an enchanted evening.

'We shall meet again, Ginny,' he said in the foyer with a little smile. 'I hope it is sooner rather than later.'

He raised my hand to his lips. I knew my eyes shone with delight and in his eyes too there was the gleam of something I dare not analyse. Then he left me and I heard his footsteps running down the steps towards the launch. I had wanted him to hold me in his arms and kiss me, but somehow his words had meant more than a kiss.

We left Venice the next morning, taking the vaporetto to where Steven had left the car outside the city limits. I was glad the vaporetto was crowded so that we had little chance of conversation. When we were in the car, Steven said, 'You were silent over breakfast. Did your evening with Riccardo Mellini give you too much to think about?'

'You would have enjoyed it, Steven. We went out across the lagoon and saw the city by moonlight, we strolled in St Mark's Square and we ate a wonderful meal.'

'And?'

'And what?'

'Are you still in love with him? Is he in love with you? I ought to write a romantic novel, I'm getting enough research — what do you say?'

'I'd stick to thrillers if I were you.'

'So, nothing happened?'

'What did you expect to happen?'

'An avowal of everlasting love, perhaps, a suggestion that one day there would be no wife with a penchant for vengeance hovering in the background.'

I winced.

'Bad as that, is it?' Steven said softly.

'Yes, and I don't want to talk about it now or ever,' I replied.

'Right, we won't talk about it. Now do you want to hear about my book?'

'Is it finished?'

'It is, and ready for you to put it into shape.'

'And you're pleased with it?'

'Yes. It was inspirational to suggest going to Venice. I've

given the reader a gruelling chase along those dingy canals and dark, dank alleyways in search of the most gruesome find at the end of it. I don't think my readers will be disappointed.'

# Chapter Twenty-Eight

One morning several weeks later I was sitting on the balcony in Amalfi surrounded by piles of work when I saw a woman walking slowly up the path from the gate. She was dressed in holiday fashion, gaily patterned trousers and a bright sweater, with a silk scarf tying back her hair. She paused when she reached the veranda, pushed up her sunglasses and said sharply, 'Who are you?'

'I'm Virginia Grantham, who are you?' I replied, faintly antagonised by her attitude.

'Do you live here?'

'No, I work here.'

'Work for whom?'

'I work for Mr Newton. Who shall I tell him is calling?'

'I'll tell him myself, you needn't bother.'

Without another word she swept past me and into the villa, and I heard her calling loudly, 'Steven, are you around? It's Gloria.'

Gloria! The second Mrs Steven Newton. I shrank inwardly, knowing he would be upset. He had talked about his wives to me over the past months, mostly after he'd drunk a bottle of wine and was feeling aggrieved. Now I could hear their voices from inside the villa, his sarcastic and faintly truculent, hers strident and filled with recriminations.

Gathering my papers together, I decided to work at home for the next few days.

When I returned to Amalfi, my heart sank at the sight of Gloria lying stretched out on a sun lounger on the balcony where I usually worked. As I opened the wicker gate, she lifted up her head and stared at me. Ignoring her, I made to enter the villa.

'Where do you think you're going?' she called out to me belligerently.

'I have to see Steven, I'm having difficulty with his notes.'

'Well, he won't want to see you, he's on a drunken spree. God knows how long it will last.'

When I turned to her uncertainly, she took her sunglasses off and her hard, penetrating eyes looked directly into mine.

'How long have you been living with my husband?' she snarled.

'I'm not living with your husband, Mrs Newton. Not now, not ever.'

'I don't believe you.'

'Then I suggest you ask him when he's sufficiently sober.'

'I already have and got no good answer.'

'You mean no answer you care to believe in. I'm sorry, Mrs Newton, I work as his secretary, nothing more. If he is unwilling to attest to my words, he can have my resignation this morning.'

I found Steven slumped in a large chair with his eyes closed, snoring loudly. An empty whisky bottle lay on the floor. I would get no sense out of him, so, picking up a notebook lying on his desk, I wrote out my resignation, tore out the page and fed it into his typewriter. Leaving my briefcase with his notes inside it on his desk, I stalked out of his room and out of the villa.

Gloria was lying where I had left her, and as I passed her chair without speaking, she said acidly, 'That didn't take long. I take it it's over?'

'Your husband is asleep, I didn't speak to him. I won't trouble you again.'

I ran down the steps to my waiting car and drove quickly away.

I was angry, but when I had calmed down and was nearing Positano, I reflected grimly that this was the end of another chapter. Where did I go from here?

I walked down to the tiny harbour where fishermen worked at their nets and boats bobbed about on the gleaming surf. The beach was deserted and for a long time I sat on an upturned boat looking out at the sea. In the distance a speedboat was hurling itself at the shore and for one awful moment I thought it would crash on the beach, but suddenly its engines died and it came to rest in shallow water. A man lowered himself into the sea and came wading ashore. I did not recognise him as he walked towards me because the sun was behind him and his face was in shadow. It was only when he stood looking down at me with a whimsical smile that I recognised Antonio Brindisi.

'Well, well,' he said, 'the lady in the flower shop, the English lady.'

I smiled.

'What are you doing here, alone and palely loitering?' he asked.

'You know English poetry,' I said in some surprise.

'Some. It was a line that came to my mind. How are you on poetry?'

'I like it.'

'You look very lonely sitting here on your own, deep in thought, not very happy thoughts. Who are you?'

'Virginia Grantham.'

His eyes widened, then he laughed. 'So you're Ginny! The poor girl who surrendered her husband to my mercurial wife. Do you regret it, Ginny?'

'Not any more.'

'You mean you don't want to take a silken scarf and twist it round her beautiful throat until there is no life left in her?'

I smiled but didn't answer him.

'But you're here to tantalise and frustrate her, should you meet in this very small place?'

'No, I'm here because I have a villa here, because I had a job here. Melissa and I have already met, and I can assure you, Signor Brindisi, it was a very civilised meeting.'

'But then you English like to be civilised. I'm Sicilian, you know, and we Sicilians are not so accommodating.'

'So I have heard.'

'My car is at the top of the path, signora. Will you allow me to drive you home?'

'My car too, Signor Brindisi, but thank you all the same.'

He waited, expecting me to join him on the climb up the path, and there seemed nothing else to do. The path was steep so

242

there was little call for conversation, but when we reached the summit he smiled down at me and, lifting my hand, brushed it briefly with his lips before walking to his car.

This time I was determined to return to England. I was busy packing when I heard Maria calling to me from the bottom of the stairs.

'Signora, there ees a mana to see you.'

My heart beat faster. Could it be Riccardo? But it was only Steven, his eyes a little bleary.

'What do you mean by this?' He waved my resignation in front of my eyes.

'It's what it says,' I answered steadily.

'But why, for heaven's sake?'

'When your wife accused me of living with you, I thought it was time to call it a day.'

'Why the hell didn't you speak to me?'

'I wanted to but you had passed out.'

'You can't resign. I need you, I want you back.'

'I can't come back. I don't want to meet your wife again.'

'You won't have to, she's gone.'

'But she keeps coming back, doesn't she? I doubt if you'll ever be rid of her.'

'This time she's gone back to America after a blazing row. Her uncle in Detroit is dying, and Gloria's gone to stake her claim along with all the other vultures in her family.'

'I've already booked my ticket.'

'Go home for a few days, just to see your folks, then please come back.' His voice had become wheedling. 'Take a week off, two weeks, but please come back.'

'I've given most of my holiday clothes to Maria and I'm already packed.' But in my innermost heart I didn't want to go home, at least not to stay.

'I'll give you an advance on your salary, and a raise,' he said, taking out his chequebook with a sudden flourish. In spite of my misgivings, I laughed with relief. I was not going home with another failure on my hands; this time I was going home on holiday and with work to come back to.

My parents and Cloonie stood on the platform waiting for me, shivering in the freezing wind, wrapped up warmly in heavy clothing. Then with a whoop of joy my brother Rodney came tearing down the platform, lifting me off my feet and whirling me in his arms.

'Let me look at you,' he said at last. 'You're still the same chubby kid I remember.'

'I am not chubby,' I said indignantly, whereupon they all laughed.

A young woman stepped forward with Mother, a smile on her pretty face, and with a proprietary air Rodney introduced her as Linda, his wife.

Nothing had changed, not the tiny shops or the cobbled square, not the grey stone church with its square Norman tower or the ancient yew tree in the churchyard. There was still the homely smell of baking bread from the bakery halfway down the hill and the swinging sign outside the village pub.

When I offered to help to clear away the dishes after Cloonie's excellent meal, everybody insisted they wanted my news first, the dishes could wait. We talked long into the night, but I did not tell them everything. I glossed over the time I had spent with Natalia and made no mention of Riccardo Mellini. But I told them about Melissa and her new husband.

Mother said angrily, 'How dare she call to see you after what she did to you?'

'Somehow it didn't seem to matter,' I replied.

Father was quick to say, 'Rodney saw Alistair in London.'

'Where?'

'In the Strand. If it had been anywhere less public, I'd have wrung his neck,' my brother said belligerently.

'Did you speak to him?'

'For a few minutes. He's back in medicine, at Guy's in London. He didn't elaborate and I didn't ask him much about it. I was as glad to leave him as he was to leave me.'

'Apparently Melissa is thicker-skinned than either you or Alistair,' Father said cynically.

'She's everybody's idol in Italy,' I said with a little smile. 'You have to admit there's nobody quite like her.'

'Oh, we admit that all right,' Rodney said.

In the days that followed, I rediscovered the haunts of my childhood. The sweeping fells and the dark mist on the mountain peaks, the narrow country lanes leading to stone homesteads, and stone walls dividing fields where Lakeland sheep sheltered from the driving sleet. Waterfalls cascaded down the mountain slopes to swell the rushing rivers, and the lakes reflected the grey skies as they dreamed under a coating of ice.

I knew that in a few months spring would bring the azaleas and rhododendrons in their showy pageantry. The birds of winter would be flying back to their homes in Iceland and Finland, but for now they filled the air with their mournful mewling. Wearing stout boots and warm clothing, I took endless walks along the margin of the lake.

Rodney and his wife decided they would travel south to stay with my sister and her family before returning to Canada. Mother said sadly, 'We shall be so lonely when you've all gone away. Can't you stay on a little longer, Ginny?'

'Not this time. You have no idea what will be waiting for me when I get back. Steven is hopelessly disorganised, he'll be counting the days.'

'How old is this Steven?' Father enquired. 'I've been looking at his photographs on the covers of his books and he never seems to look any older. He must be a lot older than you, Ginny.'

I laughed. 'Yes, he is, and if you think there's anything romantic between us, forget it. I like him, he's very kind and I enjoy the work, but he has a wife who descends upon him periodically and I'm not even remotely interested in him as a man.'

'He's a very successful man,' Father persisted.

'I know, that's why I feel very fortunate to be working for him.'

'Are you really happy without a man in your life, love?' Mother asked plaintively. 'You're still young and pretty, surely there must be somebody?'

'No, Mother.'

'Because of Alistair?'

'Oh no, Alistair belongs to the past. I recovered from Alistair a long time ago. I'm glad he's gone back to medicine, it's what he knows best. Maybe one day he'll open another clinic and make it the real thing this time.'

During the rest of my stay I was asked no further questions about Alistair and I was glad that they were respecting my privacy in the matter.

I remonstrated with them on the morning I left because I was handed a parcel filled with country butter and cheese as well as Cloonie's scones and fruitcakes. Father laughed, saying, 'Pass some of them over to Steven Newton. I take it he enjoys a good meal.'

'Well, yes, but he has a servant who is a very good cook.'

'But not in the sort of things Cloonie does so well,' Father persisted.

So I duly expressed my gratitude and found myself coping with my suitcase plus the large carton of food.

'I'll be charged excess baggage,' I said ruefully, whereupon Father produced a fifty-pound note which he tucked into my pocket, saying, 'This'll cover it, love, and anything else you need to buy at the airport.'

I remonstrated with him but it was no use. Mother and Cloonie were in tears and as I waved to them from the window of the train, I felt once more the desolation of saying goodbye.

# Chapter Twenty-Nine

There was a note waiting for me when I returned to the villa, saying simply, 'Welcome home, Ginny! Hurry back, I'm desperate. Steven.' There was also an invitation to hear Melissa sing in Milan and another for a private concert in aid of charity in Naples.

My daily woman informed me that a lady had called to see me and would come again when I returned home.

'Signora Brindisi?' I enquired.

'Ah, no, signora. The signora I 'ave seena, thees lady I nota knowa.'

I was aware of the vague fear that it might be Natalia who was not allowing me to escape her vengeance, even now when I was out of their lives; then I told myself that I was being paranoid.

I was busy packing a small box with scones, butter, cheese and cake the following morning when there was a ring on the door bell. Still a little fearful, I went to open the door. Velma stood on the doorstep, still the same Velma with her ornamental sunglasses, colourful trousers and outrageous hat.

Smiling at me cheerfully, she said, 'Your maid told me you'd gone home. I was hoping you'd be back before I had to return to Como for Easter.'

I invited her in and she eyed the box of food curiously. 'For your maid?' she asked.

'No, this is for Steven. Maria has taken her share.'

'Steven?'

'Steven Newton, I work for him.'

Her eyes opened wide. 'Steven Newton, the author?'

'Why, yes. I wrote to you, Velma, to thank you for your kindness in Rapallo and to tell you what was happening to me. Do you know Steven?'

'Does anybody? I've written to him so many times, inviting him to my charity functions, concerts and other things, but he's never once accepted my invitations. Finally I gave him up as a bad job. He is a bit of a hermit, isn't he?'

'Not really, but he works hard and he doesn't like dressing up. He's really very nice, I like working for him.'

'I didn't get your letter, honey, it must have arrived after we left for the States. I went home to see my sister and I stayed longer than I'd intended. We haven't been back to Rapallo, we're thinking of selling the villa there.'

'Oh, I'm sorry. It was beautiful.'

'I know, but we've got this one and the one near Como. How was England?'

'Cold at this time of year, but it was lovely seeing my family again.'

'You know that Melissa's here, I suppose?'

'Yes, they come and go. It depends where she's singing.'

'Have you seen her?'

'She came to see me.'

'Really? Are you friends again?'

'As much as one can be friends with someone who is hardly ever available and too involved with other things. I also met her husband.'

'That won't last, you know. Everybody's talking about them — their public rows, his philandering and her jealousy. There'll be another scandal, or worse.'

'What could be worse?'

'With Brindisi's track record, anything, my dear. Have you heard from Riccardo Mellini at all? I suppose you'll have heard that the grandmother died?'

'No! When was that?'

'About ten days ago. She was getting on in years. I don't know how it will affect Riccardo. The old lady was always there to bolster up Natalia, and now he's on his own.'

I found myself thinking about those two dark-clad figures sitting in the gondola on their way to the palazzo, one face old and lined as if it had been carved out of yellowing ivory, and the

248

other young and beautiful, etched against the darkness like an exquisite cameo.

I was suddenly aware of the silence and that Velma was looking at me curiously. 'I wouldn't be too concerned about Natalia Mellini, Ginny. She's a very rich woman and Riccardo does his best for her. I'm only surprised he hasn't cut and run years ago.'

'He probably loves her.'

'Love was never meant to withstand everything, honey.'

I made coffee and we sat in the conservatory chatting. Velma did most of the talking — about the people she knew, the functions in store, the social scene I was not a part of.

'Doesn't Melissa think of inviting you?' she asked finally.

'Yes, she has, but I haven't a lot of spare time. Steven keeps me pretty busy.'

'Well, I shall invite you to my next party here and I'll invite Steven Newton just once more. Do try to encourage him to come.'

'I'm making no promises, Velma. He wouldn't even go to the concert in Venice.'

Her eyes opened wide, and immediately I thought, Why on earth had I been stupid enough to mention Venice? But she merely said, 'My husband wouldn't go to Venice either. He says it makes his arthritis worse, all that water.'

She rose to go. 'I'll invite you round for coffee, Ginny, and I'll invite Melissa at the same time.'

When I told Steven of her visit the next morning, he grinned, saying, 'You won't get me to her bun fight. Thank God I don't have to rely on that crowd to sell my books.'

'She does a lot for charity, though.'

'I'll send her a cheque.'

The first invitation came several weeks later and I put it deliberately on the top of his correspondence, but he pushed it impatiently aside.

'Aren't you even going to answer it?'

'You decline for me.'

'I think I might go, I'm not as ungracious as you are.'

'You were ungracious in Venice.'

'I know.'

'The Mellinis are probably attending this one. Doesn't that scare you as much as the Venetian episode?'

'I haven't thought about it. Maybe they won't be there; the Contessa died recently.'

'I read about that. That shouldn't stop them. Life has to go on and he has a duty to his admirers.'

'What about your admirers?'

'I've done my share of sitting in bookshops signing copies of my novels, but they were for real people. I don't suppose Velma Forenzo's clique have even read my books.'

'You don't know that.'

'I can hazard a guess.'

I decided I'd done enough running away, and I would go to Velma's party with or without Steven.

On the day of the party I worked through my lunch hour and asked Steven if I could leave early. He looked up at me with a sly smile. 'What's happening tonight?'

'I'm going to a charity function, the one you were invited to.'

'Oh, that one. Well, have a good time. What time are you thinking of going?'

'Around nine thirty, I think. There's supper and somebody will entertain us, probably Melissa, I'm not sure.'

'Come half past ten and you'll have had enough,' he predicted.

Maria admired my gown, the rose-pink chiffon I hadn't worn for some time, and she asked if she could stay to dress my hair. When I seemed surprised, she smiled, saying, 'I worka for hairdresser once, before I marry, ina Napoli.'

She seemed to derive pleasure from shampooing my hair and setting it most expertly. I was inordinately pleased with the finished result, as was she.

Draping a wrap around my shoulders, I let myself out of the villa. As I reached my car, lights were flashing and somebody was hailing me from another car coming slowly along the road. The headlights were blinding me, but as it drew level, the driver lowered his window and Steven's voice said, 'Get in the car, Ginny. I'm glad you hadn't already left.'

As I took the seat beside him, I saw that he was wearing a

white tuxedo and looked remarkably presentable. 'You mean you're going after all?'

'I thought I should. You were very displeased with me for being such an unsociable animal. I've had to get this jacket out of mothballs, I'll bet you can smell them from there.'

'I think you look very nice.'

'Thank you, my dear. The effort was for you, not for the people we'll meet there. I'm here as your knight in shining armour, in case that harpy comes after you with a stiletto. Of course she won't — at this affair there'll be a hundred and one women she could hate.'

'You mean he could have been in love with them all?'

'I mean his wife could think he's been in love with them all. She may not even be there, but if she is, we'll stay well away from her.'

I was silent for the rest of the short journey.

After he had parked the car, he said gently, 'You're not worrying about anything, I hope?'

'No.'

'Good girl. Just walk in there with your head held up high and very proud because you've accomplished the impossible; you've persuaded Steven Newton, much against his better judgement, to be your escort.'

Velma greeted us effusively, taking immediate charge of Steven so that she could walk proudly with him around the room. I stood beside her husband, making polite conversation and looking round the room at the glittering guests. Steven appeared to be in high good humour and I felt I could relax.

'Ginny, how did you manage it?' Velma said when she returned, having left Steven to a group of admirers.

'I don't really know. He arrived at my villa this evening after saying he wouldn't come.'

'Well, he's here, and the evening looks set to make a lot of money. Melissa is singing and a young, up-and-coming mezzo. By the way, Riccardo Mellini is conducting the orchestra tonight. It's his swan song.'

'What do you mean?'

'He's giving up music for a year to stay with Natalia. Rumour has it that it was a condition the old lady made before she died. She left all her wealth to Natalia. If he finds he can do without his profession, half her fortune will go to him; if not, nothing at all.'

'Does he really need her fortune?'

'I wouldn't think so, but the burden of Natalia is very real and his sole responsibility. Ah, here they are.'

I stepped back quickly into the shadows as Riccardo and Natalia entered the room. She was wearing black for her grandmother, but black did not become her. With her blue-black hair, dark eyes and apricot-tinted skin, Natalia looked her best in strong jewel colours; emerald, sapphire and rich oranges and reds. The sombreness of her beautifully cut black gown took away her sparkle. Her face was unusually pale, and she did not enter into conversation with the people who greeted her and Riccardo.

'What a contrast from that night at my house in Rapallo!' Velma said. 'Which is the real Natalia, do you suppose?'

'You know, I have no idea. Perhaps I never found her, although there were times when I had hopes.'

'He'll be unutterably miserable without his music. How can that cold, fey woman hope to take its place?'

'Fey? What a strange word to use. I always thought that "fey" meant fated.'

'Don't you think it describes her exactly? But fated for what, I'm not sure.'

'Neither am I.' Fated to die, fated to destroy herself or someone else? I asked myself, but I did not speak the words aloud.

A voice close to my ear said, 'So we meet again, English lady. And how beautiful you look this evening!'

I turned to see the smiling face of Antonio Brindisi. The groups of women standing nearby were looking at him provocatively, but he devoted his attention to me, although doubtless relishing their interest.

'I'm surprised to see you here. Did Melissa invite you?'

'No, Contessa Forenzo invited me.'

'Of course. And who is your escort for the evening?'

'I came with Steven Newton.'

'And he is being ungallant, surrounding himself with his fans, I fear.'

'I don't mind in the least. I hope those fans buy his books.'

He laughed. 'Well, allow me to be your escort until he has the grace to return to your side. I'll get you a drink and you shall tell me how much you're looking forward to hearing my wife sing.'

'Very much,' I answered as he guided me across the room and into a smaller room serving as a bar. Handing me a glass of champagne, he raised his glass, his dark eyes filled with impudent laughter.

'Can you tell me what Melissa is singing tonight?'

'I have no idea, though I've heard her warbling most of the week.'

'You're not a very encouraging husband, Signor Brindisi.'

'I'm not, am I? Please call me Antonio.'

He was amusing, but underneath his audacity there was something ruthless. His eyes smiled but with a chill, his mouth showed white, perfect teeth but I was sure it was capable of issuing stinging words.

I was becoming paranoid again, thinking all sorts of ridiculous things about a man I hardly knew and who was putting himself out to be both entertaining and charming.

With a flourish he filled up my glass again. At that moment Steven came back to me, saying ruefully, 'Sorry about that, Ginny. They really have read my novels, they know more about them than I do. I tend to forget about them all except the one I'm writing.'

'Do you know Signor Antonio Brindisi?' I asked him.

'Only by reputation,' Steven answered with a half-smile and I noticed that they did not shake hands.

'I must confess, Signor Newton, that I have not read your novels. I like to make my own incidents rather than read about them. Why do you choose to write in Italy rather than in America?'

'I like Italy, and there would be too many distractions in America.'

'And do you enjoy the opera?'

'It's a long time since I went to the opera — a terrible admission in the land of opera.'

'Of course. I'm Sicilian, I should love opera, but one can have a surfeit of it. With me it has reached saturation.'

253

'Then you were not entirely sensible in marrying Italy's leading diva, were you?'

Antonio smiled. 'I agree, Signor Newton. You have all the perception I would expect an author of your standing to have.'

With another smile and a nod of his head he left us, and Steven said, 'Thank God for that! I don't like the Antonio Brindisis of this world, and that man's reputation is badly tarnished. Perhaps we should find a place in the room next door.'

Velma came bustling towards us, saying, 'I've kept you two chairs over there, Ginny, far enough away from you-know-who. I don't expect she even knows you're here.'

'I take it she means Signora Mellini?' Steven whispered.

'Yes. Over there.'

'I saw the lady come in with her husband. I've seen her at the clinic when I've been visiting Steiner. Don't let her presence spoil your evening.'

'I'll try not to.'

'What exactly is it you don't like about Antonio Brindisi?' I couldn't refrain from asking him.

'I flatter myself that I'm pretty good at assessing a man's worth, I only wish I was as good with women.' He grinned at me and when I smiled back, he said, 'You have to admit it, Ginny, my track record isn't good. Think about Gloria.'

'I doubt if I can forget her,' I answered dryly.

The singers came in together, taking their place on a platform in front of the small orchestra. A young tenor from the opera house in Naples was greeted with applause, and there was a baritone I had heard before, who was very well established. The young mezzo looked nervous. She was small and pretty, wearing a dark-red gown that was far too old for her. Beside her, Melissa looked confident and glowing in white chiffon, which enhanced the dark gleam of her hair and her fine eyes. There was long welcoming applause from the audience, which grew as Riccardo came forward to take his place on the rostrum.

I was totally unprepared for the power and richness of Lisa Gabrodini's voice. It seemed impossible that a voice of that calibre should emerge from that tiny, demure figure. Her voice was capable of capturing all the fire and power of roles written for the mezzo voice — Amneris, Carmen and Delilah — and with maturity I was sure she would sing those roles to perfection.

She acknowledged the applause with a shy humility which endeared her to her audience. Steven nudged me and I followed his gaze to where Antonio Brindisi stood applauding conspicuously. But when Melissa began to sing, he yawned in ostensible boredom.

'See what I mean?' Steven whispered.

This display of malice made me realise that Melissa's marriage really was in trouble.

After a short interval, Riccardo gave a solo performance on the piano. He played Chopin, exquisite melodies that were tragic with melancholy or exuberant with joy, and tears rolled down my face at the thought of what he was giving up for Natalia. What sort of love did it take for him to make this sacrifice, and what sort of love demanded it?

At last it was over and he was surrounded by a crowd of men and women anxious to talk to him. I was glad that Steven and I would be able to leave without either Riccardo or his wife seeing me. But I was unprepared for the rush of people who came to speak to Steven. As I waited for him near the door, Riccardo looked straight across the room and into my eyes.

To my consternation, he excused himself from the group around him and came across the room to stand looking gravely down at me. 'I didn't know you were here, Ginny. Have you enjoyed the evening?'

'Yes, thank you, very much.'

'Are you alone?'

'No, Steven Newton escorted me. I'm just waiting for him.'

'How are you, Ginny?'

'Very well, thank you, and you?'

'Well. We are returning to Rapallo tomorrow.'

'And your next concert?' I had to ask it, I needed to hear it from his own lips.

'Very uncertain, I'm afraid.'

He knew that I knew, it was in my eyes, and I read the misery in his.

Across the room, Natalia was watching us with a penetrating

look and I shivered, drawing my wrap closer around my shoulders.

Riccardo said gently, 'She'll never hurt you again, believe me. Goodbye, Ginny.'

He raised my hand to his lips and lightly brushed it with a kiss; then he walked back to his wife. Steven returned to my side, walking with me out of the room and across the terrace to his car.

'That was painful for you,' he said softly.

I nodded, unable to trust my voice.

'Did he say anything about his plans for the future?'

'No, our conversation was brief, there wasn't time.'

'Fans are very fickle and musicians come and go. If he stays out of the limelight long enough, he'll be forgotten.'

'Not Riccardo Mellini! He's a giant among musicians,' I retorted.

Steven squeezed my arm, saying, 'There speaks a woman in love. Time to move on, I think.'

He was right. There was no future for Riccardo and me. He had never told me he loved me. We had only shared a few fleeting moments of tenderness.

# Chapter Thirty

Summer came to the Bay of Solerno. Boats bobbed on the blue sea, holidaymakers opened their villas on the hillside, and Neapolitan melodies filled the air from the cafés and bistros in the towns. The ferries that plied between Capri and Ischia were filled with happy people in leisure clothing.

'You haven't asked for any holidays, Ginny. Are you so content working for me?' Steven surprised me by asking.

'You grumble when I take time off for shopping! Are you telling me I can take a holiday?'

'Don't you want to go home? The English lakes will be at their best at this time.'

'And their busiest. I prefer them when they're quieter.'

'So you're really not all that bothered?'

'Why are you so persistent, I wonder?'

'I have to go home to the States for a few weeks. I need to see my agent and possibly my publisher, but more than that, I've got to have things out with Gloira, as I'm sure you can understand.'

'In that case I'll be happy to take a holiday. How long do you expect to be away?'

'Not long. I'll let you know when I'm expected back. What will you do?'

'Discover Capri and the rest of these little towns, see Sorrento, Pompeii and Herculaneum, climb up Vesuvius. I've been meaning to visit these places for years.'

'Then you most certainly should.'

Steven departed for America three days later, and I drove into Sorrento the next morning. The sea rolled in beneath the towering cliffs and across the expanse of water Capri emerged shyly out of the morning mist. It was very early and the first ferry of the day was not crowded.

I could understand why the Emperor Tiberius had elected to leave Rome to spend the rest of his life in the villa he had built here on the island. Embittered by family tragedies and weary of the intrigues and treachery of the court, he must have seen Capri as a haven of peace. There was mystery in the shaded alleyways, romance in the sunlit squares, and everywhere there were flowers, trailing from ornate balconies or cascading down pine-clad hillsides.

I sailed back to Sorrento, enraptured with my day and the promise of other days equally wonderful to follow.

Two days later I stood with others looking down into the deep, dark crater of Vesuvius. A thin trail of smoke sailed upwards in the sunlit morning and all around us was the odour of sulphur. I shuddered a little. Perhaps the volcano had looked exactly like this to the people of Pompeii and Herculaneum as they went about their business, unaware that before evening the sleeping giant would awake and two cities would die under a shower of flaming lava.

Pompeii never rose from its ruins, but thanks to excavations carried out over the years, visitors were able to imagine the town as it had once been and perhaps weep a little at its tragedy. All the next day I wandered around its ruined forum and deserted villas and temples. In my imagination I could visualise the crowded theatres where spectators watched musical performances and recitals. I stood looking down into the arena of the amphitheatre, where the citizens of Pompeii had cheered the games enacted there.

It was very hot and before leaving, I sat at a table outside a wayside bistro, waiting for a line of tourist coaches to get out of the way. I was seated in the shade under the awning, sipping wine and looking at passers-by.

There was something familiar in the figure of a man stopping at the café opposite. He was tall and walked with an arrogant grace, his linen jacket draped carelessly around his shoulders. He was wearing sunglasses and carried a camera. His companion was small and slender, her dark hair held back by a brightly coloured silk scarf. I saw her looking up at her escort with a bright smile and evident infatuation.

She too was wearing large sunglasses, but when they sat at the table she took them off and her face tantalised me. Somewhere I had seen it before. The man had gone inside the café, but when he came out with a waiter I recognised him immediately; Antonio Brindisi.

He was all smiles and gallantry with his companion and I could hear their laughter. Once, when he looked across the road, I leaned back into the shadows and then changed my seat so that he couldn't see my face.

Suddenly he rose and picked up his camera. Stepping out into the centre of the road, he beckoned his companion out into the sunlight, calling, 'Take off your glasses, Lisa.' Laughing, she complied with his request and suddenly I knew her — Lisa Gabrodini, the mezzo-soprano.

I felt suddenly incensed on Melissa's behalf. All the way back to Positano I could not get them out of my mind. I had covertly observed them until they left, but Melissa would not learn from me that I had seen them standing together at his car, wrapped in an embrace.

A month passed without word from Steven. Then one evening the telephone rang and it was he, speaking from Steiner's clinic.

'I'm on my way home, but I flew into Milan and decided to spend a few days with the doc. Is everything all right?'

'Everything.'

'Good. I'll see you in a couple of days.'

That was typical of Steven. A couple of days could mean just that or over a week.

He came back three days later, calling at my villa before driving home. Slouched in an easy chair, he talked about old friends he'd met in America and the assured success of his latest novel. Then he went on to tell me that Gloria was basking in the money her late uncle had left her and congratulated himself that for the time being she would leave him alone.

'How is Dr Steiner?' I managed to ask at last.

'Very well. He asked about you, Ginny. The old man is really quite fond of you.'

The conversation flagged and he smiled wickedly. 'I know

259

you're dying to ask if Signora Mellini was at the clinic — she was not. She stayed there for several weeks after her grandmother died, but now that Riccardo has retired from public life, they're together somewhere.'

I refrained from commenting, and after a few minutes he said, 'Don't you want to know what Steiner thinks about Mellini's sacrifice?'

'I can't think Dr Steiner is in favour of it.'

'No, he's not. He says there can only be one ending — one of them will crack — and I agree with him.'

'You do?'

'I only wonder which one.'

'Natalia is already unstable.'

'That is so, but now she has accomplished what she set out to do. Can he go on day after day, year after year, pretending that she is all he needs, that his music is unimportant? And if she senses his frustration, what then? The situation is sizzling with possibilities. I could write a book about it.'

The following day I went into the florist's shop in the village. As I was paying for the bunch of flowers, a voice behind me said, 'We're destined to meet in flower shops, English lady. But why carnations when the lilies are more unusual?'

Antonio Brindisi was standing behind me, looking at my purchases with a slightly superior smile. I smiled and said good morning. As I reached the door, he said, 'Can I drive you anywhere?'

'No, thank you, I have my car outside.'

'How do you spend your time day after day in Positano? Is there enough to do here?'

'Positano is a very good centre for seeing this part of Italy,' I answered.

'Well, of course, and where have you been?'

'Capri, Sorrento, Naples, Pompeii.'

'The first three are seething with tourists and Pompeii reminds me too strongly of my mortality.'

'So you think you should stay away because you are afraid of its message?'

'I only go there on very rare occasions, when I want to remind myself that suddenly, out of a blue sky, fire and brimstone can rain on me, removing what is left of a summer's day.'

'Perhaps we should be willing to learn such lessons, signor.'

'And perhaps not. Life is for living, signora, and eternity lasts a long, long time.'

He was smiling down at me provocatively. 'If you are intent on visiting Pompeii, perhaps you would allow me to be your guide. We are by way of being family, are we not? You and Alistair, me and Melissa.'

He was holding the door so that I couldn't close it, and I was aware that behind him the shop assistant was looking faintly embarrassed.

'I'm sure you would much prefer to escort some other lady you do not regard as family,' I said with a small smile. 'Good morning, Signor Brindisi.'

His laughter followed me out of the shop, but his audacity had annoyed me.

The flowers I had bought brightened up Steven's villa. Steven settled down across the table to read the morning newspaper, every now and again treating me to titbits he thought might interest me.

'Riccardo Mellini may well have consigned his career to the past, but the media are not prepared to leave him alone,' he said dryly.

Without raising my head, I said, 'Why is that?'

'In the American press he was shown off St Lucia in his yacht, and here he is skiing in St Moritz. If one gets on a merry-go-round that never stops, it doesn't leave too much time for thinking.'

'Surely they mentioned his wife?'

'Yes, here she is skiing in the mountains, and she was present on the yacht, looking quite beautiful.'

I went on with my work. After a few minutes he said gently, 'I'm talking about photographs, Ginny. They don't say anything about how people feel. You know despair can be covered up by a smile. It's time I did some work.'

He left the newspaper on a coffee table. I waited until he left the room to retrieve the paper. There were two photographs: one of Riccardo about to ski down a slope, wearing dark sunglasses; one of Natalia looking beautiful in ski pants and brightly coloured parka.

Perhaps there was no despair. They were simply two rich,

beautiful people enjoying themselves in one of the world's most expensive playgrounds, and I wished my heart didn't ache with such overpowering anguish.

I typed Steven's book like an automaton. One afternoon he asked curiously, 'What do you think of the new novel, Ginny? Up to standard?'

'Well, yes, I think so.'

'But you're not sure?'

'I haven't taken it in page by page, I'm able to shut myself off.'

'Don't you think if the book were interesting you wouldn't be able to do that?'

'I can type what I see and still think about other things,' I retorted.

'What I am saying is that your thoughts are evidently more interesting than my deathless prose.'

'More personal, perhaps.'

'Personal? Ah.'

'You're being deliberately provocative, Steven. Don't you ever think about something else yourself when you're busy writing?'

'Not at the moment I don't, because I've reached an impasse. I am living my novel, there is nothing else. It wasn't always so. I used to put Gloria in my novels and think up all the terrible ways there were of killing her off.'

I laughed. 'There's nobody I particularly want to kill off at the moment, Steven.'

'Are you sure?'

'Quite sure.'

He didn't believe me, but with a wry smile he threw an envelope across the table with the instruction to read what was inside. It contained a gold-embossed invitation from Velma to a large function in Rome and a hand-written plea to accept it.

'Will you go?' I asked him curiously.

'Of course not. I hate Rome in the summer, it's too crowded. Wild horses won't get me there. There will be an invitation for you, too. She'll hope you can persuade me to go.'

'I have no intention of trying.'

'Well, there'll be nothing for you in Rome. Riccardo Mellini won't be there, and neither will Melissa Francesca.'

'Melissa won't be there?'

'Apparently not. It's in the paper: she's taking a month's rest after Verona. It doesn't say where, but maybe she's coming here. You might pick up your old friendship, Ginny.'

'I can't think she'll spend her time in Positano, they'll be off to more exotic places.'

'They?'

'Melissa and her husband.'

'Antonio Brindisi is not the man to keep on angling for the fish he has caught, not when the ocean is filled with others equally fascinating. She'll need a shoulder to cry on, and who better than the friend who listened to the insecurities of her childhood?'

# Chapter Thirty-One

Melissa's villa remained in darkness. By the beginning of December it had turned bitterly cold. I resigned myself to spending Christmas alone, thinking regretfully that this year there would be no Riccardo appearing unannounced on my doorstep.

I was glad of the welcoming warmth of the villa after the cold, grey day outside, and the hazardous drive on icy roads from Amalfi in the late afternoon. Maria had laid a fire ready for a match to be applied to it, and as I prepared a meal I could hear the logs crackling in the grate. As soon as I had eaten, I settled with a book in a comfortable chair.

The book failed to hold my attention and I dozed off, to be roused suddenly by a pounding on the door. Startled, I went first to the window to see if I could make out who my caller was. It was dark and I could not see beyond the shrubbery. Nervously I went to the door, calling, 'Who is it?'

'Ginny, for heaven's sake open the door! I'm getting soaked out here.'

It was Melissa's voice.

A silk scarf saturated with rain covered her hair, and as she came inside the villa she took it off, shaking it vigorously so that the moisture fell on the carpet.

'Heavens, what a night!' she exclaimed. 'I saw your light through the window. Do you have anything to drink?'

'What would you like? Gin and tonic, whisky?'

'Gin and tonic would be fine.'

She was holding out her hands to the blaze from the fire, and I said, 'Take your coat off, I'll hang it in here until it dries.'

Under her white trench coat she was wearing a blue Chanel suit. She knelt in front of the fire, fluffing out her hair in an effort to dry it.

'How long will you be staying at the villa?' I asked her.

'Until I get the urge to leave.'

'How about the opera?'

She shrugged her shoulders. 'I need a rest. Besides, there are plenty of others waiting to step into my shoes, particularly that little bitch Lisa Gabrodini.'

'Lisa Gabrodini is a mezzo, she can hardly step into your shoes.'

'Into my sheets, then.'

When I didn't speak, she jumped to her feet and started to pace about the room. I was aware of her anger in every agitated step. Stopping in front of me, she said spitefully, 'She's busy providing Antonio with all the comforts he apparently doesn't get from me. Everybody's talking about it and I'm getting rather tired of pretending I don't care. That's why I came away.'

'But it isn't serious, surely?'

'Oh no, it isn't serious. He's doing it to punish me, though the ninny no doubt thinks he's in love with her.'

'Is it him you're angry with, or is it her?'

'I helped her. She was like me in some ways. A girl from a poor family, she had nothing in the world except her voice and I felt sorry for her. She talked about an aristocratic grandmother who disowned her mother when she fell for a nobody. Remember the stories I told you about my imaginary grandmother? Lisa had no aristocratic grandmother, I took the trouble to find things out about her. Her mother worked in the kitchens in some seedy hotel in Naples. Nobody seems to know who her father was. I came to regard Lisa as my protégée, my clay to mould and fashion just as I was fashioned before her.'

'It seems to me that you're putting the blame on Lisa, yet you say Antonio is simply using her.'

'Well, I've learned to expect nothing better from him, but where is her loyalty to me?'

I sat in silence, incredulous that Melissa had forgotten so soon that she had been capable of the same disloyalty towards me.

'I should have known it'd be like this. Everybody warned me about him. I should have stayed with Alistair — he was nice, he loved me and he would never have been capable of such sadism. Oh, I've made such a mess of things! I could have married Riccardo, if only Natalia had let him go.'

I stared at her in dismay. My innermost heart refused to believe her. I had never thought that Riccardo liked Melissa, but then liking and love were very different emotions.

'There he is,' she was saying, 'tied to a woman who hates his music and wants him solely to herself, and here am I with Antonio hating every note I sing.'

'If he really hates music, why does he torment you with another singer?' I had to ask.

'Because he is cruel. He hurts me with another woman, but another singer gives me more than one reason to be jealous.'

'But you know he isn't serious about her.'

She glared at me across the room. In words that fell like drops of ice she said, 'I think one day he may kill me. He said he would.'

'Melissa! Of course he won't kill you. But if you're so afraid of him, then you should leave him.'

'Leave him!' She laughed incredulously. 'If I left him, he'd come after me. I've threatened to leave him and he says wherever I go he'll find me and he'll kill me.'

'Do you still love him?'

'I love him and I hate him. Can you understand that?'

She went to sit in the chair opposite mine, drinking her gin and tonic, slumped in misery and anger. I saw the strain in her face: the shadows round her eyes, the bitterness etched round her mouth. The fingers of one hand plucked nervously on her skirt. I wished she would go. I had faced my personal tragedies alone.

At last she looked up, and with a visible effort said, 'Sorry, Ginny, I've been a rotten companion. Why didn't you tell me to shut up instead of listening to me all this long time?'

I smiled.

'I needed to talk,' she said. 'It's all been boiling up inside me for so long now. Believe me, I've become a better actress, but the parts for sopranos seldom speak of anger, only of love.'

'When are you returning to the theatre?'

266

'In the new year. Milan and then here in Naples.'

'And Lisa Gabrodini?'

'She's too immature for Delilah and not experienced enough for Amneris. I refuse to have her sing with me, so the maid in *Butterfly* is out. As far as I'm concerned, Lisa Gabrodini is on her own.'

But Lisa would not be on her own. She would have Antonio, who would help her to spite his wife, and she had her talent.

I had to ask, however revealing my question. 'Is the orchestra happy with their new conductor?'

'I suppose so. They've had him on and off over the last few years, particularly when Natalia was well enough to be at home. He isn't Mellini, he has neither his glamour nor his presence.'

'Perhaps in time he will acquire it.'

'I don't think so, it's something you're born with. It won't last, you know, Riccardo's retirement to save his marriage.'

'If he loves her enough — '

'But she never gets enough. And wherever he goes there will be music — how can he bear to hear it and not be a part of it?'

'You understand it so well, Melissa.'

'Of course. This is how I'd feel if Antonio had his way. I'd go with him because I love him, but how long would love last when it was measured against all I had given up for him?'

'So if Antonio threatened to leave you unless you gave up your music, you would do as he asked, is that what you are saying?'

'I've thought about it. For now we fight about it and he uses Lisa to put pressure on me. One of these days I may have to make a choice, otherwise something infinitely more terrible could happen.'

I lay awake for hours that night thinking over all Melissa had said, and when at last I drifted off to sleep, dreams came to trouble my slumber — dreams of raw passions and betrayal, where Melissa and her husband were inextricably linked with Riccardo Mellini and Natalia.

Steven said, 'What ails you, Ginny? You've been miles away all morning.'

'I didn't sleep very well.'

267

'Nothing worrying you, is there?'

'No, not really.'

He fixed me with a piercing stare. 'I know you better than that Ginny, and it's my guess it's one of two things, Riccardo Mellini or Melissa Francesca.'

'I'm not worried about Riccardo, he's decided how he wants to live his life and he has nothing to do with me.'

'It's the other one then.'

I felt compelled to tell him of Melissa's visit and I expected ridicule, instead I faced his anger that Melissa should place her torment at my door.

'She was no friend to you Ginny, she stole your husband and when that didn't work out she ditched him for somebody else. Now that isn't working out and she has the nerve to trouble you with it, and to expect you to understand. She has other people she can talk to, heaven knows Melissa Francesca is the darling of thousands.'

'That doesn't mean that they are people she can talk to about intimate things. I doubt if Melissa has any real friends, only fans and acquaintances.'

'Well one of them has got to give; she's the one with a lucrative profession which drew him to her in the first place. He's probably the one who has to give.'

'Natalia didn't give,' I said softly.

'No, he did, and it's early days yet. We have to see if it lasts and if the newspapers are to believed when they say the Mellinis are on their second honeymoon.'

The raw days melted into spring and the villas on the mountainsides were opened up once more to receive their owners from Rome and Milan. Among them was Velma, who drove to see me in her large, white Bentley. She wore a floral linen suit and a large jade-green straw hat. Sunglasses covered half her face, white, shining frames shaped like the wings of a bird. When she flung her hat on a chair I saw that she had altered the colour of her hair from blonde to auburn.

She patted it, inviting my admiration. 'I decided I'd been blonde long enough. Everybody goes blonde at some time or another and I'm a brunette. The roots seemed to show more and more, and anyway, I like auburn hair.'

I smiled.

'You're still blonde, Ginny, aren't you tired of it?'

'It's the colour I was born with.'

She raised her eyebrows. 'Really? I always thought your hairdresser made a good job of keeping it the same colour, with no dark roots.'

'I only go to the hairdresser when it needs styling. I wash it myself and somehow or other it seems to fall into place.'

'Lucky you. Are you still working for Steven Newton? I sent him an invitation to my party. Any hope you can persuade him to come?'

'He hasn't mentioned it and I know he's very anxious to finish the book he's working on. He hates distractions at this stage.'

'I've been so bored in Rome over the winter. Has anything exciting happened in Positano in my absence?'

'Nothing at all.'

'Seen anything of Melissa?'

'She called to see me, but she's been in Milan most of the winter.'

'I know. She's been in Milan and he's been in Rome, with a French model on his arm. It was in the paper so Melissa was bound to see it.'

I didn't speak, and after a few minutes she said acidly, 'Of course it's petty, but with the Windsors out of the country and the Mellinis very much together, there was little else to talk about. You'll be at my party, Ginny? I'll leave you an invitation.'

I watched her depart, a colourful figure, pausing at the gate to wave, squinting in the sunlight through her ridiculous spectacles.

# Chapter Thirty-Two

Steven sat with his head buried in the newspaper when I arrived at his villa the next morning. Normally the paper lay discarded near my typewriter so that I could read it over coffee, but this morning he seemed absent-minded, staring at the printed pages and hardly bothered to say good morning.

'You seem very engrossed,' I said as he rose from his seat to go to his study.

'Mmm,' he mumbled. Taking the newspaper with him, he disappeared inside the house. Around noon, when I went into his study, he was standing looking through the window, his work momentarily forgotten.

'I wondered if you'd finished with the paper, Steven?' I said hesitantly.

He looked at me doubtfully, and I sensed that this was not a normal morning. Something had happened that he was unsure if he should tell me.

'Something's wrong — it's Melissa, isn't it? Something in the paper?'

He nodded, then in a resigned voice said, 'Yes, there's something in the paper, but it has nothing to do with Melissa.'

'Who then? Gloria?'

'No. Here, see for yourself.'

He thrust the newspaper into my hands, and I stared incredulously at the headline. Natalia Mellini was dead. She had driven her car off the Grande Corniche between Nice and Monte Carlo.

Taking the paper from me, Steven said gently, 'Their yacht was anchored in the harbour. Apparently some time during the night Natalia went ashore, took the car from the parking lot and drove at high speed towards Monaco. At a bend in the road she came unstuck — that's a picture of the car in the gully. Natalia was flung out of the car. She was dead.'

'But why?' I asked, stunned.

'There'll be questions asked at the inquest, you can be sure.'

'He'll hate it, it could destroy him.'

'Oh no, Ginny, I rather think Riccardo Mellini is made of stronger stuff. He'll be dignified and stoic.'

For days the gutter press rehashed the story of Riccardo and Natalia. Dr Steiner's clinic was also mentioned. Knowing how much he hated that kind of publicity, and how upset he would be about Natalia's death, I wrote to him, but had no reply.

Steven surprised me by saying, 'I'm going to the inquest. These are the sort of people I write about, rich, larger-than-life people. And this is a real drama, not manufactured.'

'You're going to write about Riccardo?' I cried, horrified.

'Oh, no! But this is a story I have to hear. I'll make myself as inconspicuous as possible, get back here as soon as the inquest is over and tell you all about it so that you don't have to ask someone like Velma.'

Steven left the villa two days before the inquest was to start, and I was surprised how little work he had left me to do. The days seemed to crawl. I sat in a small café drinking coffee on the afternoon of the inquest. It had started to rain, a thin drizzle that came on suddenly when I was walking on the beach, and I had gone there for shelter. The television was turned on, and the people sitting in the café clustered round it. Fashionable people were shown on the steps of the courtroom in Nice, and then a picture of Riccardo walking with his lawyer across the square. My heart lurched painfully at his handsome, remote face as he shrugged his way through the crowds, ignoring the shouts of encouragement that came from many of them.

I could well imagine that courtroom with Riccardo sitting in dignified silence, painfully aware of the room crowded with people who had adored him, women who had yearned for him, men who had envied him.

The inquest was on the radio, on the television, and at home I sat glued to it, impatient with programmes that filled the screen later, trite comedies and sport, but watching them in order not to miss the news and the groups of people discussing the inquest as if they were personally concerned.

Two days later Steven came back.

'I expect you've seen it all on television,' he said.

I could have screamed with frustration. 'Was Dr Steiner there?'

'Yes. He gave evidence about Natalia's mental health. He also made it plain that Riccardo had tried for a great many years to help her. Giving up his music had been his final hope that she would recover.'

'That evidence must have helped him enormously,' I said softly.

'Well, of course, but then there were other things. Didn't he know that Natalia had gone ashore in the early morning? Had she shown any signs that she might take her own life? Was their marriage truly happy? Had they quarrelled? Was there another woman?'

I blushed, though I was sure he had forgotten me.

'I could sense his distaste at the questions,' Steven went on. 'He hadn't known she had left the yacht because they occupied separate rooms.'

'Why was that?'

'She didn't sleep well; it had nothing to do with the state of their marriage. No, she had never shown any signs that she might be suicidal, they hadn't quarrelled, nor was there another woman. He had given up his music and shown no indication that he intended to return to it. Riccardo gave all his answers in a cool, restrained voice, but I could tell he was bitterly distressed at discussing his private life in front of a multitude.'

'Did they ask him anything else?'

'Not in the courtroom, but Steiner told me that the police have questioned him about the money Natalia received from her grandmother, which will now go to him. However, everyone knows he is already a rich man from money he has worked for.'

'But surely the police don't think Riccardo is responsible for what happened to his wife?'

'Probably not, but these questions have to be asked.'

'Surely now he will go back to his music — what do you think?'

'Give him time. In the immediate future I think he'll stay well away from old haunts and acquaintances. He'll return to the limelight when he's had enough of solitude.'

'Yes, I suppose so.'

'And how about you, Ginny? Will you be here with hope in your heart waiting for him to re-enter the land of the living?'

'I never had any hopes in my heart where Riccardo Mellini was concerned. We live in different worlds; the fact that we met at all was a twist of fate. I'm not sure what I'll do — my immediate future is in your hands, Steven.'

'We don't really belong here, do we, Ginny? I realised that when I went back to Maine for those few days — old sights and sounds, familiar faces, old friends. I came here to write because I love Italy and it gave me so much inspiration, but when I looked out at those green hills and the red maples I began to think I'd been a bit of a fool. I could go back to my roots and the inspiration would come.'

'And I could go back to England and the Lakeland fells. Is that what we're going to do?'

'I think so, but not just yet. Let's give ourselves time.'

As I drove back to Positano in the early evening, I saw the logic of Steven's arguments. He would write just as successfully in America and I would build a new life for myself with people I knew and in a country that was my own.

Across the Bay of Solerno, the sun was setting in a great red ball, turning the sea into a mass of crimson and gold. I drove the car into a lay-by on the clifftop and sat back to absorb the view. Suddenly I felt the sting of tears in my eyes. I would leave Italy with great sadness in my heart. In Italy I had experienced my greatest joy and my most acute misery, the awakening of a love that was doomed from the start. And in Steven Newton I had found a friend.

I started the car and finished my journey. Maria had placed a bowl of flowers on a small table and propped up against it was an envelope. My heart lifted when I recognised Dr Steiner's handwriting.

He said his heart had been saddened at the death of Natalia Mellini, but her life had been a waste, and he hoped in the course of time Riccardo would return to the world of music. He was glad that my job with Steven was working out so well, and he ended his letter by saying he would always be glad to hear from me or see me if I decided to visit him.

A few days later I had to break the news to Velma that Steven would not attend her party. She refused to accept it.

'I shall visit him myself. You can't have tried very hard, Ginny. I saw him at the inquest on Natalia Mellini, but he hurried off as soon as it was over. Did he go straight back to Amalfi?'

'Yes, he really didn't want to be away too long.'

'I was surprised to see him there at all. Did he know Natalia or Riccardo?'

'He'd met them at Dr Steiner's clinic, I think.'

'I see. What did he think about the verdict? Accidental death! Everybody thought she'd driven off the cliff deliberately.'

'Apparently she was driving very fast and the road is tortuous. She probably couldn't take the bend.'

'Well, nobody will ever know for sure. But what was she doing out so early in the morning, and alone? Riccardo said he didn't know she'd left the yacht. You know what that means, don't you? They didn't sleep together.'

I stayed silent, resenting her tone and her assumptions.

'Of course we all knew they hadn't really been together for years, but we thought they'd decided to try again. Apparently it hadn't worked.'

'Do you sleep in the same room as your husband, Velma?'

'Heavens, no! Not for years.'

'But you're not contemplating suicide?'

She laughed. 'I see what you're getting at, but we're not like the Mellinis. My husband's an old man with gout and insomnia. I like cream on my face and my hair tied up in rollers. Natalia was beautiful and her husband a dish in anybody's book. Questions have to be asked.'

'No, they don't. If he'd been driving the car, then perhaps somebody might ask questions, but she was alone, driving too fast on a dangerous road, and people should mind their own business.'

'Well, well, Ginny! Riccardo would be cheered to know he has such a champion in you. I wonder what he'll do with the money.'

274

'The money?'

'The money the old lady left to Natalia.'

'You know he doesn't need it.'

'Oh, well, perhaps you're right. There'll be all sorts of offers now — the opera, concerts, anything to tempt him back to his career. I hope he comes back soon — none of the others have the same pulling power as Riccardo.'

'You're thinking about your charities, aren't you?'

'Sure. The first questions people ask are: Is Riccardo conducting? Will Melissa Francesca be singing? I have to fend them off about Riccardo, say I'm not sure, and Melissa's becoming a problem.'

'Why is that?'

'She refuses to sing if Lisa Gabrodini is singing; she won't sing with one tenor because he smells of garlic and another because he upstages her. Really, these prima donnas, the airs they give themselves! Then there's her husband, flirting with everybody in sight. Mark my words, they'll be the next couple to hit the headlines.'

'They already do. I just hope nothing more serious occurs.'

'Oh, well, they fight in public, heaven knows how they behave in private. I might just call in to see Steven Newton in the morning, Ginny. Don't tell him I'm coming, I want to surprise him.'

The dismay on Steven's face the following morning was comical.

'Drat the woman!' he said huffily. 'She'll interrupt my train of thought and she'll badger me into accepting that invitation. I don't want to go and I shall tell her so.'

'Shall I send her in, then?'

'Heavens, no. I'm coming out there, I don't want to be alone with her.'

Steven was courteous, Velma was persuasive. She smiled and teased, chattering on about who had accepted her invitation, telling him that they were all great fans of his and would be devastated if he didn't show up. 'Besides,' she ended, 'Ginny really does need an escort — don't you, dear?'

'I haven't said I can come yet,' I stalled.

'Of course you'll come. You can go home to England any time. I'll leave these two tickets for you and I'll expect you around ten o'clock. I must go now, I have guests for dinner. So nice of you to see me, Steven. I hope I haven't interrupted anything, I know how busy you are.'

She went in a flurry of Je Reviens and with a gay wave of her hand.

Steven looked at me with a wry smile. 'When is this damned party?'

'Oh, it's ages away. You could be in America and I could be in England. I don't think either of us needs to worry about it just yet.'

'I thought it was imminent.'

'It was, but she cancelled so that she could go to Nice, all her guests were going too, so this one's way ahead.'

'A lot can happen before then,' he said reflectively. 'We'll live one day at a time.'

On that warm sunlit morning, neither of us dreamed that long before that party took place, tragedy would once more descend upon the hills of Positano.

# Chapter Thirty-Three

The villas were closing for the winter and people were moving away. Velma called to say she was returning to Rome and didn't expect to be back before the end of February, when her party would take place.

'Go home for Christmas, Ginny,' Steven encouraged me.

'Are you going home too?'

'I'm going to stay with Steiner. I'll take the train to Milan and somebody will meet me. Perhaps you'll come with me?'

'No, I ought to go home. I didn't go last year.'

So in the second week of December I flew out from Naples on a bright, golden morning and arrived in London to grey skies and falling sleet.

The sleet continued on my journey north, and by the time I arrived at the country station in the late evening, the snow was two feet thick and still coming down. I felt chilled to the marrow after a long wait where I changed trains, and the local train had had difficulty in coping with the incline and the snow on the tracks. My chill evaporated in the warmth of my welcome, however, as Father came towards me out of the gloom, enveloping me in his embrace.

It was wonderful to come home to slow country voices and pine logs burning in the grate. The house smelled of Cloonie's cooking — hot soups and sponge puddings, suet dumplings and the preparation of Christmas menus.

Edith and her family were staying with her husband's parents, and Rodney was far away in Canada.

We spent long evenings looking at photographs of Edith's

children, Rodney's wedding pictures, and family photographs that mother kept in well-thumbed albums.

I went with the family to church on Christmas Eve, slipping and sliding in the snow, our breath freezing on the air, our laughter echoing across the country road. Old friends were there, bringing memories of other years and the dreams of my childhood.

After dinner on Christmas Day, Father asked, 'How long are you staying in Italy? Isn't it time you came home for good?'

'Come home,' Mother said. 'Meet a nice English boy and settle down.'

'Perhaps there's a nice Italian boy she's already met,' Father suggested.

'Steven keeps me too busy,' I said lightly.

'Do you see anything of Melissa Francis?' Father asked.

'She's away a lot. She'll be home in February so I'll probably see her then.'

'So you're still friends in spite of everything?'

'What is the point of thinking about the past all the time? Besides, I rather think Melissa needs a friend.'

'Well, what do you say to going to your old school to listen to the Christmas concert? That will bring back old memories if nothing else does.'

'Oh yes, I'd like that. What are they giving this year?'

'Nothing very ambitious — they don't have the talent these days. Carols, songs from some musical or other. Your old teachers will be pleased to see you. They do ask about you, Ginny.'

Nothing seemed to have altered in the school hall as we took our places the following evening. Miss Carter stood in front of the uniformed choir with her conductor's baton and I knew I was in for a journey of nostalgia. There was no soloist, although there were duets and quartets. With young, fresh voices, the girls sang popular melodies that everybody knew and carols I had known all my life.

After the performance, we moved into the dining hall, where a buffet supper had been laid out. As we passed through the entrance hall, I looked up with surprise to see a large photograph of Melissa taking pride of place next to a painting of the school's first headmistress.

278

Seeing me noticing it, Mother said, 'Miss Carter had it copied from a photograph she saw on some poster or other. I believe the art master is hoping to paint a much larger one from it.'

This was Melissa as she had appeared in *Tosca*, her dark hair adorned by a jewelled tiara, with a diamond necklace round her throat. The low-cut bodice of her dark-blue velvet gown ended in a narrow waist, the skirt sweeping to the floor in dramatic folds. She stood on a curving staircase, one small hand holding a fan, the other resting lightly on the balustrade. I remembered her singing Puccini's haunting melodies as though they had been written for her alone.

'I saw her in *Tosca* in Verona,' I told my parents. 'She was magnificent, and the audience wouldn't let her leave the stage. I think this must be the most beautiful photograph taken of her.'

'You'll find others in the dining hall, just look around,' Mother said. 'And many of the children are keeping scrapbooks. Talk to Miss Carter.'

Miss Carter greeted me warmly, and within minutes she was asking about Melissa.

'I've kept a scrapbook about her for years,' she told me. 'It's amazing that a girl who once came to this school should be singing at La Scala in Milan and the Metropolitan in New York as well as Covent Garden. And singing with all those famous tenors and other singers — and with Mellini conducting! I think he's simply wonderful! I saw him conducting once at a concert in Vienna. I was on holiday with my sister and we had to queue for hours to get tickets. It was awfully expensive, we had to draw our horns in after that, I can tell you. Do tell me about Melissa — are you friends?'

'Yes, although I see her very seldom.'

'I was so sorry about your marriage, Virginia, and it didn't last for Melissa either. She's married isn't she? I hope she has better luck with this one.'

Miss Carter showed me other photographs of Melissa and programmes she had somehow managed to obtain. Melissa as Butterfly, Mimi and Aïda, Melissa on the gangway of the *Queen Elizabeth* on her way to New York, and Melissa with Riccardo Mellini in the Roman arena in Verona.

279

'What a great deal you've managed to find out about her,' I said eventually.

'Well, yes, over the years. And I have all her records. If you can find anything relating to her in Italy, will you let me have it, please?'

'I'll do what I can, Miss Carter.'

'Gracious, Virginia, we've spent so much time talking about Melissa, I've never even asked what you're doing. Your father said you were working for a quite famous author, an American?'

'Yes, Steven Newton.'

'I've seen his books in the shops but I haven't read any of them. I'm not into espionage and thrillers, I'm still reading Jane Austen, but I've no doubt Miss Emerson's read them. Talk to her about him.'

The opportunity to talk to Miss Emerson came later in the evening. I saw her fighting her way towards me, armed with a plateful of food. Her round, jolly face was wreathed in smiles, and she was surrounded by dozens of girls who adored her as their sports mistress.

'I've been dying to talk to you, Ginny,' she said as she reached my side. 'I saw you talking to Miss Carter so I knew you wouldn't get away in a hurry. I suppose it's all been Melissa, Saint Melissa?'

I laughed. 'Well, yes; understandable, I think, since she is the music mistress.'

'I know, but the Melissa I remember isn't the one she drools about. She was always a sulky little madam. I had the utmost difficulty in getting her to do anything, and what she did to you was quite despicable — weren't you supposed to be friends?'

'Yes, but it's history now, isn't it?'

'Miss Carter puts it all down to a theatrical temperament, but that's no excuse. I remember her the first day she came here, hadn't got two words for a cat, and quite insolent. It must be terrible for you, living in Italy and perhaps meeting her.'

'It's no problem,' I mumbled.

She carried straight on. 'Your father said you were working for Steven Newton — he's absolutely marvellous, I must have read every novel he's written. What's he really like?'

I laughed. 'Disorganised, but very, very nice. I like him, we're friends.'

'He's working on another book now, is he? When is it coming out?'

'He's about three quarters through it, I think, but I'm not sure when it's being published. Did you read his last one?'

'I did, and the one before that, and all the others.'

'He'll be very gratified when I tell him.'

'I've got a couple in my room — would you mind asking him to autograph one for me?'

'Of course. I'm here for another week, do let me have it before I leave.' I added, 'Perhaps I should get myself a cup of coffee and something to eat before it's all gone.'

'Gracious me, here I am chatting and I expect you're dying for a drink. Let me help you. If some of the plates are empty, there's plenty more food in the kitchen.'

I waited while she went round the table, filling a plate with so much food I was sure I could only eat half of it. By the time she returned, I was chatting to the headmistress, who asked no questions about Melissa.

I left England on a bitterly cold January morning when leaden clouds covered the mountaintops and people sheltered shivering under their umbrellas. The rain followed me to Naples, where the smoke from the slumbering Vesuvius mingled with the drifting clouds and the pavements were wet with rain.

Disgruntled with his lot, the taxi driver hunched over his wheel as we drove south to Positano. I reflected that on a warm summer's day he would be all smiles and geniality, treating me to a passable rendering of a favourite Neapolitan love song.

I had written to Maria to tell her when I expected to arrive home, and the villa felt warm and lived in. There were flowers on the table and a small pile of correspondence, most of it unimportant. A note from Velma indicated that she was bringing the party forward yet again and would I remind Steven in case he'd forgotten. I smiled at this sentence. Steven had deliberately forgotten almost before she'd driven away. There was no word from him, so I imagined he would be expecting me within a day or so.

Maria had left me the morning's paper, which I flicked open

as I set about making coffee. Italy was once more changing its government, and snow had fallen heavily in the skiing regions. There was nothing about Riccardo.

As darkness descended, I looked out of the windows before drawing the curtains. There were few lights on the hillsides, but to my surprise there were lights in many of the windows in Melissa's villa. I wondered whether she or her husband was at home.

# Chapter Thirty-Four

The lights continued to burn in Melissa's villa during the hours of darkness. Several times I saw Antonio's black Ferrari in the lanes around the little town. Once, when I stopped for petrol at a local garage, I saw him arguing with a swarthy man of southern Mediterranean appearance. Their words seemed to be heated, and there was a brooding arrogance in Brindisi's attitude as he got into his car, slamming the door behind him.

The garage proprietor shrugged his shoulders as the other man drove off, spreading his hands. In answer to the interest in my eyes, he said, 'He makes too many enemies, thata one. Dangerous enemies.'

Feigning ignorance, I asked, 'Who are they?'

'Signor Brindisi froma the big villa, husband of the diva. She nota here. The other man Pablo Ruguro, biga boss, make bad enemy. I nota like him to be my enemy.'

I paid him what I owed him and drove away. It seemed hard to imagine that in this sleepy town anger and violent passions should run rife, but the dark rage and hatred in the faces of the two men had been apparent.

Melissa's villa was in darkness that night so I supposed Brindisi had left the area or was perhaps dining out with friends. I felt lethargic. There was nothing of interest on the television so I had a bath and retired early with a book. I could hear the night wind sighing gently through the trees surrounding the villa.

I was startled by the sound of somebody hammering on the outside door. First, I went to the window, but no car could be seen outside the gate.

Throwing on a dressing gown, I went nervously to the door, calling out, 'Who is there?'

'Open the door, Ginny! It's Melissa.'

Like the last time, she stood dramatically in the doorway. A dark fur coat was thrown round her shoulders, her hair hanging loose.

'It isn't all that late, surely?' she said irritably. 'Were you in bed?'

'Yes. It's after midnight. Are you just returning to Positano?'

'Yes, I was going to stay the night in Naples, then I decided to drive on. Is there coffee?'

'I'll make some.'

'No, stay and talk, I'll have a glass of wine.'

The fire had died down and there seemed little chance of enlivening it so I turned on the electric fire before going to pour the wine. 'Do you prefer Orvieto or Chianti?' I asked.

'Either, I'm not fussy.'

She had opened the shutters and was gazing out at the hill shrouded in darkness.

'Have you seen him during these last few days?' she asked sharply.

'Yes, I saw him this morning at the garage.'

'The villa's in darkness, but he must be there.'

'It's been in darkness all evening. He's probably out.'

'Perhaps.'

'He doesn't know you're coming here?'

'No.'

She paced the room. Tension was visible in every line of her beautiful, brooding face. I would not ask questions; if there was anything she needed to tell me, I had to wait.

I could hear the clock ticking on the mantelpiece, and the sound of a car as its headlights swept up the hillside. I went to the window to see if it approached Melissa's villa, and felt strangely relieved when it went on along the coastal road.

She had joined me at the window. As the car swept on, she said, 'It's over, Ginny, I've made up my mind. Come over to the fire, it's cold here.'

I wished she would sit down but she kept moving around, nervously hugging her elbows. Her words seemed intended to reassure herself rather than me.

284

'I've made such a mess of things, Ginny. I thought I was in love with Alistair but what I really saw in him was familiarity. Soon I couldn't bear to watch him trying to make conversation with my fans and the others who made up my life, and they were scornfully amused by him for his conventionality. When I began to see Alistair's inadequacies, I realised how much I had changed.'

I resented her talking to me about Alistair as if I'd never known him, but I had learned not to expect any consideration from Melissa.

'Antonio was so different — bold, sophisticated, used to being adored by many women. I saw him as somebody strong and protective, but almost as soon as we were married, he changed. I was no longer the unattainable diva, I was his wife, and he had to be more important to me than my music. If I gave that up, the world would know that he mattered more. When Mellini did it for Natalia, he became more insistent. These last few months have been hell, and now I've reached the decision to leave him. Our marriage is over and I've come here to tell him so.'

That was the moment when I felt the first terrible fear that it would not be that easy. Visualising his strong, arrogant face filled with anger, remembering the ruthlessness I had sensed in him even when I was a stranger, I said, 'Melissa, you should have somebody with you when you face your husband.'

'I'm not going to show I'm afraid of him. I know what he'll be like, I've seen it all before, but I can take it. This will be the last time.'

'And afterwards?'

'I know now the sort of marriage I must have. A musician would be perfect, though I used to deny it. Riccardo Mellini will return to the world of opera one day. I was half in love with him years ago, I can be again.'

I stared at her in disbelief. She could hurt me a second time and know nothing about it. Even in my anguish, I saw the logic of her reasoning. Riccardo and Melissa could shine together like two stars in the firmament. But my tormented heart could not believe that Melissa was capable of the sort of love Riccardo needed.

She had gone to stand at the window again. 'He hasn't

285

returned to the villa,' she observed. 'He could be on the yacht or with some woman somewhere. I should go, it's late.'

It was three in the morning and in spite of the fire, the morning chill seemed to have invaded the room.

Picking up her coat, she said, 'I'll be in touch.'

I wished her luck and she let herself out of the door. I stood at the window until lights appeared in the villa on the hillside. Then I returned to my bed.

The next day, when I returned from Steven's house, Maria had left a message for me near the telephone to say that Signora Brindisi had called and I was to go up to her villa in the afternoon.

I felt reluctant, fearing I would become a witness to one of her violent quarrels with Antonio. As I drove up to the villa, I was relieved that his car was not in sight.

I had known the villa would be opulent, and Melissa showed me round with pride. Marble brought specially from Carrara covered the wide, shallow staircase that swept up from the hallway, adorned with statues of ancient gods and goddesses. Greek nymphs dipped their toes into the ornate fountain that played in the hallway, and at the head of the first flight of stairs a portrait of Melissa decorated the wall.

When I paused to look at it, she said with a little laugh, 'That's my favourite, as the role is my favourite.'

'That picture adorns the wall of our old school. Miss Carter found it in Italy on a poster, and had it copied. I agree it does you more justice than a great many of your portraits.'

'Well, I'm hardly a shrinking Mimi or a Japanese geisha, but I could identify with Tosca, with her passion and her venom.'

'Are you here alone?' I asked cautiously.

'I have servants here. Antonio came in this morning but went out almost immediately. He knows I'm here, but I haven't spoken to him. I think he must know that I'm here for a purpose.'

'I'm afraid for you, Melissa.'

'He can be violent but he isn't a fool. He'll storm and rave, perhaps hit me — once I had to wear a veil over my eyes for a week — but men like Antonio are cowards at heart.'

She took me upstairs and we looked at her gowns, her furs

and her jewels. Then we drank scented tea from delicate china cups. The sun sank in the west and dusk invaded the room.

'I should go,' I said at last, 'it's getting late.'

'Must you? Don't go yet.'

'I don't want to be here when your husband gets back. Anyway, you need to be alone with him.'

'I suppose so.'

She got up from her chair, went over to a small walnut bureau and opened one of the drawers with a key. She took out a square white box which she thrust into my hands, saying, 'I want you to have this, Ginny — now, while I'm here to give it to you. I have little faith that if anything happened to me there would be anybody to carry out my wishes.'

I stared at it curiously, and she said quickly, 'Promise me you won't open it yet. You'll know when the time is right.'

'Melissa, you're frightening me! What is all this?'

'Nothing to get dramatic about. Just do as I ask. Have you got a safe down there?'

'Well, yes, a small one, I don't have anything valuable.'

'Put the box in the safe then and forget about it. I might even ask for it back.'

She was smiling. Long afterwards, I would remember that smile on her lovely face when I had forgotten many other things about her. I had so often seen Melissa's face touched with other emotions — anger, arrogance, triumph and vanity. This smile was gentle, it meant something and held unspoken memories of a friendship we had shared.

She waved to me from the balcony of her sitting room. I was relieved that I had had the presence of mind to insist on leaving when I met Antonio Brindisi driving his Ferrari up the hill to his home.

Twice that evening I went to the window to look up at the hillside, where lights burned in the windows of the villa. I wondered if she had told him of her decision and how he had taken it.

It was just after midnight when the telephone rang. My heart hammered painfully in my breast as I went to answer it. Melissa's voice came to me in a whisper so that I could hardly hear it.

'Ginny, please come.'

'Melissa, are you all right?' I asked anxiously.

'Please come,' and then the line went dead.

My face in the mirror facing me was pale and there was fear in my eyes. I wondered if I should inform the police, but then Melissa would never forgive me if I alerted them to something that had not happened, so I decided against it.

The streets were wet with rain as I drove up the hillside; it obscured the windscreen and flashes of lightning dazzled me. I wanted to turn back but pressed on.

The downstairs rooms were in darkness, but lights shone out from a room on the first floor. As I ran from my car to the front door, I could see that a single lamp was burning over the doorway. The door was closed but it responded to my fingers turning the knob. Flashes of lightning invaded the hallway, falling on white marble figures and the gilt balustrade. I looked upwards at Melissa's portrait where the stairs divided. The darkness above was relieved by a gentle light coming from one of the upstairs rooms. I paused at the bottom of the stairs, my ears straining for any sound from above. It was so ominously quiet that when I did hear the sound of a closing door, I jumped nervously.

Footsteps echoed on marble, followed by a heavy sound and a muttered curse as if somebody had bumped against furniture. Again there was silence, and I started to climb the stairs. Suddenly from above came the sound of a door being opened, then closed sharply. A dark figure loomed at the top of the stairs and then rushed down them, almost knocking me off my feet. Antonio Brindisi passed me without a word, crossing the hall and slamming the door behind him.

I stood shaking with fear, hanging on to the balustrade, listening. I waited for the sound of his car from outside the house, but all around me there was silence.

Suddenly he flung back the door and strode over to where I cowered on the stairs. His dark face was cold, his eyes staring down at me with contempt.

'We meet again, English lady,' he hissed. 'You will find your friend in her bedroom, but there will be no greeting for you from Melissa.'

Without another word he walked back to the open door, and in seconds I heard his car driving away.

For what seemed an age, I stayed where I was, staring up into the darkness, afraid to move. His words had fallen like drops of ice into my numbed heart.

At last I summoned up all the courage I possessed and started to climb the stairs. At the end of a passage I could see light under one of the doors. Slowly I walked towards it, pausing at the door to knock and say, 'Melissa, it's Ginny.'

There was no reply. Afraid to open the door, I knocked again. What had he meant when he said there would be no greeting from Melissa? Was she unconscious? Was she dead?

Cautiously I opened the door and stood blinking in the sudden light. Chandeliers and wall lights illuminated the room. Wardrobe doors stood open and some of their contents were strewn on the floor. Articles on the dressing table, too, lay on the floor where they had fallen, and beyond in the lighted bathroom a bathrobe lay on the floor. I called out, but there was no reply.

I left the room and walked to the end of the corridor where a door stood closed, the only closed door of many, and I remembered the sharp slam before Antonio Brindisi ran down the stairs. I opened it and my hands felt nervously on the wall for a light switch.

On the bed, Melissa lay with her dark hair spread out against the white pillow. She lay as one sleeping, and it was only when I went to stand over her that I saw the thin trickle of blood oozing down her face from the round hole in her temple. Melissa was dead.

I ran out of the room and down the stairs. My first thoughts were: Suppose he came back? Suppose he wanted to silence me?

I switched on as many lights as I could find and went into the room where earlier in the day I had seen a telephone. With my teeth chattering, I lifted the receiver and rang for the police. In answer to their questions, all I could say was, 'Please come at once. Melissa Francesca is dead.'

I waited in the emptiness of the hall with the sound of the fountain around me and on the windows the pattering of rain. Then through the window I saw headlights sweeping up the drive and heard cars stopping outside the villa.

Men in plain clothes and uniformed policemen entered and searched the villa, followed by doctors, nurses and an ambulance, which took her away. Still I sat in the hall, shivering with cold and nervous tension.

The police took me away with them and asked questions. It was almost dawn and I could hardly keep my eyes open. When they finally let me go, I asked them to telephone Steven. He came and drove me home as the sun was rising and the streets were beginning to dry.

I slept with exhaustion for the rest of the day, and it was dark once more when I awoke. The memories of the night before were with me immediately and I made myself get up to look through the window, where Melissa's villa stood outlined against the sky in grim darkness.

The news of Melissa's death was in the world's newspapers, on the television and on the radio. In the early hours of the morning Antonio Brindisi was arrested in Naples. My name appeared in the papers as the friend who had found her, and my villa was surrounded with newshounds and cameramen. When Steven arrived, he chased them off angrily and refused to allow me out of the house.

Within days the villas on the hillside would fill with their owners, curious about the scandal. Velma arrived the first afternoon, telling the press that she had been a friend of Melissa's and mine. When at last she came into the villa, she said with a small, apologetic laugh, 'I couldn't get out of it, darling. It's their job, after all. How nice that you've got Steven to look after you!'

'And she's not supposed to discuss anything with anybody,' he retorted. 'You should understand, that, Contessa.'

'Oh, I do. But none of this surprises me, you know. We all knew they used to fight.'

When neither of us spoke, she went on, 'I wonder how he'll plead. A crime of passion, diminished responsibility? The Italian courts are notoriously lenient in such cases. Goodness, what a year it's been!'

After she had gone, I remembered the box Melissa had given me. I stood holding it in my hands for a long time, reluctant to open it; then, taking a small pair of scissors, I cut the string. Inside the white cardboard box was another box, this one in dark-red velvet and with a small key in the lock.

My eyes widened when I saw the emerald necklace and long emerald earrings and bracelet. They had suited Melissa perfectly, but why would she give them to me? The green stones gleamed brilliantly against the dark-red velvet and I took up one of the earrings and held it against the light. In the lid of the box was a pale-blue envelope bearing my name, and inside was a single sheet of faintly scented paper.

Darling Ginny,
I can't imagine you in emeralds but I want you to have them and wear them proudly in memory of me. I haven't been the sort of friend you deserve. Emeralds are not enough to atone for the heartache I caused you, but I am trying. In Naples a Gypsy woman told me I would die young and violently. I believed her, and I now have the feeling that there isn't much time. Think of me, Ginny! My whole life owes so much to those days we spent together in that Lakeland village and the people we knew there.
Love,
Melissa

That was the moment I wept. I had not been able to cry over Melissa, it had seemed my heart and my senses were numb from that dreadful night when I found her dead, but now for the first time the floodgates were open and for what seemed an age I sat in the emptiness of that tiny villa and mourned the loss of my friend.

For months to come they would not let her rest. At the trial of Antonio Brindisi, old scandals would resurface and their tormented marriage would be food for hungry reporters. Even in England, in our village, schoolgirls would be adding to their scrapbooks and, in years to come, would show their children that this had been Melissa Francesca, her beauty and her talent, her glamour and the sadness of her ending.

On the day of her funeral the bell tolled dismally over the sunlit stillness of the morning. Doves flew from their dovecotes, disturbed by the unusual activity, and out in the bay fishing boats dreamed on the gentle swell of the sea.

I walked to the cemetery; I had sold my car and later I would have to order a taxi to take me to the railway station. I was leaving Italy for good this time.

Avoiding the people round the gates and lining the paths, I went instead to the point jutting out above the hillside where most of the local people were congregating, wearing their sombre Sunday best. They looked at me curiously but did not speak.

Reporters stood in groups, jostling with each other to obtain advantageous positions; I suspected that most of them had been there since dawn. They were taking photographs of the famous people posing at the entrance gates, the women elegant in black, the men in dark suits.

I could almost begin to imagine that Melissa stood beside me on the hillside. I could see the amusement in her eyes, sense the cynicism in her smile. This cemetery was her stage and these people were her audience, but her part had been unrehearsed.

# Epilogue

They were leaving now. Antonio Brindisi was the first to leave, marching along the path between his two warders, looking neither to left nor right, his face impassive.

Many of those who were left were embracing each other with little cries of affection. For one fleeting moment Alistair looked up to where I was standing and raised his hand in farewell before walking alone to the gates. Riccardo Mellini detached himself from a group of colleagues and followed in Alistair's wake.

The ordinary people who lived at the little farms and worked in the vineyards were looking at the enormous floral tributes and laying their own offerings among them. They left in small groups as they had arrived, their children running ahead with laughter on their lips, unchastened by the aura of death.

At last I left my place on the hillside and went down to the path to look at the flowers, ostentatious wreaths and crosses side by side with tiny posies left by the children. Somewhere among them was a tribute from Alistair and another from Riccardo, but I did not look for them. I decided it was time I went to pick up my luggage and faced the long journey home.

All that great crowd seemed to have disappeared, but as I walked out of the gates, I noticed a car waiting on the road leading down to the sea. Leaning against the bonnet, a man stood in solitary contemplation. My heart gave a sudden lurch as I recognised Riccardo. Then he looked up and came forward to meet me.

For a long moment we gazed at each other in silence. He took both my hands in his with his sweet, grave smile, and I could find no words to greet him.

At last he said, 'I knew that you would be here, Ginny. I couldn't see you in the crowds, but when I saw Alistair Grantham wave to somebody on the hillside, I felt sure it would be you. Do you have a car?'

'No. I'm going back to the villa to pick up my luggage. I'm going home to England.'

'Today?'

'Yes.'

We walked back to the car, got in and he drove swiftly to the villa.

'Are you going home for a holiday? Or are you leaving for good?'

'I don't think I'll come back. The villa will be sold, I'll have to talk to Alistair about it. I really don't have anything to come back for.'

'It must have been terrible for you, finding Melissa like that.'

'Yes. I was so sorry about Natalia, that was terrible for you.'

'Yes. Not to know if it was intended or an accident. If it was intended, then it was the most cruel thing she could do to me.'

'But Riccardo, you'll go back to your music now, won't you?'

'I've accepted an invitation to conduct the Vienna Philharmonic in the week after Easter. To decline their invitation would not bring Natalia back. God knows I tried to be the sort of husband Natalia wanted, but that is not the person I want to be.'

'You have so much to offer,' I murmured, and suddenly I felt strangely shy.

'Do you remember what I said to you that night in Venice? That we would meet again, that it was inevitable that we would meet again? And yet when I said those words I had no means of knowing if I spoke the truth. Somehow, during all the traumas of these last few months, I believed in them.'

'You thought about me?'

'Too many times. I remembered your serenity, your gentleness and I remembered that even though life had hurt you cruelly, it hadn't made you bitter.'

'What are you trying to say to me, Riccardo?'

294

'That all these past months when I chased around the world searching for something irretrievably lost, I thought about you.'

Looking at me, his eyes were sombre and the sadness in his voice brought the tears into my eyes. I felt that I was on the edge of something tremendous, that my entire life was going to change. As he drew me into his embrace, he said softly, 'Will you marry me, Ginny?'

His kiss left me in no doubt that he loved me and needed me.

It was much later when I said hesitantly, 'What shall I do about my luggage?'

He laughed. 'We'll put it in the car, then we'll drive to Sorrento — I have a villa there. You can phone your parents and give them your news.'

I had left that Cumberland village as little Ginny Lawrence but I returned to it as Signora Riccardo Mellini. All the village was agog with the news.

My parents greeted my husband with delighted friendliness. Cloonie blushed to the roots of her hair whenever he spoke to her and bobbed quaint curtseys so that Father said with a laugh, 'I've explained that we haven't got royalty in the family, but she isn't convinced.'

In those few weeks I introduced Riccardo to long twilights and the gentle scenery of the English Lake District, to slow country voices and people who had been part of my childhood. I took him to my old school, where he caused quite a stir among the girls.

'They'll be making scrapbooks of you and your husband now, Virginia,' Miss Carter said.

'How did the girls accept Melissa's death?' I couldn't refrain from asking.

'They were devastated and tearful. And how simply awful that you had to find her! What will they do to her husband?'

'I don't know.'

'We held a service of remembrance for her in the chapel.' Her face was sorrowful. Then she smiled. 'But you're our celebrity now, Virginia. You can be sure the girls will follow your exploits wherever you go.'

'My husband is the celebrity, Miss Carter.'

'Well, of course, but you are his wife. A great many women must be envying you. I hadn't quite realised how handsome he was.'

Riccardo returned to the concert platform and to the opera. Everywhere he was received with great excitement and as his wife I went with him to the banquets and the concerts, where I met old friends and made new ones.

On each glittering occasion, the moment most precious to my heart was when he stood acknowledging the applause and the acclamation, then across the crowded room he would smile and I would know that he loved me.